Maisey Yates is a *New York Times* bestselling author of over 100 romance novels. Whether she's writing strong, hard working cowboys, dissolute princes or multi-generational family stories, she loves getting lost in fictional worlds. An avid knitter with a dangerous yarn addiction and an aversion to housework, Maisey lives with her husband and three kids in rural Oregon. Check out her website, maiseyyates.com or find her author page on Facebook.

Charlene Sands is a *USA TODAY* bestselling author of contemporary romance and stories set in the American West. She's been honoured with the National Readers' Choice Award, the CataRomance Reviewers' Choice Award and is a double recipient of the Booksellers' Best Award. Her 2014 Mills & Boon Desire was named the Best Desire of the Year. Charlene knows a little something about romance—she married her high school sweetheart! And her perfect day includes reading, drinking mocha cappuccinos, watching Hallmark movies and riding bikes with her hubby. She has two adult children and four sweet young princesses who make her smile every day. Visit her at www.charlenesands.com to keep up with her new releases and fun contests. Find her on Facebook, Instagram and Twitter, too: Facebook.com/charlenesandsbooks and Twitter.com/charlenesands

THE RANCHER'S WAGER

MAISEY YATES

ONE NIGHT IN TEXAS

CHARLENE SANDS

MILLS & BOON

First Published in Great Britain 2020
by Mills & Boon, an imprint of HarperCollinsPublishers,
1 London Bridge Street, London, SE1 9GF

The Rancher's Wager © 2020 Maisey Yates
One Night in Texas © 2020 Harlequin Books S.A.

Special thanks and acknowledgement are given to Charlene Sands for her contribution to the *Texas Cattleman's Club: Rags to Riches* series.

ISBN: 978-0-263-28277-1

0121

MIX
Paper from
responsible sources
FSC™ C007454

This book is produced from independently certified FSC™ paper to ensure responsible forest management.

For more information visit: www.harpercollins.co.uk/green

Printed and bound in Spain
by CPI, Barcelona

THE RANCHER'S WAGER

MAISEY YATES

the strangest prize of all—six feet and four inches of big, rock solid cowboy.

She couldn't have planned it better if she'd tried.

Oh, *he* didn't think he was going to lose. She knew he didn't. Because he had been betting like a fool all the way through this hand, and he had no idea that she had just gotten the absolute best hand possible.

No. He was playing like a man with a full house or a straight flush.

But she was a woman with a *royal* flush.

This final hand was always the most interesting part of this charity fundraiser, and it was the first year that Cricket had ever been in the hot seat for Battle of the Gold Valley Stars charity poker tournament.

This was the grudge game. This was the game for spectators.

Huge amounts of money had already been counted and distributed in previous rounds, all of it donated by businesses as each player had fought tooth and nail against each other, pouring cash into a pot for the sole purpose of giving back to the community. Now came the part where things got interesting.

Rivals tried to get back bits of their own, as hotly contested items that had been tussled over at rummage sales, and family heirlooms that had gone back and forth in this game for decades, were all put in the pot.

Cricket was currently wearing an oversized black leather jacket with fringes—won in the previous round from Elliott Johns, the guy who ran a water filtration company in the area. She also had an oversized black cowboy hat that she had already won from her current target. It was resting low on her head, and smelled vaguely of sweat, which was unnerving, since smelling Jackson's sweat made her feel strange. Just the idea of it.

It was a bit like that feeling she'd gotten when she was a child, and had been tempted to do something she knew she shouldn't. A strange tingling low in her stomach, that then went lower and spread down her thighs, making her feel restless and strange. She shifted in her chair, her dress slippery on the material of the seat. Another specious prize. A hand-me-down red gown originally worn by her sister Emerson to this event.

Cricket's fidgeting was just anticipation. And being so close to Jackson Cooper.

A man she usually avoided.

From afar, she had made a study of the Cooper family over the years. Something she was embarrassed to admit.

She had gotten to know Jackson's brother, Creed, a little better over the past few months, since he'd become her brother-in-law. She'd acted shocked and appalled and said any number of things about her sister Wren when she found herself involved with a Cooper. It had gone way past involved now, and they were married with a baby. And Cricket had sworn to Wren, up and down, that hardheaded, irritating, stubborn cowboys would never ever be her type.

Cricket was a liar.

Jackson made her feel strange…but he was also the only one of the Coopers who could answer the questions she needed answered.

Because of Wren, she couldn't really talk to Creed. And she didn't really want to talk to the youngest Cooper either, even though Honey was closer to Cricket's age. She'd never found the other girl approachable.

In some ways, Cricket was jealous of her.

Honey was a country girl. A tough cowgirl. And she just seemed to fit with her family. In a way Cricket did not.

Case in point, Cricket had never really had much of anything to do with the family winery. But she was a fantastic card player. And with their father officially out of commission—having been exiled in disgrace, and for good reason—Cricket had been nominated by her sisters to take his place.

And Cricket was about to take it all.

"I'll raise you," she said.

Oh yes, it was time. In that pot were a great many things she was interested in. Jackson's cufflinks. His watch. A pony from his ranch.

She'd only had to offer a diamond bracelet—wasn't hers anyway—a case of Maxfield reserve wines, and the dollar from her father's very first sale, which still hung in his vacant office, framed on the wall. Something that Jackson said he was going to give to his father.

The Maxfield and Cooper families were rivals from way back, though that rivalry had been dented some by her sister marrying Creed.

Still, sitting here across from a Cooper brought out her competitive spirit. Especially because right along with that competitive spirit, Jackson also brought out that complicated sensation she could honestly say she wasn't a fan of.

And now it was right down to the final bet.

"I bet myself," she said.

"Excuse me?"

"I bet myself. I will work for Cowboy Wines for free for thirty days."

His brows shot upward. "That's pretty rich."

"You afraid?"

He snorted. "I'll see you. And raise you. I'll work at Maxfield Vineyards for thirty days."

"No," she said. "The winery doesn't need you. You'll work at my ranch for thirty days. And sleep in the bunkhouse." She desperately needed a ranch hand. And she knew that Jackson Cooper knew what he was doing when it came to horses.

Cricket wanted as far away from the uppity confines of her upbringing as possible. And this ranch was her one way to get there.

"And if I lose…"

"You'll work at Cowboy Wines, in the tasting room. Dressed up in cowgirl boots and a miniskirt and serving our guests."

He was trying to scare her or humiliate her. But she'd grown up with James Maxfield. She'd been made to feel small and sad and unwanted for years. It was only recently she'd started to suspect why her father had treated her that way. But after a lifetime of humiliation, a miniskirt and waiting tables wouldn't defeat her. "Deal."

And she wouldn't lose. She wanted his forfeit and wasn't worried at all about her own.

She needed Jackson on her ranch. Unfortunately, she was all stalled out. Didn't quite know where to begin. That's where Jackson would come in handy.

And then there was that *other* matter.

And so she waited.

"You look awfully confident," he said.

"Oh I am."

He laid down his cards, that handsome mouth turning upward into a smile.

The smile of a man who had never lost much of anything in his life.

Oh how she would enjoy showing him what a foolish mistake that smile was.

Because not only had he lost. He had lost to her. A woman at least ten years younger than him, a woman she knew he didn't think of as wise. A woman she knew he thought of as not much of anything special.

He'd made that clear the few times they'd seen each other since they'd become kind of, sort of family.

Dismissive. Obnoxious.

"I hate to be a cliché. But read 'em and weep, cowboy."

Cricket Maxfield had a hell of a hand. And her confidence made that clear. Poor little thing didn't think she needed a poker face if she had a hand that could win.

But he knew better.

She was sitting there with his hat on her head, oversized and over her eyes, and an unlit cigar in her mouth.

A mouth that was disconcertingly red tonight, as she had clearly conceded to allowing her sister Emerson to make her up for the occasion. That bulky, fringed leather jacket should have looked ridiculous, but over that red dress, cut scandalously low, giving a tantalizing wedge of scarlet along with pale, creamy cleavage, she was looking not ridiculous at all.

And right now, she was looking like *far* too much of a winner.

Lucky for him, around the time he'd escalated the betting, he'd been sure she would win.

He'd *wanted* her to win.

"I guess that makes you my ranch hand," she said. "Don't worry. I'm a very good boss."

Now, Jackson did not want a boss. Not at his job, and not in his bedroom. But her words sent a streak of fire through his blood. Not because he wanted her in charge. But because he wanted to show her what a boss looked like.

Cricket was…

A nuisance. If anything.

That he had any awareness of her at all was problematic enough. Much less that he had any awareness of her as a woman. But that was just because of what she was wearing. The truth of the matter was, Cricket would turn back into the little pumpkin she usually was once this evening was over and he could forget all about the fact that he had ever been tempted to look down her dress during a game of cards.

"Oh, I'm sure you are, sugar."

"I'm your boss. Not your *sugar*."

"I wasn't aware that you winning me in a game of cards gave you the right to tell me how to talk."

"If I'm your boss, then I definitely have the right to tell you how to talk."

"Seems like a gray area to me." He waited for a moment, let the word roll around on his tongue, savoring it so he could really, really give himself all the anticipation he was due. "Sugar."

"We're going to have to work on your attitude. You're insubordinate."

"Again," he said, offering her a smile. "I don't recall promising a specific attitude."

There was activity going on around him. The small crowd watching the game was cheering, enjoying the way this rivalry was playing out in front of them. He couldn't blame them. If the situation wasn't at his expense, then he would have probably been smirking and enjoying himself along with the rest of the audience, watching the idiot who had lost to the little girl with the cigar.

He might have lost the hand, but he had a feeling he'd win the game.

And it was hardly dirty poker. Cricket had started it, after all.

She was in over her head, and he knew it.

When he'd heard that James Maxfield owned the property next to his, Jackson had figured he'd swoop in and buy it now that ownership of the man's properties had reverted to his family. But then Cricket had grandly taken control of the land—with great proclamation, per Jackson's brother, that she was going to be a rancher.

But Jackson knew there was no way in hell Cricket had the chops to start and run a ranch. It was hard enough when you had experience. She had none. And he knew she had some of her dad's money, but it wasn't going to be an endless well.

She was out of her league.

And a month spent as her ranch hand was more than enough time to show her that.

"Also, you should bring my pony," she said.

She was placated by the pony. He was going to end up getting that pony back. He knew it down in his bones. Because in the end, Cricket had not one idea of the amount of work that went into having animals. No idea the amount of work that went into working a ranch. Working the land.

She was stubborn and obstinate, and different than her sisters.

Their families might be big rivals, but they all worked in the same industry. He'd watched Cricket grow up. He had a fair idea of her personality. And he also had a fair idea of just how privileged the Maxfield family was.

They had a massive spread, worked by employees.

Any vision she had of ranching was bound to be romanticized.

He knew better.

He knew people looked at him and figured he was just another guy who'd grown up with a silver spoon in his mouth. Well, not literally. They didn't look at him and think that. He looked like a cowboy. But the fact was, he had grown up in a family that was well-off. At least, for most of his life. He was still old enough to remember when they had struggled.

He knew his younger brother didn't remember much of that time, and their youngest sister, Honey, didn't remember it at all. But Jackson did. He also knew Cricket had never known a moment of financial struggle in all her life. It wasn't that he thought she was stupid. She wasn't. She was bright and sharp, and a bit fierce.

He had always found her fascinating, especially in contrast with the rest of her family. Even before it had turned out her father was a criminal and a sexual predator, Jackson had always found the Maxfields to be a strange and fascinating family. So different from his own. There had always been tension between James Maxfield and his wife. Wren and Emerson had always seemed like perfect Stepford children from an extremely warped, upper-class neighborhood, cookies from the same cutter.

But not Cricket.

She had never been at the forefront of any of the events they had put on at the winery. And though Maxfield Vineyards and Cowboy Wines might have been rivals, they often attended each other's events. Professional courtesy, and all of that. And scoping out the competition. So he'd seen Cricket many times over the years. Usually skulking in the background, but then, when she got older, not there at all. One time, three years ago or so—she must've been eighteen—she'd been out on a swing in the yard, wearing a white dress he was almost certain she didn't want to be wearing. It had been dark out there, and inside, the Maxfield event room had been all lit up.

She was just lit up by the moon.

She had looked completely separate. Alone. And he'd felt some kind of sympathy for her. It was strange, and a foreign feeling for him. Because he wasn't an overly sympathetic kind of guy. But the girl was a square peg, no denying it. And in his opinion—particularly at the time—it wasn't round holes she needed to fit into. Just a family of assholes.

Now, he had changed his opinion on Wren and Emerson in the time since.

But his general opinion of Cricket's family, of her father, had certainly been correct. And just because he now thought Wren and Emerson were decent people... they were still so different from their sister. So different—it was the strangest thing.

But Cricket wasn't so different from her family that she would simply be able to step into ranching life. And he'd be right on hand to show her just how much work it was. He wouldn't have to do anything. Wouldn't have to sabotage her in any way.

She just needed a dose of reality.

And then she'd be willing to sell him that property.

He'd bought his own ranch and transitioned from working the one at Cowboy Wines after his mother died. And yes, he had people who helped him, so they would cover the slack of him not being there.

And that was the thing. Ranching never took time off. That was something he understood, and well.

"Report for work first thing on Monday," Cricket said. "And bring a sleeping bag. I don't have any extra and the bunkhouse gets cold."

She did not shake his hand. Instead, she clamped down on that unlit cigar, scrunched up her nose, grabbed the brim of the black cowboy hat and tipped it.

And right then, he vowed that no matter that Cricket had won the pot, he was going to win the whole damn thing.

Whatever that looked like.

"You *what*?"

Cricket looked at Emerson, keeping her expression as sanguine as possible. She wasn't going to get into the details of any of this with her sisters. Not now. Not just yet.

"Well, you would have known if you would have gone."

"I'm a whale," Emerson said, gesturing to her nine-months-pregnant stomach. "And my ankles were so swollen, I couldn't get my shoes on. So I didn't go."

"And I didn't tell her," Wren said, grinning. "Because I wanted her to hear it directly from Cricket's mouth."

"I won him in a poker game," Cricket said. "I won him fair and square, and now he has to come work on my ranch."

Triumph surged through her again. Her plan was working out perfectly, and she had a handle on it. All of it.

"Your ranch."

"And I won a pony," Cricket said, grinning with glee. "Why are you looking at me like that?"

"Because," Emerson said. "Jackson Cooper is a tool."

"So is Creed Cooper, but Wren married him." Cricket's teeth ground together as she said that. The whole thing with Wren and Creed had come as a shock, and like with all things Cooper-related, Cricket had kept that shock completely to herself, but she was still struggling with it a bit. "Come to that, your husband is kind of a tool," Cricket said to Emerson. "Just not to you. Also, I'm not *marrying* Jackson, I'm just having him work for me. For free."

She was practiced at pretending she didn't think much of Jackson. But this conversation pushed her thoughts in strange directions. Directions she'd been actively avoiding for months now.

"All right, I have to hand it to you, it's a little bit brilliant."

"I'm just happy to see you're doing something," Wren said. "Unfortunate double entendres aside. We've been worried about you."

"I know you have. For more than a year now. But you are both too afraid to say anything to me."

They didn't know how to talk to her. That was the truth. They might never admit it, but Cricket knew it. Fair enough, she often didn't know how to talk to them either.

"We never know what's going to make you run further and faster," Emerson said. "I'm sorry. But you know… You're not a little kid anymore. But I think it's easy for us to think of you that way. There's no reason for that."

"Glad to know that I'm finally getting a little respect."

"I did question your sanity when you asked to take on the ranch."

"It's paid for. I mean, there's definitely a lot of work to be done on it, but there was no reason to just let it sit there going to seed. And this is something I've always wanted. My own place. Wine isn't my thing and it never has been. I know you're shocked to hear that."

"Yeah, not so much," Emerson said.

"We're just different," Cricket said.

Honestly, she and her sisters couldn't be any more different if they tried. Emerson was curvy—though sporting an extra curve right now—and absolutely beautiful, like a bombshell. Wren was sleek and sophisticated. Cricket had always felt extremely out of place at

Maxfield events. It was like her sisters just knew something. Innately. Like being beautiful was part of their intrinsic makeup in a way it would never be for Cricket. And she had never really cared about being beautiful, which was another thing that had made her feel like the cuckoo in the nest.

So she just hadn't tried. Emerson and Wren had. They'd tried so hard to earn Jameson Maxfield's approval. Cricket had hidden instead. Had flown under the radar straight into obscurity.

She could remember, far too clearly, asking her father about college four years ago.

"You didn't particularly apply yourself in school, did you?"

"I..."

"What would you want to do?"

She'd been stumped by that. *"I don't know. I need to go so that I can figure it out..."*

"Emerson and Wren contributed to the winery with their degrees. Is that what you plan to do?"

There had been no college for Cricket.

She knew her dad could afford it. It wasn't about the expense. It was about her value.

Both of her parents had always been so distant to her. And it wasn't until later that she'd started to understand why.

Started to suspect she was not James Maxfield's daughter...

Well, the suspicion had made her feel like she made some sense. That her differences made sense. There were things that hurt about the idea, and badly. But she'd put those things in their place.

She'd had no choice.

"I appreciate it. I do."

"And whatever you think about our husbands," Emerson said, "they're both cowboys, and they would be happy to help you with the ranch."

"I know that. And when I've exhausted my free Cooper labor, I may take them up on it. But for now, I'll solve my own problem."

"Well done, Cricket," Emerson said, sounding slightly defeated. "I can't even see my toes."

"You're not supposed to," Wren said.

Wren's baby was three months old now, and of course, her slim figure had already gone right back into place. But even slightly built Wren had been distressed about the size of her stomach at this stage in her pregnancy.

It was weird to see her sisters so settled in domesticity. Having babies and all of that. They had never seemed particularly domesticated to Cricket, but they had fallen in love, and that had changed them both. Not in a bad way. In fact, they both seemed happier. Steadier and more sure of themselves. But that didn't make any of that racket seem appealing to Cricket.

Who just wanted…to be free.

To not feel any of the overwhelming pressure to fit into anything other than the life she chose for herself.

Maybe she'd wanted something else when she'd been young and silly and hadn't understood herself or her life.

She was the awkward sister. The ugly sister, really. She didn't mind at all about her looks. She was tall, and she was thin, and her curves weren't anything to write home about. But while that seemed elegant and refined on Wren, with her somewhat bony shoulders and knees, Cricket had always just thought her thinness seemed unfortunate on her. Her cheekbones were sharp, and she had freckles. Her top lip was just a little bit more full than the bottom one, and even though she'd had braces to solve the buck teeth situation, the gap between her two front teeth hadn't closed entirely, and it remained.

Her features were... Well, they were strong. And like everything else about her, kind of a love or hate situation.

Cricket didn't much care how she looked. She cared about what she could do. She was good at riding horses. She could run fast; she was strong. Her hair was a little bit wild, but she didn't much mind. No, she didn't mind at all. Because it made her look like she was moving. Made her look like she was busy. And that was what she liked.

That was the thing. As much as the Coopers were supposed to be rivals of her family, in some ways, she could identify a little bit more closely with them than she did with the Maxfields. They had country roots and sensibilities. That was what she understood.

It was what she connected with.

Country strong was hard to break. And that was what Cricket wanted to be.

It was what she was.

"I plan on making good use of Mr. Jackson Cooper," Cricket said triumphantly, immediately picturing the man, his broad shoulders and large hands.

Good for work.

And a good place to start when it came to figuring

out how to…how to broach the topic of what she thought might be true between them.

"Yes indeed," she said to herself.

Her sisters exchanged a glance. "Just be careful."

"Why?"

"The Coopers are a whole thing," Wren said.

Cricket blinked. "I don't understand what you mean."

"You start talking about making full use of Cooper men, and I'll tell you, it gives me ideas," Wren said.

Cricket still didn't get it.

"Sex, Cricket," Wren said. "Some people might think you mean sex."

Cricket was suddenly made of heat and horror. "No! No. Not at all. Never. How could you… Look, Wren, I'm not you. When I finally do decide to take on a man, and I'm going to need to get my actual life in order a whole hell of a lot better before I do, it is not going to be… He's *old*."

Among other things.

Wren laughed. "Right. So old. Like two whole years older than my husband."

Cricket sniffed. "And I'm several years younger than you."

Wren seem to take that as a square insult, her lips snapping shut.

Fine. Cricket wasn't old enough to take age commentary as that deep of a wound yet.

"This is strictly a business arrangement," she said. A fluttering grew and expanded in her chest. Evidence of her dishonesty. "He's going to help me with my ranch. And that's it."

"If you say so."

"I absolutely do."

"The one thing I know about you, Cricket. When you set your mind to something, you do see it done."

And what she had her mind set to, was finding out for sure if she wasn't a Maxfield at all…

And hiring Jackson Cooper was the best way to do that.

Two

The place was a mess.

To call it a ranch was a stretch. The house was… It was damn near falling apart. The porch was sloping on one side. He didn't want the place for its current assets, though.

He wanted it for the location.

This property was the best and only way for him to increase his spread, and that was what he needed to do. He wasn't going to spend his life working on his father's legacy.

He wasn't his father.

And when that screen door opened, and Cricket came out, she looked like the feral pirate queen of a sinking ship.

She had a hat on over frizzy blond curls, and a tight

white tank top and denim shorts. She also had on cowgirl boots. She was quite unintentionally the very image of a sexy, tousled cowgirl, and he knew that she hadn't done that on purpose. Not at all.

Her legs were long, endless. Her curves were slight, but they were ripe. She had no makeup on her face, but she was damn pretty. Unique looking, that was for sure. But he liked her look, he found. At least, he had been liking it more and more lately, which he didn't really care to dive into.

He wasn't here to look. He was here to educate.

In such a way that she might realize the subject matter was not for her.

"Reporting for duty," he said.

"Excellent," she responded, grinning.

"So what is it you had in mind, because this is way more than a month's worth of work, I can already tell."

She looked immediately crestfallen and he had to wonder if she was going to make it easy for him. "Why? What do you see?"

"You're liable to fall right through that porch if somebody doesn't get in there and reinforce it. I have some concerns. Are you living in this heap?"

"Yes," she said. "It's fine. I just avoid the saggy boards over there."

"Cricket," he said. "You're about to slide through the whole damn thing."

"I won't."

"Okay. Maybe you won't, because you probably don't weigh a buck and a quarter soaking wet. Somebody like me is going to fall right through."

"Well, sounds basically like the equivalent of a cowboy moat to me. And I may be okay with that."

"You got something against cowboys? Because it seems to me that you need one to get this place going." He looked around and affected an expression he hoped looked something like overwhelmed.

He'd never been overwhelmed a day in his life.

"You might need more than one cowboy, realistically," he added.

"Nothing *against*. Just don't need one in my house."

"I also suspect that isn't true. Because I'm thinking you probably need some things fixed in there."

She looked stubborn for a moment. But under that he could see…she was wary and he wasn't sure why. He'd never given her a reason to be wary. "Well, maybe a few things. But I can call someone else out for that."

"Why?" he asked. "You've got me."

Her eyes narrowed. "You know how to repair things?"

"I sure as hell do."

"Well… All right. I'll let you come take a look then."

"Lead the way. Point out the mushy boards."

He walked up the steps and through the front door, into the tiny, shabby entryway.

Cricket held her arms out. "Well, this is it." She smiled. "What do you think? Just kidding. I don't care."

He looked around, turning in a circle. "It's…something, Cricket."

To tell the truth, the little farmhouse wasn't so bad. It was worn with years, and a bit shabby, but it was definitely repairable.

What he couldn't imagine was a girl like Cricket—

who'd grown up in a monstrosity of a mansion that was doing a poor imitation of a Tuscan villa—settling into it.

"I thought so. It's a ranch. I feel like… That's what I feel like I want to do. Wine's not really for me."

"Yeah, I noticed you were never all that into any of the Maxfield events."

But there was a lot of ground between not wanting to be part of the winery and wanting to run a ranch. She might not know it yet, but he did.

He'd spent years working the ranch at Cowboy Wines. Years. Pouring blood and sweat into his father's land. His father's legacy.

Until he'd found out the truth about Cash Cooper. And then he'd just…

He'd wanted his own.

Now, he still worked at the winery. He wouldn't cause a rift. His mother wouldn't have wanted that. She'd spent years working to make sure she kept the family together at the expense of her own happiness and he wouldn't be the one to wreck that.

But he didn't have to make his father's life his own.

"No, I was really not," she said. "And this has always been kind of my dream. So…"

"Why ranching?"

Her expression suddenly went shy, then sharp. "I don't know. I feel like it's in my blood. Which is weird, because my family doesn't do it. Is that how you feel? Like ranching is in your blood?"

He shifted. Shrugged. "Can't say as I know. It's just something I do. I can't see doing any different."

"Yeah. That's exactly it. Except, it wasn't just right there for me, so I had to figure out what that meant.

What it might mean for me that I dreamed about having my own little house out in the middle of… Well, just like this. A field all around. I want horses."

"How are you going to make money? Are you breeding horses?"

"Well…"

"Cattle?" He didn't wait for her to respond. "Dairy or meat? Have you thought about dealing with slaughtering cows? With getting to the nearest USDA station and the cost of it all?"

"I…"

"If you decide to do horses are you going to keep studs or have sperm brought in?"

"Well," she sputtered again.

"Doing produce? More of a farm? Have you thought about CBD? That's a growing industry."

"The thing is," she sputtered, her manner that of a wet hen. "I haven't exactly decided. I don't really know what I want to do with the place. But I kind of feel like until I get a bit more… Until I get it into shape, I'm not going to know."

"I don't know how that's going to work," he said, like he was honestly doing her a favor. The girl had no idea what she was getting herself into. She'd be in water five feet high and rising. Before she knew it, she'd be in over her pretty head.

This was practically a rescue mission.

Yeah, don't go that far. You're being a dick. Own it.

Sure, he'd own it.

Like he'd own this ranch in the end.

But Cricket suffered from the overconfidence of the young and inexperienced. Jackson Cooper hadn't been young or inexperienced for a long time. The problem with someone like Cricket was she was sure she knew exactly what was happening, exactly what she was doing, and she was also certain no one could possibly know better than her.

"I mean, I'll be honest," she said. "I don't know if I have the fortitude to do beef. But it seems to me that the overhead with horses is really high."

"Horses are expensive. Getting into good ones… That's pricey. But it might be more what you're looking for. Breeding good horses."

"Maybe that's it." That she seemed to be considering anything he said shocked him. "I'll think about it. I'll spend some time reading." She sighed. "Fundamentally, I have time. This place is paid for. And I have some reserves."

"From your dad's estate?"

"Pretty much. I sold my stake in the winery. I wanted out. I wanted to…follow my own path, and I knew I wanted out. So… I sold my stake. I got some cash."

"And you're using me for slave labor."

"Well, since I had the opportunity, that just seems like good business. Why pay for something when you can get it for free?"

"Let's start with the house," he said, walking from the little sitting room into the kitchen. There were spiderwebs in the corner. "Have you cleaned?"

"A little," she said.

He said nothing, he just kept on looking. At the dust, the peeling paint.

She wrinkled her nose. "Okay. I'm not really used to doing any of my own cleaning. I'm not opposed to it.

There's nothing wrong with being prepared. It's just…
I haven't really done it, so I don't really think of everything. And I hate that, because I don't feel like I'm
a spoiled rich girl, but I guess to an extent I am. I feel
like I *can* do all these things, but I never have. It's all
based on… Well, basically nothing. Just my feelings
about the fact that I can do this. But that has to mean
something. Right?"

Granted, he was here to try and give her advice. Advice that would discourage her from all this. The truth.
He was here to give her the truth, but she was suddenly
looking at him like he might contain the answers to
the mysteries of the universe, and he had no idea why.

He didn't like it either.

"I don't know," he said. "But I do know that it is
always a good time to learn to take care of your own
damn self. So go get a broom and clear your cobwebs.
I'm going to evaluate." He began to walk the perimeter of the room, making note of places where it felt like
there might be water damage. Right by the sink. He
wasn't surprised. It was an old farmhouse, and it was
easy to believe it hadn't been worked on at all, judging
by the rest of the place.

He was surprised when Cricket did what he asked,
and went into the small pantry, grabbed a broom and
began to harass the spiders in the corners.

"Granted," she said. "I can keep the spiders."

"I would've thought you and spiders were natural
enemies."

"Why?"

"Don't they eat crickets?"

She rolled her eyes. "Funny."

Her name was just another thing that didn't quite fit with the rest of the Maxfields. A name with bounce and humor. And he didn't think anyone in her family had an ounce of either. "Why did they name you Cricket?"

"Why is your sister named *Honey*?"

"Well, that's easy. Mom picked it, and my dad agreed because it was so sweet to finally have a girl."

She frowned. "He sounds nice."

That was the problem. Cash Cooper was nice. A good father in many ways. It would have been easier if he was an out-and-out asshole. He wasn't. Jackson resented him plenty sometimes, carried a lot of anger toward him.

But Honey adored him. Creed had been so mired in his own issues he'd never gotten to know their mother as an adult the way Jackson had, and she'd certainly never confided in Creed.

Jackson was the only one who knew.

"He has his moments," he said. "I mean, he's a crusty old man."

"Yeah, well, James Maxfield is a little more than crusty."

James Maxfield had been unveiled as an unrepentant sexual predator. One who'd gotten a girl pregnant and cast her aside, left her a shell of herself after a mental breakdown. A man who'd blackmailed any number of employees who'd felt harassed by him. A serial cheater, liar and all-around asshole.

Cash might have his flaws, but he wasn't that.

"Right. Sorry." Then, he did feel bad, because she looked so lost.

And the way she looked reminded him of how he'd

felt when his mother had died. It had been…a hell of a thing to lose her. The entire family had done what they could to stay strong in the aftermath and they had each other. But he remembered that feeling. Cricket was hollow-eyed, and he had to wonder if James's behavior was as shocking to her as it had been to her sisters. It hadn't shocked him. The way his father had always carried a grudge against James Maxfield had made Jackson suspect there was a very serious reason for it. Of course, there would be. His father wasn't the kind of man who disliked somebody just because.

"It's okay. So, how did your dad get interested in wine? You know, since he was a cowboy first."

Jackson peeked under the sink, frowning when he saw water. Then he turned on the water so that he could try and figure out the exact source of the leak. "Well, he didn't like your dad. And I think his aim was more or less to try and prove that he could do exactly what your dad did. But better."

"That's a pretty powerful dislike. To do something just to prove you can. I mean, I respect it. That's exactly the kind of thing I can understand. Needing to prove yourself that much. It makes perfect sense to me."

"A little bit vindictive, are you, Cricket?"

She shrugged. "I think so. I mean, in seventh grade Billy O'Connor made fun of my buck teeth, and then I got braces, and two years later I made him think I wanted to go to a school dance with him, only so I could turn him down."

"That's pretty stone cold."

"He shouldn't of made fun of my teeth. Did you have buck teeth?"

He frowned. "No."

"Did Honey?"

"If so, I don't recall."

"Oh. Well, I do. And no one else in my family does. I think that's kind of weird."

"Families are different."

"Of course. I'm not saying they aren't. I'm just… I dunno. Sometimes I try to see something in common with my sisters, and I just can't. But I don't know. That feeling kind of goes away here. Spiders or not."

"Well, good to know." He knelt down, had a good look at the pipe. "I have some plumber's tape in the truck. But I'm going to need to go get a part from town to actually fix this."

"Can I go with you?"

"Sure," he said.

"Great." He headed back out toward the truck, and he could practically hear her holding something back. "Yes?"

"It just occurred to me that maybe I should go out to the bunkhouse with you. Show you around."

"Okay." He looked at her. "Are you really going to make me sleep in the bunkhouse?"

If he were another kind of man he'd sneak across the field and into his own house. But he was honorable with his dishonor. They'd had a bet.

He was sticking to it.

"Absolutely. It was part of our bet. You're going to be my ranch hand."

She didn't elaborate. Didn't offer any sort of reasoning behind why she needed him here. He just had a feeling it amused her.

Cricket was a bloodthirsty little thing.

He had to grudgingly respect that.

She led the way down a trail that had been worn into the grass, and he followed. And groaned when the very rustic-looking house came into view. "You're not serious."

"I am absolutely serious. What's wrong with it?"

"If the house is dilapidated, how bad is this going to be?"

She kicked open the door, and inside was… Well, pretty much nothing. There were bunks, but they looked like they were moldier than not.

"Cricket," he said.

He'd slept in worse, that was for damn sure. But not for as long as a month.

"Okay," she relented. "All right, I have a better idea. You can sleep in the house."

The look he gave her was full of skepticism, but his skepticism wasn't her problem. She was enjoying talking to him. Trying to get a sense of what he thought. What he knew. If they were *alike*.

And when he had talked about his dad…

She had wanted to know more. She was jealous. Because her own father had never cared for her at all. What would it have been like to grow up on the ranch? To have a place where she belonged. It had actually become something of a cherished fantasy.

The idea that James Maxfield wasn't her father. The idea that she made sense.

"Sleep in the house."

"Yes. There's an extra bedroom."

"Great."

They went back toward the house, him with his sleeping bag in tow.

"There's a quilt," she said.

"Is it full of dust?"

"Don't be silly." She waved her hand. "I beat the blankets out. I looked that up online. I've got this, I really do."

"Right."

"This place wasn't totally unoccupied until recently. The older lady who lived in it passed away. I don't really know why my dad owned it. He wasn't charging her very much in rent, which honestly doesn't seem like him. It leads me to believe that one of his business managers must've bought it and he didn't remember. Or even know. That does sound like my dad. He doesn't really notice people."

It was weird to call James Maxfield her dad. She had suspected he wasn't for at least six months. Not since she found out that the reason for the feud between the Coopers and the Maxfields was that her mother had once been in love with Cash Cooper.

It had all made so much sense then.

Her mother hadn't felt like she could get married to Cash, because he was penniless. And so, she had chosen to marry James Maxfield, and signed on for a life of misery. But Cricket had long suspected that the reason *she* existed, the reason she was a late-in-life child, was not because her parents had suddenly found a way to rekindle their romance ten years after her sisters were born. No.

It made much more sense to her that her mother had gone straight back into the arms of Cash.

It was just Cricket wanted to tread lightly in finding out the truth. Because his wife had passed away not that long ago, and she imagined it would be very painful for Creed, Jackson or Honey to accept that their father had had an affair.

From her point of view, it was pretty romantic. But then, her father wasn't heroic to her. Cash seemed much nicer. Though, she knew the Coopers loved their mother very much, and she'd seemed like a nice woman. Cricket didn't like the idea that Cash might have done her wrong.

For all that Cricket could see the affair as a forbidden romance, she imagined the Cooper children wouldn't view it in quite the same way.

So she had to tread carefully. Treading carefully wasn't her strong point. Never had been.

She tramped up the steps again. And Jackson cursed sharply. She turned just in time to see his foot go through the second step.

The only problem with all of her theories had been Jackson. And the way she'd felt about him for the last ten years. And the way her suspicions had forced her to…

Well it was a relief, really. She'd *always* hated how Jackson made her feel. Like her heart was too big for her chest and her breath was too big for her lungs. She'd felt connected to him, from the first moment she'd laid eyes on him, and she'd hated it. Especially as she'd gotten older and seen how badly a relationship could hurt a woman. Her parents' marriage was toxic. She'd never wanted anything like that, but her heart had attached itself to Jackson all the same.

That connection had made a strange, dizzying sort of sense when she'd realized. When she'd figured it out. Because, of course.

Of course she wasn't so foolish as to fall in love with him.

Of course love at first sight wasn't real, especially not as a kid.

Of course that connection was something else.

Of course.

Cricket didn't trade in uncertainty. And for years, the intensity of the emotions she'd felt around Jackson Cooper had felt *uncertain.*

It was a relief to find certainty.

It was.

"I've never had that problem," she said.

"Like I said. Not more than a buck twenty-five soaking wet."

"Can't help it." She scampered the rest of the way up the steps and into the house. He followed her, and she noticed that he didn't lighten his footsteps at all to make allowances for the fact that some of the boards were iffy. He got what he got. If he ended up severing a tendon it wasn't her fault.

"Thank you for the wild goose chase around your property."

"No, that wasn't a goose chase. We'll goose chase later. There's a pond."

"Do geese favor a pond?" he asked.

"Mine do."

"You have geese?"

"A few domestic. One Canada goose. He has a broken wing. It's flipped kind of upside down. He can't fly."

He frowned. "You have a Canada goose?"

"I do. His name is Goose."

"Creative."

She arched a brow. "Do you have a problem with a Canada goose?"

"No. Not at all. But you can't exactly make a ranch off of them."

"I'm not suggesting that it be a *goose ranch*. But my point is that tomorrow we'll go on an actual tour. No drama. This was just a walkabout."

"I can't believe you were going to throw me in the bunkhouse without ever having looked at it."

She shrugged. "I figured you're tough. And you can take it."

"I could sleep there."

"This will be more comfortable," she said. "Just down the hall."

She didn't really want to alienate him. She also didn't quite know how to wrangle him. She had a feeling that if she suddenly started being extra nice to him, he would only be more suspicious than not. So she was trying to be measured in her interactions with him. She had to… get to a place where she could talk to him. Where they had a little bit of trust. Perhaps like training a dog. She'd done that. That she understood. She might not have any experience with men, but she did know animals pretty well. Her dad might have spent a lot of years ignoring her, but she also hadn't been denied much. And when she'd asked for animals, she'd gotten them. She'd had several dogs growing up, and still had her favorite old ranch dog, Pete.

Perhaps Jackson would be like Pete.

If only she knew how to cook. Then she could feed him. Dogs really responded well to food as an incentive. Perhaps men did too.

She'd heard that. That old-fashioned saying about the way to a man's heart being through his stomach. Not that she wanted Jackson's heart.

Well, she sort of did. She needed him to feel *something* for her. Some sort of connection. Without that, he would just think she was crazy and reject everything she had to say. Without that, he might just think she was trying to ruin his family. And that wasn't it. Not at all. She had no designs on causing any kind of trouble in his family.

But her own family was broken. Smashed all to pieces. And her place, it had never been secure. She wanted to find her place.

She pushed the door open to the small bedroom. The bed was tiny, shoved into a corner, brass rails surrounding a thin mattress that might just as likely be stuffed with corn husks as anything. The quilt that was placed over the top of it was threadbare and worn.

"It's simple," she said. "But hopefully adequate."

"Adequate." He set his sleeping bag down, and looked around. "It'll do just fine."

"Yeah. I suppose." He looked absurd, too tall and too broad for the space. His feet were going to stick through the rails at the end of the bed. And the little lace curtains behind him… Well, they seemed absolutely ridiculous.

The sun shone through the window, catching his

face, highlighting the stubble on his jaw. His hair was dark, his eyes a startling blue. The same color as the bluebonnets on the quilt fabric. She didn't look like him. Not even a little bit. Her eyes were somewhere between pine cone brown and green, depending on how the sun shone. Her hair was light. But his sister had lighter hair. He was so tall. Cricket was fairly tall for a woman. About an inch above average. He was…massive. His hands were bigger, his shoulders muscular. His chest broad. He looked like a man who did hard labor all day, every day.

She felt a strange sort of cracking expansion happening in her chest.

Then he turned and looked out the window, squinting against the sun, and something in her stomach leaped. And fear gripped her.

He was just very handsome.

Of course he was. It was one of those things that was indisputable. And her feeling about that was…pride. She could see that now.

She was…proud of him.

When she was twelve years old, she'd realized it. The girls in her class were all giggling over Ryan Anderson and his floppy blond hair and she'd been fixed on Jackson Cooper. She'd been a little embarrassed about it. She'd told no one.

She knew she was a girl and he was a man and there was no way they could ever…

She'd never been silly enough or brave enough to write about him in her diary. To have a diary *at all*. But she'd thought of him every night and wove stories where they could be together, on a ranch.

Him all rugged and handsome and her riding a horse right alongside him. There had been freedom in those fantasies. In this idea that her place in the world, her real and rightful place, was alongside this forbidden man whose family her father hated.

She'd never let on how much it bothered her that Wren had swooped in and taken up with Creed. Cricket had been the one full of forbidden desire for years and years.

Wren had gone and made a Cooper and a Maxfield hooking up a thing of no particular consequence.

But now Cricket knew there was consequence after all. And anyway, she'd been twelve when she'd imagined her place by Jackson. When she'd imagined fitting into a life with him.

And it made sense now. That mystical feeling of connection, the idea that she would fit in with his life, with his family… He was her half brother. Of course. Their connection finally made sense.

A twelve-year-old couldn't be in love. The truth was just that the connection she'd felt to him had gotten muddled because she hadn't known.

It was pride she felt for him. That was all. A desperate longing for a place where she fit.

That was all it was.

That was all it could be. All it could ever be.

Get a grip, Cricket.

"Well."

"Did you still want to go to the store?"

"You know. I was actually thinking I might whip up some food. Some dinner. So why don't you go to the plumber, and I'll handle all that here."

"You cook?"

"Of course I do," she lied.

She had either been going down to town and getting a burger for dinner or eating frozen pizza for weeks now. But he didn't need to know that.

"All right. I'll see you in a bit."

"See you in a bit," she repeated decisively. He walked out, and suddenly it was easier to breathe. He walked out, and suddenly, everything inside her chest eased.

She scurried back into the kitchen, and opened up the fridge. Wren had brought her some groceries, and she'd been ignoring them. But now, staring at the leafy greens and wrapped steaks, she felt that she had to figure something out. She picked up the phone and called her sister.

"How do you cook?"

"That is a broad question," Wren said.

"Well. You gave me all this food. And I don't know what to do with any of it. And I just told Jackson that I would cook dinner."

"You're going to cook him dinner? Honestly, Cricket, are you sure you don't have some kind of crush on him?"

That would have been a horrifying thing for her sister to ask six months ago.

It was worse now.

"I do not," she said ferociously, ignoring the tightening in her stomach. "I don't. That would be…ridiculous."

"All right. I'll walk you through… What were you thinking you were going to do?"

"Make steak."

"Right. Fantastic. What else did I get you?"

"I don't know. Green stuff. Green beans."

"Okay. I will walk you through very simple pan-fried steak and green beans. Do you have potatoes? I'm pretty sure I brought you potatoes."

"Meat and potatoes," Cricket said. "Perfect."

And in the end, she barely broke a sweat over the whole thing and managed to put together something that smelled pretty darn decent.

"Thank you," she said to her sister.

"Seriously. Are you okay? Because I feel like this is the most we've talked in…ever."

"I don't know," Cricket said. "I mean, I know I'm okay. I just don't really know how to explain us not talking. Except… I spent a lot of years hiding. Running as fast as I could through childhood. Through that house. I hated it there. I always did. I never felt at home. I never felt like one of you. I don't want to be mean, but nothing with James really surprised me." She couldn't quite bring herself to call him Dad. "He wasn't cruel to me, nothing like that. It's just that he didn't care about me at all, and there was something in that way that he dismissed everything I was that… Nobody ever saw me—and it wasn't your job to. I was a kid and you were teenagers, and then you were having lives. You went off to school. I didn't do that."

"You could have."

"Maybe," Cricket said. "But I didn't know what I wanted anyway. I guess that's the thing. I've never fit. And I've been searching for the place where I do. I think I might've found it."

She might have found her family.

"And now it feels… I don't know, I feel more like talking."

Because even if Cash Cooper was her real father, her mother, Wren and Emerson were still her family. But if her suspicions were right, Cricket could finally disavow that piece of herself that had never really fit. It would all suddenly make sense.

"I can understand that. I always felt like I was being wedged into a life that I didn't fully want. I embraced it, and I care about the winery—I'm happy to work on it now—but, you know, I'm working toward my architectural engineering degree because it's something I always wanted. But I always knew I couldn't because Dad didn't want me to do it, because it wasn't useful to him."

"Believe me," Cricket said. "I do understand that being in his sights wasn't necessarily better. I really do."

"I know. It's not a competition. A tough childhood is a tough childhood. Whether you're in a nice house, whether your dad pays attention to you… Doesn't really matter. It is what it is. I mean, we were better off than a lot of people. But it doesn't take away the things that weren't great."

"I know. Anyway. I… I think I'm going to be happier."

"I'm happier," Wren said. "I think Emerson and I weren't really that much different than you, when you think about it. We started our own lives. Really and truly. And even though we are still maintaining our stakes in the wineries, we have more than that. We *are* more than that. The winery was never for you. And it's a good thing that you're finding the thing that you want."

Cricket nodded, and then after exchanging farewells,

hung up the phone. Just in time for Jackson to return with a whole bag full of supplies. He had his cowboy hat on, his jacket. He was such a striking figure. Because he was an emblem. Of what she wanted. Of the life she was hoping to find.

Because he represented something that fit. That was it. That was all it could be, and she had to really know that, understand it.

Had to understand what the extra thump of her heart meant. The jitter in her stomach.

She had to.

She had no choice.

"Smells good," he said.

Deep pride swelled in her chest. "Really?" She cleared her throat. "I mean. Sure. Impossible to mess up a decent steak."

Except she had a feeling it was very possible and if she hadn't been receiving instructions the entire time, she would've definitely done so.

"Well, I didn't realize I would be receiving payment in the form of steak."

"I do try. Food first," she said. "Then you can get to the plumbing." She served their plates and sat across from him. In the tiny kitchen, it felt incredibly...domestic.

It was such a world apart from the life she usually lived. She'd grown up with a grand banquet hall set for every dinner. Her dad all the way down at one end away from the rest of them. This little square table with peeling red paint felt homey in a way dinners never had. And Jackson smelled like soap and skin, close enough for her to get the scent. It was simple. Down-home and perfect in a way she'd always wanted things to be.

There had been a time when she'd dreamed of this. Sitting at a table with Jackson. Asking about his day, having him ask about hers.

Her Jackson fantasies had run the gamut over the years, but they'd always led to one conclusion. The only place for her was beside him.

That had terrified her before six months ago, because—as she'd gotten older—she'd realized what her feelings must mean, and she'd been unhappy with them. Ready to perform an exorcism, in all honesty.

She didn't want to get married and be miserable like her mother was.

It had been a relief to discover the real truth behind her feelings.

"What were your dinners like growing up?" she asked.

She was hungry. But not for steak. She wanted to know him. His family. What his life was like, and how hers might have been.

"Well, something like this. I mean, we started with a house that was pretty similar to this. It expanded as time went on."

"And that changed things? I mean, for all of you?"

"I guess so. I'm probably the only one who really remembers the change. Who really remembers what it was like before. Or... I don't know. Creed probably does to an extent. Not Honey, though."

"Right." So that wouldn't have been different. If she had grown up with them, she would have been like Honey. She wouldn't have known what it was like to have normal family meals around the table. She knew that being wealthy was a privilege. It wasn't that. It was

easy to romanticize things you didn't have. Easy to look
at them in a simple way. She knew that too.

She wasn't stupid.

She'd spent a lot of time by herself. And as a re-
sult, she'd spent a lot of time thinking. She thought a
lot about the way other people lived. The way families
looked on TV. And while she knew there were other
struggles involved in their lives, she also knew that
some of the good things they showed on sitcoms were
real.

"So you got a big table, probably then," she said.

"What does the size of the table have to do with
anything?"

"You know, on TV," Cricket said. "When everybody
sits around this little, cheerful table. Just like this. And
they have some kind of casserole. It's always casserole. And I don't even know anyone who's ever eaten
a casserole."

"Yeah, can't say as I've had a lot of casserole experience myself."

"Well, there's always a casserole, and they're all sitting together, and reaching for the dishes, and talking.
And we didn't have a table like that. It was big and long,
this banquet hall. As if there were fifty of us, but there
wasn't. And my dad would always sit down at his end,
miles away. And that's just… It's a metaphor. Really.
For my family. All spread out, all engaged in their own
thing and not paying attention to each other. Often-
times we would even have different food. We had a chef.
And we could basically put in an order for whatever
we wanted at the beginning of the week. We would sit
there in the same room and basically all be…separate.

And sometimes I just wanted a small table. Because I thought that would fix things."

"Well, we might've gotten a bigger table, but we all sat down at one together."

"Oh," she said, feeling wistful. "You all really love each other."

"You love your sisters," he said, and she noticed he skimmed over her question.

"I do," she said. She looked up at him, taking a chance at meeting his gaze. "My siblings are the most important people in my life."

His lips curved upward, and something in her stomach shivered. She didn't like it. She didn't like the feeling at all.

"Well, I… Anyway. I don't know. I'm just curious. About how other people grew up."

"Did you go over to anyone's house when you were a kid?"

"Not really. My sisters went to private school. They were away from home a lot. They sent me away for a while, but I hated it. I wanted a family, and being at school with strangers didn't help at all. Dorm rooms and formal dining halls and all of that. I just ended up walking the grounds alone. They brought me back. They enrolled me in a school in Gold Valley. But they didn't really want me associating with any of the local people. So I had friends. But only at school. My parents didn't let them come over. They didn't let me go over there. The stupid thing is, I'm not sure my dad would have actually known what I was doing if I hadn't asked for permission. But I've never really known how to live."

Except, she was deceiving Jackson a little bit. And

that made her feel... Well, that made her feel marginally guilty. It wasn't the most honorable thing, but her deception was all in service to something bigger.

She looked at him, and the sense of intensity, of longing, grew. She couldn't feel bad. Not now. She wanted him here. She needed him here. And some part of her knew that. On a deep, cellular level. She knew that.

"Anyway. I'm just kind of making up for lost time. For things I didn't have."

"So, you got yourself a little kitchen table."

"Yeah. And you're the first person to sit with me here."

He looked a little uncomfortable with that statement. Cleared his throat. She blinked, wondering what he thought she meant. And then she realized her words could be misconstrued.

"Only that..."

She must've sounded panicked, because he held her gaze, his expression steady then. "No drama."

"Right." His words made her feel immediately soothed and she didn't really know why.

She'd first felt this weird sort of connection to him years ago. He hadn't been as broad then as he was now. He'd been lean and rangy, and very different from his brother, Creed, who was often at winery events, fulfilling much the same job as her sister. Jackson wasn't a salesman. He wasn't the kind of guy who was in the front of the house. Much like her. He was behind the scenes. It was also very clear that Jackson was an integral part of his family in a way that Cricket had never felt like she was.

Jackson very clearly had a firm hand in everything.

He wore his authority with ease. It was so different from the way her father was. James blustered about, ordering employees around. All Jackson had to do was walk into a room. She had seen him helping with setup at different community parties on more than one occasion. He was a man who led by example. He was a man, she had always thought, to be admired.

And she had. She admired him greatly.

Wherever Jackson was, her eyes seemed to find him.

It was hard to explain how it had felt to find out there was a high probability he was her half brother.

It had been the death of a dream she'd told herself had never been real.

But it had felt like a real, actual death. Before, she might have pretended she knew he was off limits, but apparently part of her had always secretly hoped…

That connection was so powerful. That sense of need she felt when she saw him.

And the connection had only grown and intensified as she had gotten older.

As she began to realize just how much of a misfit she was with her family.

So really, finding out about her mother and his father…it made sense. And she shouldn't be sad.

"I'll help clean up," he said.

"You don't have to do that."

"You said yourself you don't know how to clean. Anyway, there's no dishwasher here."

He took her plate, which was empty, went over to the sink and started running water. She could only stare at his broad back, at the way he worked, smoothly and capably.

And then she realized she was staring at the back of him while he washed dishes with her mouth dropped open. Like he was performing some kind of Herculean effort, rather than just scrubbing a couple of dinner plates and a pan.

She scrambled to her feet and looked around the tidy kitchen. There wasn't really much to do. Not after the spiders had already been chased away and the cobwebs had been dealt with. She grabbed the broom again and began to sweep the floor, even though there was no dirt on it.

But she needed to do something, and she wasn't going to go stand over by the sink.

"Cricket," he said. "Why don't you dry?"

Well, apparently, she was going to go stand by him.

She moved over to the sink, and he thrust a dish towel in her direction. She grabbed it, her fingertips brushing his. His hands were rough.

She'd never touched him before.

She'd dreamed about it.

About his hands.

She hadn't known just how rough they would be.

She felt the lingering echo of that touch and she did her best to try and ignore it. He was warm too. She could feel heat radiating from his body as she stood beside him. Her shoulder vibrating with it as they stood with just an inch between them while she dried the dishes that he set on the side of the sink.

She looked over at him, and he turned his head. Then she immediately looked back down at the dish in her hand. She was acting weird. And he must realize that.

He must know that things were weird. But she imagined he had no idea why.

She could tell him. She could tell him right now.

You don't even know why. Do you get what you're doing?

This wasn't the reaction a woman should have to her half brother.

A pit of despair grew in her stomach.

She was supposed to know better. She was supposed to have fixed this.

No. She couldn't tell him her suspicions yet. It would only cause problems. It would only... It would ruin things. Everything. She couldn't take a chance on springing all this on him too soon.

So instead, she cleared her throat, mirroring the same gesture he'd done only a moment before, and carried the plates to their rightful spot in the kitchen.

"Well, I'm going to head to bed," he said, turning and gripping the edge of the counter. The muscles in his forearms flexed, and she made a study of the red paint on the tabletop. Of all the places that it was chipping and wrinkling.

"It's early," she said.

"Not really."

Then he brushed past her and left her standing in the kitchen. The room suddenly felt much larger without him standing in it. And that left her with a whole lot of questions she couldn't quite form. And even if she could, she wasn't sure she wanted to know the answers.

Three

This was Jackson's favorite part of the day. When the sun hadn't risen yet, and he put the coffee on. As strong as he could make it. When the world outside was quiet, and still. When the whole day had a wealth of possibilities in it.

Once upon a time, he'd spent mornings like this with his mother at the kitchen table. His father wasn't one to enjoy mornings. A rancher he was, but he also was always half stumbling out the door after the first rays of light had begun to filter over the mountains, his coffee in a to-go cup, his eyes bleary.

Not Jackson. And not his mom. Four o'clock had been his wake-up time for as long as he could remember. Plenty of time to get a jump on the day. To plan everything that needed to be done. To do it without all the damn people cluttering up the world. Let them sleep.

Those times had become especially precious when his mother had been ill.

He had lived in his own place at that point. But he still worked the family ranch. He got up, he drove over, he sat with his mother and had coffee. And then he went out to work the ranch.

In the years since, he had begun to exclusively work his own place. His father had enough hands on deck to handle the family place without Jackson. And anyway, once his mother had been gone, there had been no real reason to stay. There had been no one to have coffee with in the morning.

Jackson had realized at that time that the only reason he had stayed was that he was hanging on to something in his past that he had known wouldn't last forever.

And once she was gone, it had been time for him to move on too.

Anyway. His father was still barely dragging his ass out of bed and making it out to work on time.

Jackson didn't mind having coffee alone.

He walked down the hall, taking note of each squeaking board as he went into the kitchen and started the pot of coffee. This was not the kind of coffee maker he was accustomed to. But in truth, he could make coffee anytime, anywhere. He could MacGyver coffee with nothing but a tin can, a cheesecloth and a campfire. He could do what needed to be done. He could make this little plastic job work. But he preferred his programmable machine at home. Which had everything waiting for him as soon as his feet hit the ground.

He might enjoy this hour of the day, but there was

nothing wrong with wanting everything to be in its place, and as easy as possible. At least, not to his mind.

He thanked the good Lord that Cricket had coffee, and got it all started, his mood lifting immediately as the sound of the water beginning to heat filled the room, as the scent of the freshly ground beans hit him.

He really did love mornings.

He had a feeling Cricket didn't. Because she wasn't up. That actually suited him just fine.

He still couldn't figure out what the hell she actually wanted.

For a woman who said she couldn't wait to run a ranch, she really didn't seem to have a concept of what it took. And then there had been the way she'd behaved last night.

Like you don't know what it is?

Dammit. It really wasn't worth examining. He had been sure that when she wasn't in that dress, when she was back to being the Cricket he had known since she was awkward and had those buck teeth she'd been talking about earlier—which he did remember—those feelings of lust that he'd felt the night of the poker game would vanish.

But the problem was, now he'd seen the potential in Cricket. And he didn't much like it.

He wasn't a man for relationships. He had arrangements. Satisfying, adult relationships with women his age who, for whatever reason, didn't want relationships either. Divorcées, single mothers, busy women who traveled through in a group of friends, or with a bachelorette party. City girls looking for flings with a cowboy.

Yeah, he was down for all that.

But not young, earnest looking girls who had roots in this valley as deep as it was possible to have, who had already been wounded by her father, and who clearly had issues. Daddy issues.

That made him grimace. He supposed being a bit more than a decade older than her put him squarely in the territory of daddy issues.

And what did that make him?

Just a man, he had a feeling. Men were basic. And while he prided himself on maybe not being as basic as some of them, the fact of the matter was… He wasn't any different. He liked arrangements because he liked sex. And he didn't go without.

Come to think of it, though, he'd been without for a while.

He'd had to increasingly spend more time at the vineyard. Their father hadn't really gotten better since their mother had died, he'd only gotten worse. He was withdrawn. And he wasn't functioning in quite the same way that he used to.

Which pissed off Jackson, since he wasn't quite sure why his dad had fallen apart so much, all things considered. But the blowback was hitting the vineyard, and it was hitting Honey, and Jackson didn't want that to happen.

He had no idea how to fix it. Not when he had never really reconciled his own grief, or the accompanying anger at his dad.

His mother had been the single most important person in his life.

She had been a strong woman. And she'd sacrificed

everything for Jackson. Everything. He hadn't realized just how much until he'd gotten older. And he'd never had the chance to repay her. He'd been planning on it.

But there hadn't been enough time.

Grief about all that was always close at hand. But here in the silence of the morning, he could remember his mother as she'd been.

And he felt a little closer to her, instead of impossibly far.

He waited until he had his first sip of coffee. A smile touched his lips and he looked out into the yard. Everything was quiet. There were still stars in the sky. Then, once the caffeine had begun to do its work, he decided it was time to make his move. He went down the hall, doing nothing to modify the sound of his steps, and threw open the door to Cricket's bedroom.

"Get up, princess. There's chorin' to do."

"Mfffmmmmmmgh."

"What's that?"

The indignant figure in the bed moved, then sat up. It was dark, but he could see that her pajamas consisted of a white T-shirt. And he wondered if there was anything else. Or if she was bare underneath that thing. Then he quickly turned his focus away from that.

"Go away!"

"It's time to start doing work."

"It's…" She whipped her head around to look out the window. "It's midnight."

"It is 4:30."

"Basically midnight."

"Not in my world. And not in your world either. Not

if you want to be a rancher. I thought this was in your blood?"

He couldn't see her face. Obscured as it was by the fact that the light was off. And she was lucky. Because if he'd been in a really mean mood, he might have turned it on. But while he enjoyed harassing Cricket, there was no real reason to poke at her quite that much.

"I think sleep might be in my blood at this hour of the day."

"Too bad. If you have animals, you're going to have to get up and take care of them."

"I…"

"Sorry. That's how it works. You gotta get up early to be ready to work."

"That seems obscene."

"I grant you, I like an earlier morning than most."

"Go away. Morning people are suspicious."

"I made coffee."

She made a rumbling sound again.

"I'm going to go into the kitchen and pour you a cup. Don't make me come back in here and wake you up."

He turned around and walked down the hall. He did not need to see her get out of bed. He did not need to answer any of the questions he had about what she was or wasn't wearing under that T-shirt.

He didn't like the whole thing. This whole sudden, errant attraction to Cricket. It could definitely be argued that it would be a fine enough thing in theory. Because it wasn't like they weren't both adult people, even if he was a bit older. But he couldn't give her anything. And that… That didn't seem fair. She was young and scrappy and trying to make it on her own, and the last thing he wanted to do was…

Well, none of it bore thinking about because he was a grown man. And thinking a woman was pretty didn't mean acting on anything.

He wouldn't do it. Most especially because he was here to talk her out of her ranch. He had his limits.

He got a small, chipped mug out of the cupboard and poured some coffee in it. Just in time for Cricket to appear, in what he thought might be the same T-shirt, her blond hair resting on top of her head in a messy knot, jeans and a pair of boots.

"Good morning," she groused.

"You said you wanted to be a cowgirl."

He handed the coffee mug over to her.

"I was unaware that being my own boss would involve being woken up at a specific time. Hey. I'm your boss. You're not my boss."

"Yes. But the land waits for no one, Cricket. That's your first lesson in being a real, bona fide rancher."

"I don't like it."

"Doesn't matter. Why do you love the idea of being a rancher?"

"I don't know," she said.

"You have to do better than that."

"I feel… I don't know. I feel weird and wrong most of the time. I feel like I don't fit. But outdoors, I always felt like maybe I belonged. You know, I was better at riding horses, at dealing with bugs and dirt and all of that kind of stuff than my sisters. It was something I was just naturally more comfortable with. And maybe that's not right or fair. Maybe that's a little bit smug. To like something simply because I was better at it, when I couldn't be better at school, or being pretty."

"Better at being pretty?"

"Oh, come on. Wren and Emerson are naturally elegant and completely and totally perfect in every way."

"They're perfect when it comes to their particular kind of pretty, I'll give them that. And I'm not going to say people don't tend to have their favorite kind of flower. But all flowers are pretty."

"Surely not all of them."

"You're messing with my metaphor."

"It's too early for metaphors."

"It's never too early. Drink your coffee."

He didn't know why he felt the need to be nice to her. It was just that she seemed…utterly lost. He related to the feeling. He supposed that in some ways, losing whatever connection with her father that she'd had— though she claimed that it wasn't a very deep one—was a lot like a death.

And he knew what it was like to lose a parent. It was hard. It had left him feeling… Honestly, he hadn't known what to do after his mother had died. He hadn't been ready for it. No one was ever ready. But he had felt deeply and profoundly unprepared for the way the grief had rocked his life. For all the things he'd left unsolved and unsaid. For all the regret he felt on her behalf.

He knew she'd felt stuck in a loveless marriage. Even though she'd loved their family. Loved the kids.

Sometimes he felt…responsible for her unhappiness.

His dad was mired in grief, as if she'd been the love of his life, but sometimes Jackson thought the real reason his dad was mired in grief was that he'd known they *weren't* the loves of each other's lives and they'd trapped each other.

Sometimes, as a family they'd been so happy…

It didn't matter. All he knew was there was something in Cricket that he recognized. Didn't matter that she was a completely different creature than him. He knew what she was feeling.

And he might resent the position he found himself in, but honor prevented him from backing out. Anyway, now that he was here, he wanted to help her.

She sat at the table, her shoulders hunched up by her ears, and sipped her coffee a bit too slowly for his taste. He liked a leisurely morning, but you needed to get yourself out of bed a bit earlier if you were going to be that sluggish with it. Granted, they didn't actually have specific chores. But this was her lesson. Her lesson in ranching. And if she really thought she was going to do it… Well, then she had better get used to this.

He didn't think she would, though.

In fact, he had a feeling he was a step closer to being able to make his move than he'd thought he'd be at this point.

"Come on, little Cricket," he said as soon as she had drained the last drop of her coffee.

"I'm not little," she said.

"You are to me."

"I'm quite tall," she sniffed.

He looked down at the top of her head. "Again. Not to me."

"Well, you're ridiculous. Height runs in your family," she commented.

"Honey is short."

"But you and Creed are very tall."

"Yes," he agreed.

She seemed suddenly renewed, and he opened the front door and held it for her, and she went past him, going straight down the steps. "What are we going to do?"

"Well, why don't we start by looking at your pastures and your fencing. Then we're going to take a look at the barns and see what kind of shape they're in."

"That's all a very good idea," she said.

"Well, that is why you hired me. Or rather, won me."

"Yes," she said, frowning. "I suppose you are the expert."

"Say that again?"

"You're the expert," she said, but this time angrily.

"Just remember that."

He opened the door to his truck.

"What are you doing?"

"I figured we'd drive."

She got in, grumbling the whole way. They started driving out on one of the access roads that went toward the back end of the property. They would start there, and work their way back. At that point, the sky was beginning to lighten, and turn a bluish gray. The mountains were like sloping ink spills bleeding down into the fields. It was a beautiful piece of land. Hell, if Cricket didn't want to keep it, he'd be happy to add it to his own portfolio.

"Except," she said. "You do kind of have to admit that there is no actual reason for us to be up this early since there are no animals."

"Again," he said. "Practice. And also to give you a little dose of reality."

"You think I need a dose of reality?"

"Before you go committing to having lots of animals, I do think you probably need to have an understanding of what you might be in for."

"Bully for me."

"Yeah, well. You chose me to be your consultant."

"Ranch hand," she corrected.

"Yeah, who's calling the shots?"

She sputtered. But at that point, he put the truck in Park and got out. "Oh boy," he said, going up to the edge of one of the fences. It was light enough to see now, now that the sun was rising, the sunlight spilling rapidly over the landscape. "This fence is a mess. You're going to have a lot of work ahead of you."

"Well, we need a crew."

"We're going to have to figure out your budget."

"Don't talk to me like I'm a child. I do understand that. I know I haven't lived on my own, and I know that I come from money, but I also know there has to be money. Don't worry. Like I said, I sold my stake in the vineyard. So I have a bit of cash."

"Great. You're going to need quite a lot of cash."

"I'm sure you have an idea of how much a winery like Maxfield Vineyards is worth."

"True." Cricket was probably a fairly rich woman at this point. Even selling a quarter stake would've probably netted her quite a lot. "But it still wouldn't hurt you to have training. There may be an emergency, and you may not be able to get someone out here in time. What's going to happen if part of your fence comes down and you've got horses everywhere? You're going to have to know how to solve some of your own problems. Fortunately, I have tools. This," he said, indicating the whole fence line, "is going to be a hassle. And you're right. We're going to need to get a crew out here. But we can start it together."

"That sounds unpleasant."

"No, sweetheart. It's ranch work." He handed her a hammer and a pair of wire cutters. "Living the dream."

Cricket was exhausted and sore by noon. But at least then Jackson produced beer and sandwiches, and she found herself sitting happily on the tailgate of his truck, eating and watching as he continued to work. He never stopped.

"All right," he said, "let's head to the barn."

"We're not done?"

"Nope. And this is ranch work when you haven't got any animals. I'm just letting you know what you're in for."

"I feel like you're trying to actively discourage me."

He lifted a shoulder. "If you can be discouraged from being a rancher, then you should be."

"What does that mean?"

"That it's a hard life that often produces very little profit. And if you don't love it, you should do something else."

"Why would you say that?"

"Because it's the kind of thing that needs to be said, Cricket. If the work doesn't deter you… Then it doesn't. But you know, you could still live here without being a rancher. You could lease the fields to someone. Or you could sell up, get yourself a nice farmhouse and a couple of chickens."

"I don't want to do that," she said, feeling resolute. "I want to have my own life. My own land."

That statement was clarifying.

Because honestly, he had worked her ragged enough today that she had begun to question some things. And yeah, she was having to admit that she was a little sheltered. That she hadn't done all that much work in her life. She had done a lot of running around in the country, and she had managed to equate that with doing this kind of work. But it wasn't the same.

She just wished that she could do things half as effortlessly as he could. His body was a machine. Every muscle, every movement contributing to the other. She felt like she was all thumbs. That it took her five hits of the hammer to create the same kind of movement he got out of one. He was more efficient, more precise... It was frustrating. Maddening, even.

Though watching him was...

Well, she was learning a lot. She felt her cheeks get prickly. But she chose not to think too much about that and got into the cab of the truck with him as they drove to the barn.

He parked in front of the old, run-down building, and the two of them got out.

He walked over and pushed the door open, muscles straining. And yet again, she realized she was standing there gaping at the back of Jackson Cooper.

She mobilized herself, scampering through the open doorway as soon as it was wide enough for her to get through.

He came in behind her, and she could feel him. It was the strangest thing. Like there was energy crackling between them. It was more than just his body heat; it was something else.

She turned, and was looking up underneath his jaw. At the square line there, the stubble on his chin, his lips.

His lips were really very compelling. They were turned down slightly, naturally, which gave him a bit of a grim look. An intensity. That was one of the things that had always fascinated her about him. That quiet, brooding intensity. Something she did not have in common with him at all, because there was very little about her that was brooding. She wasn't quiet, she just avoided things by choice.

She took a step away from him and moved deeper into the barn. "Well," she said. "This is it."

He made an amused sound. "Not much," he said. "Is it?"

"No. I mean, all of it can be revamped." She looked at him sharply. "I know that it costs money."

"I know you do."

"Well, you do a lot of lecturing. So I can't exactly be sure."

He walked past her, and she noticed, not for the first time, that he had a very particular scent to him. His skin and soap and the wild. The pine from the trees, and a bit of the earth. "This could be a decent facility, with some upkeep. Don't get me wrong. I'm not trying to discourage you. I promise."

"Well, that's good to know," she said.

"There is a whole lot of moldy hay in here, though. We need to get it cleaned out. Why don't you grab a shovel?"

"More chores?"

"Yes," he said. "Actually, thinking of it as chores is kind of counterproductive. It's part of the gig. Part of life. Everything in life that you care about, whether it's your house or the land, has to be taken care of by somebody. I understand on the Maxfield family spread that somebody else does a lot of the caretaking. At our place, the Coopers do the caretaking."

"And you're currently caretaking your own ranch?"

"Obviously I have help," he said. "Which is good for you. Because if I didn't, I wouldn't be here."

"Right, right."

"Grab a shovel."

That was how she found herself feeling sweaty and indignant, moving great piles of moldy hay out into the bed of his truck.

"It will make decent enough compost. But you don't want it in here," he said.

"It smells," she said.

"A whole lot of things about ranch life smell."

"I don't mind it," she said, resolute.

"Sure."

"I really don't. I was just saying."

He arched a brow, half of his lips curving up into a smile. "You do a lot of questioning for somebody who just knows, and is fine with everything."

Her cheeks burned. She didn't really know why. "I'm fine," she said, stepping into the corner and grabbing another shovelful of that vile hay.

"Yeah, you seem totally fine."

"It's just a lot to learn. I'm happy to. I want to. That really is why I…" Except that would be a lie. She was about to finish the sentence with *it was why I wanted you here*. But it wasn't why. The words caught in her throat, and then her gaze caught his and held. She couldn't seem to look away. And he didn't look away either. He was close.

Closer than she had realized a moment ago. Or maybe the space around them had shrunk. She didn't know which. Except, of course that was impossible. But there was something about his nearness that felt impossible all on its own. Like she had been dropped onto an alien planet, into an alien body.

But there was no guide for how this should feel. Living with this man who had captivated her for the better part of a decade. This man who was so unlike anyone she'd ever known, and who she didn't really know, but who felt like he might be the answer to *something* all the same.

This was not what she'd dreamed about. But…she had to make what she was feeling something else because the only other option was for everything she'd suspected to be nothing and she couldn't bear that either.

To have her life just be the same.

To have her whole self just be the same as she'd always been.

His gaze flickered downward, and she realized that he was looking at her mouth. And that was when the tension in her stomach twisted, making her organs roll. Causing her heart to stutter.

And suddenly, her mouth felt like it was on fire. She was just so very aware of it. Had never, in all her life, been quite so conscious of the fact that she had lips.

But she was now.

Because he had looked at them. Because he was standing there, so close. Because they were sharing this space, sharing the air. Because he fascinated her in a way no one else had.

Because he had the answers.

Her heart started racing.

No.

No.

She had never been this close to him. And last night his hands had brushed hers and now he was standing right there. She knew she had to think of him differently now, and not as a man, like she'd always seen him. But she couldn't make him that. She just couldn't. Couldn't force her body to acknowledge what her brain suspected, no matter what she'd tried to tell herself about their connection.

He was there. And she *wanted*.

It couldn't be.

But then the light went on in those eyes, and even she could recognize the expression there, because she'd eaten dinner with the man last night.

Hunger.

And she felt it. She felt an answering appetite low and deep.

He moved, and she didn't know if it was toward her or away from her, because she dropped her shovel and ran out of the barn.

Ran.

Like the devil and all of hell was coming after her. Ran and didn't look back. Ran past his truck, through the fence, and out into the middle of the field. She stopped, panting, her forehead damp with sweat. She planted her hands on her knees, and only then did she realize what she'd done.

She had run from him.

He must think she was insane. She was acting insane. Except…

Why?

The word was more a groan in her soul than a real, actual word. A deep, enduring sadness that made her feel like she might be crushed with it.

It wasn't fair. It just wasn't fair. How in all the world was he…

The one man, the *only* man, that she had ever felt this for?

She was sick. There was something wrong with her. *You always knew there was something wrong with you.*

Yes, but she hadn't thought *this.*

She made a rough sound of distress. Out loud, and she didn't care if it carried all the way back to the barn. She couldn't care.

She looked around suddenly, wildly, to see if he was behind her. He wasn't.

Why was this happening to her? She had thought she had finally been on her way to finding her place. She had been resolute in winning over Jackson, in getting to know him so she could approach him about their potential connection…

And what if he had been moving toward her? What if he had been about to kiss her?

Well, then everything was ruined. Absolutely everything.

Cricket wasn't one to cry. She wasn't one to give in

to despair. But she wanted to now. Yes, she did. She wanted to now because she had thought she'd found a way out. She had thought she'd found a way to change her life. To change everything. But she hadn't. She was just weird, awkward Cricket, who would never find a place that felt comfortable.

Because this certainly wasn't comfortable. This was an abomination.

And you're not a baby. You're going to figure out how to face him, apologize and get your head on straight.

Yes, but she couldn't face him now. So she spent about an hour picking through the field and ignoring the fact that she was going to have to face him eventually. And when she finally went back to the barn, his truck was gone, and so was he.

And it left Cricket to wonder if she had hallucinated the whole thing.

Four

Jackson had decided to go to town to get some things for the ranch, and check on his own spread. Anyway, a drive to town was good for a little bit of self castigation. Obviously, he had terrified Cricket earlier when he'd moved in on her. He could pretend that he hadn't been about to kiss her. But he had been. And he knew better. Earlier, he had decided that he wouldn't. But for a minute there, she had seemed like she wanted him to, and his reasoning had gotten lost.

He hadn't felt like an ass for having ulterior motives for agreeing to the bet, knowing he'd lose. Knowing it would put him in a prime position to convince her to sell. Until now.

Because one thing he wouldn't do was get into a personal relationship with her while trying to get her land.

That was a step too far.

He had thought about going after her, but he had figured it would only create more problems. She had run for a reason, after all. It was pretty clear she didn't want him to go after her.

Now, of all the reactions he'd had from women he'd made a move on, running full tilt the other direction wasn't one of them. Sure, sometimes they might decide they weren't into it, and then all it took was a simple no thanks. He wasn't a man to push himself on anyone. And anyway, he didn't have to.

But Cricket had run like he might. And that made him wonder things about her. And he didn't want to wonder about her. Not any more than he already did.

He also figured that while he was out, he should go and check in on his father. Honey still lived at the ranch, and he knew she took on a fair amount of responsibility. Probably more than she should. It suited him that she was relatively sheltered, he had to admit.

And that got him right back into guilty thoughts and feelings about Cricket. She and Honey were roughly the same age. And if a man his age made a move on Honey, she wouldn't be the one running away. *He* would, with Jackson right after him.

He maneuvered his truck down the driveway, up to the winery show room. The place was no less grand to him now than it had been when he was a boy. It always would be. But he would also always picture his mother standing there, waiting with a smile. No matter how many years she was gone, that's what he would see.

But she wasn't there. It was Honey.

"What brings you around?" his sister asked, pushing the door open to the tasting room. "Aren't you in indentured servitude to Cricket Maxfield currently?"

"Currently."

"Honestly, I'm glad you lost the bet. I can't imagine having her working the tasting room."

"What do you have against Cricket?"

Honey shrugged. "I just don't really know her. Anyway, she's not all that friendly."

He frowned. "She's not particularly unfriendly."

"I don't know. She's weird. Don't you think?"

He thought about all the things Cricket had said. About feeling out of place. And that his sister's take, that she was weird, made him feel...

Sorry for her, he supposed.

"That's not a very nice thing to say."

"Since when do you care?"

"I don't."

"You must, a little."

He shrugged. "She's a nice kid. Anyway, I feel bad for all of them."

"Maybe someday I'll get there. I still can't believe Creed married Wren."

"You like Wren."

"I know. But... Isn't it weird? Switching allegiance like that."

"The problem was James."

"I don't know. I think it's deeper than that. Dad really..."

"Dad's not perfect," he said. "Dad's feelings on something don't have to be the final say."

"I know that."

Poor Honey had only been a teenager when their

mother had died. And Jackson felt like she had thrown herself in a relationship with their dad even deeper, trying to please him much more than she would have if that hadn't happened. There was no gray area with Honey when it came to Cash Cooper. While Jackson's relationship with him came with about fifty shades of it.

"Speaking of Dad," Jackson said. "Is he around?"

"Yeah, he's just back in the office."

The main office for the winery was at the back of the tasting room.

"You have any groups coming today?"

"A couple. Stick around, it's a bachelorette party."

And he found he had no interest at all. He found he was soured on the thought of it. Maybe his reaction had something to do with a woman running flat away from him not that long ago.

Or maybe it had something to do with Cricket herself, and her deep, seeking eyes. And that pretty mouth of hers.

Well.

He waved a hand toward his sister, then walked back to the office, his boots making a hard sound against the reclaimed barn wood floor. He knocked once, then opened the door without waiting for his dad to respond.

"The prodigal has returned," Cash said.

"Just to check in," Jackson grunted.

"Jericho came by yesterday and made it sound like you are pretty busy with your new boss."

"Yeah," Jackson said. "Jericho can shut it." Jericho was basically another brother to Jackson. They had grown up thick as thieves, and had started their own ranches about the same time. Like a brother, Jericho could also be a spectacular pain in his butt.

"Why exactly are you here?"

"I came to check in on you. I don't like being away for so long."

"You don't sound happy about it."

"What's going on, Dad? Look, I've never called you out. Not once. Not in front of Creed, and not in front of Honey, and I won't. Not even in front of Jericho. You might not be his dad, but he looks up to you. But I was closer to Mom, and I know that... I know that you're grieving. I believe that. But I don't get exactly what you're grieving. Because I don't think she was the love of your life."

"Jackson..."

"I know that things weren't always great with you."

"I loved your mother."

Jackson paused, a muscle jumping in his jaw. He wasn't going to argue with his dad about what he felt or didn't. "I'm sure you did. But enough that you're still nonfunctional five years later?"

He sighed. "It's complicated."

"I'm sure it is."

"You've never loved a woman in all your life, Jackson, let alone two. So what would you know about the kinds of things that I've been through?"

Jackson's senses sharpened. "Two?"

"I'm not going to discuss it with you. All I can tell you is nothing in my life has been right since I lost your mother. There are a variety of reasons for it. And maybe you're right, but to me it's not so simple. And maybe you don't think I deserve to have the grief and regret that I do. But I do. You know what's worse than grieving the love of your life? I think it might be grieving a person you wronged."

"What exactly…"

"Not up for discussion. Why don't you get on back to the Maxfield property? Used to be you were all so against them."

"*You* were against them," Jackson said.

His father cleared his throat. "Yeah. I was."

"Not anymore?"

"James was the problem."

"I figured as much."

"Turns out he was a problem for everyone."

"Again, not a surprise."

Though, Jackson wondered if her dad's problems had been a bigger surprise to Cricket than she let on, and if that was maybe part of *her* problem.

He had no idea what his problem was. Why was he overthinking every interaction with Cricket? He didn't overthink anything. If anything, he tended to underthink. He was a man of action. If there was something to be done, he liked to get it done. But maybe that was the problem. He couldn't quite figure out Cricket's aim in having him work at the ranch. Yes, she needed some guidance, but she often seemed to bristle beneath it, and she seemed more interested in him as a person then she did in his ranching expertise half the time.

But then, when he'd nearly kissed her, she'd run away. He would have thought that if there was a motivation, her having a crush would make sense.

Still, he preferred to take his chances with Cricket

than trying to stand here and reason with his father.
Trying to understand his father. "I'll see you around.
Just... Why don't you go to the bar tonight or something? Do something. Honey shouldn't have to cook
you dinner every night."

"She doesn't have to. I could easily get food from
the winery."

"She doesn't want you to do that. She wants you to
take better care of yourself. And you not doing it is
keeping her here."

"Didn't keep you here."

"Yeah, well, I don't feel responsible for a stubborn
old man. And she does."

He put his hat on his head and walked out of his dad's
office. Honey was standing in the middle of the room,
and Jericho was there too.

"Don't you have your own place?" he asked his
friend.

Jericho grinned. That particular grin of his, the one
he got when he wasn't being genuinely friendly. "Yeah.
I do. Just came to see how everyone was faring. Saw
your truck, and thought I'd see how you were doing
with your life as a ranch hand."

"What is it exactly that you find that so funny?"

"Because long as I've known you, you've never taken
orders from anyone. And I hear you're taking orders
from her."

"Not exactly."

"And sleeping in a bunkhouse," Honey said. "If I recall the terms of the bet correctly."

"Turns out the bunkhouse was in disrepair. I'm sleeping inside."

That earned him openmouthed stares from both Jericho and Honey.

"Really?" Jericho asked, a dark brow lifting.

"Really," he said, giving his friend a flat look.

Jericho frowned. "I didn't take you for a cradle robber."

"I'm not." He shoved his discomfort aside, shoved the memory of a couple hours ago aside. "Anyway, I didn't take you for a busybody."

"Well, it's not every day my best friend is suitably lowered to such a position. I'd be lying if I said I wasn't enjoying it."

"Some friend."

"I never claimed to be a *good* friend, just the best one you have."

"No kidding," Honey said. "Just an exasperating one. Anyway, I have work to do, unlike you two lazy cowboys. I actually still work here."

"And the place is hopping," Jericho said, looking around the empty space.

"I have a bachelorette party coming in twenty minutes. And no, I've decided neither of you can stay. I can't bear watching you go for the low-hanging fruit. I'd like to have more respect for you."

"I never pick low-hanging fruit," Jericho said. "The sweetest ones are at the top of the tree."

"Well, put up your ladder somewhere else, cowboy. Because you're not picking off this one." She made a shooing motion with her hands. "The ladies deserve to have a party in peace."

Both he and Jericho allowed Honey to kick them out

of the room, and he walked out toward his truck with his friend. "What were you really doing here?"

"I... I have a meeting with your dad."

"You have a meeting with my dad?"

"Yes. About the vineyard."

"Really?"

"You and Creed are silent partners. At least, more or less these days. Your dad is... Well, he's not enjoying this as much as he used to. He wants to get out of it."

"Are you buying my dad out?"

"Talking about it."

For some reason, that bothered Jackson. "You didn't think to talk to me about it?"

"It's a business deal, Jackson. I don't have to talk to you about my business."

Jackson knew that Jericho had been very successful with investments. His friend was a rancher, but he was a great deal more than that. Successful, extremely so, and not because he sat on his hands, or did things with caution.

"No. But you are my friend."

"Yes. I'm talking to you now. But I figured I would have a conversation with your father before I did that. I haven't finalized anything yet."

"What's the deal?"

"I'm buying half. And I'm going to transition to running the day-to-day."

"That means you're buying Honey's portion."

"She hasn't come into it yet. Because of her age. So yes."

"She's going to be..."

"She should be free of this. Don't you think?"

"Now you're going to tell me that you have nothing but my sister's best interest at heart?"

Jericho shook his head. "No. But I care about her too. I'm not just acting without thought."

Jackson shook his head. "She's going to kick you in the nuts."

"She might. Like I said. It's business. It's not personal."

"It kind of has to be personal. Given that our relationship is personal."

"If it were personal, I would be buying him out for a good deal. I'm not. I'm overpaying."

"Well, at least there's that."

His dad hadn't told Jackson, of course. Bottom line, there had been a wedge between his parents whether his dad was ever going to address it or not, and by default Jackson had ended up on his mother's team. They had all rallied when they'd needed to. His dad had been there for his mom. He couldn't fault him for that. No. If only it were more straightforward. If only things had been toxic. Because if they had been toxic then Jackson could have disavowed his dad. If his father hadn't been there for his mother, then Jackson could easily cut his father out of his life.

But it was never going to be that simple. His dad wasn't a bad man. But as far as Jackson could tell he'd been a bad husband.

He'd also been there when it had counted.

"Look, I gotta get back to work. I'll see you around." Jackson got into his truck, leaving Jericho standing there, leaving his conflicted feelings there at Cowboy Wines, because it was easier than staying and confronting them. Honestly, dealing with Cricket was much easier than all of this.

Five

Cricket was bound and determined to pretend that nothing had happened earlier. Though, when Jackson arrived in his truck, she was a little bit chagrined. She had hoped that she might get a small reprieve. After all, he hadn't said why he'd left, and it was entirely possible that he figured, since she had run away from him like someone not thinking straight, he had every right to back out of their agreement. But no, he was back.

She flung open the door to the house, and stood there with a grin fixed permanently on her face. A grin that dared him to comment.

He got a couple of paper bags out of the truck, and held them. Standing there staring at her.

"Glad you're back," she said.

"Yeah," he said. "I'm ready to fix the sink."

"Well great," she said.

"Yeah, I said I would."

He slammed the door of the truck shut and began to walk toward her. She scampered back through the entryway, but still stood there, with her hand on the door. She didn't want to look like she was running scared. Not again. She needed to get a grip. That was the thing. She needed to stop acting this way.

"I really appreciate it."

"Yeah, I mean, you said."

He brushed past her, and she held her breath. Because she didn't want to smell him. Didn't want to get the impression of his scent again, because it did weird things to her insides and she heavily resented all the weird things Jackson did to her insides. She couldn't think about it right now though. Because she had to act... She had to act like everything was okay. She just really desperately needed to pretend like everything that happened earlier hadn't happened.

He set the bags on the table and she stood in the doorway, watching as he got out pipes and tape and tools.

"Do you want to learn something?"

"Well, you are ever the teacher."

They had found a way back to their earlier rapport, so there was that.

"That I am."

"Where's the water shut off, Cricket?"

"I don't know that," she said.

He shook his head. "Well, we're going to have to turn the water off or we're going to end up with a flood."

"Okay. Maybe it's... Maybe it's in one of the cabinets."

"The water shut off is in the cabinet."

"No, I mean the instructions. There's some paperwork that has information on the house. In this cabinet." She walked past him and reached up into a cabinet that was full of papers. She didn't have enough dishes or utensils to bother moving them. She had plenty of space in the kitchen that they could stay right there. She pulled out the paperwork and spread it out on the table, rifling through the sheets, but he had already walked out of the room. She heard the door shut, and a few moments later he was back.

"Found it."

"How?"

"Logic. Experience," he said. "Anyway. It's fine now."

"I should probably know where the water shut off is," she said, still standing there holding the papers.

"I'll show you afterward." He got down underneath the sink, tools in hand, and began to dismember things.

"Can I hand you stuff?"

"Sure."

They set up an assembly line, where he asked for things, and she handed them to him. When he was done, he would give it back, and she would put it on the table.

Things felt not quite so fraught. And it was easy for her to forget that earlier today had gone so horribly wrong.

"Come down here," he said.

She started. "What?"

"I want to show you something."

Slowly, cautiously, she knelt down beside him. It

wasn't him she was afraid of. It was herself. He wasn't the one who knew why earlier was such a disaster, and he probably didn't even…well, she hadn't stayed to find out if he'd even been leaning in toward her. It was all in her head, that was the thing. So she resolutely got down next to him and made a valiant attempt at not breathing the same air, since that had caused her some serious problems earlier.

"What are you showing me?"

"I'm going to have you fit the pipe."

"Oh…okay."

He handed her a wrench. "Lean in and tighten it right here."

She leaned in and she couldn't help but breathe. And when she did…

When she did, she was overwhelmed by him.

Why did he have to smell so good? Why was he so compelling? She looked at the square line of his jaw, the straight blade of his nose. The intensity in those eyes. Those eyes that had always been so fascinating to her.

It *had been* a crush but now it *couldn't* be.

It couldn't be.

It couldn't be.

She still couldn't breathe.

She looked down. But then… She could feel him looking at her, and she couldn't keep herself from looking back.

And when she did, he was so close. His eyes were so intent on hers. She had run away earlier. And she had been smart to do that. She had needed to do that.

She should run. She should run. She should move

away. Because this was wrong. And it was crazy. *She* was crazy.

And for some reason—anger, rebellion against what she was feeling—she didn't run. Instead, she leaned forward.

Instead, she closed the distance between them.

She was going to prove, once and for all, that she did not want him.

This would disgust her.

It would burn all those feelings to the ground.

And for the first time in her life, Cricket's lips touched another person's.

Because she was sure she'd find that once she kissed him, once she took the mystery out of it all she'd be disgusted. She had to be, right? Because surely, *surely*, nature would take care of this and she'd recoil in horror when their mouths met.

As soon as her lips touched his, though, she knew she was wrong.

It was like a flash bomb had gone off inside of her stomach.

And Cricket ignited.

He moved, large, rough hands cupping her face, holding her steady as he consumed her. His whiskers were rough, his mouth hot. He smelled like heaven.

She was shaking. Guilt warred with desire as her mind went blank of everything. Of what she should be doing. Of who he was. Who she was. And what she suspected. It was all gone. There was nothing left but the intense sensation of being touched by him, kissed by him.

How had this happened?

How had she… How had she ended up desiring him?

You don't know? As if it hasn't been halfway to a crush all this time?

She'd been fascinated by him but she'd never called it that. She'd been interested in him, intrigued by him, but she'd never…

And then she'd found out about their parents and… and…she'd thought what she'd been feeling was something else.

She didn't know anything.

She'd moved to this ranch convinced that she was finally figuring things out. Finally making a move toward having a life that she wanted. But here she was, drowning in confusion. Drowning in desire. A desire she had no business feeling. Not at all. Here she was, making the biggest mess of everything that she could possibly make.

She was less certain now than she'd been before. Less of anything, less of everything. And more too.

Jackson Cooper. This is Jackson Cooper.

And he's probably your half brother.

She jerked herself away from him, gasping. "No."

"Cricket, it's okay," he said. "You don't have to run away."

"No," she said. "I might."

"You don't need to be afraid of me."

"It's not you I'm afraid of."

"What?"

"It's me," she said. And much to her horror, tears sprang to her eyes. And they started to fall before she could even consider holding them back. Cricket didn't cry. And here she was, weeping like an inconsolable child in front of Jackson. He must think she was insane. She thought she was insane.

"What is it?"

"It's us," she said. "Jackson," she said. "I think you might be my brother."

Six

Jackson was on his feet and halfway across the room as soon as that last word came out of Cricket's mouth.

He didn't know what the hell she was on, but she was wrong.

He knew that down to his soul.

He had a sister. He knew what that felt like. This did not feel brotherly at all. Not in the least. Absolutely nothing about what he felt for Cricket could fall under the heading of familial. She was a beguiling little minx who had essentially been a source of irritation for him for the last several years, and then had turned into a wholly irritating, and far too attractive, woman.

Then she'd kissed him. And now she was telling him that she thought she was his sister.

"You better explain yourself, and quick."

"I just… I found out something about our parents. My mother and your father… They used to be… Did you ever wonder why your father hated mine so much? I mean, beyond the fact that James is a real piece of work, there had to be something else. And I knew there had to be. Well, my mother started talking about it more. And since she and my father got divorced… Well, she told us. She told us that she used to be with your father. She was in love with him, but he was poor, and she chose to marry James instead. Why am I so much younger than my sisters? It doesn't make any sense. I don't fit with them. I fit with you."

"Cricket," he said. "You are not my sister."

"I pretty much have to be," she said.

"You pretty much don't," he said. "There is no way, no way in hell, that you could possibly be my sister."

"Why not? I think it makes plenty of sense. Seems to me that it's reasonable enough."

"There is nothing reasonable about any of this."

"I have always…thought that I didn't fit. And I think this is why."

"So why did you psychotically decide to kiss me?"

"To prove it would be gross!"

The way his blood was burning through his veins made a mockery of that statement. He just stared at her.

"Hey," she groused. "*You* almost kissed me earlier. Why do you think I ran away? It's wrong, Jackson. And I was just trying to make it right and now I messed it all up!"

"Get in the truck."

"What?" she squeaked.

"Get in the truck. There's one person who can settle this."

"I mean," she said, using that same arch, certain tone she'd used many times she'd been certain, but wrong, in the time he'd known her, "there are DNA tests that can settle it. Many men in labs could settle it…"

"We're talking to my father."

"Oh…"

"I'm going to have him tell you, once and for all, you couldn't be his daughter."

"I…"

"Did you talk to your mother?" he asked.

"I… No. I didn't ask her directly. But you have to understand that she… It took her so long to tell me any of the specifics about her life. About her relationship with your dad. We're not really all that close. And I just didn't… Talking to her won't mean a lot to me. I won't believe that it's true."

"I'm sure that if you told her you were considering jumping my bones, she might give you the straight answer."

"Don't say that. Anyway, I never said I wanted to do that. I just kissed you."

"You're not in high school, Cricket, when does it end with just a kiss?"

"Well." She didn't know what to say to that, and it was clear. And he was being mean, but he…

Hell. His father had cheated on his mother…

Would it really surprise you?

He didn't think Cricket was his sister. End of story. He knew too much about women and chemistry to think it, even for a moment.

His certainty in his libido was sound.

His certainty in his father? Less so. And even though he knew Cricket had the wrong end of the stick here, he was worried that one piece of it might be true.

He had enough of a hard time with his old man without having to believe he'd been unfaithful to his mother.

"Get in the truck," he said. "I'm not repeating myself again."

They marched out to the truck, and he jerked the passenger side door open for her.

"Thank you," she said softly.

"No problem."

He started the truck and pulled out of the driveway much faster than necessary. "Why didn't you tell me? Why didn't you tell me right away when you had a suspicion?"

"Because. Because I knew that... It doesn't bother me to think about my mom cheating on my dad. I wouldn't blame her. I think she loved your dad, and she made a terrible mistake. And I can see how... When someone gets under your skin, Jackson, it's not that easy to get rid of them. I can understand that."

"Can you?"

"Yes," she said, filled with fury. "I can. I don't judge my mom. Except... Except on behalf of yours. Because I know how much you love your mom. And she was a lovely woman from what I remember. And she's gone, and I just didn't want to... I wanted to get to know you better first. I wanted to figure out the whole situation."

"Why didn't you just ask Creed?"

"I'm not even that close with Wren and Emerson. I'd like to be closer. But... That's the thing. We're not a

normal family, and we never have been. They're close
with each other because they're close in age. Because
they had more in common in their upbringing. I'm different. I always have been. So I'm not just magically
close with Creed because he married my sister. I'm not
even magically close to my sister."

"What? You thought you'd become magically close
to me?"

She made a sputtering sound. "I've always... I... I
don't know. Forget it."

He thought back to how she'd trailed after him. Like
a damn puppy when she'd been young. Had she thought
he was her brother even then? No, she'd said that it only
occurred to her recently. And all his thoughts, all his
intentions toward buying her ranch, everything...just
kind of faded away.

Because handling this was what mattered.

Settling it was what mattered.

He pulled up to the winery and saw that there was
still a light on in the tasting room. He was sure that his
dad was still in there.

"Come on."

"Okay," she said, clearly filled with trepidation.

He gripped her arm, and propelled her forward.

"Can you not touch me?" she said, jerking her arm
out of his hold. She was as disgusted by the whole thing
as he was.

Except.

Except, the problem was his body wasn't all that
disgusted.

His blood was on fire from that kiss. And while
there had been a momentary dampening caused by the

shock of what she'd said, it had not created in him an instant disgust.

They needed to get this settled.

He needed her to be as sure as he was that there wasn't any truth to her suspicions at all.

Fact was, he was sure he had more experience than Cricket when it came to sex. So maybe she was naive enough to think they could be related, but he was not confused about connections, chemistry and attraction.

And he knew what was happening here.

None of it was familial.

He opened the door to the tasting room and walked in. Cash Cooper was standing at the back of the room, examining the stock.

"Dad," he said. "We need to talk."

His father turned, shock registering on his face when he saw Cricket standing there. "What can I do for you?"

"Oh…" Cricket started to fidget. "I just had a question to ask."

"What's that, young lady?"

"Well, I kind of need to know if I'm… If I'm your daughter."

It had happened. *It had happened.*

She was standing there in front of Cash Cooper, and she was asking him if she was his daughter. Except now… She hoped that it wasn't true.

Because Jackson was in her blood. And she…she wanted him. And she had been so sure she could overcome that. That she could put all these feelings in their proper place, but she hadn't managed to do it. She didn't know if she ever could. She just didn't know. She had tried. She had tried, and it had ended with her kissing him on the floor of her kitchen.

Everything was a disaster. It was an absolute and total disaster. But then it had been from moment one, hadn't it? Because there were only two scenarios here.

One, she was hopelessly and utterly attracted to Jackson Cooper who was unobtainable in every way, who would never want her, and who would never keep her even if he enjoyed kissing her, and she was just out of place in her family because she was.

Or the second one, which was that she was unforgivably, irrevocably attracted to her half brother.

No, she couldn't win.

"What made you think that, young lady?" Cash asked.

And he was so kind, it made her heart ache. It made her chest feel like it was being cracked in two, because James certainly wouldn't have been this nice. She wanted Cash to be her father, but she did not want Jackson to be her brother, and she didn't think that there was…

There was just nothing.

"My mother told me. She told me she was in love with you. She told me that she married James Maxfield and it was the wrong choice. And I've just never felt like I belonged. I've never felt like I fit. When she said that it all made a lot of sense. That… That maybe I'm not a Maxfield, and that's why I don't fit. That maybe I was supposed to be here the whole time. Because I want to be a rancher. I don't want to spend my life in a stuffy winery. Because I want different things and I look different and I act different and I… I just thought maybe that was why."

"Cricket," Cash said, and his voice was so kind and gentle she thought she might break apart. "I'm not your father."

She wanted to cry. In despair, with relief.

Jackson wasn't her brother.

He wasn't her brother. So that was… There was that.

Beside her, she heard him let out a huge sigh of relief. And that brought a skeptical look from Cash, but he didn't say anything. Then he looked back at Cricket. "I did love your mother." Then he turned to Jackson. "I… That was the problem, Jackson," he said. "I loved Lucinda. And I never quite got over it. You know… You know that your mother and I got married because she was pregnant with you. I acted rashly because I was heartbroken. She and I both paid for it for years. We tried. And we love you kids. With everything. I cared for her. I cared for her a whole hell of a lot. But you know what makes me the most sorry? That I could never be the husband she needed. That she died being with someone who always had feelings for someone else. That's what kills me."

Cricket felt guilty. Standing there listening to this.

It was clearly a private conversation, one that needed to happen without her presence. But here she was.

All because she had been…

Because she had been so desperate to fix this thing inside of her.

What was wrong with her? Something was wrong with her. And there always had been something wrong, and this was just further evidence of it.

A tear slid down her cheek and she felt horrified. Horrified to be displaying this kind of emotion in front of not just Jackson but Cash. This man who wasn't her father, who should feel nothing for her at all.

"You look like your mother," he said softly.

She hadn't expected that. It was like an arrow to the heart.

"No, I don't," Cricket said. "My mom is elegant. And pretty. And her hair never…does this," she said, gesturing to her curls.

"She used to be like you, Cricket. And she was my first love. Just like I was hers. But love wasn't enough. Not for her. That's fine."

"It wasn't fine though, was it? She was miserable. She was absolutely miserable being married to him. I hope you weren't miserable."

"I wasn't miserable," he said. "I think I might've made my wife miserable. But I wasn't. Still, I have a lot of regrets."

"My father doesn't have any. His only regret is that he's lost everything. He doesn't care about anything or anyone else. When I say everything, I don't mean us. James Maxfield never cared about a damn thing. And he's…he's my father."

Sadness settled deep in her stomach. Because for just a little while she had hoped. She had really, genuinely hoped…

"Did you ever cheat on Mom?" Jackson's voice was granite.

"No," Cash said, addressing his son. "I swear it. I swear to you I never did."

"Well then. I guess that answers all those questions."

"I'm not sure if I should apologize or not," Cash said.

Cricket shook her head. "I should. I assumed something about you that wasn't fair. And I did it because I… I'm not happy with my family. I'm not happy with my place in it. But that's just the way it is. There's no answer for it. So… So. That's it."

Then, she turned and ran out of the tasting room, back to the truck. She leaned against the door, breathing hard.

She was doing so much running.

And all she could think was—what a mess she'd made out of everything. She'd revealed to Jackson that she was interested in him, revealed that she had suspected he was her half brother… Every single thing that she'd been so bound and determined to have control over, she had gone and just made a huge mess of. He was never supposed to know that she was attracted to him. And she was supposed to time this whole thing… better. But did it even matter?

He came out a few moments later, looking like thunder. And she knew that the truth didn't matter. She had managed to absolutely and totally… She felt stupid. And small. And wrong.

Every bad thing she had ever felt, it was magnified now.

"I can walk…"

"You cannot walk. Get in the damn truck."

She didn't even argue, because she felt too guilty. Too bad. So she got into the truck, and they made the drive back to the ranch in total silence.

She was going to send him away. Send him back to his place, because there was just no… There was no point in anything. She wasn't a rancher. It wasn't in her blood. She had spun herself all manner of fantasies about Jackson Cooper when she was a girl, when she didn't know anything about anything. And then, when her family had imploded, she had spun different fantasies altogether. She had watched her beautiful, elegant sisters win over handsome cowboys, and Cricket had realized that her own darkest, most cherished secret— the thing that she had lied about for years—would never come true. Because Wren had gotten the interest of Creed, and Wren was…well, she was beautiful.

Elegant and sophisticated and refined and everything Cricket could never be.

And not only was Cricket too young for Jackson to ever evince an interest in, she was also just… She was just her. And so yes, it had been convenient to weave a new fantasy. About all the reasons why she might feel wrong. All the reasons why she might have felt connected to Jackson, ways that explained away the feelings that she had, but that would still mean he mattered.

She stumbled out of the truck when they got to the house.

"Jackson…"

He rounded the front of the truck quickly, his eyes filled with liquid fire. "First things first," he said.

And before she could react, before she could open her mouth or say anything, his lips were on hers. And he was kissing her again. Deep and hard and longer than the first time. There was rage in this kiss. An intensity that she had never known a kiss could possess.

Wrong.

Small.

Ugly.

All the words that she felt inside—all the words she

had used to describe herself—slowly began to fall away, each pass of his mouth over hers stripping them back. Creating something new inside of her. Something different. Something she had never experienced before. Like an avalanche. One of need and desire and hope.

It was the hope that stunned her. Suddenly that yawning, cavernous thing in her chest was filled with light. Suddenly it was lifting her, propelling her forward. Up on her toes and more firmly into his arms.

He angled his head, his tongue passing over hers.

And she felt right.

Because this had been the feeling all along. That first connection that she'd felt to him. When she had first known what it meant that she would be a woman some day, and that she would want to be in the arms of a man, and that she was certain that man was Jackson Cooper. In that one blinding moment he had taken everything that felt wrong and turned it around.

Because he had kissed her.

She wasn't wrong about that. He was kissing her, and he was doing it with just as much passion as she felt inside of her for him. And if he felt that, then she wasn't wrong.

She hadn't been wrong.

Life had been wrong.

And she had altered her expectations, changed what she felt to make it easier to digest. She had been trying to create a story that was easier to live with.

One where her father didn't love her because she wasn't his.

One where her mother found her difficult because Cricket was a reminder of sins.

One where she was so different from her sisters because they were only half of each other.

And one where Jackson mattered not because she had an unobtainable crush, but because he was her long-lost brother.

One where she wanted to be a rancher because she came from a family of them, not just because she did.

But this was proof.

That she had her own dreams just because.

That she was herself, wholly and singularly, for better or for worse. That she wanted him, maybe because—like ranching—he was too big, too unobtainable and too impossible to have.

Maybe that's who she was.

A pioneer. A person who saw what was possible and asked for that little bit more.

A person who looked around and said this doesn't have to be just enough, I can have more, I can have better.

Maybe that was who she was.

It was a revelation. Just like his arms, just like his mouth.

But then, just as suddenly as he kissed her, he was pulling away.

"That had to happen. Because I had to... I couldn't leave it at that last one. Not with what you said."

Cricket launched herself back into his arms. Because she didn't want to be anywhere else. Because she wanted to feel. All these things that he and he alone had made her feel for all these years.

It was done. That was the beauty of it. The beauty of having made such a damn fool of herself already. There was no going back. There was nothing to protect.

The crushing reality was that James Maxfield might be her father. Or he might not be. But the one thing that mattered most was that Jackson *wasn't* her brother.

Her long-held crush had no doubt been revealed by her earlier actions, but that was freedom in many ways. She had wanted him—she had wanted this—for so long, and there was no reason to not simply…take it now. None at all.

So she did. She drank deeply from his mouth like she was a dying woman and he was the source of life-giving water.

His whiskers were rough beneath her palms, where she grabbed hold of his face and stretched up as hard as she could, on her toes, kissing him with all the breath she had in her.

"What exactly do you want?" he said, large hands grabbing her hips and setting her back on the ground. "Because you've got to know, little Cricket, that you're playing with fire here. I don't want you to get burned."

She scoffed. "I'm not afraid of fire."

"You're not?"

She tilted her face upward. "I'm not afraid of anything."

"You're trembling."

"Yeah, that happens sometimes, when a woman is turned on, didn't you know?" She spoke with a bravado she didn't necessarily feel.

"You might have to educate me on the subject."

"I'm not afraid of anything, do you know why? Because… I already can't have the approval of my family. And you know, I was really scared of what it meant that I wanted you, suspecting what I did. I was really scared to look foolish, but you know what? I did. I do. So where is there to go from here? I guess I could fear for my own physical safety, but I don't. Not when you hold me. I spent my whole life wanting things I couldn't have. Wanting my parents to care about me in a way that they didn't. Wanting to fit in a way that I couldn't. Wanting to be part of a family that I wasn't." She felt like it was the better part of valor to maybe not mention that wanting him was part of what she'd been denied for all this time. She might not have a whole lot of pride, but she had a little, and she was going to protect it.

"I'm tired of that. No, I'm not afraid of this. I'm not afraid of you. I'm just afraid of living more of the same."

"Marriage is not for me," he said. "Just right up front. Relationships aren't for me."

"That's real flattering, cowboy, but did I propose?"

"I'm just getting that out there, Cricket, because I can't ignore the fact that you had a hell of a day, and from the sounds of things, a hell of a few weeks. On top of that, you are younger than me. And I just need to make sure that we are both completely aware of what this is."

"I want you. I'm very tired of not having the things I want."

"Seems fair."

It was deeper than that. But it wasn't really his business. She had a feeling, though, that Jackson Cooper was a mountain she had to climb if she was ever going to figure out what lay on the other side of him. On the other side of this. Because honestly, the weirdness of the last few months was all bound up in him, and before that, years of a crush that had quite overtaken her life.

So, there was no magical, mystical connection to the Cooper family.

But Jackson was still a thing. And that needed to be sorted out before she could be the new Cricket. This woman who was going to make a way apart from her family. This woman she wanted desperately to be. Needed to be.

He was so tall and strong and beautiful. And she had no idea what he was getting out of this. But that wasn't her concern. Her concern was...*her*.

It didn't matter what anybody else thought. Didn't matter what anybody else wanted from her, what they thought of her. It didn't matter what he thought. She had been dragged into Cash Cooper's very own tasting room, and she had accused him of cheating on his wife. Had asked if *he was her father*. She had reached the height of humiliation. So she was all in on this, because there was nothing left to protect or destroy.

She was Cricket, reduced.

And she wanted to build herself back up again.

"I'm tired of talking," she said.

Talking wasn't her thing. She had spent so many years just off on her own, daydreaming about the life she might have someday. She had done more talking with him over the last week than she had ever done with anyone, really. She didn't want to talk. She just wanted him.

"Suit yourself."

That was how she found herself being lifted off the ground, his large hand on her ass, around her back, as he picked her up and kissed her, hard and deep. She could feel his body, firm and insistent against hers, evidence of his arousal. And it thrilled her. Thrilled her down to her soul. To know that he wanted her the same as she wanted him. To know that, of all the mistakes she'd made, and all the things she might have done wrong today, she hadn't dampened his desire for her.

He did want her.

He did.

His kiss was wild now, far beyond anything she'd ever fantasized about. She'd done a lot of fantasizing about Jackson Cooper, but it had been gauzy, and it hadn't been half so physical. She hadn't really known about the heat of another person's body pressed against hers, the rough feeling of his whiskers, the firmness of his mouth. That slick friction of his tongue against hers. The way their breaths would mingle, the way she could feel his heart raging through his chest and against hers. Those rough hands, moving over the fabric of her T-shirt, and then under it, against her skin. His body was so very hard.

No, she hadn't counted on this. The intensity of it. The reality of it. It was blindingly brilliant and beautiful, and was making her into a version of herself she hadn't known was possible—a wild creature, which in many ways she'd always been, but with aim, with purpose.

Because her wildness was pouring out of her and over him. She didn't feel embarrassed. Didn't feel nervous.

There was no inhibition at all. She bit his bottom lip and he growled. And she didn't know why she'd done it, only that it had felt right. And she didn't question it. Didn't question anything. This felt natural. This felt right in a way that nothing else ever had in her entire life. He felt right, fitted against her, the softness of her body seemingly made for the hardness of his, and she couldn't recall a time when she had ever felt so…right. So real. So complete.

So certain that the things about her that were different were what made it all so good.

For all her life she'd felt like the lone misfit toy on an island of beauties, and now, she didn't feel misfit at all.

No, she fit just right.

He carried her up the front steps, stumbled slightly on a board, then braced her hard against the door, and she gasped. His erection pressed firmly between her thighs, hitting her right where she was the neediest for him. At the place where she was desperate with longing.

He rocked against her, growling as he took the kiss deeper. She gasped, letting her head fall back, arching into him, rubbing her breasts against his chest, reveling in how sensitive she was.

She had been so ashamed, so embarrassed of her every desire for a great many years—to feel a total lack of that shame was a revelation she hadn't known she'd been waiting for.

He pushed the door open, then propelled them both down the hall and toward his bedroom. Toward the little twin bed there.

She doubted he fit on it by himself, she had no idea how the two of them were going to fit. But her bed wasn't any larger.

He didn't seem concerned at all. Just like a loose

board hadn't caused him to make a false move, the bed size didn't do it either.

With knowing, competent hands, he pulled her top off over her head, and with one deft motion took her bra with it.

She was standing there, totally topless in a pair of jeans, and mesmerized by the look of abject hunger in his eyes.

He wanted her. More than a little. He wanted her, and it was obvious.

And she, with all her slight curves and frizzy hair, felt desired. Felt beautiful.

She closed the space between them, pushing her hands beneath his shirt, loving the feel of his hard muscles, the rough hair that covered his hot skin. She'd never thought much about sex in general. Only sex with *him*. But he was far and beyond anything she'd ever fantasized about. Far and beyond anything she'd ever dreamed she might have.

She pushed his shirt up and over his head, revealing his body. So much more beautiful and perfect than she could have ever imagined. That broad chest, lean waist and perfectly defined muscles. He was all things masculine and glorious, and everything feminine within her bloomed with glee.

And suddenly, she wanted to cry. Because Cricket Maxfield never got what she wanted. Cricket Maxfield never got the best or the brightest. She had the leftovers of her family's gene pool. She wasn't brilliant or beautiful, particularly ambitious. She wasn't the one the sun shined down on with favor.

But she had wanted Jackson Cooper for as long as

she'd known what it meant to want, and she was getting him.

Whatever happened after this didn't really matter.

Because this was the most perfect moment she'd ever felt. Ever experienced.

Oh, she'd tried to pretend that her feelings for him could be something other than this, but they couldn't be. This was the connection. For her, this was what it was. What it always would be.

"What?" he asked.

"You are just stunning," she said.

He laughed. Honest to God. A chuckle rumbling in his chest. And then she found herself caught up in those big, strong arms, her bare breasts brushing against his hot, rough skin.

"Well I'm glad you think so."

She found herself being kissed again, and all the while his hands worked on getting rid of her jeans, her panties, socks and shoes.

Until she found herself stretched across the bed with his big body over the top of hers. She completely naked, he still in his jeans. The denim was rough between her thighs, the delicate skin there scraped by the raw material. And she could feel him, right there, so hard and insistent and…

She ached.

And he just kept on kissing her. And kissing her. He shifted slightly, putting one hand between her thighs, finding her slick and wet, each pass of his fingertips over that sensitized bundle of nerves creating a white, electric heat that nearly left her blinded.

She had never felt anything like this before. And

yes, she'd put her own hand between her legs plenty of times, but it wasn't like this. His skin was rough, and she had no control over how fast he worked, how slow. How much time he took. And when he pushed a finger inside of her before drawing her wetness back out over the source of her desire, she gasped. He did it again, and again, adding a second finger to the first, until she was sobbing. Until she was begging. For what, she didn't even know.

She fumbled for the front of his pants, tried to get his jeans open.

He chuckled. Husky and knowing.

"Not yet," he said. "I'm not done with you."

He dropped off the bed and she found herself being dragged to the edge of the mattress. Her thighs draped over his shoulders, the heart of her completely open to him.

"Jackson," she said, her voice trembling.

She might be a virgin, but she wasn't innocent. In that she fully knew all the things men and women did to each other. Her sisters had never been particularly shy about their sex lives, or their desires. And beyond that, she hadn't kept herself sheltered in terms of what she watched or read.

But having a man right there, looking at her, with no way to hide herself, that was a different proposition altogether than simply knowing. And when his mouth touched her, she jumped back, only to find herself pinned firmly against his face, his strong arms wrapped around her thighs, holding her there.

She wiggled as he lapped at her, as he tasted her like she was a decadent dessert.

"Jackson," she said, a feeling like flying building in her stomach, making her certain that she was no longer being held to the bed, but somewhere among the stars.

She couldn't breathe.

She didn't want to. She just wanted this. Forever.

Him. His hands. His strength. His mouth.

The pleasure she felt wove around all those things and created the magic tapestry that wrapped itself around her, cocooning her, making her feel safe even as she was brought to the edge of an intensity like she had never known before.

She rocked her hips in time with the motion, and when he pushed two fingers inside of her again, she broke apart. Her internal muscles squeezing around his fingers as he worked them in and out of her body. As he continued to tease her with the flat of his tongue.

She was left desperate and panting, begging for more.

"There's more," he said, his voice rough. "Don't worry."

He stood, and she watched transfixed as he undid his jeans, lowering the zipper slowly, the strong column of his arousal coming into view.

And he was... Well, much larger than she had imagined. Not that she had a great frame of reference. Or a very good idea of scale. But he was as beautiful as he was intimidating. And he was a lot of both.

Everything about his body was glorious. Strong and well defined and damn near miraculous.

And she didn't have time to cling to her worry, because then he was positioning himself at the edge of the bed again, wrapping his arms around her thighs, this time lifting her hips up off the mattress as he positioned himself at the entrance of her body, and thrust home.

The pain nearly blinded her.

She cried out, hand scrabbling for purchase, but she couldn't reach any part of him. And she wanted to hold on to him, wanted to dig her nails into his skin to keep herself from crawling out of her own.

His eyes widened, and for the first time, he looked truly at sea.

He adjusted their positions, bringing her legs around so that her feet were pointed toward the end of the bed, bringing himself onto the mattress the right way, still inside of her, but over her now, and she gripped his shoulders, squeezing her eyes shut tight.

"Cricket," he growled.

"Don't stop," she begged. "It's already done."

"Cricket…"

"Just please don't stop." And then, she opened her eyes, grabbed his face and kissed him.

And that seemed to work.

She could feel his control begin to unravel as he started to move slowly at first, gently even, until the pain began to recede. Until it was replaced with a full, complicated pleasure that made her want to cry as well as scream with desire.

She began to move her hips in time with his, as they found a rhythm that pleased them both. As they found each other.

And then, he took control, his movements no longer measured, his skin slapping against hers. The primal edge to their joining so much more than she had ever imagined it could be. So much better.

Desire built inside of her until she was trembling again, like she had done outside, like she had done after their kiss. He reached between their bodies, moved his fingers along the sides of where they joined, then back upward, pinching her gently as he thrust in, and light—bright and brilliant—flashed behind her eyes, pleasure breaking over her like a wave.

It was unlike any reality she'd ever known. Deep and unending as she pulsed around him. And he thrust inside of her, once, twice more, and on a growl gave himself up to his own pleasure.

She felt rocked. Stunned. The aftershocks of everything that had just happened continuing to move through her, little tremors of need that caused her to cling to him with each passing ripple.

"Well," he said. "You should've told me."

"Oh, about being a virgin?"

"Hell yes," he said.

"I figured that was pretty evident."

"Not evident enough, Cricket," he said.

"Well. It wasn't really any of your business."

"It was exactly my business."

"I didn't want it to be. I just wanted it for me. Please don't ruin it by lecturing me or scolding me or yelling at me, because I just don't care about your opinion, okay? It was good." She let herself fall backward onto the bed, her head resting against the pillow. "It was good, and that's all I care about."

"Cricket… I shouldn't stay."

"Why?" She scrambled into a seated position, leaving herself completely uncovered. She didn't know why she was so at ease being naked in front of him. It felt

right though. Natural. In a way that being clothed in
many other situations never had. She felt… Well, she
felt essentially Cricket. Like the baseline nature of who
she was was completely and totally reinforced by this.
Like the essence that made her her, that had always felt
wrong and out of place, suddenly fit. In this house, in
this bed. With this man. And, she didn't see any point
in feeling regretful or shy. In apologizing to him for the
fact that she'd been a virgin.

Really, if it didn't bother her, it shouldn't bother him.

"Because there are things you don't know about why
I agreed to come and work here."

"You lost a bet, cowboy. Seems pretty straightforward to me. Though, the bet had nothing to do with
this, so don't go and try to cheapen it now."

"I'm not going to," he said, his eyes level. "Cricket,
why do you think I bet myself as your ranch hand?"

"You thought you were going to win."

"No. I thought I was going to lose. I *knew* I was going
to lose. Your level of bravado was not that of a woman
who had an iffy hand."

"How…" She felt utterly aghast. "How can that be?"

"It just is, sweetheart. I knew for a fact that you were
going to win, and I agreed to these terms because I
wanted to be here. Because I wanted to… I wanted to
show you that you didn't have the chops to be a rancher."

"You what?"

"I wanted to talk you out of it. Because I wanted to
buy this place."

She frowned. "You… You were tricking me?"

"Yes. Though, in fairness, I never lied to you, not
once. I never lied about how much work it takes to run

a place like this. Everything I said to you was the absolute truth. The morning wake-up time was real. The amount of work and money and time that is going to be needed for this place is all real. And nothing I said to you was off base there. But I certainly didn't do anything to encourage you. Not really. Because what I wanted was for you to give up and throw in the towel, and for me to be there ready to buy you out."

"Jackson…"

"Yeah. And now I feel like an ass. Because I didn't know that all this was going on. That you thought we might be related. And I…"

"So wait a minute, were you going to…seduce me to try to get the ranch away from me?"

"No."

"Just please tell me this was real. If nothing else, Jackson, just tell me this was real."

"It was real. But that doesn't mean it can be anything but tonight."

"Why not?"

"Because it's a disaster. Because I'm not the kind of man who can give you what you want. You've already been hurt by too many people in your life, Cricket, and I don't want to be another one."

"Well, too bad. Because this is hurtful."

"I'm sorry about that. I didn't want to hurt you."

"No. You just wanted to crush my dreams and make me think that I wasn't up to them, and then buy my dream piece of property out from under me. Jackson, you did want to hurt me. It was just that you didn't know me, so you didn't particularly care. And if you feel guilty now, it's only because you've seen what a pathetic human being I am, and I was a virgin on top of it."

"I don't pity you."

"Then what is it?"

"Having seen you naked, having been inside of you, I can't take advantage of you. Okay? Because yeah, I can stand here and justify my actions, and say that I didn't lie to you like that makes it all okay, but I know it's not, Cricket. I know it was a shady thing to do. And the fact of the matter is, I could ignore what a shady thing it was when I wasn't personally involved with you, but after tonight I think it's pretty safe to say that personal involvement has happened. From dragging you in front of my dad to getting into bed with you."

"Well, then how can you stand there and say it can't be anything else? If we are already personally involved…"

"It's a mess."

"Oh, no argument here. Believe me. I've been pretty much mired in the mess this whole time." She let out an exasperated sigh. "Don't you know that I have had a crush on you the size of the Willamette River for… I don't know, years? So finding out that you were possibly my brother was about the worst thing I could think of. Do you have any idea what it's like to spend years lusting after somebody, and then find that you might share a dad? It was horrifying. I'm sorry, but I needed to know, and then once I did know… I needed to be with you. Because I felt so wrong, in so many ways, for so many years—I think this had to happen for me to…get over it. To start feeling some things that are…a little bit more normal. Like, believe me, none of this was how

I saw...the hookup between us going. But that whole trying to get my ranch thing... That was pretty awful. And, you know, not something I thought you would do."

"Cricket, I didn't know you had a crush on me. But I'd venture to say that you might have a slightly better view of me than is realistic. I'm just who I am. I'm not a particularly bad man, but I'm not a really great one either."

"Why my ranch?"

"I'm right next door. It just makes sense. If I want to expand..."

"Why do you need to expand?"

"It's what people do."

"I mean, to what end? For more money?"

"No," he said. "For more of something that's mine."

"Oh. Well, I mean I understand that. Wanting something that's yours. But this ranch is mine. And you can't have it. And I don't really care how hard it's going to be to make it work. It's going to be mine. You underestimated me. You had no idea about everything that was going on in here." She tapped her temple. "Honestly, it's been a wasteland of horror for the past...six months at least. So, don't go trying to scare me away."

"I'm going back to my place tonight. Let's just... cool off."

She sputtered. "I don't want to cool off."

"I need to."

She stared at him. "We had a deal," she said. "And none of that's changed because of what just happened tonight. Are you the kind of man who backs out of the deal?"

"Things have..."

"Changed for you. Because you were lying to me. But I was never lying. I was always being honest, and…"

"Except for the part where you thought that I was your brother, and you figured that you needed to… I don't know, what were you trying to do exactly?"

"Get close to you, enough that I could say, 'Do you suppose it's possible your father cheated on your late mother, and he is perhaps my dad?'" He barely moved, but a muscle in his cheek flinched. "Yeah," she said. "Exactly. It's awful. And there's really no good way to approach it. At least, not one I could think of. And believe me, I tried. I tried to think of something better than that. So yes, I guess I had ulterior motives too, but I also just want to run my ranch. And I need your help. And you promised me thirty days. Staying here. Free labor."

"You're in my bed."

"So, you have a couple options. You get back in bed with me, you go to the bunkhouse with the spiders, or you go to my bed, where I may just end up."

He sighed heavily, then came back down onto the mattress. "You don't know what you're playing with here, little Cricket."

"There's only one way I'm going to find out, though, isn't there? By continuing to play."

She took a deep breath, focusing on the tenderness in her chest. "In all honesty, Jackson, I am just really sick to death of feeling like I'm fundamentally wrong. And this felt right. So…why don't we just keep on?"

"I lied to you," he said.

"Yeah. But so what? I mean, we're not friends. You lost a bet. End of story. You're not my family, so we don't have some kind of mystical connection like I thought we might. We are not…anything. So what does it matter? Your plan would've only worked if you could have talked me out of my dream, and quite frankly, if you could have talked me out of it, I would've deserved what I got."

"Is that really what you think?"

"Yes. As it is, you were never even close to making me second-guess it. Because you know what's harder than figuring out how to do chores and work a ranch? Growing up in a mausoleum. An altar to your father, when you don't even like or respect the man. Being made to feel like you have to fit in, when you don't particularly want to, or see the benefit of it. Yeah. That's hard. And, well… I decided not to do it. I decided to figure this out. So I did. So I took it upon myself to figure this out. A few early mornings weren't going to scare me off."

"You're a whole thing, aren't you, Cricket?"

"Not by choice. It just kind of seems to be the way I am."

He lay down next to her, and gathered her up against his body. She put her hand on his chest, tracing shapes over the broad expanse of muscle. "You seem like a man who might be able to handle a whole thing. And you kinda make me feel like less of one. Or at least like… this might be the place for it."

"Sure, if you want to play… You know I'm here to play. But playing is all I got."

"That's okay. I'm trying to figure out my life. I'm trying to figure out what I want to be. Who I am. What it means… James is my father, most likely."

"Are you going to ask your mother directly about it?"

She nodded. "I am. Because I need to know the truth. I'm afraid this is probably it."

"Sometimes, you have to contend with things you don't like about your parents. And I grant you, your dad is a hell of a lot worse than mine."

"Your dad seems… Well, I mean, to me he really seems not bad at all."

"He's not, I suppose. But his relationship with my mom… I wouldn't have been surprised if he'd cheated."

"I'm sorry."

"None of it's your fault."

"Well. I kind of put you in an awkward situation tonight."

He shrugged. "My dad's own behavior actually put him in that situation."

"For what it's worth… I used to look at your family and think… Well, I really wished that I could be part of it."

"I guess that's the thing, then. I never wished that I was part of your family. I suppose that's the difference."

"Yeah, there is imperfect, and there's dysfunctional. Believe me, there's kind of an important distinction between the two."

"We might be skirting the edge of dysfunctional, here," he said.

"Yeah, but I think we can both handle it. And we're not dragging anyone else into it."

He huffed. "True."

"Might as well enjoy this. I have twenty-one days left of indentured servitude from you."

And then suddenly she found herself pinned to the mattress, his large body over hers, his eyes glittering. "Might as well," he growled.

And then, they were done talking for the rest of the night.

Seven

Jackson felt like an ass. He should have left last night when he'd said that he would, but Cricket had looked at him like she was a wounded puppy, and he couldn't bring himself to do it. Still, there hadn't been much of an excuse to stay. Except that he was weak. And human, and basically just a man. And she had presented a temptation he couldn't turn away from.

Though it wasn't just being a man, that was the thing, because if it was, then it would've been about her just being a woman, and fundamentally, he could have turned down any other woman. It was Cricket that was the problem. Cricket was a damn problem.

He was marinating on that as he drove into town for more lumber the next day. She had been up early, at the crack of dawn, without so much as a complaint, while he had been the one who'd had a hell of a time getting his ass out of bed. He was driving back out toward Cricket's spread when he noticed his brother's truck in the oncoming traffic lane. Creed waved his hand, and Jackson found the nearest turnaround and followed his brother, both of them parking by the side of the road. It wasn't extraordinarily unusual to randomly run into his brother about town. Gold Valley was a small enough place. And they were off running similar errands, considering they were both ranchers. They had the same haunts, the same basic routines.

"Fancy meeting you here," he said.

"Likewise," Creed said. "I was figuring on coming out to see you today anyway."

"Oh?"

"Yeah. My wife has been after me to check in on you."

"Why?" Jackson asked.

"Just to make sure nothing untoward is happening between you and her little sister."

Jackson kept his face flat and immovable as stone. "Is that so?"

"Yeah. She told me that Cricket called her the other night inquiring about how to make steak. Because she was cooking for you. And that got Wren stirred up."

"I fail to see what your wife's feelings have to do with me."

"Well, the funny thing is, then I went by the winery this morning, and I talked to Dad, he said that you and Cricket stormed the place last night, and she demanded to know if he was her father."

"Oh."

"And that you said it was really important to know for sure."

"Look, she had a valid suspicion."

"Why? Dad was crazy about Mom. He would never have cheated on her."

Jackson's frustration finally boiled over. Maybe it was Cricket and all the nonsense with her, or just the vast unfairness of his brother's complete and total obliviousness over something Jackson had borne the weight of for years. Whatever the reason, he was at the end of his patience.

"Are you blind, Creed? Dad was not crazy about Mom."

"The hell you talking about? He's been deep in the throes of grief for her for…five years. Completely messed up. Not right at all. You can't tell me that's a man who was not crazy about his wife."

"He's a man who was crazy with guilt." Jackson let out a harsh breath. "Look, I was closer to Mom than you."

"I…feel bad about that. But I was pretty deep in some of my own stuff there for a while."

"I know. It wasn't a criticism. I'm just saying… Believe me, what Cricket thought was valid enough. Did you ever wonder why Dad hated James Maxfield so much? Not just because he's a prick."

"Yeah, I mean it crossed my mind a time or two."

"Dad was in love with *his* wife. Always. And I think, whatever he felt for Mom never overshadowed what he felt for her. It wasn't… It was never fair. Ever. It's not just grief that has Dad a mess. He has a mountain of regret. And he should."

Creed huffed out a breath. "That doesn't make any sense. Why would Mom... Why would she be with him?"

"Why do you think? They stayed together for the kids." He looked at his brother. "That would be us."

"Why did they get married in the first place?"

Jackson sighed and shifted his weight. "Me. She was pregnant with me. Haven't you ever done that math? I have. And anyway, I don't have to rely on math. She told me. I thought... Damn, you know, I thought we had this great, happy family. And then I found out... Not so much. A forced family, and then they tried to... Honey was their attempt at making things better. But that doesn't work. Or at least, it rarely does. Anyway. That's what everything was about with Cricket. She suspected, given that she, like our sister, is a late in life baby... That maybe she was the product of an affair. An affair her mother had always wanted to have. But no. Dad said no."

"Oh. Well, that is entirely different from what Wren was afraid was going on. And I can't say I could really figure out what I thought was happening..." Creed stared past him, off at the thick grove of pine trees that lined the highway. "I don't know what to make of any of this. I... I didn't know that Mom and Dad..."

"They didn't want us to know."

"Why did Mom tell you?" Creed sounded hurt. Jackson didn't have the capacity to deal with his brother's hurt. Not now.

"She had to tell someone. She was lonely. And..."

"Dad was there for her though. He was. He didn't leave. And if he didn't have an affair..."

"You're a married man, Creed, don't tell me you wouldn't feel a difference between being the love of your wife's life, or knowing there was someone else out there that she wanted first."

"Right. But you know…" Creed chuckled. "Wren and I got married because of her pregnancy."

"Given your background, I understand that."

He nodded. "But it's not why we stayed together."

"Yeah, but I think it was why Mom and Dad stayed together."

"Well, I just pulled you over to give you a hard time, I didn't figure you'd give me this depressing as hell story."

"I'm just explaining the last twenty-four hours, which believe me, have been a little weird for me too."

"Well, be careful with her. Wren is really worried."

It was Jackson's turn to stare at the trees.

He could feel his brother's eyes burning into the side of his face. "If you're sleeping with my sister-in-law… I might have to punch you. I'd rather not."

"I'll be careful with her."

"That's not a denial."

"Can't give you a denial."

"Really? Really. *Really? Cricket. Really.*"

He shot his brother a look. "Say it one more time."

"So…she thought you were her half brother, and somehow you ended up… You know what. I don't want to know." Creed lifted his hands and took a step back. "The less I know the better, because I'm going to have to explain it to Wren. And I don't want to be the keeper of that information, because God knows I love my wife, but she is the kind of woman to shoot the messenger. And I like all my body parts where they are."

"So do I."

"And *really* don't let Holden find out." Creed's brother-in-law, married to Emerson, the middle Maxfield sister.

"Why is that?"

"My loyalty is torn. You're my brother. Holden… Well, his loyalty is in one place firmly. And, also, I get the feeling he's done some things."

"Look, nothing happened that Cricket didn't want."

"I'm confident in that. I'm still confident it won't matter to Wren."

"Just let us sort it out."

"I can't keep secrets from her. But I can keep her busy." Creed grinned.

"Great. Do that. And keep this to yourself. What's going on with me and Cricket is nobody's business but ours."

"I just don't get why. I mean, she's cute enough, sure. But…"

Jackson felt a violent surge of…protectiveness? He didn't even know. Just something primal and overly irritable. He couldn't explain what appealed about Cricket. It was not simple. But… She was special, and when he saw her as something other than an adversary to be defeated, he could truly see that. She was tough. And beautiful. Naive in some ways, sure, but in others… Like a person outside age or time. Not like anyone or anything he'd ever known. He came back to that vision he'd had of her the first time he'd rolled up to the ranch.

When he thought of her as a feral pirate queen on the

deck of her ship. And he should have known then. She wasn't a woman to take prisoners, and neither would she be one to negotiate. She wasn't going to give up on what she wanted half so easily as he had hoped. And now, he didn't even want her to. Because somewhere in all of this, he'd begun to root for her. He wanted her to win. That vulnerable, delicate piece of herself only he'd seen was something he wanted to protect now, not exploit.

"Don't worry about me. And don't worry about Cricket. She can more than handle herself."

And he was…well, dammit all, he was going to help her.

Jackson had been gone for most of the day, and it was probably for the best, Cricket had to concede. She wished he was in bed with her instead of seeing to ranch chores. But the ranch chores were important and all. It was kind of the whole point of having him on the property. But now she wanted the point to be more of him in her bed, and honestly, who could blame her? Having an orgasm was a lot more fun than doing chores.

But…she also needed to do something other than chores today. Which was how she found herself driving to Maxfield Vineyards.

She usually avoided the place as much as humanly possible. But it was weird. Today, with a bit of distance from her family, from everything that they were, and all the pain and isolation she had experienced growing up here… She was not feeling trapped by it. It felt…better. She felt able to appreciate the beauty of it. The rolling vineyards, the vast, Tuscan-style villa. The elaborate pavilions and tasting rooms. It was a beautiful facility, when she wasn't a prisoner.

"Prisoner" wasn't really fair. But she had felt trapped in her circumstances, that was for sure. And now that she had another place to be, now that she had...

Honestly, had a night with Jackson changed her so much? She looked the same. She had checked herself over in the mirror this morning just to see if this change was visible, that shift that had taken place inside of her last night. But as far as she could tell it wasn't. She took a breath, and put her car in Park, right in the circular drive just in front of the massive entry to her family home. A place that had never, ever felt like home to her. But she didn't have the same knot of dread that she used to have when James was in residence, didn't have the same feeling of discomfort. So there was that.

She knocked, because she didn't live here anymore, and when one of the members of the staff opened the door, she was led in as politely as if she were a guest.

She stood in the foyer, waiting for her mother to appear.

When she did, Cricket could only stare. Her mom was still every inch the lady of the manor, even though the circumstances at the manor had changed pretty drastically.

"Cricket," Lucinda said, smiling brightly. "What brings you by?"

"I... I really need to talk to you. About..." She took a breath. "I spoke to Cash Cooper last night."

"Oh," her mom said, faltering.

"I asked him if he was... If he was my father."

"Cricket..."

"I know that you are in love with him. And I know that he was in love with you. And I know you didn't marry him because you chose money over love. I just thought that maybe…"

"He's not your father."

"That's what he said."

Her mom looked…embarrassed. "Was he…"

"He wasn't mad. I mean, not much. Jackson was kind of mad, but… I don't know. I was just embarrassed. But I really thought… There's something wrong with me? I think? Because I'm not like anyone in this family, and I just thought that maybe I would fit better with the Coopers. And I thought that after I found out that you were in love with him…"

"I was always in love with him. I always will be. I gave things up, Cricket. For a life that I thought would make me happy. But I was very foolish. I was very wrong. And it has taken me all this time to be able to admit it. All this time to be able to understand. Just how… Just how wrong I was. I thought this house could take the place of love. I thought money could do it. And then I thought social standing, because Cash managed to go and make all that money, just to show me what I was missing. I won't tell you I wasn't tempted by him. I won't tell you *we* never were. There were times… We had opportunity, and it was hard. Because I remembered what it was like with him. And it wasn't… I shouldn't tell you all of this. You don't want to know about my love affairs, I'm sure."

Cricket didn't really, it was true. But she could be a whole lot more understanding about them now that she'd experienced a bit of it herself. Would it be like that with

Jackson? Forever and ever? Staring at him from across crowded rooms and knowing how it was? If he married someone else… Would she still always remember what it was like to have his hands on her body? What if she married another man?

Frankly, she couldn't imagine it. She didn't really have dreams of being a wife and mother. She had always had dreams about him.

"But you didn't. That's the important part."

"No."

"And did you… With anyone else?"

"No."

"So James Maxfield is my father." It wasn't a question, but a heavy confirmation.

"Yes."

"Okay." Cricket turned, her chest feeling weighted with answers. The fact was, she hadn't wanted to ask her mother before because she had been afraid that this was the answer. And it turned out…it was. There was nothing half so romantic as a hidden family out there waiting for her. Nothing half so wonderful as an explanation for why she was the way she was.

She just was.

And she was going to have to find a way to cope with that, to understand herself.

To be okay with that.

"He said that…" She took a breath. "Cash said that I looked like you." She turned around again to face her mother, looked at her smooth, unlined skin, her sleek blond hair. "I don't see how. He said I reminded him of you."

Her mother's expression became soft. Wistful. "Because back then I did. You're probably the most like me, Cricket, of any of the girls. I was wild, and I was headstrong, and I couldn't be told a damn thing. I made a sport out of daring him. Of pushing him, I felt like I was meant for bigger and better things than I could get in Gold Valley. Bigger and better things than he could give me. And I would yell that at him. I would tell him that if he really wanted me, if he really loved me, then he would figure out a way to give me the kinds of things I wanted. Because you see… I really believed that the man who would make me happy would come with all the things I wanted, and I didn't think about the kinds of things I would give to him. And that was how I ended up in a one-sided marriage where I didn't ask any questions, and I just took everything that came my way. I didn't have dreams of my own. Not beyond what I could have. And when I realized that I was stuck with a man who didn't love me, with a man who wasn't faithful to me… I had you girls. And I wouldn't do anything that might jeopardize my having you. And he used the three of you to threaten me." She closed her eyes. "I'll be completely honest, half the time the only thing that kept me away from Cash Cooper was knowing that if your father found out he would do his best to make sure I never saw you again."

"I'm sorry, Mom," Cricket said. "And I'm sorry I never realized how unhappy you were here."

"Yes, well. I'm the one who made this place." She looked around. "It was my prison. And I built it for myself, and locked myself inside. And you right with me. I never felt like I had a right to offer you any comfort."

Cricket didn't know what to say. Except… She remembered what Jackson had asked her, that first day he had come to her house. "Can I ask… Why did you name me Cricket?"

Her mom smiled. "Because it reminded me of who I used to be. A hot summer night sitting outside and listening to the crickets. Of simpler things and simpler times. And by then I knew… I knew I wasn't ever going to find happiness here. The only happiness I had was you girls, and I didn't… I was distant, because I let my guilt and my fears determine how we connected. I'm sorry for that. I really am. The divorce—this has been like a slow waking up. I'm not liking everything that I'm seeing around me. My own flaws. My own…failings in all of this."

"James Maxfield is kind of an evil bastard."

"Well, there was a time when I was suited to him. And that doesn't fill me with any great joy."

"I don't understand how you could… I don't want to pile anything on, Mom, and for the most part, I just think… We were all victims of his. But one thing I don't understand is how you could marry him knowing that you loved Cash."

"Cash didn't come after me. He let me marry him. And up until the wedding I imagined him riding up on a white horse and taking me away from it all. I really did. I thought he would rescue me. And he didn't. Instead he found someone else, and they had children right away. Much faster than your father and I did. And I threw myself into loving the money. If Cash hadn't gotten married, I don't think my marriage to your father would've lasted. But my other option was gone."

"Have you ever thought that…now it might not be?"

She smiled sadly. "He's a proud man. I don't think he would have me. I can't say that I blame him."

"I don't think you can know that. Unless you try. And don't you think we all deserve a chance at being happy? Whatever that looks like?"

"I know that you do. I think for me it might be too late."

Cricket left her mom's house with a lot to think about. And she wasn't sure that she liked any of it. It sounded to her like her mother's relationship with Cash had been more than a little dysfunctional. And she couldn't deny that her mom had a decent sized stake in the way things had gone. But she also didn't see the point in the two of them continuing to be sad forever. They both clearly had feelings for each other that they hadn't resolved. But one thing Cricket couldn't imagine was...

She could never marry another man.

The conversation with her mom had solidified that thought. Not after Jackson. She couldn't have another man's children. Chances were, she would grow old with her ranch. But at least she would have her own dreams.

When she pulled up to the house, he was on the porch, hammering boards in place. Each swing of his hammer was hard and decisive, every muscle and tendon in his body working harmoniously toward its goal. He was a thing of beauty. And the porch was... It was practically brand-new. In the few hours since she'd left, he had transformed the place. It was no longer sinking, no longer looking dilapidated. It was incredible. And it was all him.

He was incredible.

Her heart lifted in her chest, and she felt... She didn't

really know. Renewed in some ways. Her mother's story was tragic, but it was also a reminder that there was no circumstance Cricket could simply sit back and accept.

She was James Maxfield's daughter. That hadn't been her choice. But everything she did with her life... that was her choice. James didn't own her. Didn't have a claim on her. She was Cricket. Named after the simple summer nights her mother loved and remembered. After a time in her life that had been special to her. After memories that had mattered. And Cricket was made of those things as much as she was her father's DNA.

It made her feel rooted, grounded to this place, and certain of her decisions. Much more so than she had ever been before.

"Horses," she said as soon as she got out of the truck.

"Excuse me?" Jackson looked up, his gaze meeting hers, sending her stomach into a freefall.

"Horses," she reiterated. "I want to breed horses. That's what this ranch is going to be. I've decided. I want to start right away."

"We're going to have to build stables."

"Then let's work out a budget. And I can find a contractor. I know it might take some time, but I'm willing. Because my life is going to be what I want it to be. It doesn't matter what my DNA is. I talked to my mother today. James is my father. For sure and for certain. But that's not even really the biggest thing. My mom lived a life that she didn't love for years because she felt trapped in it. Because she felt like she didn't have a choice. I never want to feel like I don't have a choice. I'm not one determined thing because I'm James's daughter, and not Cash's. I'm not anything but what I decide to be."

"Good for you."

She pointed her index finger at him. "But you can't have my ranch."

"That's okay."

"And you still have to finish out the terms of the bet. I'm not going to have you back out early, just because you can't do your whole secret…thing. I have nothing but your own honor as a man to hold you to it."

"You got me."

"And I want to keep sleeping with you," she said, suddenly resolute in that decision too. "Until this is over."

"You sure?"

"I'm sure. I'm building my life. And this is who I am. I don't sit back having crushes on men and not saying anything. I don't just dream about having a ranch. I'm going to have all those things."

"And then at the end of the thirty days?"

That made her chest feel sore. But she was resolute either way.

"You go your way. I'll go mine."

And she wasn't going to worry about all the things he could and couldn't give her. She was going to focus on what she could do. Who she could be. What she could give to herself.

Because she would never be her mother. A passive participant in her own life.

No.

She was the one who decided.

Nobody else. She would have a ranch, and a man. And sure, it would be temporary. But it would be hers. The start of something.

And she was so very ready for her life to begin.

Eight

The crew had started work on Cricket's stables. It was weird, now that his focus had shifted. He actually wanted her enterprise to be a success. And that meant looking at things from an entirely different point of view. That meant teaching her about ranching, rather than just making overarching statements and watching her stumble around. It meant bringing her alongside him for repairs, not just to show her how hard it was, but to show her that she could. And with each improvement on the property, he saw her become more firmly rooted in her sense of who she was, and there was a great sense of accomplishment inside of him that he couldn't quite explain. Except that... Except that he'd felt useless to fix the sadness that he saw inside of his mother, and being able to do something to give Cricket a better life did something to help heal that sense of failure.

Somewhere in the back of his mind, he always thought that if his mother had gotten better, maybe he would have helped her leave his father. Given her a place to stay, proved to her that it didn't matter whether they were together like a traditional family. What really mattered was her happiness. She didn't need to stay. Not for him. But he'd never said it to her. She'd died before he ever could. Before he'd gotten his own place up and running. And maybe part of him had still been working toward that with wanting to expand to Cricket's property. But he didn't need to do that now. What he could do was help Cricket find her way to a dream.

And then maybe that would help put something to rights in his own life. Cricket wasn't out with him today, she was off bustling around the house. He told her he would check in on the building site, and then he was going to drive up to the upper pasture, and get the lay of things. It really was a beautiful property.

He thought back to what she'd asked, if ranching was in his blood, as he stood out in the middle of the bright, patchwork field, filled with brilliant green mixed with patches of dark olive and backed by rich pine. As he looked at the sprigs of yellow that clustered around the perimeter interwoven with waving fire-colored Indian paintbrush and dappled orange fritillaria, at the pale blue sky that would be a richer blue come the height of summer, he knew the answer was… It was deeper than blood. It was down in his bones. He was part of the land, and it was part of him. Something that went further than want.

And he'd never thought about it that way before. Only when Cricket had asked, did that thought grow into a feeling.

And he understood. He understood why she wanted this. Why she was here. It was true. When it was part of you, it simply was. Nothing you could do about it.

He heard the sound of a truck engine and turned, and there was Cricket, rumbling up the dirt road, driving that big beast of hers.

That was another thing that was getting down into his blood. Because he hadn't just been helping her on the property.

No.

They'd spent long nights in beds that were too small, exploring, tasting, and he loved to say that he was teaching her there as much as he was around the ranch, but it was more than that. Because Cricket was a whole new landscape, one he'd never seen or explored or imagined before. She was strong, and she was energetic.

She had no limit as far as he could tell. Nothing embarrassed her.

Rather, she touched and tasted with full enthusiasm, never shying away from anything. That wild girl he'd seen out on the swing at the Maxfield Vineyards brought that sense of the unrestrained into the bedroom, and there were no lessons involved in any of it. No. He was just on the ride. At the mercy of it. And he loved every minute.

He gritted his teeth. There was no getting attached to it.

Why not?

He pushed that thought aside. Cricket got out of the

truck, wearing a white tank top and tight jeans, holding a blanket and a picnic basket. And she looked like far too much of a temptation for him to handle.

And hell, she wasn't a temptation he had to resist over the last couple of weeks, so why should he start now? He crossed the distance between them, and wrapped his arms around her slender waist, pulled her into his arms and planted a kiss on her lips.

"What are you doing?"

"I brought lunch," she said, a pleased smile curving her lips. "I've been practicing being a good pioneer woman. I made bread, I cooked a ham and I've made sandwiches."

"You really made bread?"

"Yes," she said, her face shining with triumph. "And two of the four loaves turned out. So, you have sandwiches."

"Cricket, that was awfully nice of you."

"I know," she said. "And often I'm not very nice, so it surprised me too."

"You're plenty nice."

Or at least, her particular brand of sharpness was nice for him. Didn't really matter either way.

She spread the blanket out in the meadow and took a seat, and he stared at her, the golden glow of the sun shining on her face. And he couldn't figure out quite why she'd done it. Quite why she'd given him this. He couldn't recall anyone else doing similar for him. Sure, his mom cooked for them. But… She was his mom. Family.

Cricket wasn't family.

She wasn't beholden to him in any way. He'd lost a

bet to her. That was why he was here. And his education hadn't included cooking. She had just done this. Just because.

And it did something to his chest that made him want to growl, because he wasn't a sentimental man. And he didn't concern himself much with things like this. But it was…unexpected, and it was a hell of a lot more than he'd ever wanted or gotten from another person.

It shocked him how good everything she made was. Though he supposed it probably shouldn't surprise him. Everything Cricket set her mind to she did with her whole self. And it didn't mean she couldn't fail, but she was determined enough that he had a feeling she would have baked ten loaves of bread in order to present him with just one. Because what she wanted, she went and got. And that was something. It was really something.

He liked to watch Cricket eat, among the many things he enjoyed about her. Because she did that with the same level of ferocity and intensity she did everything else. She was sitting on the blanket with her elbows propped up on her knees, her sandwich gripped tightly in her hands. She had brought cans of Coke for the two of them, and when she had eaten about half of her sandwich, she brushed her hands off and picked up the Coke, tipping it back like a beer.

She looked over at him. "What?"

"What?" he repeated.

"You're staring at me."

"You're pretty." That made him sound like a dumb high school boy. Come to that, he kind of felt like one.

But Cricket blushed. Cricket, tough little thing that she was, blushed, and he found that was all the payment he needed for the worse moment of feeling like an idiot. Something he wasn't accustomed to.

"Well," Cricket said. "So are you."

"Really?"

"Yeah. I mean, I've always thought so."

"Yeah," he said. "You mentioned something about that." He wasn't sure he wanted to know. Because already he felt some kind of strange obligation to her. Deeper than his obligation to any other woman he'd ever had a physical relationship with. And he wasn't sure he wanted to dig in any deeper, but sitting there under that brilliant blue sky, eating her homemade bread and ham sandwich, he didn't know if there was any other option but to dig in. He didn't know how *not* to be involved with her, and it was absurd. It had started with a bet, an assumption on her part that they might be related, a nefarious plan on his part to talk her into selling him her ranch...

But maybe that was it. The whole thing was so bizarre—how could they come away from it with neutral feelings about each other? Maybe it was impossible. Maybe the only option in a situation like this was to develop some kind of attachment. Maybe it was the only way.

"I'm pretty sneaky," Cricket said. "I mean, I'm used to hiding what I feel from people. And you were no exception. I mean, the way that I felt about you. I would just tell my sisters that I thought cowboys were annoying. And that I didn't want anything to do with any of them. It was a pretty convincing ruse, if I say so myself. Plus, I knew you were way off limits. A thousand years older than me."

"Hey. Not a thousand."

"Well, it seemed like it at the time. The gap feels a lot smaller now." She smiled. "Oh, I didn't like any of the boys at school. None of them. But how could I, when I already liked a man? And a Cooper at that. I knew nobody would understand. But nobody understood me, so that didn't really bother me. And so I just…kept it a secret. And then I was so mad when Wren hooked up with your brother, because I felt for so long that being attracted to you was this great, impossible thing, another sort of deeply rooted difference in who I was. In my genetic makeup versus the rest of my family. And then she got to Creed before I could get to you. Honestly. It was an insult. But still, when she told me that I would maybe find my own cowboy… I played it off. I told her no. That I didn't want anything to do with a man like Creed, and I didn't. I just wanted you. So it feels right, you know? To start this new phase of my life with you… Though I'm not asking you for anything. I promise."

"Well, happy to help."

Except it made him feel… He didn't even know. It kind of made him angry, because she was the younger one. She was the one without experience, and she made him feel like he had no idea what he was doing. It didn't seem right. That was all.

He should be the one who knew what he was doing. He should be the one who had total confidence in everything taking place between them. But he couldn't say that he did. He couldn't give a reason. Couldn't give a speech about what he was doing here. He had written it off as being male and basic and taking the sex that

was on offer, but he knew that wasn't true. It wasn't
how he did things. It wasn't how he looked at women.
And he had been telling himself a story, all this time.
Cricket's story made a lot more sense, and had a purpose behind it. And he just… He just wanted to touch
her. It was a hell of a thing.

"You know, the way you were talking to your dad
that day… Tell me about your mom. I mean, tell me
about all that. Because you know about my dad, and
you know all about my mom…"

"They were obligated to be together. And it was pri-
marily because of me," he said. Because he might as
well tell her. She was right. He'd had a front row seat to
all of her issues. He'd talked to Creed about it, sure. But
Cricket? She could hear it all. Because she didn't have
a connection to the family, so why not? It was a safer
place. This moment out here in the meadow.

"One day when I was sixteen, she was crying. Then
I asked her what was wrong. We were the two that got
up early. And we used to spend mornings together. I
loved that. So I would have all this extra time with her.
And one morning, I asked her what was wrong. And it
was like everything I ever thought about my life broke
to pieces. My father married her because she was pregnant. My father was in love with another woman. He'd
told my mother that. Before they got married. He was
honest, if nothing else. And she thought that he'd fall in
love with her. But instead, it had just become years of
the two of them stuck. Because they had a family. Because they had a business. Because they had all these
things that were obligated to come before having feelings. Before love.

"And you know, I'm not over-bothered by my dad anymore. I think that was enough for him. He couldn't have your mom, so he made himself a life he enjoyed. But I'm not sure my mother ever got to fall in love with anyone. Not for real. Not and have them love her back. She was just stuck. With a partner, sure. And when she was sick... I can't fault my dad for how he was. He *was* a partner. He cared for her. And he stayed with her. And you know, plenty of marriages that are founded on love, they don't end up that way. Somebody gets sick and they go through a years-long battle, and the other person leaps. It's too much for them. And sometimes I wonder if maybe my dad not being in love with her made him more able to take care of her during that time. It's complicated as hell. Because there was a very real partnership between the two of them, but sometimes it made my mother feel broken, and I will never not feel responsible for that. Like I should've found some way to fix it."

"They made their choices," Cricket said. "That's what I'm realizing about my mother. For all her own misery, for all that I feel bad for her sometimes, for all that my father was an unforgivable asshole, my mom made her choices. She wanted money. And she thought that would be enough. She wanted to have things, and thought that would transcend love, but it didn't. And then she didn't leave. She stayed. Because she was afraid. And all her reasons, they were real enough, but they were still excuses. Even if they were pretty valid ones. My mom stayed with James for us. Because she was afraid that he would find a way to take us from her.

But she also could've had the fight. She weighed her options. And she chose."

"I have some sympathy for that," he said. "If she thought she couldn't win…"

"It was still a choice. Just like your mother had one. It's not like it was the 1800s. They could've gotten a divorce. They could have. Nobody had to be unhappy. They sat there in rules they made for themselves, and lived lives they made for themselves, prison walls they decided were okay. That isn't your fault, and it isn't mine."

"Yeah, but on the other side, now your mom has a chance to make something new. Mine doesn't. It's a hell of a thing."

"I know." She shook her head. "I'm not saying it would've been easy. I'm just saying you can't take their choices and blame yourself for them."

"You're twenty-two years old."

"Yeah. And you're what? Thirty-four? Thirty-five? So what? I'm not stupid. I've had a lot of time to think. That's what comes of being the isolated, odd one out in your family. You have way too much time to think. And believe me, I've had tons. I don't need experience to have figured that out."

"So you have the whole world all figured out, do you?"

"I mean, I'm not gonna say the whole world. But maybe my piece of it."

This girl. This woman. She didn't know when to question or doubt. She dove headlong into everything. Bets at a poker table, wild conclusions and into his bed. And he just…he liked that about her.

"Bold claim, little Cricket."

"I don't know, things make more sense now than they ever have. I didn't think that was possible. I just walked through the messiest, weirdest time of my life. And it's really not so bad. And yeah, I basically do have it all sorted out."

He wrapped his arms around her, and pulled her on top of him, laying them both back on the blanket. He looked into her earnest face, and desire stirred in his body. "You have everything figured out, is that it?"

"Basically. The mysteries of sex are even solved."

"Every last one?" he pressed.

He didn't know why he needed this right now, but he did. It was deeper than lust, that was the problem. He couldn't write it off as simply basic desire. He'd wanted to. He'd tried to. But it was so much more than that. That was the thing. With her, it always would be. And whatever was happening between the two of them, she didn't have to be here. They didn't have to be here. They were choosing it, out here under the unending sky. With the land and the ranch in their blood, and his need for her pumping hot and insistent through his body.

"Bet you can't teach me anything," he said, his voice rough.

And Cricket, true to form, sat up, her thighs on either side of him, and stripped her white tank top up over her head without pause. She was wearing a plain, matching bra, her lean, athletic body a sight to behold. "Is that a *bet* bet, cowboy?"

"Sure."

"You know, historically, you lose bets with me."

"Yeah. I feel like a real loser right now." With her

sweet ass perched on top of him, and all her beauty blocking out the sun.

"Well."

"Just remember that there are some bets I lose on purpose." He gripped her hips, sliding his hands up to her slim waist, then up further still, brushing his thumbs over her breasts. Then he reached around and unhooked her bra, flinging it off somewhere in the grass.

She made a small sound that might have been indignant, but he didn't much care. Because she was bare and gorgeous and perfect and he was dying for a taste.

He pressed his palm firmly against the center of her back and brought her down toward him, toward his mouth. He sucked one perfect, ripe bud between his lips, and the cry that escaped her lips wasn't indignant this time. Not at all. It was one of pleasure, one of desire, and he reveled in it. She wrenched his shirt over his head, wiggling away from him as she did. And he pinned her down on her back, her arms up over her head, and kissed her deep.

"Little Crickets with smart mouths get themselves in trouble," he said.

A challenge glimmered in her eyes. "Do we? I sure hope so."

"Do you?"

"Yes. I lack discipline."

"Is that so?"

"I've mostly been neglected. I need a firm hand."

"I could probably provide you with one."

"So many promises. And yet…"

He growled, unsnapped her jeans, unzipped them and pushed them down her thighs, and she helped eagerly. Then she wiggled downward, kissing his chest, his stomach, still on her back beneath him as she undid his pants and freed him. She peered up at him, squeezing his length and making a sound of purely feminine satisfaction.

"You're really kind of a work of art," she said, leaning forward and rubbing her cheek against him. He could honestly say a woman had never done that. And the look on her face made him so hard he thought he might burst.

She shoved lightly, and he moved, going onto his back as she bit her lip and looked down at him. Then she knelt over him, taking him slowly into her mouth, the sweet, wet heat an assault on his senses. She tortured him. And she wasn't practiced or knowing or anything like that. Didn't have a parade of well coordinated tricks, but she made up for it with enthusiasm. Pure and simple. She was a woman in full enjoyment of his body, and he didn't think he'd ever experienced anything quite like that. And hell, looking at her, at the elegant line of her spine, her ass up in the air as she pleasured him, was something more powerful than he'd ever experienced.

This moment was free of obligation. Something in his chest began to unravel, as if each pass of her tongue, each movement of her mouth over his body, was working to loosen something inside him, unraveling something he hadn't been aware was there.

Who knew that sandwiches and a blow job out in the middle of a field would be enough to make a man almost believe in romance? He sure as hell hadn't. But it was something. *She* was something. Far and away beyond anything he'd ever known or experienced or figured he might want to understand.

Cricket.

She pleasured him until he thought he couldn't take it anymore. Then he reached in his back pocket, grabbed his wallet and took out the condom, tearing it open and guiding her up his body as he sheathed himself with one practiced hand.

She seated herself on top of him and took him inside of her slowly, achingly so, her mouth dropping open, her head falling back. She flexed her hips, a ragged sound on her lips, and then she began to move, slowly at first. Then more quickly. But it still wasn't enough for him. He grabbed on to her hips, moved her up and down over his body, driving them both crazy. Pushing them both until she cried out her pleasure. And then he reversed their positions, pounding into her, unable to hold himself back any longer. It was primal and urgent, and exactly what he needed to compound that strange unraveling in his chest. Only then, she opened her eyes and met his.

And he couldn't breathe. Not then. Just as his climax took him over, he was lost. In Cricket. In the look of wonder on her face, the absolute trust there. He was her first lover. The only man who had ever touched her like this. He was bound up in all of the strange things she'd been going through for all this time, and he didn't want to be even more turned on by that, but he was. And he lost himself then, just went over the edge, growling out her name as she cried out his and convulsed around him. As she stared up at him, the look of absolute contentment in her eyes undid him. She didn't know better. Didn't know a different man.

He had taken her crush and used it to his advantage.

He had taken her inexperience as a rancher, as a poker player, and had used it to his advantage there too.

He felt… Well, he felt like shit, actually. Because there was something in him that knew instinctively he could never answer the depth of longing in her eyes. There was something in him that knew he had bound her to him. Her childish feelings, her awakening desire—she would feel connected to him in a way she shouldn't. That was a fact. That was the problem. And he would… He would what? Take her away from this place that she was turning into her own? Away from this life she was making and into his? He would just be another man taking a woman's dreams and putting them underneath his own.

They would be done at the end of the month. That was the deal. And whatever possibilities he felt out here in the wilderness… They just weren't to be.

That was good. It was right that he knew that, felt that. Everything would go back to the way it had been, when all this was said and done. That was for the best. Because he wouldn't be able to give Cricket what she wanted. Not really. And when she realized that, then they would both be trapped in the exact same hell their parents had been trapped in.

And he wouldn't have that.

Not ever.

But he didn't say anything. Instead, he kissed her forehead, and she snuggled against him. And right out there in the open, completely naked, the two of them fell asleep.

What happened at the end of the wager was a problem for their future selves. Because right now, they had this.

And Jackson's last thought before he drifted out of consciousness was that he couldn't remember the last time he'd felt quite this content.

Nine

It was the thirtieth day.

Cricket hadn't had the heart to ask if he would be staying the entire day, or leaving right away, or… She didn't know. And she was afraid to find out exactly what the answer was.

She was a coward.

She desperately wanted this to keep on going. She desperately wanted him to stay with her.

Right. So you're going to beg him to stay in your little ranch house? And for what? You're trying to find your own way…

No. She couldn't beg him to stay.

But they woke up the morning of the thirtieth day in the same bed just as they had every morning since they'd begun sleeping together, and he had gone out to work the same as he had from the beginning.

And so when he returned that evening, dirty and disheveled, she breathed out a sigh of relief.

Maybe he wasn't ready for things to change either. Maybe things wouldn't change. Maybe it would all stay the same, just for a little while. Maybe they could put off all the hard conversations for another time. They could say goodbye another day. She had cooked. Just in case. And she had been rewarded. It was funny, how much she enjoyed cooking. And she would have been more annoyed about the fact that she liked such a traditionally feminine pursuit, except that he seemed to enjoy it so much, and he appreciated it. She thought back to the day she'd made bread and brought out ham sandwiches. Oh yes, he'd appreciated that a whole lot. She felt a dreamy smile cross her face when she thought about it. These times with Jackson had been... Well, they'd been everything.

He'd been everything she'd ever fantasized about.

She knew this moment was supposed to be about moving on. About moving into the next phase of her life, but...

No. It doesn't bear thinking about.

Except, he was here.

And she kept thinking that, even as they each built hamburgers out of the ingredients she had laid out.

"Jackson," she said softly as they finished eating. "How was your day?"

"Good. And yours?"

"Good and—"

She cut herself off. Because she didn't care. She didn't want to have this conversation. She really didn't. She didn't want to talk at all. Because her insides were jumbled up and everything hurt. Because this was the last day, and she didn't know how to ask him if he would stay. She didn't know how to explain to herself, in a way that made her not feel silly, why she might ask him to stay.

Because I want to marry him.

And I want to have his children.

Because I would be his ranch wife in this house or any house.

Because he was her dream. And that was the bottom line.

She was young, and she was supposed to go out and live. She knew that. She wasn't supposed to want a man she had been completely hopeless over since she was twelve. She was supposed to experience more. Have more lovers. Travel. Something.

But she just didn't want to.

And she had the sick, terrible feeling that—much like her mother—there was really only one man for her, and there would never be anything that would take away her feelings. So she didn't want to waste time talking.

She flung herself into his arms, climbing up on the same chair as him, her legs on either side of his, the heart of her right up against where he was rapidly growing hard. And she kissed him. Kissed him until she thought she might die. Kissed him because she thought if she *didn't* she might die.

He stole her oxygen and became it all at once, and she couldn't have explained that feeling if she'd been put before a firing squad. She had never thought in terms of fate. She had always believed she was a pragmatist. But he felt like fate. This moment felt like fate.

And she really couldn't deny it. Didn't really want to. Didn't want it to end.

He stood up from the chair, and he swept their plates to the side, breaking them on the floor. "I owe you a set of dishes," he said roughly.

"I don't care," she said.

Oh she *really* didn't care. Because she just wanted him, wanted this. And nothing else mattered. Not plates, not anything. And she gave thanks that she had worn a dress, which she so rarely did, because it made everything easily accessible for him. Because then he had his hands at her hips. Had his fingers between her thighs, stroking her, stoking the fires of her desire. This was like madness. This was like every fantasy she'd ever had.

And she had a terrible feeling that it had been love she'd been feeling from the very beginning. Love and fate—and that was why. That was why it had been him from the time she was twelve years old. And it didn't matter how much she wanted to deny it. It simply was. It simply, simply was. But he was here. He was here.

And he had broken dishes and cleared the table and was kissing her on top of it.

This table that had been an emblem of everything she'd been missing.

And she'd thought what she'd wanted had been some generic idea of a sitcom family. And she'd tried to shoehorn Jackson into that picture. But that wasn't what she'd wanted. It hadn't been quiet dinners that she was missing. It had been him. Just him. It wasn't an aching for domesticity that she felt that first night they'd sat down to dinner together, it was a life spent with him. It had been things shared with this man that had called to her from the very first time she'd ever seen him.

It didn't matter if the idea was crazy. It didn't matter if she was younger than he was. It didn't matter if she was just starting out. Because she knew.

He'd made fun of her the other day, when she'd said she'd understood all these things, but she did. She understood this. Now, suddenly, in his arms—she understood.

She loved him.

And that was all there was to it.

She loved him and she wanted to be with him. And whatever else she needed to experience, it didn't matter. Because this was the one thing her heart and her body had known from the beginning. A lifetime spent feeling like she might always have to be second best, not quite so spectacular as her sisters, had seen her trying to find another explanation for how she felt. To find a way to protect her heart. But there was no protecting it, not now. She felt exposed. Cut open. She couldn't hide or protect herself even if she wanted to. So she didn't try. She surrendered to this madness between them.

And then he was inside of her, the table hitting up against the wall with each and every thrust. And he was amazing. In every way. And she let herself feel it. All of it. The love she felt for him expanding, growing in her chest, so much so that she thought she might burst. So much so that she nearly wept, and when her orgasm finally broke over her, she did. She shook and cried and held him, as his own release took him over.

And when it was done, he stood, and she just lay

there, wrecked. The dishes on the floor a metaphor for her body.

"I…"

"Jackson," she said, at the same time.

"Cricket, this has been… It's been… The bet's over."

She just lay there, frozen, her arms spread wide, like a butterfly that had been pinned in place in a collection, unable to move, her back against the table.

"Are you leaving?"

"It's the end of the bet," he said again.

"Day thirty," she said. "You almost left me that first night too. Why don't you just…not."

His eyes looked tormented then, pained. "I should have left you then. That's the thing. Better late than never."

"No…"

"But it has to be some time. I've got a ranch. I've got a life, and so do you."

"Well, maybe don't leave me with my fucking dinner plates on the floor, you asshole," she said.

He didn't flinch. Instead, he righted his clothing and went over to the corner, grabbed the broom and the dustpan. His actions reminded her so much of the first night he'd been here, when he had fixed things and she had swept, that she nearly cried. And she just lay there, naked, while he swept up the glass on the floor, but left all the pieces of her heart.

"If you ever need anything—if, when the horses come, you need something… You just let me know, Cricket."

"No," she said.

Because what she wanted from him, he wasn't going to give.

The words were lumped in her throat, and she couldn't bring herself to ask for them. And when he left her house, and she was there, nothing but misery, she had to wonder if she had changed at all.

Because she hadn't said what needed to be said. She hadn't. She'd just left it all there, in her chest, afraid of rejection.

What was the point? What was the point of any of it if she hadn't gotten strong enough to say what she needed?

What was the damn point?

But she didn't go after him. And for the next several days, she did nothing at all. Until she started to realize that something wasn't right. Not just the loneliness or her heart. She was pretty upset by Jackson leaving, and by his not coming back, but not enough to screw with her cycle. And when she showed up at her sister Emerson's house, practically shivering from the cold and clutching a bag that contained a pregnancy test, she was in a daze.

"What are you doing here?"

"I couldn't go to Wren. Because she is married to Creed."

"Yes," Emerson said, stepping back away from the door. "She is."

Cricket stepped inside, and held up the test.

Emerson touched her stomach. "I'm actually good. But is there something you need to tell me?"

"Yes," Cricket said. "I mean, maybe. I need to use your bathroom."

"You know you can."

"Please don't tell anybody," Cricket said.

"I won't."

She went into the bathroom, and didn't come out for way longer than the prescribed number of minutes. It didn't take long for Emerson to knock.

"I feel like your lack of communication indicates the test results were not what you wanted." Her sister's voice was soft through the door.

"No," Cricket said. But even as she said that, she didn't feel like it was true. She wasn't devastated. She wasn't even sad. It felt…right somehow. That there was no way she was going to get out of a relationship with Jackson without keeping something of him.

Without being changed.

"Honey," Emerson said. "Open the door."

And Cricket did, knowing she must look every inch the bedraggled insect her name suggested she might be.

"Whatever you need. I'm not here to judge. If you need a ride to anywhere, if you need me to provide you with an alibi while you collect a weapon to go kill someone…"

"No," Cricket said.

"No to…"

"Any of those things. I'm fine. I mean, I will be. I've just got to…tell him."

"And by him, do I take it you mean Jackson Cooper?"

"The very same. And I didn't want Wren to tell Creed to kill him."

"Well, I'm fixing to tell Holden to kill him, so all you're really doing is sparing Creed's conscience."

"Please don't kill him. I've got to tell him."

"Sure."

"I'm not upset."

"You look upset."

"Well we're not really…together anymore. So that kind of sucks."

"Well, you don't need him. You've got us. Whatever you want to do, you've got us."

"I want to have a baby," Cricket said. "And I didn't think I did. But now that it's happening… I mean, I guess it's not a bad thing that I'm not horrendously unhappy about it."

"Yeah," Emerson said. "I guess so."

"I just need…to see him. Before anything else."

Emerson had been protective, but Cricket managed to extricate herself from her sister and get herself on her way to Jackson's place. She had never been there before, and she was stunned by how impressive the modern ranch house was. All black windows, reddish wood siding and charcoal paint. An extraordinary collection of shapes and angles. So very different from the classic little farmhouse she had.

They were so different.

But…

At their core, they had plenty in common.

There was a reason they were in this situation, after all. Chemistry, for sure, but more than that.

She would never forget that day they had spent out on the picnic blanket. He might have been stern and cold the last time they made love. The last time she'd seen him, but that wasn't the sum total of what they were as a couple.

A couple.

But they had never been that, had they? They'd been two people bonded together by a bed, by her pain and…

And glimmers of his. Which he had shared, but so sparingly. And she knew there was more to him. She did. Knew there was more to who he was and everything that he carried around inside of him, even if she didn't know quite all what it was.

But this was the time, she supposed. This was where the rubber met the road and the…well, the positive pregnancy test met with their present reality.

She took a deep breath and got out of her truck, making her way up the paved walk that led to the large, flat entryway. The door was huge, and it made Cricket feel tiny. She stood there and took a breath, trying not to be reminded of feeling tiny in other circumstances. Standing outside the door to her father's office. Sitting way down at the end of a long banquet table, feeling lost in the family villa.

No, this was different. Because she was standing there a changed woman from who she'd been back then. When she'd just been a girl. When she hadn't known who she was or what she wanted. When he called her little Cricket, it wasn't a bad thing. And she didn't mind. When he said it, it somehow made her feel special, protected. And right now, she was protecting a life inside of her. And that made her feel strangely powerful. Renewed and changed.

She'd never really thought about being a mother. And in fact, in passing, had thought she wouldn't be. After all, her own experiences with family hadn't been any good. But she didn't feel tied to that. Not now. Not anymore. Whatever the Maxfields were, it didn't make Cricket Maxfield one of them. It didn't mean she had to repeat their legacy over and over again. Somehow, that little inner boosting helped buoy her on, and she raised her hand and knocked on the solid oak door. She shook her hand out, because it hurt. And she wasn't even sure it had made a sound in the gigantic space.

But then, the door opened, and she jumped back. Because there he was, standing in the doorway wearing a tight black T-shirt, jeans and a black cowboy hat. And he looked…well, amazing.

"Hi," she said.

"Cricket," he responded. "What are you doing here?"

"Well, that's not the friendliest greeting."

"Sorry. Do you want to come in?"

"Probably should."

He opened the door, and let her into the room made of the same wood as the exterior of the house, glossy black details punctuating the rustic look, making it feel somehow modern. The room was huge, square, with a ceiling so tall it brought her back to that place of smallness.

Of course, Jackson and all his height contributed to that, as well.

"We need to talk," she said. "The way you left me… I wanted you to stay."

"Yes, and I explained that I couldn't." His jaw was tight, his expression firm.

"Yeah, and you didn't give me a good reason. So I'd like to hear it. I really would."

Before she told him what she had to say, she wanted to know what he might say to her without that information.

"It's complicated."

"No. Complicated is having a crush on a man for years, then finding out he might be your half brother, then wanting to sleep with him anyway. Then finding out he's not your half brother and sleeping with him for the duration of a thirty-day wager. That's complicated. So, we've been through complicated already, so whatever else you have on your mind, whatever else you have to tell me, is not going to touch that. I think we can figure it out. Trust me when I say I'm pretty resilient."

"All right, Cricket," he said. "You really want to have this conversation?"

"Yes. I do."

"I don't want to get married. I mean, what's the point? It just two people being tied together for no particular reason that I can see."

"So, why does there have to be marriage? Why can't we just be together?"

"I would never want to be responsible for not loving someone enough. For doing to them what my father did to my mother. And at the end of the day, whether I admire or look up to him or not, I'm Cash Cooper's son."

"And I'm James Maxfield's daughter, but I'm not going to sexually harass anyone. I'm not going to treat my kids like an afterthought and my wife…well, husband, like a trophy. It doesn't matter whose son you are. What matters is what kind of man you are. And that's your choice."

"Okay then, it's my choice not to put myself in a position where I could hurt someone that way."

"So you don't think you could love me."

She stared at him, willing herself not to break his gaze. Not to be a wimp. She would brazen this out. She just would.

"It's not you."

"Oh, it's not you, it's me. Very original. You know, Jackson, I expected better from you. Better from us. For us. We are not like anyone else. So don't be a cliché now."

"I'm not trying to hurt you…"

"Another good one. Who writes your dialogue? Because it's not very good."

"I'm sorry."

"And I'm pregnant."

Ten

Jackson felt like a bomb had been dropped in the middle of his living room. It was like watching a horror movie. Looking back on the last few weeks. Sitting there, wanting to tell the idiot not to go into that house, but he'd gone in anyway. And now here he was. Exactly the thing he'd been trying to avoid.

She was pregnant.

That was absolutely everything that he hadn't wanted to happen.

"When did you find out?"

"Literally an hour ago? I went to my sister's house—not the one who is married to your brother—and then I came straight here."

"What the hell are we going to do?"

"Well, the unfortunate thing is I was kinda hoping

you would have something better to say than what you just did."

"You understand that we can't get married."

"Well, fantastic," Cricket said. "I figure I'll just find another man to marry, then."

"You damn well will not."

"But you don't want to marry me. Then maybe somebody should. Because maybe I care about that kind of thing." She took a big, deep breath. "Maybe I care about tradition and I don't want my child to be a bastard. Did you ever think about that?"

"Well, do you?"

"No. What I care about is the fact that you're being ridiculous. We are good together."

"And this is exactly the kind of thing I wanted to avoid. This obligation. This idea that two people have to be together. For the sake of the child. Do you know what it does to a child, Cricket? I was worried about you. About what I might do to you if I couldn't be what you needed... But a kid. Dammit, that kid is basically me. You know what it's like to find out you're the unhappy glue that held your parents together for better or for worse? Mostly worse?"

"We already talked about this. It's all about choices and—"

"But I've seen what it does. If I committed to that, if I committed to you... I would never let you leave."

"Great. I don't want to leave," she said. "I want to be with you. I want to stay with you. Why is that bad? Why would it be so wrong?"

"I don't love you," he said, the words scraping his throat raw, and he knew they felt wrong. He knew they *were* wrong. But he couldn't find any other words. Couldn't figure out what else to say, what else might come from that hammering feeling in his chest.

"What if I said I loved you?"

"That's what we can't do, Cricket. We cannot have that. We would make each other miserable. I would make you miserable."

"I want to be with you. I'm choosing that. What about my choice? Maybe I want to be with you even if I would be sorry that you didn't love me. Maybe I'd rather be with you than not."

"Cricket…"

"No. Be honest. Be honest about what you want and what you don't want, Jackson. But don't blame it on me, and don't blame it on your need to protect me. Because that's not what's happening here. You're not protecting me. You're…protecting yourself. I'm standing here, and I'm not scared. I'm not scared to love you. I'm not scared to have this baby. And you know what? I'm not scared to do it alone, either. I would rather not. I mean, flat out, I'd rather not. But that's just because I'd rather share my life with you. Because I have never felt so happy as I did living in that farmhouse with you. And so I would weather anything to figure out how we could work. You're the one who doesn't want to. And I can't quite figure out why.

"You think because I'm young, because I was inexperienced, that I can't understand what I want. But I do, Jackson. I do. I have always known what I wanted. A place in this world where I fit, and to be with you. It seems to me that what you're after is a life where you won't regret anything. And I don't think anyone can guarantee you that, Jackson, I really don't. We could be together, for better or worse, like you said. And maybe sometimes it would be worse. But I think it would still be a better kind of worse than being apart."

"Because you don't know what that looks like. Not really. I do. I watched my mom… I watched her wish for another life. And I was the cause of her not having it."

"So, we can get married. And if you were miserable, we could get divorced."

"Cricket…"

"No, really, what's your problem? You're afraid of what? You're afraid of failing? Because we're not trapped. We wouldn't be. It would be up to us. But you're afraid of something. Otherwise…this would be a different conversation. You're acting like I didn't grow up around a dysfunctional marriage. So why don't you stop hiding behind the one you grew up around. I thought cowboys were supposed to be brave."

Her words were like a dagger through his heart. He did feel like a coward. He felt like the worst kind of coward, standing there and offering her absolutely nothing. Standing there and failing her, except…

He knew what he knew.

He knew what it was to be a child who had been part of a marriage of obligation. More than that, he knew what it was to be the child who'd caused it. And maybe Creed had been willing to do that to be with his kid, but his brother had been through something entirely different. His brother had been barred from seeing his child.

His child.

So Jackson was going to live in a different house than his kid?

This was why they'd done it. He could understand it. That was the thing. Standing there staring at her, and the enticement of the future they could have…

But Cricket hadn't said she loved him.

She was standing there, asking for something that would make their lives easier on a surface level. The thing that so many people did. To try and make a family for a child.

But he knew that beneath the surface of the happiest-looking nuclear family there could be rot and decay. A kind of desperate sadness that nobody saw but the people on the inside of the arrangement.

And whatever he was, he didn't want to be her obligation. Whatever he was, he didn't want to be her regret.

You're protecting yourself…

How? He didn't feel protected. Not now. What he felt was angry. Infuriated and just damn helpless.

He hadn't done any different than his parents. And that was a galling thing. But he would do different now. He would. He would do better, for them both.

"Do you even want to be this baby's father?"

"I'll be a father. If I made a kid, I'm going to take care of the kid."

"It's a shame you can't feel a little bit of that for me."

"Whether you see it or not, Cricket, this is me caring."

"No, I don't see it," she said, her tone as icy as her expression.

"We'll find a way through this."

"To what? Coparenting? Sharing custody? Will we trade our kid back and forth in the parking lot of the grocery store?"

He didn't like anything about the future she painted with those words. He didn't like any of this. What he wanted to do was grab her and pull her up against him, pick her up in his arms and carry her upstairs and make her his.

He wanted to keep her.

And she would stay.

For the child.

And he would still be that obligation he'd always been.

He gritted his teeth, shoved that aside. "Whatever you need."

"Except a husband."

"It's better."

"Well, if you say so. But if I were you, I don't know that I'd lay a bet on it. Since you'd only lose. Because you know what, I got the better hand." She stopped and looked at him, her expression almost pitying. "The thing is, Jackson. You keep thinking that you know exactly how this is going to play out. You keep thinking that you know better than me. Even from the beginning. When I won, you felt like you had another plan, and so you didn't really lose. But you did, though, didn't you? I got my way. So if I were you, I would maybe try to figure out what all I know that you don't."

And then Cricket left.

Turned and left him there, driving off in her great truck down the hill, taking some piece of him with her. But she didn't understand. She didn't understand that this was how it had to be. Because in her mind she could will all these things into fitting together, and he knew better. He'd spent his life as an obligation.

But now he was standing there, feeling like he'd cut his own heart out of his chest, and he knew he was a liar.

He couldn't love her...

He already did.

And he was every bit the coward she had accused him of being.

Cricket didn't go back to the ranch. She couldn't. Instead, she went to Emerson's. And it didn't take long for Wren to show up. At this point, there was no protecting Jackson from the wrath of her brothers-in-law. And Cricket didn't intend to try. She was too angry at him. He was being...ridiculous.

He didn't have a damn good reason for any of this.

Cricket had never sulked so hard in her life. But she was doing her best to work a groove into her sister's overstuffed, white fluffy beanbag chair with the weight of her indignant sighs.

"So, when do we get the whole story?" Emerson asked.

It all came pouring out of Cricket, from her lifelong crush to their love affair, to the half brother thing, and all the way to what had just happened at his place.

"Well," Wren said. "Creed is going to kill him."

"I know," Cricket said. "It's why I went to Emerson first. Because I didn't really want him to die. I'm feeling more flexible on that subject right at the moment."

"So he said he can't love you?"

"Yes. He did. And you know what, if I believed it... then maybe I would think he was doing the right thing. But I don't believe it. I do think he can love me. I really do. I think he might love me already. And I think he's being afraid."

"Well," Wren said, "love makes fools out of men. Trust me."

"Even Creed?"

"Oh, Creed was the *worst*," Wren said.

"No," Emerson said, "I think Holden was the worst. I told him that I loved him and he lost his mind."

"Yeah, Creed was not exactly receptive to me loving him either."

"Oh," Cricket said, frowning.

"What?" Wren asked.

"I didn't exactly tell him that I loved him."

"Really?" Emerson asked. "But you do, right? I mean, you have for years."

"I… Yes. But I…wanted to see what he would say, and I didn't want to…"

"Cricket," Wren said gently. "I'd like to kill him. With my bare hands. If he didn't think that he could give you something real he never should've touched you."

"No. I told him it was okay. He was honest with me. He was upfront. He was. He never lied to me. It's just… I thought I could be with him and then move on. I thought I could be with him and then make it part of a phase that I moved past. But I couldn't. I was lying to myself. He was never a phase. He was always fate."

"Then you need to tell him."

"He *humiliated me*."

"Yeah. And…sometimes we have to be fools for love."

"I don't like that at all."

"I don't either," Wren said. "But I love my husband.

And I would debase myself for him a thousand times to keep him. But he doesn't make me. Maybe the real problem is that Jackson needs to know how you feel. The Coopers are… They're hard men. And I don't know all of Jackson's issues. But I do know what it looks like when a Cooper runs scared."

"So what? I don't wait for him to come to me? I don't…wait for him to say it first?"

"You can. But I think you have a good head on your shoulders, Cricket. And you always have," Emerson said. "You know who you are. And it would be great if relationships could be fifty-fifty, but they can't be. Everybody has to give everything they've got all the time, and sometimes you're going to have to be the one carrying your partner. No, it should never look like Mom and Dad's marriage. Where one of them dies emotionally, without any kind of love or support. But sometimes you have to be the first one who's willing to break. The first one who's willing to be vulnerable. And it might be tough, but it's best. Because otherwise you end up in a stalemate forever, and nobody wins."

"Maybe it's just a bad hand. All around."

"No. Don't say that. Look, he's a good man, and you're a good woman. And I don't believe for a minute that the two of you can't find a way to make something together."

"But…"

"It sucks," Emerson said, "but anything that matters is tough sometimes. The only person who ever has it easy in a relationship is someone like Dad. Someone who doesn't care enough to be hurt. Who doesn't care enough about someone else's feelings."

Those words resonated inside of Cricket and sank down deep. She had always wanted to be protected, but being part of her family, in the way that she had wanted to be…it had been a bigger risk than she was willing to take. It hadn't mattered enough. It hadn't mattered enough because she hadn't aspired to the kind of life her mother and father had anyway. So contorting herself to become part of it had seemed the opposite of a good idea. But Jackson… He was different. The life they could have—she could see it. She ached for it. A life together, one with their child. And that hadn't been her fantasy. She had thought about Jackson, about having him. Not about domestic bliss or anything of that kind. But she wanted it. It was a future that burned bright and hot in her mind. A future that mattered.

Because she loved him.

And where in the world did pride fit in with love? She *couldn't* protect herself.

That was what he was doing. Whether he would admit it or not, that was what he was doing. And she wasn't going to do that. She wasn't going to sacrifice love on the altar of her own pride. Because this was deeper than that. It was in her bones, in her blood. Like the land. Like ranching.

Some things simply were.

And for her, loving Jackson was one of those things. And she was going to fight for it. Fight for him.

Because her life mattered too much to let someone like James Maxfield twist her sense of who she was enough to prevent her from being happy even when he wasn't around. And it was the same for Jackson, whether he knew it or not. His parents' mistakes didn't get to decide what he was.

She burrowed out from the large poof she'd been sitting on. "All right," she said. "I'm going to tell him that I love him."

"A good idea. Maybe not at nine o'clock at night, though," Emerson said.

"Why not?"

"Formulate a plan. You got this. But it wouldn't hurt to take some time with it."

Cricket nodded. "Okay. Time."

And that was when she did start to form a plan.

"I'm going to need to borrow your dress again," she said to Emerson.

"Whatever you need."

Eleven

Jackson was no stranger to grief. But what surprised him this time was that the situation with Cricket felt more like death than he'd anticipated anything like this could feel. He had reached the end of his rope and he knew he had two options. Reach for the bottle of whiskey, or reach for his car keys. He opted for the car keys, and found himself driving down from the ranch and heading to where his father was, at the tasting room, and that was how Jackson ended up pounding on the door. He knew he'd woken up the old man, but he didn't really care.

"Jackson? Is everything all right?" Cash asked, tying his robe hastily as he pulled open the door.

"Cricket is pregnant," Jackson said.

"Well hell," Cash said. "You really did need to know who her father was."

"I told you I did."

"You didn't waste any time."

"It was inevitable. But it doesn't matter. I need to know something else from you, and I need to know it now. Why did you marry Mom if you couldn't love her? Why did you do it for me? Because you know what, it doesn't feel very good to be the reason your parents are miserable. To be the reason that they're together. To know that you're why they are not happy."

"You were never why we weren't happy," Cash said. Then he sighed wearily. "Come in."

Jackson stepped inside, enveloped by the sense of strangeness he always felt when he entered his childhood home. He had sat at the dining table countless times with his mother. He had opened Christmas presents in the corner, right there by the fireplace where the tree always was. He had read to his mother while she lay on the couch, while she wasn't well. While he was losing her, watching as she slipped away.

He couldn't be in here and not…feel.

"You need to understand that we weren't unhappy," Cash said. "Not always. Just like we weren't happy always. And look, the pain that your mother felt, that was my fault. We had a bad fight. Must've been…fifteen, sixteen years in, and she told me how much she hated the winery, and at that point, it had made us so much money, it felt like the best thing I'd ever done. But she said it just reminded her that my whole life was built on the foundation of trying to win back another woman."

Cash shook his head. "And I… I let that sit inside me. I let that fester. And I figured… It would've been a lot easier to be married to Lucinda Maxfield. But I know better than that. I mean, I know better than to believe that being with Lucinda would've fixed all my problems. Because you can't compare a childish infatuation to a marriage that spans decades. You just can't do it. Every what-if supposition your mother and I ever had about if we hadn't been together... We were never with anyone else for all those years. I didn't have children with anyone else. The stresses and pressures that time in a family put on you can't be compared to anything else. We grew up with each other, for better or worse. We changed together, in sickness and health. We were part of each other."

"You were together because you felt obligated," Jackson said.

"Is that a bad thing?"

"Yes. You should be with someone because...hell, because you love them."

"Where the hell did you get the idea that love didn't come with obligation? Loving a child is full of obligation. A marriage is filled with obligation. *Obligation* is not a bad word. It's bad people that turn away from it, don't you think?"

"I can't say that I ever thought of it that way."

"We weren't perfect. We weren't blissfully, perfectly happy. And I carry so much guilt for all my feelings. For the kind of husband I wasn't. It's not that I couldn't have loved her, it's that I chose—*we* chose—to let certain things affect what we believed. To let certain feelings grow rotten and determine how much and how little we could feel and forgive."

"When she told me that you only got married because she was pregnant with me—"

"Maybe," his dad said. "Maybe that's true. But she doesn't know that. Not even I know that. We could say that, shout it at each other at the worst of times, and we certainly did. But that doesn't make it true. That doesn't make it a sure thing that we can know. We loved each other then."

"Well, you were only with mom because Lucinda Maxfield married James."

"This is the problem," Cash said. "I don't know the way things would've gone, or could've gone if we'd done things differently. If we'd been less stubborn. Less self-righteous. But we weren't. And that's my burden. It's not yours or anyone else's, and she shouldn't have put it on you. But there's a lot of things I shouldn't have put on her… You shouldn't have been the person she had to talk to. But the problem is—this is all 'should have,' 'could have.' And you drive yourself crazy with it, Jackson. Believe me. I've done it. For years and years, I've done it. And most of all since she passed."

"Why since then?"

"I told you. Guilt. And regret. Because at the end of the day, I loved your mother very much. And what I didn't do was show it. Because I kept expecting it to feel the same as something I felt when I was young, something I felt that was impossible and painful, and wonderful in its way…" He shook his head. "And then, I wonder what could have been between us now and that makes the regret even worse. Because I can hear her in my head, saying I was just waiting for her to die so I could be with the person I really wanted. But that's not the truth of it. It just isn't."

Jackson let out a long, slow breath and rocked back

on his heels. He didn't know what the hell to do with any of this. Cricket looked at him and talked about fate. She had talked about him and her as if they were something preordained. And his dad was making this all sound a lot like choice. And a whole collection of hard ones at that.

But something else Cricket said burned bright inside of him.

They weren't their parents.

And they weren't. It was true.

Because Jackson didn't feel conflicted or confused about whether or not he should be with Cricket because he had feelings for someone else. He'd never had feelings for anyone like he did for Cricket. And he wasn't young and naive. But what he was, was damn tired of feeling like a sacrifice. And if he was truly honest with himself, he was angry at his mother. Because she'd made him feel that way. Whether she'd meant to or not. And hearing his dad say he wished she hadn't dumped that on Jackson gave voice to all these things he'd tried not to think about.

"You know, son," Cash said. "She was sick, not a saint. A wonderful woman to be sure, but flawed like any of us. I know she didn't mean to hurt you. But the fact of the matter is…she did. Doesn't mean she didn't love you."

"I know," Jackson said.

"For what it's worth, she would've walked into fire for you. Marrying me was only a hardship for part of the time."

"Do you regret the way things happened?"

"I regret the way I handled them. I regret that I didn't

find a way to be a better husband. I've never regretted you. I've never regretted the life your mother and I built together. But I didn't let go of the past the way I should have, because your vows say you forsake all others. And I never cheated, but I kept that desire and those memories in a special place inside myself. You make choices every day, Jackson. And I don't know that you'll ever be able to live a life with no regrets, but you should make sure you live a life that's honest. Those games we all played, they were games. And games don't amount to much. Nothing more than needless heartache, anyway."

"I don't want to feel like she has to marry me."

"She seems like a modern enough girl."

"I told her I wouldn't marry her."

"Well hell, boy," Cash said. "I didn't raise you to wimp out on your responsibilities."

"I'm not. I'm trying to make sure she doesn't see me as another responsibility."

"Well, ask her if she does. Don't just try to protect yourself. Ask her how she feels."

"How will she know?"

"How will she know?" Cash repeated. "You want too much. You're going to have to trust her. You're going to have to believe her. Trust would've gone a long way in fixing my marriage. Trust, faith and honesty. If I could do more of any three things, it would be those. And we would've had a different life."

Jackson loved Cricket. He did. He was sure of that, standing there in this house filled with all these memories. All those weighted, hurtful memories that had seen him silently carrying around a whole lot of baggage he hadn't realized was there.

And she had been right. He was protecting himself. Because the burden of feeling like an obligation to his mother, a debt that he'd never been able to repay, haunted him. And the last thing he wanted was to be that burden for Cricket.

But he would have to ask. And he would have to trust.

And he would have to hope that…well, that Cricket really did know everything. And that she had faith in all those things she'd shouted at him before she left.

She was right. He'd lost the bet.

But it was one he was glad to lose.

The next morning, when Cricket opened her door wearing that red dress from the poker tournament, that oversized leather jacket, cowboy hat, but no cigar, Jackson was standing there. He looked haunted, like a man possessed. Like a man who hadn't slept all night.

"What are you doing here?"

"What are *you* doing?"

"Well, obviously I was on my way to stage a very serious scheme."

"Very obviously. Do you have a pistol on you?"

"No pistol." Her heart hammered, hard, as she looked up at him. As she tried not to hope what his presence meant.

"I fold," he said.

"You…what?"

"I fold, Cricket. I'm done. I surrender to this, to you. And you're right. I was afraid. I was a coward. A damn coward. Because I didn't want to face the fact that I wasn't really afraid of being my father, I was afraid of being my mother. Sitting all bitter and hollow at my kitchen table and telling my teenage child I was only in a marriage for their sake. That there was no love. No, the real thing I was afraid of was being the one who felt unloved. Because I have to tell you, when my mom said all that to me, that's how I felt. Like a burden and an obligation that she should never have had to take on. And I couldn't stand being that for the rest of my life. Not with you. But I love you, Cricket. And I'm willing to be that. I'm willing to do anything if it means being with you, having you. I'm willing to be an obligation, and to earn your love later. I know you want to be free. I know you want to start a life, and I know that having a child right now, and settling down with me, doesn't have much of anything to do with that. But I think… this is fate. And far be it from me to go against her."

"Jackson," she whispered, her heart expanding in her chest. "You're not a burden to me. I went to my sister's house last night and I complained to her about how you rejected me. And then they asked me if I told you that I loved you, and I realized that I hadn't. That was me protecting myself. I wanted to know what you felt, what you thought, before I put myself out there. It was easy to talk about marriage, and so much harder to talk about my heart. Because I've never done it. I've never seriously talked to anyone about how I felt. Except for you. And I've done more of that over the past month than ever in my life. Told you more about who I am, what hurt me, and what made me who I am. The bottom line is, above all else, and with everything else shoved aside, I love you. I have loved you for years. And I would want to be with you, pregnant or not. It was just the thing that got me up the mountain. It was just the thing that forced me to be as brave as I was, and even then, I wasn't all that brave. So I didn't really have a right to yell at you."

"You had plenty of right."

"Jackson," she whispered. "I really, really love you. And I have never wanted much of anything in my whole life enough to fight for it. Except for you. Only you. I can't imagine another person, another feeling, another anything that would ever be worth all this hassle. You're not an obligation. You're my inevitability."

"Cricket Maxfield," he said, wrapping his arms around her waist and looking at her, square in the eye. "You're the surprise I didn't see coming. Little Cricket, you're the thing I've been missing. I didn't know the right place to look to fill the hole in my heart. But you've known all along. You are wiser than me. Smarter than me. Braver than me. And I am going to love you today, and every day after. I don't care if some days are hard. I don't care if there are sleepless nights, or if I have to move out of my house and into your farmhouse. Because nothing matters but you. And that's… My dad said to me, that obligation and love often go together, and I expect that he's right. Love is what makes you want to fulfill that obligation. But this is different. Everything else feels like an obligation. You feel like breathing. And that's as deep as I can explain it."

"Is it in your blood?" she asked, her voice a whisper.

"Yes," he responded. "It's in my blood. My bones. My heart."

"Mine too."

And then he kissed her, and she couldn't think anymore. Couldn't breathe. She could only feel. And somehow, she knew she felt the same thing he did. Somehow, she knew that in this moment they were one. And it wasn't a pregnancy or marriage vows that would make it so. They could never have parted even if they'd wanted to. Because it was too late. The chips had already gone down. The game was over.

And in the end, they had both won.

Cricket Maxfield had won any number of specious prizes in her life. And she had often felt uncertain about her place in the world. But the biggest and best prize she'd ever won was loving Jackson Cooper and having him love her back. And if all the years of feeling misfit and frizzy and gap-toothed and like she didn't belong was what it had taken for her to get here, then she counted them all worth it.

She wouldn't change a single thing, not about herself, not about anything. Because it had brought her here. To this man, to his arms.

And that was truly the greatest prize of all.

* * * * *

ONE NIGHT
IN TEXAS

CHARLENE SANDS

To my author pal and assistant, Dani Gorman.
You are the best. Thanks for all you do!

One

She looked at herself in the mirror and saw the same girl she'd always seen staring back at her. Gracie Diaz of Mexican American descent, whose immigrant father had worked for the Wingate family on their ranch, whose mother had taken up waitressing once Gracie's father died. She saw the same young girl with smoky brown eyes, olive skin and long dark hair who was still swept up in romantic fantasies of Sebastian, the more serious of the devastatingly handsome Wingate twins. The same starry-eyed dreamer with lofty aspirations of developing an events business and having a family of her own one day.

But she wasn't *just* that girl anymore… She was much more. Twenty-eight years old now, and the winner of a sixty-million-dollar lottery—a woman with means to do as she pleased.

"And you did that, Gracie," she said to her reflection. "You did as you pleased."

At the Texas Cattleman's Club masquerade ball. Nearly three months ago, she'd fallen for a tall, masked stranger, unable to resist his enigmatic charm. There was something in the way he'd held her, danced with her, *kissed* her. He was masterful and passionate, and it all had been so thrilling. She'd tossed away her inhibitions that night and had given in to the cravings of the body and mind. His scent, his deep, low voice, the way he moved—their chemistry had been off the charts. Their secret tryst had happened quickly, in a hidden spot where they wouldn't be found. But mere moments after they'd made love, voices coming from the hallway had interrupted their erotic interlude, and she'd fled. Taken off without so much as getting his name.

The mystery had intrigued her for months.

Because Gracie didn't know who he was.

Until now.

Her cell phone rang and she picked up on the second ring. Smiling into the phone, she said, "Hi, Beth."

She'd been Beth Wingate's assistant before she'd won the lottery, and now they worked side by side on special events. But mostly, Beth was her dearest friend. She hadn't told her friend the truth yet because she hadn't had enough time to process what she'd discovered two weeks ago. But she knew she couldn't keep it under wraps forever. "I'm glad you called me back."

"I know why you're worried, hon," Beth replied. "But believe me, you buying the Wingate Estate isn't gonna put my nose out of joint. I'm actually *glad* you're doing it, Gracie, because ultimately, it's good for everyone. My family needs cash to get Wingate Enterprises up to par. And selling the estate is the best way to get the new Wingate hotel chain on its feet."

Gracie was grateful to Beth for her encouragement. Though she had always dreamed of living in this amazing estate, she'd never believed it would happen. She'd chalked it up to one silly girl's childhood fantasy. After all, she'd been the daughter of a ranch employee, her father working for the Wingates most of his life. So now it was a pretty strange feeling having this monetary reversal, to be in the position to buy the estate. She'd never thought herself worthy and maybe she didn't feel that way now, either. But her mentor's supportive words had helped. "Thanks for making me feel better about it, Beth."

But it wasn't just the Wingate heiress's opinion that mattered. Soon Gracie would have to deal with Beth's brother Sebastian. She *so* wasn't looking forward to that.

"It's the truth," Beth said. "I'm happy you and the baby will be living there. How are you feeling lately?"

"My morning sickness is gone, thank the Lord for that. And I feel pretty good. No baby bump yet, but the doctor says I'm healthy."

"All good news. You've been wanting a family of your own for a long time now. It's finally happening."

Gracie closed her eyes, filled with mixed emotions. After she'd won the lottery, she'd tried dating, but she was never sure if it was her or her money that attracted men to her. After several dating mishaps, her trust had evaporated and she'd pretty much decided to have a baby on her own. She'd seen Dr. Everett months ago for fertility treatment, planning to do in vitro, but a glorious one-night stand during the masquerade ball had taken care of that. Now she was three months pregnant by a man she'd crushed on during her youth, a man who'd never seemed interested in her in the least, a man whose identity she'd finally figured out. "Yes, it finally is."

She placed her hand over her belly, imagining the new life growing inside her. What a miracle it was. She'd wanted a family of her own so much, and now those cherished dreams were *finally* coming true. She loved this baby already, but she didn't love the strings that would eventually become attached.

She'd have to think about that tomorrow.

Today, she had an estate to purchase.

"Beth, I'm glad we spoke. You've been such a good friend, and I didn't want to do anything that would make it awkward between us."

"Nothing ever will, girlfriend."

"Same here. Well, gotta run. I'll call you in a few days, okay?"

"Sounds good. Oh, and, Gracie…good luck."

"Thanks."

Gracie set the phone down and chewed on her lip. She was at loose ends here, and needed to gather her wits. After all, she had a meeting at the foreclosed Wingate Estate in one hour.

With her Realtor, her attorney…*and the father of her baby.*

It was damn cold inside the house, the January chill sweeping into the walls of the empty estate. Sebastian shuddered. From the frigidness? Or was it from a sudden feeling of loss? All the furnishings inside the house were gone, most items hauled off to an estate company where they'd gotten a fair price, but nowhere near the cost of his family's memories.

Sebastian wasn't the sentimental type—he was a realist and this sale was a good thing—but still, he was hit with a wave of unexpected nostalgia from selling his childhood home. There'd been an abundance of love here, plus silly and not-so-silly arguments. Not to mention wild shenanigans, especially between him and his twin brother, Sutton. His other siblings—Miles, Harley and Beth—hadn't exactly been angels, either. Sebastian grinned, thinking of his brothers and sisters when they were kids. He'd allow himself a moment to reminisce about the good times, the pranks they'd pulled, the trouble the five of them would get into. There was never a dull moment in the Wingate household.

But their good name had almost been taken down by sabotage. All the Wingates had worked toward this past year had nearly been destroyed.

In a big way, their home was the answer to the Wingates' prayers. Once this place was sold, Sebastian would have cold hard cash to put into the relaunch of the Wingate name and reputation, as well as the financial means to invest in a hotel chain geared for romantic getaways, wedding events and resort-style fun.

For years, their hotels throughout the world accommodated the corporate class. They were straightforward residences meant to temporarily house business and industry travelers. Now, with the money from the estate sale, conference rooms would be converted into grand ballrooms, cafeterias would become gourmet dining rooms and cooks would be replaced with culinary chefs. The atmosphere and attitude associated with Wingate would change entirely. It had to work. The Wingate empire was banking on it.

The door opened and in walked Gracie Diaz. Oh, man, she looked *good*—her lustrous dark hair down and parted to the side, and her delectable body rocking a clingy dress. With those big, almond-shaped eyes, she could practically destroy a man with one sultry look. Sebastian inhaled a deep breath, giving his addled brain a mental shake. He'd always been attracted to the olive-skinned beauty, but he'd never gotten close. Never acted upon his urges with her, because Gracie had always been off-limits. She was the daughter of an employee. *And* his sister Beth's best friend. Succumbing to his desires spelled disaster at every turn, and Sebastian was smarter than that. But if things were different, he'd be knocking on her door until she let him in.

As soon as Gracie spotted him, she stopped in her tracks. She seemed really shaken, her usual confidence apparently hitting a bump. He understood why.

She was the one with power now. With money enough to buy their family home, and she wasn't comfortable with it. It was, in a sense, a complete reversal of fortunes.

Sure, the sale was awkward, but completely necessary... and welcome.

"Come in, Gracie. I don't bite."

He smiled, but that only made her mouth turn down.

He walked toward her, taking tentative steps. "Whatever you're thinking, don't," he said. "I can assure you, no one is upset about you buying the estate."

"I understand," she replied tentatively. "Beth told me the same thing."

"Okay, then. Come in. There's a table and chairs set up in the dining room. Your attorney thought it best for us to go over any concerns you have here, so we can address them as they come up."

She stepped inside, skirting around him. "I have no concerns."

"Just in case." And maybe *he* did. As CEO of Wingate Enterprises, he wanted to oversee the sale, to protect his family interests, as well. Old habits died hard.

Gracie took a seat at the table, setting her briefcase on the chair beside her. She'd become quite a businesswoman, from what Beth had told him. Not only had she helped his sister with planning galas and events, but she'd also funded a new eatery in town. She was looking for other investments, too, he'd learned.

But she sure seemed jumpy around him today. Maybe it was the sale of the estate, or maybe it was her pregnancy. Though, by looking at her in a body-hugging soft gray sweater dress that exposed her perfect shape and brought out the lovely tones on her olive skin, she didn't look pregnant at all. No, she looked gorgeous and *hot*.

His mind wandered to a place it shouldn't go. A place he tried to never let it go. He'd become pretty darn good at pushing aside his attraction for Gracie Diaz.

Luckily, he didn't have to think on it too hard, because the attorneys and Gracie's Realtor, Tom Riley, walked in just then, and within a minute, they'd made introductions and gotten right down to business.

The negotiations went smoothly, if you could call them that. Gracie had asked for nothing out of the ordinary. And they'd agreed to all the terms laid out by both attorneys. Gracie had even agreed to rehire some of the staff and groundskeepers for the property. She was a woman who understood hard work and didn't take anything for granted. After her father passed, she'd started waitressing to put herself through online college. Sebastian admired that trait. He was a hard worker, too, sometimes to a fault. At times, his staff would remind him of the late hour, and his twin would tell him to take a damn vacation. Sutton never kept his thoughts to himself, especially around his older brother by three minutes, but Sebastian wasn't one to listen.

"So if both sides are happy, I'll draw up the necessary papers," Tom Riley said. He gave Gracie an encouraging nod, as if to say all was in order and the deal would be done soon.

She smiled softly. Which had Sebastian oddly on edge. He should be satisfied—after all, it was what Wingate

Enterprises needed, a financial boost in the arm. Yet, he couldn't take his eyes off Gracie. She'd barely said a word throughout the talks, and her smile just now was the first one she'd cracked since she'd gotten here. Instead, she'd tapped her fingers on the table, toyed with the hem of her sweater dress—something he'd *tried* not to notice.

But those long tan legs weren't easy to ignore.

He'd known Gracie for years. She was a family friend and they'd always been civil with each other, despite his hidden fascination to her, yet he'd never seen her looking so nervous.

"I think we have a real workable deal," he said to her Realtor.

His attorney, Todd Woodbury, seemed pleased. "I think everything's in order." He began to gather the papers, stuffing them into his briefcase.

"Well, then, I guess we're good to go." Sebastian smiled at Gracie, but she didn't make eye contact. What was with her? Why wouldn't she give him the time of day?

"I'll show you out," he told the men. Not that he had a right to usher them out; he didn't own the house any longer. And hadn't lived here for months. He was living in a rental house now, but he had to make sure Gracie was okay with this. "I want a minute to speak to Ms. Diaz alone."

He walked them out and turned to find Gracie, who was snatching up her briefcase and a pile of papers. She then made a mad dash for the door, but halfway there she fumbled, and the papers went flying, practically landing at his feet. He bent to retrieve them. "I'll get these."

"No, it's okay," she said, dropping down on her knees to gather them up. Their heads nearly bumped as both grabbed for the papers, and that was when he caught a whiff of her hair as it fell forward in long, glimmering straight sheets. He breathed deeper, taking it in. That floral scent reminded him of something…

And then a hint of her perfume reached his nostrils. It was wildly erotic. The mysterious scents that had haunted him for weeks were all here.

He hadn't stopped thinking of that woman, of their one-night stand, which had been crazy and amazing and *intoxicating*. He'd lain awake nights wondering who she was, and why he couldn't figure it out. Wondering if he would ever find her.

And wondering if he'd ever have better sex. He'd relived that night in his mind so many times, recalling how creamy smooth her skin was, how delicious her lips tasted, how silky her hair was. All of it came rushing back now. The scent of her hair, the texture of her skin, the soft moans as she came apart in his arms…

In his gut, he knew he'd found his mystery woman. And it was none other than Gracie Diaz.

He looked at her flushed face and downcast eyes, which blatantly refused to meet his. He was close enough to feel her presence, to react to her nearness. Like some damn high school boy with raging hormones, he was instantly aroused. And that could only mean one thing. He took a moment to tamp down the blood rapidly heating his veins. His senses on overload, his mind began to spin.

"Gracie?"

She stole the papers from his hands and rose quickly. "I've really got to go. I'm late…for an appointment."

Before Sebastian could stop her she was gone, leaving him kneeling there as she sprinted out the door. More memories flashed in his mind of the masquerade ball. Those erotic scents, the sensual aura of her. He wouldn't have ever guessed it. But he'd never reacted to a woman like that before.

He stood up and swallowed down his misgivings. Blinking his eyes, he knew only one thing. He had to get to the bottom of this. He had to *know* for sure.

And the only way to do that was to confront her.

Gracie paced the floor in her living room, wringing her hands, feeling anything but hungry. But it was dinnertime now and she had to eat, for the baby's sake. So she'd called for takeout, something she could stomach, and the pizza delivery guy was due here any minute.

At least she'd ordered a healthy veggie pizza with all her favorite toppings. Maybe her appetite would come back. Right now she was bordering on nausea. Not from her pregnancy, no, she'd been pretty healthy lately on that score. But from the fact that she was fairly sure Sebastian had put two and two together today, and figured out she was the woman behind the mask, the woman he'd made love to with unequaled passion.

What else had he figured out? It wasn't exactly rocket science. They'd been together three months ago, and she was three months pregnant.

Her heart skipped a beat every time she thought about him being her mysterious lover. She'd found out quite by accident during a party just weeks ago, when Sebastian had been tossed into a pool and she'd seen the scar on his back, the one she remembered feeling while they were making wild, passionate love that night. She'd been shocked to her very core, totally blown away to learn that Sebastian, her teenage crush, was the guy who'd fathered her child.

Sebastian had never thought of her as anything but a family friend. He'd never given her a second look. In the back of her mind, she'd always thought it was because she wasn't worthy. There was a definite class difference between them. Even if the Wingates didn't make it obvious, Gracie had always *felt* it. She wasn't good enough for a Wingate, and she'd never once thought her fantasies of Sebastian would ever come true.

The knock at her door made her jump. Gosh, she was a nervous Nelly today. She grabbed her credit card and strode to the door, her appetite at an all-time low. But she thought of the baby's health and gently opened the door.

"Pizza delivery." It was Sebastian, holding the square box.

Her eyes widened. *What on earth?* Then she heard the rumble of an engine, and saw the delivery guy take off in his tiny blue car.

"You can put your credit card away, I paid for it."

"I…don't understand. Why are you here?"

"For pizza?"

She shook her head.

"Okay, I think you know why. We need to talk."

"Showing up unannounced isn't polite."

"Neither is lying," he said brusquely. "Are you going to let me in?"

She paused. She had no choice. "I suppose I have to. You have my dinner." Not that she could eat a bite now.

She moved aside and let him into the foyer of her small, tastefully decorated rental home. His presence filled the space, surrounding her, making her nerves bounce. They stared at each other for a split second, then Gracie grabbed the box. He didn't let it go. Four hands on one pizza box. "I've got it," he said. "Where's the kitchen?"

Her shoulders slumped as she released the box, pivoted and led the way into the kitchen. The instant gleam of white cabinets and sparkling countertops contrasted with her gloomy mood. She was totally unprepared for this sudden visit. Because, in truth, she was still processing this baby-daddy bombshell, and hadn't thought far enough into the future to know what to say to Sebastian if ever confronted. But here he was, his eyes probing, his very kissable mouth looking thin and hard.

He slid the box onto the table and put his hands on his hips, as if he were the ruler of the kingdom or something. A ruler dressed in black slacks, a white shirt rolled up at the sleeves and tight enough across his broad chest to leave any sane woman breathless. Aside from the way his presence unnerved her, she wasn't going to let him get the best of her.

"You're her, the woman from the masquerade ball, aren't you?"

"I was at the ball, yes." She turned away from him and opened the pizza box. The scent of bell peppers, olives and tomatoes wafting up curled her stomach. She closed the box.

"Don't dance around the subject, Gracie. Look at me."

Gracie didn't like to be ordered around. She didn't like that he'd trapped her. Especially since she hadn't sorted this all out in her mind yet. When she didn't turn around, he walked over to face her fully, his presence looming. He was in her space, inches away, probing her with eyes that demanded an answer, with his tight, firm mouth. It was hard to imagine that mouth on hers, like it had been months ago. It was hard to believe she'd given him so much that night and now he was here interrogating her.

"I already told you I was at the ball." She lifted her chin.

"It's the reason you've been so skittish around me today."

"I'd just spent a fortune on your house. So yes, I was anxious."

"Gracie, dammit. Answer my question."

She had nowhere to go. No way to put him off any longer. She didn't want to admit this to herself, much less to him. But she hesitated too long.

Sebastian put a finger to her cheek and his soft touch melted her instantly. She hated that he could do that to her, crumble her defenses that way. "Gracie, it was you, wasn't it?"

She swallowed and gave a nod.

Breath blew out of his mouth and he stepped back, looking differently at her now. As if he was reliving that night in his mind, thinking of the sexy, erotic things they'd done to each other. He seemed truly shocked. As if he couldn't believe *she* could cause that reaction in him. Her pride could barely take the insult.

"When did you know?" he asked gruffly.

"What does it matter?"

"When?"

"I found out at the launch party. I saw…the scar on your back when you got out of the pool. I remembered it." That night, in their secret alcove, there was no light, only heat and passion, and their heightened senses. She'd remembered tracing her fingertips over that scar, recalled wondering how he'd gotten it.

For a second, Sebastian looked away, as if touching upon the moment he and his brother Sutton had been celebrating the launch of their new hotel. One second he'd been standing by the pool, and the next he'd been tossed in. It had all been fun and games, until Gracie saw him strip off his wet shirt and get naked from the waist up, and that was when she'd noticed the scar.

Sebastian turned and stared into her eyes. "I've never forgotten that night, Gracie."

Neither had she. It was the night she'd had incredible sex. The night she'd conceived her baby. "Getting tossed into the pool?"

"I'm not talking about that night, and you know it. I'm talking about the masquerade ball."

"Oh, right." Playing dumb wasn't her strong suit. She was stalling.

"And the baby you're carrying…it's mine?"

She set her hand over her belly. It was *hers*. All hers. Sebastian wasn't her fantasy man any longer. She didn't want a man who didn't want her and he'd proven that to her over the years. He'd never given her a second look before. He'd never flirted or seemed the least bit interested in her; and now to think Sebastian was the man who'd made wild love to her was all so confusing. His questioning rattled her brain. She wasn't ready to sort through her muddled thoughts—she needed more time. "The baby is mine. We want nothing from you."

"What?"

"Sebastian, that night we were two strangers meeting. It wasn't planned. And so you owe us nothing."

"Hey, listen to me, Gracie. Maybe that night was a mistake, but I don't run out on my mistakes and obligations. And you have no right—"

"This…baby…is…not…a mistake." Heat rose up her neck. Her face felt flush. "It's wanted. By me."

"I didn't say the baby was a mistake, Gracie. It's just that you need to think about this more rationally."

"You think I'm not being rational? I'm being very rational. I want what's best for my baby."

"*Our* baby."

Gracie sucked in a big breath. She felt faint. Probably because she hadn't eaten all day. So what she needed now more than anything was to show Sebastian the door.

"Why don't we sit down and discuss this?" he asked.

"No, I'm tired. I think you should go."

"Gracie?"

"Sebastian, just go. I need to rest." She was playing the pregnancy card, but it was true. The day had taken a toll on her.

"We haven't finished this. Hell, we haven't even started it. I'll call you tomorrow."

She nodded and marched to her front door, leaving him to follow. All she wanted right now was to get him out of her house. She needed some peace.

At the entrance, Sebastian faced her, his expression somewhere between panic and remorse. Already he'd insulted her, said she was irrational and called the baby she was carrying a mistake. "Gracie, I, uh… I'll call you," he repeated.

"Fine." It was so *not* fine. But she wanted him to go, and if agreeing to talk to him tomorrow would do the trick, then so be it.

"Get some sleep." He gave her a sweeping look that touched every nerve in her body. Then he walked out.

Two

Gracie spent the morning in her pajamas, looking online for baby furniture. Sipping decaf coffee and eating a blueberry scone on her bed was a good way to distract herself from the confrontation she'd had with Sebastian last night. She fully expected him to call her first thing this morning, but it was already eleven o'clock and the phone hadn't rung once.

She clicked on page after page of cribs and dressers, of high chairs and strollers and all things baby. It was clearly daunting. She'd always wanted a child, but now with all these choices in front of her, she definitely had homework to do. At some point she would take a class on parenting and childbirth. Gosh, her tummy rumbled in excitement and a little fear.

Though Sebastian Wingate had played a role in her fantasies from childhood, it was a mere silly young girl's dream. Gracie wanted the kind of unconditional love her parents had had for each other. It was clear Sebastian didn't have feelings for her.

And the fact was, she really didn't know him at all. Was he the man of her childhood fantasies or the mystery man who'd swept her off her feet and made love to her? How often had she thought about that one wondrous night with Sebastian, and the wild woman she'd become in his arms? It had been so out of character for her, to have sex with a stranger. But the pull between them had been strong. Undeniable. *Uncontrollable.* He'd given her an unforgettable night of mind-blowing passion.

And a baby.

She had to think about what that all meant.

She was still processing it when her cell phone rang, jerking her out of her musings.

Her stomach ached. This was the call she'd prayed wouldn't happen, but as she dared a look on the phone screen, Lauren's face popped up. The breath trapped in her throat slowly escaped and her shoulders slumped in relief. Lauren Roberts was her friend, and now they were business partners anticipating the grand opening of The Eatery in just one week. The restaurant was almost ready, the staff hired. Lauren was an amazing chef, someone who'd started a food truck business that kept her hopping. Now she was selling those trucks to commit to one place, and one man. Sutton Wingate, Sebastian's identical twin brother. The couple were head over heels in love and planning a wedding, but she wouldn't hold that against her friend. Sutton was actually a pretty cool guy.

"Hi, Lauren. I was planning on meeting you in a few hours at The Eatery. What's up?"

"Uh, that's why I'm calling. Something's...come up, and I was hoping you could come by maybe a little earlier?" Her voice squeaked. "I'll make your favorite lunch. The baby will like it, too, I promise."

Lauren seemed unusually anxious. "I have no doubt. You wouldn't have it any other way. Let's see, I could be there by noon. Does that work?"

"Yes, thanks. That'll be…um, perfect."

"Lauren, is everything okay?"

There was a short pause on the other end of the phone. "Yes… I think so."

"We're still going to go over the plans for the grand opening, right? I have some ideas to run by you."

"Y-yes. We'll do that. Uh, okay, gotta run."

Gracie held the receiver long after the call ended, thinking her friend sure had acted odd over the phone. She'd find out what was going on once she saw Lauren face-to-face.

A few minutes after twelve, Gracie unlocked the back door of The Eatery and let herself in. She passed the small room where Lauren and her sous-chefs would taste-test new items on the menu, then walked into the state-of-the-art kitchen. After the appliances had been installed, she'd teased Lauren that their sparkle and shine could blind a person when they walked in. Even now, she could smell the newness of the place. "Lauren, I'm here," she called out.

Lauren walked in from the main dining room, wearing an apron. "Hi," she said, out of breath.

"Hi."

"I was just serving your lunch at your favorite table."

"You mean *our* lunch, don't you?"

Lauren's face colored to a rosy pink and she reached for both of her hands and gave a squeeze. "Gracie, we're good friends now, aren't we? And you know I value this partnership very much, right?"

Where was all this coming from? Lauren seemed super serious and it worried her. Gracie nodded. "Of course."

"Good, because I really care about you."

"I care about you, too."

She heard someone walking into the main dining room and glanced out the kitchen doorway. "I didn't know Sutton was meeting us for lunch, too."

Lauren closed her eyes briefly. "That's not Sutton."

Gracie dropped her friend's hands. "What?"

"It's Sebastian."

"I don't want to talk to him right now," she whispered in a rush. She wasn't ready; that was why she'd sent him away last night. The last thing she wanted to do was speak to him face-to-face. Seeing him in the flesh confused her even more. Because he was undeniably handsome, and when she looked at him, memories flashed in her mind. Of him kissing her, caressing her, making love to her like she was the only woman on earth. It had been so good between them—being totally in tune with her body, Sebastian had given her the best night of her life. But she feared him, too, because he could interfere with her plans for the baby. He could change everything. And that worried her.

Before she could utter another word, Sebastian walked into the kitchen. "Don't blame Lauren. She didn't want to do this. Honestly, it took all my powers of persuasion and then some to convince her to help me."

She glanced from Sebastian to Lauren. "Did he hold a gun to your head?"

Lauren smiled softly, her eyes filled with compassion. "No, just a baby. Gracie, I'm sorry. Please forgive me."

"So...you know?"

"I do. Sebastian confided in me. And honestly, I think it's pretty amazing."

Gracie blinked. She was trapped by her friend's good

intentions. The truth was bound to come out eventually.
She and Lauren had discussed their special masquerade
ball encounters with each other. Lauren and Sutton had
also met under the guise of a mask at the gala, and there'd
been a case of mistaken identity between the twin brothers. But they'd fallen in love despite the mix-up, and now
were embarking on their happily-ever-after. "But, Lauren, you took Sebastian's side over mine. We're supposed
to be partners."

"I didn't think of it as taking sides. You both need to
talk and you can do it here. In private. With no interruptions. Will you do that?"

She shrugged, defeated. "Only because I have no
choice."

"Okay, sorry. You two have some lunch together. And
if you're still speaking to me after that, I'll come back and
we can talk shop."

Gracie tipped her chin up toward the ceiling, shaking
her head the way her mother would often do when she
was faced with a difficult situation. Both coconspirators
awaited her response. "Fine."

"Okay, well, I'll disappear now." Lauren gave a tentative smile. "Everything is set out and ready for you. I made
your favorite, Gracie."

"Thank you," she said quietly. It was a really sweet gesture, one that might just let Lauren off the hook.

Gracie tried to ignore the earnest look on Sebastian's
face—the small smile, not of triumph, if she was being
honest, but of optimism. He strode by her side, almost
making an attempt to put his hand to her back, but then
corrected the move. Smart man. She wasn't in the mood
to be charmed.

At the table, he pulled out the chair for her and she took
her seat. Around her, unique Southwestern artwork deco-

rated the top half of the walls, while ocean-blue glass tiles added color and light and sparkle to the lower half. Fresh and clean, a place for open minds and palates, The Eatery encapsulated Lauren's vibrant personality to the letter.

"Looks delicious," Sebastian said, glancing at the lobster roll bathed in a reduction of lemongrass sauce and paired with skinny fries and zucchini spirals.

"It is. Lauren's creations got me hooked and I wanted to help her. When I worked with Beth, I'd leave the Wingate Estate at night and head over to one of Lauren's trucks. Those meals were my go-to and I was never disappointed. I'm excited for her, for this place."

"Yeah…about Lauren," Sebastian murmured, taking a breath. "She's a friend of mine, too, and I put undue pressure on her to make this lunch happen."

"You have a rep for getting what you want."

He let that comment slide. "So it won't hurt your relationship with her?"

"I'm not happy, but her intentions were good."

"I'm glad you recognize that."

"Yeah, well, at least it's one thing I recognized." She stared straight into his eyes. How could she not know she was making love with Sebastian, when she'd dreamed of it so many times?

"You could say that about me, too," he said. "Listen, I think we got off to a bad start yesterday. Can I have a mulligan?"

"Golf terms are so not persuasive."

"Sorry. How about giving me a second chance?"

"I don't have much choice, now, do I?"

"Maybe we should break bread together. That would be a start. Are you hungry? Or did you lose your appetite when you saw me?"

She laughed. Though she hated to, because yesterday

he'd called the baby a mistake. But he had charm. What woman would look at him and lose her appetite? "I need to eat."

"Yes, you do."

They sat quietly and chowed down, and every once in a while, their eyes would meet. Sebastian had the most unique green eyes. She'd memorized the change of colors, in her head. Sometimes they were soft and pale like a shallow river, and sometimes they were probing and deep like a lush forest, depending on his mood or the color he wore.

Today he was dressed in casual, well-worn jeans and a white shirt, looking terribly handsome and manly. An unwelcome thrill scurried through her body while sitting with him, sharing a meal. They'd done far more than this as two disguised strangers, getting naked and making love in secret, giving to each other unselfishly. She's never been that bold before, and her masked lover had encouraged her with his whispered words, his guttural groans. That, too, had been thrilling, but *this*? This was surreal. Ever since finding out that Sebastian was the father of her child, she'd been overwhelmed and riddled with confusion and deep emotion. And now she was dining with him, just like she'd often daydreamed.

She nibbled on her sandwich and picked at her baked skinny fries. Sebastian had already finished his food and was watching her. "Just to clarify," she said, pointing a fry at him, "this baby is *not* a mistake."

"I was the one who made the mistake, Gracie. I didn't mean what I said yesterday."

"Good."

"So you accept my apology?"

"I haven't heard an apology."

He reached across the table and covered her hand, looked straight into her eyes. "I'm sorry, Gracie. I truly am."

The instant he touched her, her pulse pounded and an electric jolt shot through her. He squeezed a little harder, closing his eyes as if…he couldn't help himself. As if he felt the connection, too. He muttered an oath and she couldn't blame him. They seemed to share something combustible. So it hadn't been just the excitement of the masquerade, or the thrill of a clandestine tryst. Their attraction was as real now as it'd been that night. Gracie tugged her hand away, conceding that one touch from him was all that was needed to unravel her.

Sebastian stared into her eyes. "Do you forgive me?"

Oh, gosh. She didn't want to. But her mama had taught her to forgive if the asker was sincere, and Sebastian's deep green eyes spoke of sincerity times a thousand. Which meant she would have to give him the benefit of the doubt. "Yes."

"I want to be a part of your life, Gracie. Part of the baby's life. He's my…"

"Don't you dare say she's your responsibility."

"She?"

"He or she. I won't find out for a while."

"I hope I'm there when you do."

Gracie didn't have a crystal ball and had no clue what the future would bring. After all, when she'd set out on a path to be a businesswoman and a mom, she hadn't figured on dealing with the baby's father. She was supposed to conceive this child by a medical procedure. But clearly, fate had other plans in store for her. "I can't make any promises."

His brows rose, and the softness in those green eyes vanished. "I'm not asking for promises." His lips tightened, all color draining out of them as he gave his head a shake. "Well, hell…yes, I am. You seem to want to do this all on your own. Why is that? Is it because our roles have reversed, and you have the means to raise this baby all by yourself? Tell me, Gracie. Is that it? The Wingates are down right now and you're a millionaire and so it's okay to cut me out of my baby's life?"

The chair slammed back as Gracie instantly rose from her seat. "How dare you accuse me of that!"

Sebastian lifted up, too, gritting his teeth. "Is it true? Are you too damn independent and stubborn to realize that the child deserves two parents in its life? Even if one of them is broke."

Fierce anger bubbled up and she let her hot Hispanic temper fly. "You have no clue about me, Sebastian. You never did." And maybe that was the problem. All those years she'd spent looking up to him, admiring him, measuring all men against him, even when he'd never given her a second glance. Oh, what a fool she'd been. She was the help, or rather the child of the help, and she'd always felt she wasn't good enough to be included in his inner circle. But to accuse her of that very thing was wrong on all kinds of levels. In her heart, she was still the same girl, minus the money, of course, that she'd always been. A girl who deserved to be loved for who she was inside and not for any other reason. "This conversation is over. I'm leaving. Don't even try to follow."

"Wouldn't dream of it."

"Fine."

"Fine."

Gracie marched out the back way, and right before she slammed the door, she heard Sebastian mutter, "Ah, crap."

That was exactly how she felt right now.

As well as remorseful and angry and ten other emotions she didn't care to name.

Is it okay for me to return? Lauren sent the text to both him and Gracie. Apparently, his brother's fiancée was an optimist. She'd believed one sit-down would do the trick. And had been thoughtful enough to give them privacy to talk, arrange a delicious lunch for them and set the atmosphere. However, Sebastian had blown it, but only because Gracie had been unreasonable. She wouldn't give an inch.

He'd texted Lauren to come back anytime. They were through.

Literally.

Ten minutes later, Lauren entered The Eatery through the back door. "I'm back," she called as she walked into the kitchen. She faced him at the stainless steel sink. "What are you doing?" She looked at the dish towel in his hand.

"I'm cleaning up. It's the least I can do. I messed up your meeting with Gracie."

"I heard."

"Already?"

"Gracie and I had a brief conversation. She's not happy with you." She eyed the dish towel again. "Give me that." He handed it over. "For heaven's sake, you don't need to clean up."

"I wanted to do…something."

"Well, talk to me. Gracie didn't go into detail, but she said you and she—"

"She rattles me, Lauren. I mean, I look at her now, and I see the woman I can't stop thinking about. That night we spent together was…" He wasn't a kiss-and-tell kind of guy. "Let's just say I've never had such a hot night, never felt such an instant connection with a woman." He wanted *that* Gracie, the one who wasn't so damn proud and stubborn. The one who'd given him the best night of his life but whom he couldn't go after, because he'd labeled her off-limits. And now he didn't give a damn about that. He wanted her…and the baby.

"Was it because you didn't know who she was?"

"I won't say that didn't play into it. But there's more to it than that. I mean, it was crazy good between us, like two live wires touching. And afterward, I racked my brain trying to figure out who she was, but I never came up with an answer."

"And Gracie never came to mind?"

He shook his head. "If I'm being honest, no. I've always been attracted to her, but for years I pushed those thoughts out of my head. She wasn't ever an option. She was Beth's employee and a good friend for one, and her father worked for us. So I put her completely out of my head. And then at the meeting yesterday, she dropped some papers and we both bent down to get them. The scent of her perfume, the smell of her hair, the closeness we shared, clued me in."

"Wow."

"Yeah, *wow*."

"I heard it had been pretty amazing between you two," Lauren said. "Gracie didn't go into detail when we spoke of it in the past, but by the way her eyes would glow and her voice would become breathless, it was special for her."

She touched his hand. "What did you say to get her so upset?"

Sebastian sighed. "I got angry and hinted that she had no use for me because my family has been dragged through the mud."

"Hinted?"

"Okay, I accused her of it, but only because I was frustrated. She wasn't giving an inch, and well, I'm not used to being at loose ends like this. I'm glad our name has been cleared, but it's unnerving trying to hold on to Wingate Enterprises. It's been a struggle, but we've managed to retain most of our US holdings, and then a beautiful masked woman comes into my life, bringing some brightness. And I find out Gracie's the one tying me up in knots, buying the

Wingate Estate and carrying my child. It's a lot to handle."
Sebastian's gut tightened.

"I'm sorry the meeting didn't go as we'd hoped," Lauren said. "But I'm afraid you're going to have to fix this on your own. I risked my partnership and friendship with Gracie by going behind her back. I can't do it again."

Sebastian squeezed her hand. "Don't think I'm not grateful, Lauren. You went above and beyond. My brother's a lucky man, getting a woman like you."

"Thank you for saying that. So what are you going to do?"

"I'm not sure yet." But one thing was certain, he wasn't through with Gracie Diaz yet. Not by a long shot.

"Mom, thanks for coming over," Sebastian said, looking at his mother, who was dressed impeccably in a pastel plaid blazer and beige palazzo pants of the finest material. Her hair was up in her usual fancy bun. There was not a hair out of place on Ava Wingate, ever.

"Hello, Sebastian. How's my son today?"

He smiled and kissed her cheek. "I'm fine, Mom."

He led her into the great room of his rented house, and they both took a seat on the couch. His mother was usually a dynamo, someone with incredible energy and gusto, but he'd noticed her slowing down. She seemed worn out lately, and this past year, learning she'd been deceived by her trusted friend had taken a toll on her. Keith Cooper, who'd been his dad's best friend, had been hopeful of gaining Ava's affection after Sebastian's father died. And when that didn't happen, he'd ended up embezzling funds and nearly destroying Wingate Enterprises. Luckily, he'd been caught before the entire empire went under, but the fiasco with Keith had taken the wind out of his mother's sails. She'd always been strong, the Wingate rock, a woman who always spoke her mind. But now, she seemed defeated in some ways, taken down a peg. It pained him to see it. "Can I get you anything, Mom? A drink? Something to eat?"

"I'm fine, but it's clear that you're not. I can see it in your eyes, Sebastian. Something's troubling you."

"Actually, I do have news."

"More problems with the company?"

He smiled. "No, Mom. Everything is moving along well with the business. It's not that."

She sat back in her seat. "So then, it's personal?"

"Yes, it's *very* personal. And good news. At least I hope you'll think it's good news. You're going to be a grandmother again."

His sister Harley's son, little Daniel, was four years old. But Ava didn't know him too well. Harley had never really gotten along with their mother. She had left home to raise Daniel overseas and stayed away until just months ago, when she'd come back home and finally told Dr. Grant Everett, Daniel's father, the truth. Now Harley, Grant and Daniel were a family and planning on moving to Thailand.

His mother's mouth dropped open as surprise lit up her eyes. "That's…very good news, I suppose." Then her forehead wrinkled. "I didn't know you were dating someone."

Sebastian scratched his chin. "Yeah, well, about that… It's a long, involved story and I only just found out myself a couple of days ago. But the bottom line is, Gracie Diaz is pregnant, and the child is mine."

"Gracie?" His mother's brows rose. "Why, we've known her for years. You never… I don't think you ever gave her a second glance, Sebastian. Am I wrong about that?"

"No, you're not wrong, Mom. But things change. And well, I'm afraid now things aren't going too well. Every time we try to talk, I get tongue-tied, and it ends up with one of us walking away."

Ava smiled. It was rare to see his mother look so amused.

"It's funny to you?"

"No, not funny. But that's exactly how your father was with me when we first met. He said I made him jittery. And either he'd lose his tongue altogether or say the absolute wrong thing to me."

"Really? I never knew that."

Though his mother always did come off as intimidating, and his dad might've been thrown by her strong personality. But it was probably more their powerful attraction to each other that caused his dad's nerves, just like when Sebastian got near Gracie.

"So what's the plan?" his mother asked.

"I'm not sure. She's pretty set on doing this all on her own."

"You have legal rights, son."

He shook his head. "I'm not willing to go that far. At least not right now. I think she's overwhelmed. And I don't want to destroy whatever relationship I have with her."

"You have a relationship with her?"

"Not at the moment, but I've got to fix that. She won't answer my calls. Won't respond to my texts."

"Want me to speak with her?"

He studied his mother's serious face. He couldn't ask Ava for help. While well intentioned, she might just make things worse. She wasn't the most tactful person in the world, but he knew she was trying hard to help her family and win them back. "Thanks, Mom, but no. I'll manage. I do have a favor. Only a handful of people know I'm the father, so please keep this a secret. I don't think Gracie needs any more pressure right now. Can I trust you to keep it quiet?"

"Of course."

"I thought you had a right to know," he said.

"Well, you're more thoughtful than Harley was."

"Mom, she was young and very mixed up."

"Yes, I know. What's important now is to keep the entire family together. And that includes the little one you're about to have. Do you know if it's a boy or girl?"

"No, it's too soon for that. When we find out, you'll be the first to know."

"I would appreciate that. Tell me, what do you suppose Gracie wants more than anything?"

"What are you getting at?"

"You want something from her, so give her something that's important to her."

Sebastian paused for a second, deep in thought. She may have something there.

His mother rose from her seat. "I've got an appointment in half an hour. I'm afraid I have to be going."

Sebastian walked over to her. "Thanks for listening, Mom."

"You'll be a good father, Sebastian." She kissed his cheek and took hold of his hand. "I'm confident you'll find a way. You always do." Then she smiled again.

His mother had more confidence in him than he had in himself at times. With Gracie, things were off-balance and that flustered him.

And then a thought struck. His mother's words came back to him. *What do you suppose Gracie wants more than anything?* She'd bought the house on the first day it went on sale. She wanted to live at the estate and raise the baby there. Damn, he did have a little bit of leverage with Gracie.

It was risky. It might backfire and he could end up losing everything. But he wasn't willing to give up on Gracie

Diaz just yet. He was drawn to her for so many reasons, and he desperately needed more time with her.

Bottom line? He had to try *something* and this was the best he could come up with.

Gracie had spent the entire week helping Lauren get The Eatery ready for tomorrow's big grand opening. She checked on the menus, made sure the staples, supplies and all the orders were correct. Lauren was a pro, and what Gracie didn't know about food service, her partner made sure to school her in with quick lessons. Gracie did know how to promote, however. She had taken out ads in Royal's newspaper, paid teenagers to distribute flyers in the community and reached out to Lauren's food truck fans to spread the word about The Eatery's grand opening.

There were a few other investments Gracie wanted to look into. For starters, she was set on raising horses, to see her father's dream come true. He'd worked as ranch manager for the Wingate family and often spoke of having his own ranch one day. And it was always her goal to start an event-planning business. After working with Beth on galas and charities, she'd caught the bug. She had a knack for planning, design, decoration and making her vision come to fruition. But today, her focus was all about Lauren and The Eatery.

"It's all so exciting," she said to Lauren. "And a lot of hard work. But I'm sure it'll pay off."

"Exciting and nerve-racking," her friend replied. "This has been a dream of mine for a long time. I only hope I haven't forgotten anything."

"You haven't forgotten a thing. You're a pro and I know it's going to be great. I'll be with you all day tomorrow."

"I appreciate that." Lauren smiled. "You and Sutton have given me so much support."

"You deserve it. You've worked hard for this."

"Thanks."

"Now I think we should lock up and go home and get some rest," Gracie said.

"It's only six."

"And knowing you, your day will start at six in the morning."

"You're right. Let's go." Lauren wrapped her arms around Gracie's shoulders and hugged tight. "The three of us need our rest."

The reference to the baby immediately turned her thoughts to the baby's father. Sebastian was making her crazy, saying the wrong things, and his last accusation had really rattled her. She'd always seen him as a kind, thoughtful, hardworking member of the Wingate family. Where was the man she'd crushed on for years? Was he gone now, taken over by someone she didn't recognize or trust?

Later that evening, Gracie hung up the phone from her Realtor in disbelief. Last week she'd gone to his office to sign the necessary papers for the purchase of the Wingate property, hoping for a short escrow period. After all, the house was just sitting there empty. She was anxious to settle in and the Wingates were eager to get their money. Money that they desperately needed to build back their business. But Tom Riley had just told her there was a holdup. Or rather, a hold*out*. Sebastian was stalling. He'd given her Realtor one excuse after another regarding signing the final papers for the sale of the house. It'd been eight days already. Without his signature, the deal wouldn't go through as planned.

Sebastian had her back up against the wall. He'd called her every day, and every day she'd put him off. Now he'd fixed it so *she* would have to call *him*. She could go through her attorney to get to the bottom of this, but Sebastian was well versed in business dealings. He knew how to get what he wanted, and she understood he wouldn't cave until she spoke to him.

Gracie squeezed her eyes closed. All the man had to do was touch her and she melted on the spot. It wasn't fair that he had that kind of power over her. She didn't like not being in control…didn't like not knowing which Sebastian she was dealing with. The decisions she would have to make for the future were too important, and she couldn't allow her confusion and, well, yes, her *desire* for him to get in the way.

If that made her a control freak, okay, she'd own it. She had a baby to consider and she'd do everything in her power to protect her child.

So far, Sebastian had called their night together a mistake, making the child she was carrying a mistake, too. He'd accused her of social climbing, thinking so little of her that he thought she would actually push him away because of his recent lack of wealth. And now he was blackmailing her, for lack of a better word, by holding back the sale of the house.

"Not a way to win friends and influence people," she muttered.

If she was a mean girl, she'd teach him a lesson and back out of the deal entirely, to call his bluff. But backing out would mean hurting all the Wingates, and she didn't want to do that. It would also mean denying herself a beautiful place to live. She'd come to love the estate and had spent a lot of time there while growing up. To throw that all away because Sebastian was being obtuse didn't seem right.

Her cell phone rang, breaking into her thoughts. She glanced at the screen and picked up immediately. At least

Sebastian did one thing right—he called her. Just like he had for the past week.

"You do know you're jeopardizing the sale of the estate," she said to him.

"Hello to you, too, Gracie."

"Sebastian, I know what you're doing." Her foot began to tap the floor.

"That's good, because I don't have a clue."

"What are you talking about?" she demanded.

"I mean it, Gracie. I *am* jeopardizing the sale of the estate. Because that's how much I want you. If things go sour, I'll be sabotaging the company's success."

"I'm glad you recognize that."

He huffed out a breath. "I've been trying to get your attention all week."

"So blackmailing me was your answer?"

"*Blackmail* is a strong word."

"What would you call it?"

"I'd say it was…a subtle nudge."

"*Subtle?*" She groaned loud enough for him to hear. "You are delusional."

"*Determined* is a better word."

Gracie was tired of this back-and-forth already. He'd found a way to have things on his terms, and she hated that, but in order to move on with her life, she needed to hear him out. "Okay, fine. What do you propose?" Oh, boy, that was such a bad choice of words. "I mean, what do you want?"

"I think we should talk. The sooner, the better."

"Why, are you afraid I'd back out?" she prodded.

"Maybe. Would you?"

"No, not unless you gave me a good reason to," she answered.

"I won't, I can assure you."

Gracie sighed. "And can you assure me you'll sign the documents?"

"Yes, I'm a man of my word."

Maybe he was, but she didn't like his tactics.

"How about we meet tomorrow?" he asked.

"Tomorrow is impossible. It's the grand opening of The Eatery."

"Oh, right. I forgot."

"I can meet you on Monday."

"That's three days away."

"Yes, and…?"

"Okay, fine," he said grudgingly. "I'll come to you. Monday morning."

She closed her eyes. "Monday morning. And I'll meet you at your office."

He paused, clearly not happy, but he kept his tone neutral. "We'll talk Monday, then."

She could only push so far. "Yes, goodbye."

"Good night, Gracie."

His deep, low rasp brought an onslaught of full-body tingles. That voice with its beckoning tone did things to her. The attraction between them was undeniable, like nothing she'd ever felt before. She couldn't quite separate the man blackmailing her from her childhood crush. It gave her a headache and kept her up at night. She'd been avoiding him for that very reason…kept waiting for her head to clear. Only, it wasn't cooperating.

"Sleep well."

"Same to you," she whispered back, before she even realized her mouth was opening. Sebastian was masterful in so many ways, and even though she was angry with him, she couldn't quite get the night of the masquerade ball out of her mind. His touch, his kiss, the way he made love to her. It had been surreal, and something she would never forget.

She had three days before she had to speak to him. She wouldn't dwell.

Tomorrow was all about The Eatery's grand opening, and helping Lauren realize her dream.

Three

Royal 7 News showed up during the lunch rush to interview Lauren about her transition from her Street Eats food truck business to her very own eating establishment, the news van parked front and center on the street. Gracie didn't have to do much arm-twisting to get them there. Whenever the Wingate name was bandied about, it made news. Most of the press for the past year had been negative, their good name and reputation ruined, but the Wingate family had pulled together, cleared their name, recouped some of their embezzled cash and were now on the road to recovery.

Gracie stood off to the side listening as Lauren continued speaking to Daniella Moon from Royal 7 News. "I was proud of Street Eats, and loved having those food trucks, but opening my own restaurant has always been my dream," she told the reporter.

"Well, judging from the line outside, your restaurant is going to be a huge hit. Royal can use another dining hot spot. And you're engaged to Sutton Wingate. The Wingates were involved in a big scandal not too long ago. Do you have anything to say about that?"

Lauren paused a second, then gave the reporter a big smile. "I never had any doubt that Sutton and his family would clear their name. They were framed and have been vindicated. That's all behind us now."

"Rumor has it you have a silent partner, none other than Gracie Diaz, the recent winner of the sixty-million-dollar Powerball. How much has her support meant to you?"

"I couldn't have done any of this without Gracie's help. She's backed me in every way, believed in me, and I'm very grateful to her."

The reporter walked over to Gracie. "Miss Diaz, looks like you found a good investment in The Eatery. Business seems to be booming."

Gracie didn't love being in the limelight—she'd had enough of that when she'd first won the lottery—but she answered Daniella Moon's questions and then they took off in their news van.

Back in the kitchen now, Lauren wiped her brow. "Thanks for setting that up. I don't think that interview will hurt business," she said with a grin. "Sorry they put you on the spot, Gracie. I know you don't like being in front of cameras."

"For you and The Eatery, I'll endure a camera in my face."

Then Gracie's happy mood soured when she spotted a tall Texan with blond hair and green eyes striding through the back door.

Until she realized it was Sutton. He waved hello to her and walked straight into Lauren's arms. It was nice to see the two of them so happy. Her friend's dreams were all coming true. Good for her.

Cam and Beth stopped by for a late lunch and Gracie seated them at a table near the kitchen. Beth was not only her dear friend and mentor, she was Sebastian's sister. Beth was marrying rancher Cam Guthrie in a matter of weeks and she couldn't be happier for them. Cam was one of the good guys.

"It's great to see you two. I'm really glad you're here, and, Beth, I miss our brainstorming sessions."

Gracie had worked with Beth for years at the estate, helping her plan events, galas and parties, and she'd enjoyed it so much she hoped to open her own events company one day. Back then, it had been a lofty dream, but today it was actually a possibility.

"Yeah, I've heard about those brainstorming sessions," Cam deadpanned. "According to Beth, they'd turned into margarita parties for two." He gave her a wink.

"Giving away our trade secrets, Beth?" Gracie asked.

"Well, it was when we did our best work," she answered.

Beth turned to speak only to Cam. "Gracie gets a drink in her, and then she lets loose."

Gracie chuckled. "With *ideas*, Beth. And I could say the same about you."

"That's why we made such a good team."

"Well, Lauren will be thrilled that you two are here."

"Of course," Beth said. "Lauren is family. Where else would we be?"

"Uh, planning your wedding, maybe. You guys don't have that much more time." Cam had built Beth the home of her dreams, and they were having a private wedding there in two weeks.

"Beth's got it all covered," Cam said, smiling. "Who better to plan a party than my beautiful fiancée?"

"So true," Gracie admitted.

Beth beamed. "I'm all set." Then her brows gathered. "I think."

"Knowing you, everything will be perfect," Gracie reassured her. "But if you need any help, you can always count on me."

"Thanks, and I might take you up on that. We'll talk later."

"Okay."

Beth scanned over the entire restaurant. "I think I love this place already. The artwork is beautiful." Beth had an eye for those things. Gracie had always admired her good taste.

She handed each one of them a menu. "Check out the menu and I'll have a waitress take your order."

"Sounds good. And, Gracie, congrats. The Eatery is… something. You played a big part in getting this place opened. I know it's going to do well."

Gracie gave Beth a hug. "Thanks for saying that. Means a lot. Now I'd better check on Lauren. She needs to pace herself or she won't make it to dinner."

By eight thirty the dining room was starting to empty out. Gracie's feet ached and she could only imagine how Lauren felt. She took a seat at a corner booth, coaxing Lauren to do the same. Her friend was on an emotional high, but fatigue registered on her face. "You're beat, but in a good way, Lauren."

"You're right. I am beat. But excited, too. There weren't any glitches today, except for running out of cheesecake. I didn't think it'd be so popular. Tomorrow I'll be better prepared."

"No one complained. You gave everyone free dessert. Can't argue with that."

The front door opened and in walked Sutton. "Maybe

not entirely over," Gracie said. "Looks like you have to feed this guy again."

Lauren grinned and rose from her seat. She wrapped her arms around her handsome fiancé and then asked him to sit down. That was when Gracie realized it wasn't Sutton this time, it was Sebastian. He'd caught her off guard once again. She didn't like it. She wasn't too happy, either, about the way her stomach flip-flopped every time the man entered the room. Images of their sizzling hot night flashed in her head and she had trouble purging it, trouble forgetting what it felt like being with him that way.

"Thanks for coming, Sebastian," Lauren said.

"I would've been here sooner, but I had meetings most of the day. Congratulations to both of you. I heard your grand opening was a huge success."

"It was more than I could've imagined," Lauren said on a lovely sigh. "Really awesome."

"Yes, it was pretty amazing." Gracie didn't want to burst Lauren's bubble or in any way put a damper on this night by being rude to Sebastian. He had every right to be here, she supposed. But the second he sat down and pierced her with those melt-your-heart green eyes, her pulse pounded and her breath stuck in her throat.

"I bet you haven't eaten, Sebastian. And I know you haven't had a bite to eat since lunch, Gracie. You both need sustenance. Let me get you something wonderful from the kitchen."

"I don't want to put you to work," Sebastian protested. "I'm fine."

"Me, too," Gracie said. "I'll eat later."

"Nonsense. Gracie, you've been a godsend today, and you *need* to eat."

Her point was well taken without the mention of the

baby. Although Sebastian's eyes did immediately rivet to her belly. She flushed, her skin prickling under his scrutiny.

"And, Sebastian, I know how you Wingates roll. I bet you're hangry."

He stared straight at Gracie, giving her another unnerving moment. "Okay, I guess I could eat."

"Thanks for not making me argue," Lauren said. "I'll be back in a few minutes."

After Lauren walked off, Sebastian smiled. "She's perfect for my brother."

"I agree."

"Well, that's good. We agree on something. It's a start."

"Sebastian, please let's not talk about anything tonight. I'm really tired."

"You've been here all day?"

She nodded. "It's been fun, seeing a business start off from its very roots. I've never been a part of something like this before."

"You have a mind for business, Gracie."

She shrugged. "Maybe. I have some investment ideas."

"Care to share?"

She shook her head. "Not at the moment. You know, it's uncanny how I almost can't tell you and Sutton apart. He was here today, and when you walked in just now, I thought you were him for a second."

"Yeah, we've gotten that all of our life. You said, *almost*. Does that mean you can tell us apart sometimes?"

Gracie hesitated, biting her lip.

"Well?"

"I, uh…"

"You feel it, too. This pull between us. When I get close, you know it's me."

She closed her eyes briefly. She didn't want to say it aloud. She didn't want him to know.

"I guess I have my answer," he said quietly.

No triumph, no smugness. Just truth.

She nodded. It was the most she was willing to give as admission. Up until now, she hadn't spoken of it, hadn't acknowledged the draw between them. But it was there. It was *real*. She felt it every time he walked into the room. But she still really didn't know Sebastian, the father of her baby. She still didn't know what he wanted from her. Or if she could trust him.

"Gracie," he whispered.

But before he could say anything more, Lauren arrived with a savory chicken-and-rice dish with yeast biscuits and a quinoa salad for them to share.

Sebastian took his eyes off her to glance at the meal. "Looks delicious."

"Yes, uh, thanks." Gracie's stomach growled in a delicate way, but enough to turn their heads. She gasped and put her hands over her tummy. And everyone laughed. "I guess I'd better eat, or this little one is going to be making more noise."

It was the first light moment she'd had with Sebastian, and the brightness in his eyes and on his face was appealing as hell. They smiled at each other, and suddenly, a weight seemed to lift from her shoulders. The boulder that sat there was being chipped away, so she could look at him and see someone she'd known, the boy from her youth, the thoughtful, kind, yet aloof guy she'd had fantasies about. He'd been the quiet one, the more serious of the Wingate twins, and she'd liked that about him.

"Feed that kid, would you?" Lauren teased.

"I plan to."

"And I plan to make sure she eats all of…"

Gracie raised her brows.

Sebastian took one look at her and cut off his own sentence. Was he about to say something to tick her off again? "Nothing, never mind."

"Okay, well, enjoy the meal," Lauren said and walked away again.

After that, Sebastian measured his words carefully and they made it through the meal without a problem.

The kitchen closed by nine thirty and an exhausted Lauren was grateful Sutton stopped by to pick her up. They offered to walk Gracie to her car out back.

Sebastian spoke up instantly. "I'll do it, you two go on home."

"No one needs to walk me," Gracie said. "I'll be just fine."

The look on Sebastian's face said he wasn't going to give in. "I'm going to make sure of it. Put on your jacket and let's go. No arguing, okay?"

Gracie had little choice. She grabbed her jacket and Sebastian helped her put it on.

Lauren locked up The Eatery and then both couples headed in different directions in the parking lot.

Within a few moments, Gracie reached her car. She turned to face Sebastian. "This is it." She drove a sporty cranberry-red Lexus with a small back seat and trunk. But as much as she loved it, she knew it simply wouldn't suffice once the baby arrived. Buying a family car was on her long list of things to do.

There was a chill in the January air and she shivered a bit.

"Cold?" he asked.

"A little. I'd better get going." She gestured to her car.

"Just one more thing, Gracie."

Sebastian touched her hand just as she was reaching for the door handle. His hand on hers did silly things to her insides. She put her head down, closed her eyes. "What is it?"

"Talk to me, Gracie."

"We'll talk on Monday."

"Gracie," he said softly, as if her name was something precious, something beautiful. "I want to see you before Monday."

She looked up and gazed into his clear green eyes. "Why?"

"You know why."

"But I don't...not really." She had questions. Not quite trusting this.

"Maybe this will help you understand." And then his fist gently lifted her chin, and he bent his head, slowly inching toward her. She couldn't pull away, even if she wanted to. It was crazy, this attraction, this magnetic pull she had toward him. His breath touched her cheek, his lips closed in and the anticipation nearly undid her. She sucked in a breath and he caught that breath with his mouth as his lips careened down onto hers. It was as perfect a kiss as she'd ever had—the perfect taste, the perfect pressure, the perfect sensual mating of their mouths.

His scent surrounded her, his warmth protected her and his arms wrapped around her. She was taken by the power of his kiss. Her body hummed inside and the easy slide of attraction heated her up.

"Sebastian," she whispered, breaking off the kiss. "This isn't a good idea." But it was too late. The kiss marked her, the kiss made her want more. Even as he stopped and pulled away, the damage was done to her soul.

"Gracie, what if you're wrong?"

What if she was wrong? Would she miss out on something wonderful?

Her chest was pounding. If she fell for this guy, it could all go bad quickly. Wasn't it better to keep her distance? Wasn't it better not to give in to this fierce temptation?

The fire might burn out and then where would she be? Whenever Sebastian was near, whenever he kissed her, her mind muddied up. She didn't like being confused like this. "What…what do you want from me?"

"A chance to get to know you, Gracie. That's all," he rasped.

"What does that mean?"

Sebastian's smile devastated her. Her heart pounded even harder. "It means I want to date you, Gracie. I want to see where this goes. You owe me."

She blinked. "How do I owe you?"

He sighed deeply, and she sensed his frustration. "You found out it was me at the masquerade ball, and you never said a word. You conceived my child that night, and I had to find out accidentally. You were never going to tell me it was you. You were never going to tell me about the baby."

"That's not true—"

"Isn't it? You had plenty of opportunities to tell me. When we were negotiating the sale of the estate, or maybe all the times since then. Why didn't you say anything?"

"Because, I—I was confused and worried. I don't really know you, Sebastian. I don't know if I can trust you."

"There's only one way to find out, Gracie," he whispered.

It was ironic and all backward. First, she'd had mind-blowing sex with him, then she'd conceived his child and now he wanted to date her.

"It's crazy."

"We do crazy well, Gracie."

His thoughts must've coincided with hers. They did do crazy well, starting with that night at the Texas Cattleman's Club masquerade ball, then Gracie finding a shirtless Sebastian by the pool, only to discover he was her mysterious lover. And then Sebastian finding out Gracie was carrying his child quite by accident.

She couldn't argue the point with him. She smiled. "True story."

He smiled back. "I'll pick you up at seven tomorrow night." Then Sebastian opened the car door for her and she slid into her seat. After he gave a slight shove to close the door, she started the engine with the push of a button and drove off. A glance in the rearview mirror gave her one last look at hunky Sebastian Wingate.

Her date for tomorrow night.

Sebastian gave himself a dozen mental warnings before knocking on Gracie's door. He didn't want to blow it again by saying anything that would alienate her. Because the truth was, he desperately wanted to get to know her better, to see the woman behind the mask, per se. So far, all they'd done was argue, and he didn't want more of that. He'd have to walk on eggshells all night and not let his physical attraction to her get in the way of their date. Which meant he planned on being a perfect gentleman, even if it killed him.

He knocked and Gracie's housekeeper answered. Funny how the roles were reversed now. She had the servants and he was on the outside looking in.

The older woman let him in and then Gracie stepped into the foyer. Oh, man, it *was* going to kill him. She looked amazing, wearing a cinnamon-red hip-hugging dress that landed at her knees. Her olive skin peeked through the delicate red lace at the arms and back. Her hair, lustrous and long, teased her breasts. The night of the TCC masquerade ball, she'd also worn red, a shimmery gown that knocked him upside the head. He'd been drawn to her then, as he was now, the pull so strong he had no willpower around her.

Just last night he'd kissed her, tasted her lips again. It had been three long months of wondering, of trying to find his mystery woman, of not knowing who she might be. But that incredible kiss had brought back all the reasons why he couldn't get the woman in red off his mind. It hadn't been a fluke; it hadn't solely been about the forbidden thrill. It had been about the woman.

Gracie. Bold. Sexy. Unforgettable.

He cleared his throat. "You look…nice."

"So do you." Her response was automatic.

He'd spent extra time choosing his clothes. His slacks were pressed and he wore a shirt in deep purple, a color his mother called eggplant. But instead of a sports jacket, he wore a black suede bomber jacket. "Are you ready?"

She nodded, though she seemed hesitant and unsure. Beth had once told him that after winning the lottery, Gracie had been swarmed with male attention, and she could never be certain if the guys showed up for her or for her money. Though Gracie hardly knew how pretty she was, how sultry she appeared with that slender figure, those long legs and perfect breasts. Her eyes were large, expressive and black-coffee dark. Her skin was so smooth he hadn't forgotten how silky it felt beneath his palms.

But that was months ago, and now he had to show her a different side of him. He wanted to gain her trust and win her over. He wanted to be a part of their baby's life. His thoughts flashed to Lonny, and the role Sebastian had played in the young boy's life. Lonny was his ex-girlfriend's teenage brother, a boy deeply troubled, and Sebastian had been there for him. He'd tried to give the boy his love and support, because heaven knew Lonny needed it. And he had for a time, but then Sebastian and his girlfriend had broken up and he'd lost touch with her younger brother. He'd always felt bad about not being there for the boy anymore.

Sebastian didn't want to let his own child down that way. He wanted to know his baby, be a positive influence in his or her life. He wanted so much not to screw up his child's life.

"Great, then let's get going. Do you have a coat? It's chilly outside."

"Yes," she said. "Right here."

She put on a knee-length sweater coat the same color of her dress and her distinct body language told him not to offer to help. It went against his instincts and the manners drilled into his head since he was a kid. But his mission tonight was to stay out of trouble and get to know her better.

He opened the door and they were hit with a blast of winter cold. "Ah," she said. "Smells fresh and clean out there."

She stepped outside and he waited for her to lock up the house. Then, without wasting another moment, he put his hand to her back and guided her to his black BMW. There was no question about him opening the car door for her. He went about it easily and she slid into the seat. By the time he got behind the wheel, she was belted in.

"I hope you like Italian."

She glanced at him. "Who doesn't?"

He laughed. "It's a bit of a drive, so sit back and relax."

"Where are we going?"

"Amore, just outside of town," he told her. "The chef is a friend, and he's very talented. Have you ever been there?"

"No, I don't think so. But it sounds good."

He winked. "I think you'll like it."

Gracie smiled in response.

"Care for some music or would you like to be quiet?"

"I wouldn't mind music," she said.

He clicked on the radio and Reba McEntire's powerful voice came through the speakers, singing along with Kelly Clarkson about pain and trust and hurt.

"I like this song," Gracie said, laying her head back against the headrest. "It touches me with its truth."

Sebastian nodded. "Yeah."

Every second spent with Gracie taught him something new.

"Music tells the truth better than any other medium," she mused. "Don't you think?"

He'd never really thought about it before. "Could be. Maybe."

Gracie was touched by a song that spoke of heartache and mistrust. She was a cautious one, wary of involvements, as the song inferred. That much he knew about her, since she hadn't told him immediately about carrying his child. She'd been protective, and he was still trying to get over her not revealing his paternity until she was confronted. Maybe he had trust issues, too.

Five songs later they were seated in a private dining room with a table set for two inside the restaurant. "Thanks, Chef," he said to Tony Perrino. "This is nice."

"Of course, anything for you, Sebastian." Tony was a silver fox, a sixty-year-old man who'd lived a few lifetimes already and had finally settled in Texas. They'd had business dealings in the past and had developed a friendship over golf and pasta through the years. "I only wish you would let me feed you more often."

Sebastian turned to Gracie. "Gracie, this is my friend Tony. He owns Amore. The only thing better than his golf swing is his homemade pasta. He's bringing a little bit of the Old World to the Southwest."

Tony laughed and greeted Gracie with a bow of his head. "Pleasure to meet you, Gracie."

"Thank you. I love your place."

Gracie seemed to have an eye for design, and approval shone in her eyes as she scanned the small, intimate dining area. The restaurant spoke of European elegance without being cliché or overdone. The tablecloths were pristine white, the place settings hand-painted Italian ceramic, the glassware cut crystal and the centerpieces an array of pillar candles. There was also a mini stage set up, where sometimes a band played and sometimes singers entertained the patrons.

"It has so much charm," she said.

"I appreciate the compliment." The chef smiled.

"Gracie and a mutual friend just opened a restaurant called The Eatery, in the heart of Royal," Sebastian told him.

"Of course, the town's buzzing about it," Tony said. "Are you a chef?"

"No, not me. My friend and associate, Lauren, is the culinary genius. I'm more the investor."

Tony eyed him briefly. He must've put two and two together and recognized Gracie as the big Powerball winner, but he was discreet enough not to mention it. "Well, I'll have to visit your establishment one day and see for myself."

"Please do," Gracie said with a sincere smile.

"If the chef's as talented as you say, then maybe I should be glad your restaurant is across town."

"I think I'm glad, too," she said, charming the chef into a grin.

"If you would allow me, I'd love to make you both a special meal," Tony offered. "It would be my pleasure."

Sebastian glanced at her. "Is that okay?"

"Of course, that would be terrific, if it's okay with you."

"Yeah, it'll be a treat." He gave Tony a nod. "Appreciate that, Chef."

"Shall I send over a bottle of our signature Amore vino?"

Sebastian didn't have to think twice. "No, not tonight."

Gracie spoke up. "Please, don't let me stop you. If you want a glass of wine, go ahead."

Sebastian shook his head. He wasn't about to drink wine when she couldn't have any. It would be that way for six months at the very least. "Thank you, Tony. But I'll pass."

Gracie studied him intently. "That was nice of you."

"I'm a nice guy."

Her brows went up, but she remained noncommittal. She didn't like to give an inch, but he was wearing her down. He could tell by her tone. It was much more gracious tonight.

"I hope you're hungry. You don't want to miss any of Tony's creations."

"My appetite is finally coming back. I had a little bout of morning sickness earlier in my pregnancy and had to force myself to eat. But I'm better now."

Sebastian looked away for a second and sighed. He'd have wanted to be there for Gracie and his child during that time. Maybe he could've helped out somehow. But that was water under the bridge now. There was no going back.

A server came by with a full basket of garlic knots. Gracie breathed in the aroma.

"Those smell soooo good."

"Try one."

"One? I may eat the whole basket, but since you're being nice, I'll save you one." She grabbed a piece of bread and began nibbling. "Yum… They taste as good as they smell."

And after they indulged in several, the server reappeared to present an eye-catching antipasto platter. Olives, artichokes, tomatoes and salami amid a variety of cheeses, all drizzled with olive oil over a nest of arugula and romaine lettuce.

Gracie looked impressed, because, well, Tony's creations were impressive. "I think I'm in heaven."

Sebastian looked her in the eye. "Really? Because of the company?"

"Yes."

He jerked back in his seat. Was this progress? Did she actually enjoy being with him?

"Chef Tony is pretty talented."

He shook his head. "Very funny."

"And this food is amazing."

She popped an olive into her mouth and his eyes followed the movement as she chewed delicately. Everything about Gracie moved him and made him hunger for more than food. "Well, at least I know you have good culinary taste. I'll check that box off."

"What other boxes are you planning on checking off with me?" she murmured.

That was a loaded question, but he'd opt for the safest bet. "I was hoping to get to know you better, Gracie."

"We've known each other a long time."

"Yes, but that doesn't mean we know things about each other. For instance, do you have hobbies? What was your favorite subject in school? Who do you admire most? Those are basics and yet I couldn't answer any of those about you."

She quirked a brow. "Would it matter?"

"It'd be a start."

"Horses, I love horses. I love riding, though lately I haven't done much of it. Favorite subject, history. I like learning how we got to this point in our lives. There's so much still to learn. And as far as who I admire most? My father. He was a hardworking, honorable man. I miss him very much."

He liked the way her eyes lit up as she spoke of her father. She clearly loved and admired him a lot. Alberto Diaz was a good person. "Your dad was highly respected when he worked for us. Everyone remarked about how good he was with our horses. He was much more than a ranch manager. He had a special connection to the animals. It must be why you have such a fondness for horses."

"Maybe it's genetic, or maybe he taught me to love such regal animals."

"Could be a little bit of both," he said.

She smiled. "What about you?"

"Me? What about me?"

"Same questions."

"I like to ride, too. I have a great affection for all animals, but I've been around horses all my life, and they seem more human at times than the real thing."

"I know, right? What else?"

"I'd never refuse a round of golf, either. I take it as a personal challenge to better my game. I guess you could say those are my hobbies." He blew out a ragged breath. "But this year has been rough. I've spent most of my time trying to clear the family name and keep the company going. As you know, we were dealt a raw hand with Keith Cooper. That guy nearly destroyed Wingate, but we've been able to relaunch the hotel chain with a new brand and we've kept WinJet strictly in the US now. It's really helped our public image."

"Beth filled me in on some of it. I know it was tough on the family."

He nodded. It'd been all over the news, but the worst scandal was when the Wingate name was associated with drug runners. Thankfully, that was disproved pretty quickly. "Well, then you know the truth."

"I do, or I wouldn't be here right now."

"Fair enough."

"Go on. What's your favorite subject?" she asked.

"Gracie 101."

She shook her head and fought a smile. "Corny."

"Yeah, it was, but you did smile. A little."

That made her smile more and it was beautiful, as was seeing her eyes lighting up with pure, unabashed joy. She didn't smile enough around him.

"Okay, I'll be serious. Don't hate me, but math is my favorite subject. It comes easy to me, though Beth says it's a four-letter word. I remember tutoring her after school, but either you get it or you don't. I like that the answers are all there in black-and-white, and there are no gray areas."

"If only life was that simple," Gracie said on a sigh.

Somehow, he got the feeling they weren't talking about math anymore. Was she in a gray area in her life? She didn't have to be. He reached across the table and took her hand. She didn't flinch or pull away, but a quick gasp escaped her mouth when he lifted their entwined hands and brushed his lips across her knuckles. The connection sparked life between them. Made him want her more. "It can be, Gracie."

Skepticism touched her eyes. But the pull they had was real. He felt it sizzle through him. One touch and he was a goner.

"There's more to life than physical attraction," she said softly.

"That's very true, but it helps." Sebastian grinned and then tugged his hand away. He promised no pressure and he had to abide by that even as his body heated up from having her so irresistibly near.

The waiter brought over an array of dishes—pastas and eggplant and shrimp scampi. It was all beautifully arranged on several platters, more food than they could possibly eat in one sitting.

"Thank you," Sebastian said to the server.

Gracie took a look and opened her eyes wide. "I know I'm eating for two, but this is enough for a football team. It's amazing."

"I hoped you'd like it. Wanna dig in?"

She nodded. "I shouldn't. I've already eaten so much. But I've got to have a little taste of everything."

Sebastian refrained from helping her fill her plate. Gracie wasn't the wilting-flower kind of girl. He had to remember that. She helped herself and then offered to serve him. Since she already had a big serving spoon in her hand, he agreed. She was generous with her portions, giving him much more than he needed. He enjoyed watching her pick out items to set in his plate.

They ate quietly, Sebastian sipping lemonade, Gracie's drink of choice. It felt good being in sync with her, even if it was just by sharing food and drink. They spoke about her day at The Eatery and how the place had fared on the second day of business. The conversation was light, nothing too intense. And just doing these normal things together made him feel closer to her, closer to the baby.

A three-piece band walked onto the stage, and soon old Sinatra classics filled the dining room. The lead singer had a deep voice, his pitch-perfect tone catching the attention of everyone in the restaurant.

A few couples got up to dance. It was intimate and cozy, and the need to hold Gracie, if only for a few fleeting minutes, overpowered his good intentions. He rose from the table and offered her his hand. "Dance with me?"

Gracie glanced around the restaurant, as if measuring

her options. Then she gazed at his outstretched hand and looked into his eyes. She sighed, as if losing a mental battle, and placed her hand in his.

He led her to the dance floor and took her in his arms, leaving a decent amount of space between them. It was harder than he thought, holding her and not drawing her close, not feeling her soft, supple body nestled up against his.

"Are you having a nice time?" he asked huskily.

She hesitated for a moment. "Yes."

Their eyes met then, and he nodded. "Good. Me, too."

"Is this another box you wanted to check off?"

"Dancing with you? I've thought about how we danced the night away at the ball so many times, and I can hardly believe we're doing it again. I was convinced I'd never find you," he whispered.

"You were shocked to find out it was me," she whispered back.

"Surprised, yes. But I was also glad it was you."

To his relief, Gracie began to slowly relax as they both found themselves swept up in the music. Her scent flavored the air around him, her body moved with rhythm and grace, and every so often, some part of her would touch him somewhere. Sebastian relished it all—her hair brushing his shoulder, her breasts grazing his chest, her legs teasing his thighs…

There was no doubt heat and desire had lodged between them, prickling his skin, making her skin flush. Like a slow-building fire, the longer he held her, the hotter it grew…until he felt a desperate, frenzied need to act on his impulses.

"Gracie," he whispered in her ear. And then she snuggled his neck and lifted her head up, locking her eyes with his. There was an openness on her face that he hadn't seen before, a sweet invitation.

He bent down and kissed her, a gentle tasting of her lips that sent him reeling. He had to remember where he was and stick to his promise to keep it chaste tonight. But she indulged in the kiss, keeping a tight grip on his neck as their lips brushed again. He wanted so much more from her. If only he could keep holding her and kissing her all night long. If only he could weave his fingers through her long, shiny hair, and inhale her delicious scent. If only he could make love to her again. Knowing full well who she was.

When the song ended, their eyes met again, searching, pondering and then silently acknowledging their incredible chemistry.

He cleared his throat. "Looks like Chef is ready to serve dessert," he said, as Tony came out personally with a dish of Italian pastries. "We shouldn't keep him waiting."

"Uh…no," she agreed, a little breathless. "We shouldn't."

He took her hand, leading her back to the table, and then greeted the chef again. The pastries were out-of-this-world appetizing. Yet, no matter how delectable the dessert, tonight nothing would match the taste of Gracie's lips on his.

Four

After Sebastian walked her to her front door, Gracie put the key in the lock, realizing this was a pivotal moment for the two of them. If she invited him in, she was pretty sure what would happen. And she didn't know if she was ready for that. She didn't know if she could forgo all of her misgivings about getting romantically involved with him.

This date tonight was a chance to get to know each other better. It was a way to find out who they both were. She wasn't that mystery woman any longer. And he wasn't her mysterious lover. That fantasy was over; she now had to deal with the real-life Sebastian. Was he someone she could let into her life? Her child's life?

Tonight had been scary good. Sebastian had been a perfect gentleman, except maybe for the kiss on the dance floor. She had to be honest with herself, though—it wasn't all his doing. She'd *wanted* him to hold her close, she'd wanted him to kiss her again. The emotion wrapped up in their encounter had been mind-blowing, so she couldn't fault him for something she'd subtly invited.

"I had a great time tonight," he said. "I hope you did, too."

She spun around to face him. Oh, boy, her fifteen-year-old self would hardly believe she'd actually gone on a date with Sebastian Wingate. That *he* was actually pursuing *her*. But she wasn't fifteen anymore. And things were different now.

"I did. It was…fun."

He nodded, his eyes gleaming. "I want to see you again."

She figured. And the idea wasn't making her stomach ache.

He went on, "What are you doing tomorrow?"

"I plan to be at The Eatery helping out. I'll be doing the books."

"Will it take all day?"

"Why?" she asked.

"Because I have something in mind. Can you clear up your afternoon?"

"I…think so."

"Great, I'll pick you up at two. And dress casual, although you do look amazing tonight." His gaze moved over her, a quick glint of approval, and a river of heat rushed down her body. "But tomorrow, just jeans and a jacket."

"Aren't you going to tell me what we're doing?"

"No, you're just going to have to trust me. Can you do that?"

She slanted him a look. "I'll…try."

"Great," he said, leaning forward and giving her a little peck on the cheek. "Sleep well, Gracie."

"You…too," she murmured, somewhat dumbfounded. But before she could utter another word, Sebastian had already turned away and was walking to his car.

So much for worrying about putting him off. She didn't

know if that was a good thing or a bad thing. With Sebastian, her heart always warred with her head. But when it came down to their date, this was by far the best one she'd had…ever. But dating wasn't the issue. She worried about blurring the lines between her deep attraction to Sebastian and doing what was right for the baby. It was something that still confused her, still caused her ill ease.

Half an hour later, after she'd had a luxurious soak in the tub, her cell phone rang. She threw her arms into the sleeves of her cozy pajamas and picked up on the third ring. "Hello."

"Hi, it's Sebastian." The deep, sexy Texas drawl in his voice threw her off-kilter. Her heart began to pound.

"Hi."

Was he calling to break their date tomorrow?

"Am I disturbing you?"

Always. Despite her caution and worry, she'd had him on her mind all evening. Her body still hummed from their date—from dancing in his arms, from laughing with him and *kissing* him and secretly dreaming of so much more. "No, not at all. Just got out of the tub."

There was a long pause on his end. Dummy, why did she tell him that?

"I won't say what I'm thinking right now."

She chuckled. She deserved that. "Thank you."

"Gracie, as I told you earlier, I had a great time tonight. And well, I could make something up, a reason for the call, but the truth is, I just wanted to hear your voice one last time before I turned in. Hope that's okay."

She was taken aback by his sincerity. "Yes, actually that's very nice."

"I told you I'm a nice guy."

She paused. She knew it deep down in her bones, her instincts telling her so, but could she trust them right now?

There was too much doubt and caution warring with the good stuff in her head. He could be charming, but he could also be quite ruthless. She wasn't forgetting his ploy to hold back the sale of the estate to get what he wanted. So no, she couldn't give him everything right now. A phone conversation, yes; other things, no. "You keep telling me that."

"Maybe if you hear it enough, you'll start to believe it."

She chuckled again. "So that's the strategy?"

"I wish I was that clever."

"You're not?" she asked.

"Not when it comes to you, Gracie. I'm actually a little…thrown off by you."

She felt the same way about him. Only, he'd been throwing her off for years. He'd never shown an interest in her or given her even a little reason to flirt. She'd grown to believe she wasn't in his league—he'd dated some high-profile women in the past—and had resigned herself to the fact that she just wasn't up to his standards. It'd hurt her and made her feel less worthy. And so all of this sudden adulation was hard to measure. "I could say the same."

"I never want to give you a reason to doubt me," he admitted gruffly.

She didn't know what to say to that. "Thank you," she whispered, for lack of a better answer. Yet, she did still have doubts. And one late-night phone call wasn't going to change that.

"Well, I'd better let you get some rest. Sweet dreams, Gracie," he said softly.

"Good night, Sebastian."

She had to admit, this man sure knew how to get what he wanted. He was chipping away at her resistance, slowly but surely.

Was he true-blue, or was it all a ploy to secure what he wanted?

* * *

Sebastian hung up with Gracie and sighed. He couldn't stop thinking about her, the way she'd looked tonight, how it felt to hold her tight in his arms. She was so pretty, but pretty wasn't enough. He was really trying to get to know her. She was the mother of his baby, for one. They both had an equal stake in this, but he wasn't going to deny Gracie had the upper hand. Slowly, she was letting him in. It wasn't fast enough for him; he wasn't a patient man. He wanted more than one night with her. But right now, that wasn't happening.

His cell phone rang and he glanced at the screen, puzzled to see his ex-girlfriend's name come up. "Hello."

"Sebastian? I'm so glad I reached you. I've been trying you for a few hours."

He'd shut his phone down during his date with Gracie, wanting no interruptions or distractions. "Hi, Rhonda. How are you?"

He hadn't seen Rhonda Pearson in over a year, but they texted from time to time. Her supermodel status had taken precedence over their relationship, and things hadn't worked out between them. But it had been an amical breakup. "I—I need your help, Sebastian. Can we meet somewhere?"

"Now? It's late. Can it wait?"

"It's about L-Lonny."

Sebastian's nerves rattled, hearing Lonny's name come up. There was desperation in Rhonda's voice. "What about Lonny?"

She was raising her fifteen-year-old brother all by herself, and the boy seemed lost at times, not having the stability a teen needed. Sebastian had taken to the kid, and the boy looked up to him. Not staying in touch with Lonny was one of Sebastian's biggest regrets. He'd planned to, but then Rhonda had thought a clean break would be better for the boy. Then Sebastian's business had gotten into trouble and suddenly he was persona non grata. So he'd stayed away.

"He's out of control. I don't know what to do with him. I just need someone to talk to, you know? He's always admired you. And well, you were really good with him."

"Rhonda, I can meet you tomorrow night. I wish it could be sooner, but I've got a full day of appointments."

"Tomorrow night is good. Thank you, Sebastian," she said gratefully. "I want to keep this as private as possible. You know my life's an open book, but not Lonny's. I don't want this to get out."

"It won't… I promise." Damn, Sebastian had always worried about the boy. He should've stayed in contact with him despite his business woes. Despite Rhonda thinking severing ties would be best. That boy needed direction and focus, and Sebastian had let him down. "Come to my office at eight o'clock and we'll talk. The place should be cleared out at that hour," he said.

"Okay. See you then, Sebastian. And thanks again."

The knock came precisely at two o'clock and Gracie was ready. She'd gotten home just twenty minutes ago and changed into a pair of skinny jeans. How long would she be able to wear them? Right now, the fit was perfect. She also wore a taupe ribbed sweater under a rust leather jacket and matching midlength boots.

She opened the door to Sebastian, who was dressed pretty much how she was—boots, jeans and a jacket over a tan shirt. He looked smoking hot. Her heart began to race and she mentally cursed. He hadn't said a word yet and she was already losing it.

"Afternoon, Gracie."

"Hi, Sebastian. You're right on time."

"Did you get your work done today?" he asked.

"Most of it. I brought some home to look at later." She gestured to her attire. "Do I...need anything else?"

"You look perfect, Gracie. I have what we'll need for the afternoon."

She scrunched her brows, suddenly not feeling so sure about this. "Are you going to tell me where we're going?"

He smiled. "You'll see. If you're ready, let's go."

She locked the door behind her and he led her to his BMW. A minute later, they were heading toward the Wingate, uh, the Diaz estate. "What're you doing?" she asked. She had no idea what he was up to.

"You are a curious thing, aren't you?"

"Yes, when my sanity is at stake."

"Believe me, you're going to like this. And no more questions. Deal?"

Was she ready to make a deal with Sebastian? She already had, really. She'd bought his house, and was having his child. What was one more? "Oh, all right. Deal."

He grinned, bringing the sexy lines around his mouth out to play. She turned away from him to look out the window. She didn't want him to know how much he tested her sanity, *for real*.

He bypassed the mansion and drove a little farther to stop at the stables. She gave him a long look.

"Horses," he said. "We both love them. How would you feel about a ride?"

"I would love it." Gracie hadn't been atop a horse in a long time. She missed it, and missed being around the stables. Technically, she was on her own property, though escrow hadn't gone through yet. But she'd promised not to displace the ranch horses and had kept on the wrangler and his one-man crew to oversee the stables.

"My horses are still here," Sebastian said. "Duke and Duchess."

"I know them. They're beautiful animals."

"I thought we'd give the royal pair some exercise, let them know they haven't been forgotten." It was also part of the sale of the house, that Sebastian could board his horses here until he could find another home for them. There were six other riding horses on the property, as well.

They got out of the car and walked over to the corral. Sebastian whistled, the sound perking up all the horses' ears, but it was Duke, the dapple gray gelding, and Duchess, the bay mare, who trotted over and hung their heads over the fence.

Sebastian patted them each between the ears, his low, deep voice resonating with the pair, who seemed to be taking his love and giving it right back. "Oh, hey, I've missed you two."

Gracie walked into the stable, filled a bucket with carrots and apples, just like she'd do when her father was working here, and strode back to the corral. Within seconds a huddle of horses began eating out of the palm of her hand.

"Well, look at you," Sebastian teased, "stealing my thunder."

"Food will win them over every time," she said, happy to be among the animals. It only reinforced her desire to one day breed and raise horses on the property.

"True," he concurred, walking over to her.

After the horses had their treats, Pete, the wrangler, walked out of the stable and greeted them. "Give me a minute or two, and I'll have them saddled up and ready to ride," he said.

Sebastian peered at her, and she nodded. "I think this time, Pete, we'll do it ourselves."

"Fine by me. I'll be in the office if you, uh, need me," he said, looking from Sebastian to her, perplexed. As if this whole arrangement was above his pay grade. She couldn't blame him. Things *were* a bit confusing around here, since she was the one signing his checks now.

After Pete walked off, Sebastian brought out both sets of saddles and tack, one at a time. Gracie hadn't forgotten how to get a horse ready to ride. She enjoyed every second of it, until it came time for her to lift the saddle onto Duchess.

"Whoa, there, Wonder Woman," Sebastian said. "I'll do the honors. This sucker is heavy."

Before she could say a word, Sebastian hoisted the saddle atop Duchess. She didn't mind one bit seeing his muscles bunch and his neck strain. There was something innately sexy about Sebastian in this setting.

Once the horses were saddled up, Gracie tried to slide her left boot into the stirrup, and as tall as she was, she still couldn't quite manage without a little help. Sebastian gave her rump a push up, his hand lingering a bit longer than necessary on her butt cheek. "Watch it, bud," she said lightly.

"Oh, I am. Trust me, I am."

Gracie peered into his twinkling eyes and shook her head at his shameless attempt at flirting. Once fully seated, she grabbed the reins.

"Something's missing. Give me a sec," Sebastian said.

He marched to his car and came back with two hats and a duffel bag. He mounted Duke and guided him toward Duchess. "Here you go," he declared, plopping a tan hat on her head. "Cute." Immediately, her eyes were shaded from the sun.

He didn't look *cute* in his hat. *Mesmerizing* was a better word, but then she'd always had a bias when it came to

Sebastian. How often she'd gaze at him from a distance, the tall handsome Wingate twin saddling up his horse, riding out onto the land he owned. She'd often daydream about this very thing, riding out with him. And now here she was.

"What's in the bag?" she asked.

"Snacks."

She flashed him a grin. "Wow. You think of everything."

"This is our second date. There'll be no skimping."

"Good to know," Gracie said, making a clicking sound and encouraging the mare to get going, which Duchess did right on cue.

Sebastian caught up with her, and they were quiet for a while as the horses moved in sync with each other. She glanced over at him every now and then, watching as he took command of the animal, of the land. His jaw firm, his eyes focused, he made her jittery inside while the rolling landscape and beautiful scenery calmed her. The contrast wasn't lost on her, And yet, there was peace here. And sanity. She concentrated on that.

"How're you holding up?" he asked, breaking their silence.

"I'm loving this."

"I thought you would."

She quirked a brow. "And you knew this because of our conversation the other day?"

"Only partly. I used to see you with your dad, the joy on your face whenever you'd come back from a ride. I figured this might be something you'd enjoy."

"Those were good days," she admitted, feeling a little nostalgic. "I would look forward to those rides. They didn't happen often enough for me. Dad was a stickler about work, and only once he was caught up would I get to mount up with him. But oh, it was fun."

Sebastian smiled. "How adventurous are you feeling today?"

"Why?"

"There's something I want to show you. But it'll take us another thirty minutes to get there."

"And you're not going to tell me what it is?"

He thought about that a second. "It's a secret place I'd go with Sutton. There's an old shed my brother and I turned into a clubhouse. There's a running stream nearby. It's been years since I've been there. Don't know if it's still there. What do you say? Are you up for it?"

"Sounds like fun. Sure, I'm up for it."

"Great." Sebastian pointed west. "That way." He reined Duke in that direction and Duchess followed.

In less than thirty minutes, they reached a clearing, coming upon a rustic building erected several feet from the banks of a rushing stream.

"Would you look at that," he marveled, taking it all in. "It's still standing."

She imagined the twins playing in there as boys, laughing, raising a ruckus, telling scary stories. It wasn't a total wreck—the structure seemed relatively sound—yet the wood planks that served as protection from the elements were severely weathered. "It sure is."

The stream was gurgling, the water flowing by and catching sunlight. It appeared narrow enough to wade through on foot. Lush green trees beyond served as a verdant backdrop. It was truly a lovely spot.

"Let's dismount and check it out," he said.

He was off his horse quickly and then came around to Duchess. Gracie lifted her right leg over the saddle and held on to the saddle horn as she slid down the mare's left side. Sebastian caught her around the waist and guided her down the rest of the way, until her boots hit solid ground. She swallowed a deep breath as his hands applied slight pressure. He didn't back away...wasn't letting go. "Gracie," he whispered in her ear from behind.

Their connection sizzled, and as she turned around, she was fitted snugly in his arms. Hot desire arced between them. Her breathing grew heavy. There was a look of unmistakable hunger in his eyes. And when she lowered her gaze to his mouth, a rumbling groan rose from his throat.

At the sound of his restraint, something sparked within her. She couldn't figure out why all of a sudden she was okay with this, but she was. More than okay. Her body ached for him, for a release of the tension he provoked every time he walked into a room.

"Sebastian," she whispered.

And then his lips crashed down on hers, tasting, *devouring*, making her head swim in crazy delight. Beyond reason now, she pushed aside her misgivings. All she knew was that she wanted Sebastian.

Desperately.

Gracie poured herself into the kiss, tugging on his neck and squeezing closer to him. His body radiated heat and energy, warming every inch of her. Duchess shifted, becoming impatient, and stepped away from them, snorting. Her move left them both to realize they were out in the middle of a clearing, with no shelter other than a broken-down, cobwebbed clubhouse.

Sebastian hugged her to his chest for one last moment, then broke their connection, pulling away. "Seems Duchess has more sense than I do."

"Does she?" she asked.

"Don't tempt me, Gracie. This isn't easy."

"What's not easy?"

"You're gonna make me say it?" he rasped.

She nodded. She wanted to hear everything he had to say.

"I want your trust, Gracie. I don't want to mess this up by rushing you into anything. I lost my head for a moment, but more than anything now, I want to get to know you better. I want to build a bond with you."

"So you're on your best behavior?"

A sly grin crossed over his face. "You've already seen my best behavior."

"Ah," she replied, catching his meaning. The night of the masquerade ball immediately came to mind. The way he'd danced with her until they'd needed much more than casual touching. The way he'd whispered in her ear to leave the dance floor with him and the sizzling hot tingles that had her nodding her head. The way he'd made love to her that night had been nothing but the *best*. "But this is a close second?"

"Only if I'm winning you over. 'Cause believe me, if I had my way…" He shot her a hot glance that made her entire body twitch. She had no words.

He sighed and took her hand. "C'mon. Let's have something to eat."

He pulled a lightweight blanket out of the duffel and spread it a few feet from the creek. "Have a seat."

She sat cross-legged and he came down to face her.

She looked inside the bag and found all kinds of snacks. She helped him pull out a small loaf of bread and chunks of gourmet cheese, fresh apples, tortilla chips and two over-size chocolate cookies from The Eatery. "Hmm, I think I recognize these," she said, still tempering her heated body.

"Lauren's best," he murmured.

"I agree."

Together they munched on the snacks, Gracie totally

aware of Sebastian. She liked the way he chewed, the way he swallowed, the way his eyes stayed focused on her even though there was beautiful scenery all around them.

"It's peaceful here," she said, taking a bite of the cookie.

"My brother and I would come here often when we were kids. It was our secret place, or so we thought. Turned out your father knew about it, too. We found out years later that he would come out here and make sure the building was kept up and solid, free of spiders and webs. Did he ever tell you about it?"

"No, never. But that sounds like something my father would do." She stared at the structure, picturing her dad making a point of stopping by every so often to make sure the boys were safe. "Dad was always good with horses, but he was also a softy when it came to children. Thanks for telling me, Sebastian. It makes this place special to me, too."

He nodded, giving her time to reminisce.

She appreciated that. No wonder she loved the estate; it was a part of her parents' lives as much as it was her own. She'd loved everything about the Wingate property—the land, the house itself. And now that she owned it, she realized there wasn't anything she wanted to change about the place. It was perfect. She'd always thought so.

When they were through eating, she started cleaning up and putting things back into the duffel bag.

"Are you ready to go?" he asked, a question in his eyes.

"Aren't you?"

He stood up and reached for her hand. "Take a walk with me?"

"Oh, uh, sure." Guess he wasn't ready to go, and honestly, neither was she. She was having a good time getting to know Sebastian better. As she placed her palm into his hand, he held it firmly in his grasp. There was something possessive in that gesture, which said, *You're with me.* It was thrilling and almost too good to be true. Did she deserve all of this good fortune? It was a question she often asked herself. It was hard for her to accept the way her life had changed, when in her heart she was still that same young girl who'd been on the outside, looking in.

They walked along the stream and she put her head on Sebastian's shoulder. It was a bold move, yet it felt right. He relaxed his shoulder and stopped walking to give her a delicious kiss.

It was perfect and easy and so natural.

"I'd love to see you tonight. For dinner," she added, surprising herself. When had the pursued become the pursuer?

Sebastian smiled, his eyes gleaming bright, but then his lips curled down into a frown as he seemed to remember something. "I'd love to take you up on that. But I can't tonight."

"Is it work?"

"A meeting. I'm afraid I can't get out of it."

He brushed a strand of hair from her cheek. That simple gesture and the caring look in his eyes moved her to distraction. "How about tomorrow night?" he asked.

"Yes," she said softly, immediately. "I accept."

He smiled, taking her hand, and they headed back to the horses.

Sebastian poured himself a rye whiskey from the small bar in his office. If he didn't have this meeting with his ex-girlfriend, he'd be with Gracie now and he'd be one step closer to getting what he wanted. He couldn't believe she'd actually asked him on a date.

And he'd had to refuse her.

Her trust was important to him, but he just couldn't bring himself to tell her about this meeting tonight. He'd promised Rhonda that he'd keep this meeting private. He understood her motives. She wanted to spare Lonny any more grief. The teen's problems didn't need to make the ten o'clock news. And Sebastian was a man of his word, so he'd told a little white lie to Gracie about what he was really doing tonight.

Rhonda Pearson, famous supermodel and his ex-lover, made headlines around the globe. Her photos had graced more than a dozen magazines, and she had a long list of accomplishments in the modeling industry. And all during that, she was trying to raise her much younger brother.

He took another swig of whiskey, and at precisely 8:00 p.m., he opened the door of the Wingate offices to Rhonda.

She smiled, but her eyes didn't reflect anything but sadness. "Sebastian, thanks for seeing me."

"Rhonda, come in."

He returned a smile, noting that his former flame hadn't changed since they'd dated. She was the same gorgeous, leggy blonde-haired beauty she'd always been. Rhonda had a natural grace about her, and yet, it hadn't been enough for him. She'd been too much in the public eye, too much into herself, to be the kind of woman he wanted. In the end, he'd allowed the press to believe she had called it off with him, so she could save face amid her fans. Sebastian had made the right decision in breaking it off with her. He hadn't once regretted their breakup, except for losing touch with Lonny. He'd been like a father to Lonny, a mentor of sorts, and then it had all ended. Sebastian hated that he hadn't fought harder to keep that relationship going.

He led her through the lobby and into his office. The staff had all gone home now, and he offered her a seat. She sat down on the sofa. "Care for a drink, something to eat?" he asked.

She glanced at his whiskey glass, not quite empty yet. "I'll have what you're having."

He lifted a brow and nodded. "That bad, uh?"

"That's why I'm drinking, but why are you? Is the company still having problems?"

He sighed as he walked to the bar to pour her drink. "Some. We're not fully out of the woods yet, but we're getting there. It's hard to gain back a reputation, you know?"

"I do know. That's why I try my best to stay away from scandal."

He poured whiskey into a tumbler and handed it to her. Then he took a seat at the other end of the sofa. "And yet here you are, in the sinful Wingates' den of thieves."

She chuckled at his theatrics. "I never believed it."

"That's what people say now that we've made it over the hurdle. But you're not here to talk about me. Tell me about Lonny."

And for the next half hour she filled him in on what was going on with her brother. Sebastian had always known that losing his parents at such a young age had affected Lonny, but now apparently it was causing the troubled teen to spin out of control. Rhonda told him Lonny was acting out whenever he could, getting in with the wrong crowd at school, to the point of almost being expelled. She had used all her powers of persuasion and superstar status to save him from the expulsion. The principal was giving her brother one last chance to change his ways—or face the consequences—and Rhonda was at her wits' end.

"I've already turned down more work than I've accepted, in order to be home more. If Lonny gets expelled, it'll be a black mark that will travel from school to school with him. He doesn't understand that, or he doesn't care. Either way, I have to do something with him. I threatened him with boarding school, and all he said to that was he always knew I wanted to get rid of him. Sebastian, I don't know what to do." She sipped her whiskey and sighed, tears welling in her eyes.

"You're not a bad sister, Rhonda," he said softly. She was just out of her element raising a young boy while trying to maintain a career. "As I recall, you put that boy first as much as you could. Has he seen a therapist?"

She gestured with her free hand, putting up fingers. "Three of them. He doesn't give an inch, won't open up. That's why I'm here, Sebastian. When we were together, he was the happiest I've seen him. He bonded with you."

"Yes, but he was younger then. I'm no therapist, but..."

"He'll listen to you. I *know* he will."

He shook his head. "No, that boy doesn't need a lecture."

"But will you try to talk to him, Sebastian? Will you come over and see him?"

Sebastian had a lot going on in his life right now, but he couldn't refuse helping a distressed young boy. Lonny just needed a chance—Sebastian knew that in his gut—and the way he'd let the boy down before still gnawed away at him. That was why he was so adamant about working things out with Gracie. He couldn't stand to lose another relationship with a child, *his* child this time.

His baby.

"I'll call you and set up a date. But it shouldn't look like we planned it. That'll turn Lonny off for sure."

"You mean we should accidentally run into each other?"

He nodded. "Something like that."

"Thank you," she breathed. "I feel better already." She put down her glass and rose. Sebastian took her elbow and walked her outside to where her car was parked. He opened the door for her, and before he knew what was happening, Rhonda kissed him, planting a grateful smack on his lips. Because he'd been with her for two years, he knew the difference between passion and gratitude. The kiss was purely innocent, but she'd landed it right out in the open. And a sudden pang of guilt hit him as Gracie's image came to mind, but he shoved that aside. The two situations, the two women, were totally different.

He glanced at his watch. It was quarter to nine. Not too late to visit Gracie.

He hoped not, because he didn't have it in him to stay away.

Five

Gracie rubbed her backside, easing the soreness that lingered there from the ride on Duchess today. And even though she was paying a small price, the ride and the man had been perfect. She sighed. Sebastian had been open and honest with her as they spoke of their lives while growing up. They'd shared more about themselves on the ride and she'd laughed at some of the stories he'd told about his antics with his twin.

It seemed that in their youth, Sutton and Sebastian had a history of fooling people into believing one was the other. Teachers and friends had all fallen victim to their identical looks. And more recently, Lauren had been unintentionally misled that Sebastian had been the man she'd met during the masquerade ball, when it had really been Sutton. Once all was sorted out, Lauren and Sutton had fallen madly in love with each other.

If only she and Sebastian…

Gracie was just about to take the stairs when a knock at the front door startled her. Then her security alert chimed, and she glanced at the live feed on her phone.

Quickly, she fussed with her hair, straightened out her clothes and then opened the door to Sebastian.

"Hi," he said, charming her with a smile…and, well, his presence.

"Hi." Her heart pumped hard.

"I hope it's not too late to stop by. I wanted to give these to you," he said, and that was when she noticed a lovely bouquet of winter flowers in his hand.

He transferred the flowers to her. "They're beautiful," she murmured, bringing them to her nose for a sniff. Pine and cinnamon mixed with the sweet scent of roses, reminding her of the holiday just past.

"They're a thank-you for today. I had a good time."

"Yes, it was a nice day. Did your meeting end early?"

He hesitated a second too long and a part of her wondered if he'd been lying to her, though why he'd find the need wasn't quite clear. "It didn't take as long as I thought."

"Well, uh, would you like to come in?"

"It's not too late?" he asked.

She doubted she'd get any sleep tonight if she sent him away. "No, it's not too late." She opened the door wider and allowed him entrance.

He stepped into the house and turned to her. She fingered a silky rose petal and smiled. "This way. I'll put these in water." She led him into the kitchen and set the bouquet down. As she reached up on tiptoes to get a vase from the cabinet, Sebastian was there behind her, lifting it off the shelf easily. He handed it to her. "Here you go."

She stared into his green eyes, those same eyes that had melted her and made her do crazy things, like shedding her clothes and making love with him in an alcove at the Texas Cattleman's Club. She nearly dropped the darn vase as that image revealed itself yet again. Could he tell what she was thinking? Were his eyes reflecting the same thoughts?

Sebastian took the vase from her and set it down, never once taking his gaze off her. He whispered, "Gracie," and she trembled from deep down and acknowledged what was happening. What she wanted to happen. "I swear I only came here to say thank-you."

"I know." The pull between them was powerful, and despite his motives, he was here and she didn't want him to leave. "I'm glad you did."

Maybe her hormones were out of whack. Or maybe they weren't. All she knew for sure was that she could no longer control herself around this man. She wanted to feel the same exquisite feelings she had before when Sebastian was simply a mystery to her. As she was to him. And maybe, just maybe, she liked the man she was getting to know, which, in turn, was adding even more fuel to their sizzling hot attraction. "Hearing you say that is music to my ears," he growled, wrapping one arm around her waist and bringing her up against him. The soft material of her skinny jeans pressed against his rougher denim as their bodies collided. Sebastian shook his head as if he couldn't help himself, as if not touching her was torture, and then brought his mouth to hers and kissed her until they both needed oxygen.

He cupped her head and kissed her again and again, each kiss stirring her up, making her hormones dance. Soon, her blouse was off, then his shirt. Their hands found skin, warm, inviting, the touching as fevered as their kisses. Sebastian's caresses destroyed her and she hungered for more...

He reached under her and she was lifted in his arms,

his strength, the way he held her so effortlessly, the ultimate turn-on. She didn't mind this caveman act; she was like putty already and doubted she could walk. "Which way?" he rasped, between kisses.

"Up the stairs, to the right," she said breathlessly. "Hurry."

Sebastian groaned as he kissed her again, making his way up the staircase. Her big bed loomed large in the room. He lowered her down upon it and she lay there quietly as he removed her clothes. "Hot," he remarked about her cherry-red underwear, taking precious care with her bra and then sliding the panties down her thighs slowly, savoring every second. She was naked and so damn sexy he could barely breathe.

"I never saw you like this, Gracie. You are so beautiful." The last time, it'd been too dark to see much, and they'd only gone by feel. But tonight was very different.

"My turn," she said softly, rising up from the bed with a smile. She pulled the zipper of his pants down and helped him kick them off. Next came his boxers and then he was bared to her. She laid her hand on his shaft, stroked him and then put her mouth on him. His knees nearly buckled under him. He loved Gracie's confidence, her unbelievable boldness, but it was almost too much. *Almost.*

And when she was through, he offered her the same, grazing the apex of her thighs with his tongue, his hand. Mattress sounds didn't rival Gracie's moans of pleasure as he brought her to utter completion. He loved that she didn't hold back, didn't hide her enthusiasm. Her whimpers in the aftermath bolstered his ego. When her breathing slowed, he pulled her into his arms. "We haven't even gotten to the good part yet," he whispered wickedly in her ear.

She chuckled and folded her body closer into his, her

long, thick hair teasing his sensitized skin. It hadn't been a fluke the last time. It hadn't been just the thrill of the unknown. Gracie was the best lover he'd ever had. And he wondered about other men in her life. How many? Who? Had it been this great with them? He didn't want to think about Gracie with other guys. Twinges of jealousy surfaced. He'd never felt this way before. Not with Rhonda or any other woman.

But those thoughts were short-lived. Their night was not over yet. And when he made a move toward Gracie, she shook her head. He had a moment of panic at her refusal, until she climbed atop and straddled him. Staring up at her, with her olive skin glistening in the moonlight and her lustrous hair falling gloriously past her shoulders, he felt completely spellbound by this woman. Man, oh, man, how had he managed to keep away from her all these years?

"Sebastian," she said softly as she came down onto him, squeezing her eyes closed, giving him an unforgettable image of her naked beauty making love to him. He gritted his teeth as she moved slowly up and down, setting a sensual pace and rocking him to his very core. When it became too much to take, he grabbed her hips and their eyes met as he sped up his thrusts. She followed his beat, his rhythm, the bounce of her body exquisite to watch. Then her mouth gaped open, her breathing hitched and her eyes shuttered as her release washed over him. The beauty of that moment shattered him completely, and he couldn't hold back another second. He experienced the best damn orgasm of his life.

Afterward, they lay quietly in bed for a while, both staring up at the ceiling. "Was it—"

"Yes," she said. "Now we don't have to wonder anymore."

"You wondered, too?"

"Of course, I did," she admitted. "I've never made love with a stranger before. I'm not usually that…wild."

"I like wild. But you're not?"

"No. Not even close."

"So it must mean something."

"It means we have great sex," she whispered.

"Right." They did. So why was he disappointed in her answer? Why was she still wary of him? Still unwilling to admit they had more than great sex.

He stared at her abdomen, the place where his baby was growing and thriving. He wanted so much for that child. But he didn't want to press his luck with Gracie, either. He took hold of her hand, entwining their fingers. "Be my date for Cam and Beth's wedding."

He was going to be the man in Gracie's life. And it wasn't all about the baby. It was her and the way he was beginning to feel about her. He waited for her answer, and finally, after she was quiet for several seconds, he asked, "Is that a problem?"

She rolled over to face him. "It's just that people will think…"

"That I'm the baby's father?"

"No… Yes."

It stung that she didn't want people to know the truth about the baby. Sebastian was ready to let the world know. He didn't like lying to his family this way, or at the very least, omitting the truth from them. He wanted Gracie, but she was still gun-shy.

"It's just that… I'm not ready. I don't know where this is heading and I don't want to explain the situation to everyone, when I don't, uh, *we* don't, have answers."

He had answers, but she didn't want to hear them right now. "You're going as my date. It's as simple as that," he said. "No one's going to presume anything, or even if they did, I doubt they'd ask you."

Eventually, everyone would find out the truth. He was going to play a role in the baby's life, that was a given. Gracie couldn't keep his paternity secret much longer— he had rights, too, and he wasn't going to back off. That said, he was trying to give her some latitude here, by not putting undue pressure on her. But he did want to bring her to the wedding.

To stake your claim, said the little bug in his ear. Having her on his arm would be a step in the right direction. "I'd love to take you," he said, stroking her arm up and down.

She laid her head on his chest. "Okay, then, yes," she whispered.

"You'll go with me?"

"Yes, I'll go to the wedding with you."

He nodded. Finally, he'd have a chance to get to know Gracie a little better. To find out if what they had that night was real. He wanted her, but he also wanted to discover what made her tick.

Gracie woke to the sound of Sebastian's light breathing. It was dawn or a short time after, she couldn't tell. She was still in a daze about what had happened between them last night. She glanced at him sleeping next to her in bed, his broad muscled body that had worked magic on her now relaxed in sleep. Making love with Sebastian was unequaled, she didn't doubt that. But she could easily let him into her heart, and that was what scared her. She wanted to, so badly, but her instincts told her not to go all in with him. Life wasn't so neat and tidy that she'd have all of her fantasies come true. A man she'd always wanted, a baby she already loved and riches beyond her belief. At some point, this merry-go-round would stop to let her off.

She still had doubts in her mind about Sebastian. Even after last night. Physically, they were in tune, but what about everything else?

The bed creaked as she tossed off the covers and rose, stretching out her arms. She walked into the bathroom quietly and turned on the shower. Stepping inside, she shivered from the chill in the January air, until the hot spray rained down, spreading a delicious warmth. She'd had a workout last night, too, and she welcomed the heat that soothed her muscles.

When the glass door opened with a click, she spun around. Sebastian stood naked behind the door, a devilishly charming smile on his face. "Mind if I join you?"

Another fantasy coming true. Was she dreaming, or was this as real as it got? "Come in, the water's perfect."

He stepped inside. "You're the one that's perfect." He laid a hand on her tummy. Was there a little bump emerging? "So is this little one."

He kissed her then, under the hot spray of water. And then his hands were on her, soaping her up, touching her in private places, sliding seductively over her swollen breasts. She trusted him with her body, and so far, she hadn't been disappointed.

She kissed him back, using the bar of soap to lather him up good. And when she was just about done, and the lather was washed off, his large hands came around to her rear end and he lifted her slightly onto him. She tucked her legs around his waist, fully secure in his grip. There was no doubt this was going to happen again. She'd known it the second the shower door clicked open, but the intensity of their lovemaking always surprised her. Her heart beat fast, her body heated up, the water lapping over them giving her a thrill. He held her tight, moving deeper inside, taking the burden of the thrusts upon himself. It was too passionate, too torrid, and she couldn't hold on another second. She gripped his neck and spun out of control, her release mind-blowing.

Their lovemaking was raw and beautiful, just like the two times before. With no worries about the actual act, since she was already pregnant and they'd both confessed to not having any prior physical relationships for a long while, she harbored no regrets. Sebastian kissed her again and then shut off the water. They held each other for long moments, regaining normal breaths and coming back down to earth.

"Do you like bacon and eggs?" she asked him.

He chuckled. "That's the last thing I thought you'd say right now."

"The baby needs to eat. And it'll be egg whites and turkey bacon, but I make a mean omelet if you're hungry."

"I accept." He kissed her nose, and it was the simple things like that that captivated her. "Only if you let me help."

"Can you make coffee?"

"Of course," he answered.

And twenty minutes later, they were dressed and working in the kitchen, the flowers he'd given her last night adorning the center of the kitchen table. It was a cozy scene, a fact that didn't escape her as they went about making breakfast together.

Another one of her youthful imaginings coming to life.

But that was fantasy and this was real.

She didn't for a minute know how long it would last.

Gracie walked into The Eatery later that morning and greeted Lauren in the kitchen. Her business partner was hard at work, developing her special of the day, basil herb chicken with roasted vegetables. "Smells good in here."

"As it should," Lauren said, putting the finishing touch

on the dish with a drizzle of extra-virgin olive oil. She looked the part in her uniform jacket and toque blanche, as she called her chef hat, a historical name from years gone by.

"Looks like word is spreading. We've got a decent lunch crowd."

"Yep, some of my regulars from Street Eats are coming in and helping spread the word," Lauren replied. "We're busy, which makes me extremely happy."

"Oh, I thought Sutton was the only one who could do that."

"Very funny! Good food and a good man rank up there on my happy scale. And you should talk… Sutton tells me Sebastian didn't come home last night. Which may very well explain the healthy glow on your face."

Was it that obvious? "It's amazing what prenatal vitamins can do."

"They can only do so much, Gracie."

"And how would Sutton know about Sebastian's comings and goings? I thought he spent his nights with you."

"He goes home every once in a while, to water the plants." She winked.

"You're so bad."

"It's okay if you don't want to tell me." Lauren feigned a pout.

Gracie didn't want anyone to know about her budding relationship with her baby's daddy. But Lauren was a good friend, and she knew about the night of the masquerade ball. She supposed if she told anyone, it would be her business partner. "Maybe Sebastian and I went on a date, and maybe he just stopped by last night to bring me a bouquet of flowers."

"Sounds interesting. Go on."

She rolled her eyes. "Can't you use your imagination, Chef?"

"I do, with my creations, but when it comes to friends, I want to hear it all."

"Okay, fine. Since I need a favor from you, I'll tell you that Sebastian made me happy twice last night."

Lauren's eyes bugged out. "Wow," she mouthed. "That's awesome. Are you two…"

"Dating? Sort of. He's taking me to Beth and Cam's wedding. And I don't know what the heck I'm doing."

"You don't have to know, Gracie. Just let things happen naturally."

"I don't want to be pressured, that's all," she admitted.

"Sebastian knows that, I'm sure. But it would be absolutely per—"

"About that favor," she interrupted. She knew it would be perfect if Sebastian fell in love with her, but that might not ever happen, and she had the baby to protect. For as hard as she tried, she couldn't shake off the constant, nagging suspicion that she'd never been good enough for a Wingate, and that was why Sebastian had never even considered her an option. But no matter what, she wasn't going to settle for anything less than true love. She wanted the kind of love that made birds sing and flowers bloom.

She wanted the fairy tale.

"When it slows down in here, will you help me shop for a dress for Beth's wedding?" she asked.

"I'd love to. Give me two hours to serve the lunch crowd and I'll go with you."

"Great, I'll plant myself in the back office and do some work until you're ready."

Lauren dug her teeth into her lower lip. "You know, you already have a gorgeous red gown."

Gracie began shaking her head. "No way. I can't go in the dress I wore to the masquerade ball, Lauren. Not anymore than you can." They'd both worn deep red gowns and gold masks on that night, part of the reason there'd been a case of mistaken identity.

"I know." Her friend shrugged. "It was just a thought."

"If you need me for anything, just give a shout. I'll be in the back."

And three hours later, Gracie and Lauren walked into a high-end boutique in Royal and, with the help of a very astute saleswoman, narrowed down Gracie's choices to three. In between try-on sessions, they were served passion fruit herbal tea and cookies. Both passed on the cookies but sipped the tea. Gracie and Lauren both came from humble beginnings, and this type of not off-the-rack shopping was new to them. But it was fun, and Gracie felt a little bit like Julia Roberts in *Pretty Woman* choosing a dress this way. Only, she was using her own credit card for the purchase.

The saleswoman, Edith, couldn't be nicer, even though Gracie opted for a dress on clearance that was slightly more money than she'd earn as a waitress for a month. "It's fabulous on you," Edith said.

"I think it's the one, Gracie," Lauren concurred.

Gracie glanced at herself in the triple mirror, admiring the amethyst lace dress from all angles. It had off-the-shoulder sleeves, a sweetheart neckline decorated with delicate rhinestones that traveled down to a tapered waistline and a high-low hem hitting her well below the knee. She knew it might just be the last time she'd squeeze into a garment like this. Her tummy was still flat, but her breasts were fuller and her waist was thickening a little. All in preparation for the baby, so it was a good thing. "I think so, too."

"Wonderful! Shall I get it ready for delivery?" Edith asked.

Gracie looked to Lauren, and she nodded enthusiastically. "Yes, I think so."

"Great! If you don't mind me saying so, I'm thrilled to have met you, Miss Diaz. To think Rhonda Pearson came in just before you. Two celebrities in just one day."

"I'm hardly a celebrity," Gracie said, humbled. "So Rhonda Pearson shops here, too?" She knew Rhonda had dated Sebastian for a long time. Rumor had it they were to be married, but then they'd had a very public breakup. The supermodel had dumped him and the tabloids had a field day with that story. Now Rhonda was back in town. To see Sebastian?

"Why, yes, she does. She has excellent taste in clothes, if I do say do myself. And why wouldn't she? She's an international supermodel and just a lovely person."

"Y-yes, I suppose she is, though I've never met her," Gracie said.

Rhonda was gorgeous, from high cheekbones and perfect bone structure to a sweet-as-sugar smile. Plus, she had a mane of stunning blond hair that any woman would envy.

Gracie wasn't going to lie to herself, she didn't like the memories flashing in her head of Rhonda and Sebastian. They'd made headlines often. And maybe a streak of jealousy flitted through her system, as well as self-doubt. She's never been in Sebastian's league, and Rhonda Pearson could make even the most confident woman feel the lesser.

She tried not to think about it, yet feelings of unease still wedged their way in.

"Thanks for the tea, Edith," Lauren said. "And for your help today. I'm afraid I have to get back to work. Gracie and I just opened The Eatery in town. Perhaps you've heard of it? We'd love it if you stopped by one day, and be sure to bring your family."

Edith smiled warmly. "Thank you. I certainly will."

Gracie changed into her street clothes and handed the dress back to Edith. "Thanks again."

"Sure thing. I'll have it sent to your home by tomorrow."

"I appreciate that," she said.

"All part of the service." Edith beamed. "And thanks for shopping at Goodwins. Goodbye, now."

Lauren took Gracie's arm and ushered her outside. "That was a blast! I like spending your money, Gracie. Does that make me a terrible friend?"

"I don't think of it that way, Lauren. We're friends and *partners*, so in a way you're making me money."

"Okay, I'll take that. And OMG that dress—it's stunning on you! Sebastian won't know what hit him. The only trouble is, now I have to find something to knock Sutton's socks off."

"Lauren, you're engaged to him, and he thinks the sun shines on your shoulders. You have no worries."

"I know." She giggled and kept the smile on her face all the way back to The Eatery.

Sebastian straightened his charcoal-and-black paisley tie in the mirror. He couldn't believe his sister Beth was getting married today. Cam Guthrie was a good guy, a hard worker and a man who'd been building Beth a dream home on property that was intended to be their working dude ranch resort. They were getting married in a private family ceremony today and Gracie was going as his date.

"What're you smiling about?" Sutton poked his head into the room.

"Beth," he lied. "She's the happiest I've ever seen her."

"So are you lately. Must have something to do with a certain pretty woman we both know."

"Maybe." He glanced at his brother. "But for years while growing up, Gracie wasn't someone I thought I could date or even think of that way. She's a little skittish around me, too, so we'll see how it goes tonight."

"Got it. But otherwise things are going well?"

He nodded. He didn't want to go into detail, so he kept his mouth shut.

"Hey, I have some news," Sutton said. "Not to put a damper on the day, but you should know about this. Chloe had a hunch about Keith Cooper's involvement when Dad was recovering from his stroke. She thinks that while he was supposedly *helping out* with the company, he might've dipped his hand into the till, too. Miles is doing some digging now. And you know our brother—he won't rest until he finds out the truth. He wants us to sit tight and see what he comes up with."

"If anyone can sort through the BS, it's Miles." Chloe was Miles's fiancée and both were delving into the family's past finances.

Sebastian scratched his chin. What a corrupt man Keith Cooper had turned out to be. "It's not the kind of news we want to talk about at the wedding."

"No, I agree. But I wanted to keep you up-to-date."

"Got it," Sebastian said. "We'll just wait to hear what Miles finds out."

"Right. But in any event, this is gonna be a happy day. The family needs a fun celebration to remember what life was like before all the negativity and deception."

Sebastian glanced at his watch—it was almost time to pick up Gracie. His heart thumped hard, a current familiar reaction whenever he thought about her. This date was more than a date, because it was Beth's wedding, and both he and Gracie loved her, wanted to see her happy. They had that in common. But for the first time, the family would see Gracie on his arm. He wanted that. He wanted to step up instead of hiding his paternity. Maybe today would be a start toward making that happen.

"Time to run, bro," he told Sutton.

"Yeah, me, too. I'm picking up Lauren in a few minutes. Can't wait to see the house, now that it's all finished. Should be a special night."

He slapped his brother on the back. "And not just for Cam and Beth, but for all of us."

A short while later, Sebastian stood on Gracie's threshold in total awe, mesmerized by the smile that lit up her entire face. The dress she wore was a knockout, fitting her form perfectly. Its deep amethyst color highlighted her olive skin tones and the smoky brown of her eyes. Her hair was up in a do that looked both complicated and trendy, held together by a rhinestone clasp in the back.

"You look…" Delicious. Gorgeous. Stunning.

"Thank you. You look nice, too. Let me just get my coat. Come in."

He stepped into her foyer. She was back with a cream-colored faux fur coat and a clutch purse. As he helped her put it on, the delicate scent of flowers tickled his nostrils. "Love that perfume," he whispered as he tucked her into the coat, holding her lapels tight. "Reminds me of the other night." *When they'd made love…*

"You mean the way I smelled after getting off Duchess." She sent him a coy smile.

"Right, that's exactly what I meant." He tilted his head and leaned in to brush a quick kiss to her lips. It was something he needed to do, for his own sanity. He'd have to be a perfect gentleman tonight, in front of his family, and that was plain no fun.

"We should go," he said softly, stealing one more kiss. "Sorry, that's gonna have to hold me through the night."

It was getting harder and harder to keep this slow pace with Gracie. He'd never been a patient man, and his baby mama was testing his limits.

Six

Gracie had seen the plans for the renovation of the two-story house, but nothing compared to seeing it in person. As Sebastian drove up, the entire ranchland was spread out before them, and smack in the center was Cam and Beth's glorious home constructed with river stone, an amazing glass-and-wood double-door entry and a red tile roof. The architecture, a harmonious mix of Spanish style and Craftsman, spoke of casual elegance. The first floor had a wide veranda that could probably hold every single guest at the wedding, while the second floor sported a wraparound balcony, and she could only imagine the view from there on a clear blue-sky day.

There were also bunkhouses and outer buildings and a gorgeous redone barn painted the color of fresh meadow grass.

The invitation said cocktails in the main house first, before the ceremony, but the actual wedding would take place in the barn. It was Cam and Beth's way of holding an open house as well as a wedding. Sebastian turned his keys over to a valet and waved the attendant off, opening the door for Gracie himself.

He took her hand and led her up the steps of the grand home. Inside, they explored the rooms, checking out a dining room set with a large pine finished table and enough seating for ten. The great room was just that, *great* and large, furnished with an array of bulky furniture toned down by Beth's soft, feminine touch. Gracie's eyes drifted to the stone fireplace, which captured the room's essence, floor-to-ceiling and massive, but again was not overdone, as a mantel displayed family photos backlit by pillar candles. Beth and Cam had good insight into making this space homey and comfortable.

Waiters came by offering champagne and appetizers, and Gracie was touched when Sebastian took two flutes of sparkling water instead, offering her one with a smile. Seeing the food, her stomach growled, and she had no trouble accepting bacon-wrapped shrimp and a mini beef Wellington from another server. Sebastian watched her eat, his gorgeous green eyes on her as she chewed with gusto.

They spent time admiring the house, and then Harley and Grant spotted them and walked over with little Daniel. "Hi, you two," Harley said, giving them both quizzical looks. Grant, too, seemed surprised at seeing the two of them together. He was the doctor who'd been helping her with hormone therapy so she could have an in vitro procedure.

Sebastian gave his sister a kiss on the cheek. "Harley, you look very pretty tonight." He shook Grant's hand, and then patted Daniel's head. "Hey, buddy, how's my favorite nephew today? Excited for Aunt Beth's wedding?"

"Uh-huh." The four-year-old bobbed his head up and down. "And cake."

They all laughed. "I bet your mom will let you have as much cake as you'd like tonight."

"Well, I wouldn't go that far." Harley gave her brother a quelling look.

Sebastian smiled at the boy. "Daniel, can you say hello to my girlfriend, Gracie?"

Daniel looked at her with big innocent eyes, while Harley and Grant exchanged glances. She'd never thought of herself as Sebastian's girlfriend, yet it sounded right, and she wouldn't refute it. "Hi, Daniel. I like your bow tie. You sure look handsome today. Maybe you and I can have a dance later on."

Daniel wiggled his nose, as if that was an awful idea. "May...be."

Harley took her hand and pulled her into a warm embrace. "Hi, Gracie. It's pretty cool that you're dating my brother now."

"Yes, we've, uh, been on a few dates." She turned to Dr. Everett. "Hello. Nice to see you again."

"Hello, Gracie. It's good to see you, as well," he said discreetly. He was her doctor, and he must know that she'd gotten pregnant the natural way, since she hadn't gone through with the in vitro.

"Grant and I have some news," Harley said. Her eyes beamed bright and eager, as if she couldn't contain herself. "I'm not going to make a big deal of this, since it's Beth's big day, but we've decided to leave for Thailand in two weeks. We're anxious to get started on our work overseas. We just can't wait. We've told Daniel, and he's excited about having this grand adventure."

"Wow, that's pretty quick," Sebastian said. "I'm sure you'll do a lot of good over there. But we're really gonna miss you."

"Thanks. And we'll miss you all, too." Grant put his

arm around Harley's shoulder and drew his son in close. "But now is the right time for us to go."

Gracie thought their commitment to go to a foreign land to bring change to the health care of the underprivileged was such a selfless and generous undertaking.

The rest of Sebastian's siblings and their significant others circled them, along with other relatives—Miles and Chloe, Sutton and Lauren, Piper and Brian, Luke and Kelly, and Zeke and Reagan. Once again Sebastian took her hand and made sure she was included, as his date and family friend, as they wished Grant and Harley good luck on their travels.

Right after, it was announced that the ceremony was about to begin, and everyone filed outside and headed to the barn.

As she and Sebastian stepped inside the wide doors, they entered into a wedding winter wonderland. Beth had done much of this by herself, and Gracie was honestly floored by what she'd accomplished, transforming a large, rustic barn into every bride's dream. Half of the barn was set up for the ceremony, and the other half with tables and chairs ready for the reception. They walked toward their seats, separated by a snowy white aisleway.

"Wow," she said. "Beth has outdone herself here."

Sebastian gazed around and nodded. "Yes, she has."

Above them, sheets of sheer fabric swooped down from the rafters, and twinkling lights overhead softly illuminated the entire barn. Candles centered pedestals and were surrounded by greenery and red roses. The chairs were gold, with big ivory bows wrapped around their backs. It was a small private wedding with only family and close friends in attendance, and all thirty of the guests had admiring eyes as they took their seats.

Gracie was thrilled for Beth, who deserved every bit

of this happiness with Cam, the widower rancher. They would have a good life together. Gracie sighed, and Sebastian picked up on it. "What is it?"

"Nothing."

His brows rose. "No? Sounded like something."

"It's just all so beautiful. I'm happy for Beth and Cam."

"So am I." He stared at her for such a long moment that she had to turn away. Because she saw something in his eyes that worried her, something that said they could have this, too. But no, Sebastian didn't love her, and that was her bottom line. After the love and trust her parents shared, and now her good friends Lauren and Beth had found, how could she settle for anything less? How could she trust what she herself was feeling? Aside from her hormones acting up, she had pregnancy brain. It was a real thing, her friends had told her, and along with it came muddled confusion. She was beginning to believe they were right.

Gracie returned her focus to the decor and the detail Beth had put into transforming the barn. It was a much safer thing to think about. Weddings made her sentimental, and she was a big fat softy when it came to seeing a groom up at the altar awaiting his bride.

When the music from a three-piece orchestra began, everyone rose and turned. And there was Beth, her smile shining, rivaling the sparkling lights. She looked gorgeous in an understated ivory gown that flowed Cinderella-like around her. Whispered oohs and aahs from the guests filled the room. Beside Beth stood her mother, Ava, the matriarch of the family. Someone who had issues with all of her children, it seemed, but in light of recent events, was trying to make amends. She was dressed in azure blue, her thick silver hair down in a flip, the lines in her face softening as she began her walk down the aisle next to Beth.

It was an olive branch to her family, a way to show them she had their backs from now on.

Cam looked handsome in a black tuxedo and bolo tie. The good-looking rancher was the ideal match for Beth. They spoke vows to each other solemnly, but not completely void of humor. Through tears and laughter, they became husband and wife.

Sebastian squeezed her hand when the newly married couple turned to each other and sealed the deal with a kiss.

Gracie's eyes were watering, and Sebastian was there, handing her a handkerchief. She dabbed at her eyes, and then, as the minister pronounced them Mr. and Mrs. Guthrie, she applauded along with the others.

A little later on, Gracie met up with Cam and Beth at the receiving line. "Congratulations, you two!" She hugged Beth first, then Cam. "It was a beautiful ceremony."

"Thank you." Beth's eyes were misty, too. "It went just as I'd hoped."

"It sure did! And I couldn't be happier for you."

Sebastian was only a step behind, giving hugs out to his sister and shaking Cam's hand. "Good luck and congrats. Sis, you look amazing." He kissed Beth's cheek. "Love you."

"Love you, too."

Sebastian took Gracie's hand then, holding her possessively, and Beth's eyes widened. "Did you two come together?"

"Yes," Sebastian was quick to say. "We came together."

Beth's gaze met hers, and her look said, *We have to talk later.* She did owe her friend an explanation, but now was not the time. "Well, it's about time you dated someone we all like," Beth told her brother.

Sebastian only smiled and led her away. They found their dining table, one of six decorated with white linens and golden utensils. A mini chandelier hung above each of the tables, providing sparkling light overhead, and winter sprigs laced with deep red roses made for a lovely centerpiece.

"What did Beth mean when she said you were dating someone they all liked?" Gracie asked.

"It means you're very likable."

He totally avoided her question, but she was too curious to let him get away with it. "Who didn't your family like?"

Sebastian sighed and shook his head. "I guess they didn't think Rhonda Pearson and I were a good match."

"But you dated her for two years," she blurted.

His eyes widened, surprised by her knowledge apparently. "How do you know that?"

"Well, it wasn't exactly a secret. You and Rhonda made the Royal news a lot." Some of the entertainment pieces were positive, but there were other articles about them that didn't paint a rosy picture of the pair. And when Rhonda walked away from the relationship, she'd laid all the blame at his feet.

"Don't believe everything you read," he quipped.

"I try not to."

He nodded. "We had our up and downs, Rhonda and I."

"I hear she's back in town." Darn, her curiosity was getting the better of her.

Sebastian looked her square in the eye. "Is she? I wouldn't know."

"Must be hard. I mean, she broke your heart."

Sebastian made a face. "It's old news, Gracie. Let's not go there. It's my sister's wedding day and it's a happy occasion for my family."

Gracie cringed, wanting to take the conversation back. He was right. This was a happy day and she shouldn't let her insecurities about Sebastian get in the way of that. "Of course. I'm sorry." She took his hand, entwining their fingers, feeling the powerful connection. "Aren't you giving the toast soon?"

He glanced at their hands, looking pleased. "I am. Very soon."

"I can't wait to hear it."

He nuzzled her ear and brushed his lips to her throat. Something stirred in Gracie's heart. Desire, yes, they had that down pat. But it was more. The beginnings of…trust.

A short time later, Sebastian, being the eldest brother by three minutes, left the table they shared with Piper and Brian Cooper to toast the bride and groom. He sang Cam and Beth's praises, telling a few funny stories about Beth in her youth, amusing the guests. He was as charming as he was gracious and loving in his devotion to his sister. "Everyone, please raise your glass for Beth and Cam. May their lives be forever touched with happiness."

"Hear! Hear!" many of the guests chanted.

It was a beautiful moment, and Gracie, too, clinked glasses with Piper and Brian and then sipped her sparkling water.

"My nephew always knows the right thing to say." Piper's eyes beamed as Sebastian made his way back to the table. "I loved your toast," she told him.

"Yes, it was perfect," Gracie said.

Sebastian took his seat next to her again and thanked everyone. It was a little odd sitting with Brian and Sebastian's aunt Piper, Brian being Keith Cooper's nephew and all. But Brian had a hand in bringing his uncle's treachery to light, and had proven himself to be true-blue to the Wingate family. So much so he'd fallen in love with Piper, a woman eleven years his senior, and now they were a solid couple.

Gracie noticed Piper wasn't drinking champagne, either. She'd opted for sparkling water, as well. Every once in a while, Piper would put her hand on her tummy and make a face. Gracie knew that look.

Piper glanced at Brian, looking a little tentative. "I'm just a little bit…"

"It's okay." Brian took her hand and the love shining between them was truly beautiful. "We can tell them."

Piper smiled softly. "We didn't want to steal any of Beth's thunder today. We'd planned on telling the family later on, after the wedding…but I think it's okay to tell you. We're pregnant. Brian and I are having a baby."

Something flickered in Sebastian's eyes for a moment, before he caught himself and smiled. "Well, this is…" He searched for words.

"It's wonderful," Gracie filled in for him. "Congratulations, this is really great news."

"Yeah, congratulations, you two." Sebastian shook Brian's hand and leaned over to kiss his aunt's cheek. Piper was the cool, younger-minded aunt, from what Gracie could gather.

"I wasn't even sure I could have a child, but it appears sometimes miracles happen."

Brian kissed Piper's cheek. "*You're* the miracle," he said.

Gracie sensed Sebastian's eyes boring a hole in her back. They had news, too, but it would have to hold.

"I don't think Beth and Cam would mind hearing your news tonight," Sebastian said graciously.

"No." Brian shook his head. "Cam and Beth should have their day. We can wait to tell the rest of the family."

"I agree," Piper said. "I'm still getting used to the idea myself."

Gracie knew the feeling. No one had mentioned her pregnancy tonight, but she noticed inquisitive eyes watching her at times. His family was too discreet to confront her and ask questions, but what other conclusion could they come to, seeing her with Sebastian? It wasn't as if they'd ever shown interest in each other before this. And to be honest, it wasn't exactly Sebastian's style to date a pregnant woman. So yes, she supposed them being together today was cause for speculation. It was what she'd been afraid of, what she'd suspected would happen.

"Your secret is safe with us," Sebastian told Piper, glancing at Gracie.

"That's right. Our lips are sealed." Gracie zipped her fingers over her mouth.

"Thank you both," Piper said.

The three-piece orchestra took their places again, and soon music filled the barn.

"That's my cue," Brian said, rising up and taking Piper's hand. "Are you up for a dance?"

"Of course."

The two took off to the dance floor, and Sebastian rose, as well. He didn't say a word, simply put out his hand. Gracie accepted it, and they, too, walked onto the dance floor. Under soft chandelier lighting, Sebastian spun her around slowly, holding her close, keeping their bodies connected. In his arms, the complications of her life fell away and everything seemed simple and easy. There was no need for words.

The rest of the night flew by in a blur. Gracie enjoyed the dinner, the dessert and more dancing with Sebastian. And finally, once the lovely wedding reception was over, Sebastian stood on her doorstep with no uncertainty that he would be coming inside.

Gracie took him by the hand and led him up the stairs and into her bedroom, both shedding their clothing along the way.

* * *

"I love waking up with you," Sebastian whispered, taking Gracie's hand and kissing each one of her knuckles. Dawn light streamed into her window, and she remembered falling asleep naked in Sebastian's arms after quite an exciting night.

"Mmm."

"I can't seem to get enough of you," he whispered. But the cliché didn't bother her, because she shared that sentiment. Slowly but surely, her walls of fear were crumbling. She was willing to open up more, to put aside her doubts and begin to believe.

"I feel the same way," she murmured.

"You do?" He touched a hand to her thigh and began stroking. Instantly her body reacted.

"Oh…yeah."

She was spooned next to him. Her heart pounded against her chest, her insides turned to mush and every part of her she'd thought was sated was now calling out for him, craving him again.

"Gracie, is this even possible?" he asked in total awe.

"Feels like it is," she said, only half teasing.

He cupped her head and kissed her flush on the lips, hard, demanding, claiming her as his own. At least in the moment, as she went willingly, loving the taste of him as he brushed their tongues, the scent of him as she breathed him in, loving the power of him as he held her hands above her head. He made love to her with his mouth and his hands, caressing her breasts, stroking her until she could barely take any more and then dipping down to please her below the waist.

She whimpered at his touch, the way he knew exactly what drove her wild, and when he brought her to completion, he kissed her again, riding the wave with her. And then he entered her, his power tempered by her body's limits, thrusting until he couldn't take it another second. He moved with grace and potency, and all the time giving to her as much as she was giving to him.

She came down to earth along with him, both of them breathless. "Gracie." He whispered her name like a solemn oath and hugged her to his chest. "Where do we go from here?"

Wasn't that her line? Except that she was too afraid to ask, too afraid to answer. "Now I make you the best breakfast you've ever had in your life."

She broke contact and moved quickly, tossing on clothes. She was running from her emotions, and Sebastian seemed to be struggling with his patience. He wanted to lay claim to his child, just as Piper and Brian had done last night, and she was the big mean culprit holding them back. At least that was how she felt. "Breakfast will be ready in thirty."

Sebastian clunked his head against the bed frame, defeat in his eyes. "You don't have to feed me."

"I want to. And you'll be glad I did."

"I'm sure. I'm glad of most of the things you do for me."

Gracie flushed at his deep rasp, the sexy way he was looking at her. He rose from bed, stark naked. Her eyes were riveted to his ripped chest, his narrow waist. A man couldn't be more beautiful. "I'll help."

She swallowed and lifted her eyes to his. "Okay."

She turned around and headed to the kitchen. Then heard him rummaging through his clothes, his footsteps just seconds behind her.

"Have you ever had my mama's chorizo?"

His brows gathered. "No, how would I?"

"I thought maybe my papa would've brought some to your family once." She shrugged. "I guess not." She shoved a coffeepot into his hands. "Make coffee, please. I'll do the rest."

Gracie put a little butter and oil in a big cast-iron skillet, heated it up and added the chorizo, a mildly spicy variety, perfect for breakfast. Next, she tossed in day-old potatoes, cut into tiny chunks, and a cup of cooked black beans.

With the coffee brewing, she turned to Sebastian, who was sitting at the table watching her work at the stove. "It's important," she told Sebastian, "not to make a mush of this. We push the potatoes down carefully and try to fold everything together. Every family makes their own version of chorizo, with different spices and ingredients, and this is my mama's recipe." The scents rose up in a rush of steam, and she helped them along with waves of her hand. "Oh, smell that. It brings back such good memories for me."

She smiled at him. He was being sweet and she couldn't deny the incredible twenty-four hours they'd had together. "I wish I had time to make homemade tortillas. It's best with chorizo."

"Another time, maybe?"

"Yes, maybe."

A few minutes later, they took their seats and Gracie served up the meal. Sebastian gobbled up every bite. The baby craved chorizo, too, and Gracie made quite a dent in her big dish. "So good."

His gaze lowered to her plate. "I like that you eat, Gracie."

"Most people do." He was too easy to tease.

"Not all women do."

"And you know *all* women?" she murmured.

"No. But…"

"Ah, most supermodels don't eat. Is that what you meant to say?"

"I take the Fifth." He put up his hand.

Funny he should compare her to his ex-girlfriend, right after the night they'd shared.

"It's really delicious, Gracie. Thank you for making it."

"I'm glad you—"

"What are you doing tonight?" he rushed out.

She shrugged. "I don't know, other than going by The Eatery and putting in a day's work."

"Have dinner with me. I want to take you someplace nice."

In her heart of hearts, she wanted to go. She wanted to spend more time with Sebastian, but it was all happening so fast. She was spinning, and she needed to stop and get off the ride for a little while. To regroup and think. Funny how, as a teen, she'd dreamed of being swept off her feet by Sebastian, and now that it was really happening, she had to slow it down. He was using a full-court press, which at any other time or situation she'd welcome. But not now. She didn't want to be rushed. She didn't want to make a mistake. Her baby and her future were at stake, and having great sex with Sebastian was only muddying the waters. She couldn't think clearly after being with him.

"I can't tonight."

The light in his green eyes dimmed. "Why not?"

"I need…some time."

He sighed loud enough to make her shudder. His patience was running thin. "Then when?"

"Tomorrow night?"

"Fine. I'll pick you up at seven."

He walked out of the room then, without another word.

Seven

The next day, Sebastian searched the grounds of the Royal park, his eyes honing in on every person he spotted. There were joggers and people walking their dogs at a brisk pace. He also spotted two toddlers bundled up in bright blue bibbed jackets on the swings, their mother's pushes sending them flying as their squeals of laughter rang out. A lone gray-haired man sat on a bench, his arms crossed to ward off the cold.

Sebastian looked at the text message Rhonda had sent earlier today. He's playing football with his friends at the park after school.

"No, he's not," he murmured. Lonny wasn't here. There were no football players at the park. Sebastian had been here watching and waiting for the better part of an hour. He'd offered to help the boy and he thought it best to make it a chance encounter, but Lonny was a no-show. Sighing, he eyed the park perimeter one last time, making sure he hadn't missed anything. Still no sign of Lonny. He headed to the parking lot. Rhonda was there, leaning against his car, waiting for him.

"Rhonda? What are you doing here?"

Distress marred her perfect face and tears ran down her cheeks. "Lonny ditched school today, and we had a big fight and he stormed out. I can't find him anywhere. I thought maybe he'd be here. You know, with his friends. I had to come check for myself."

"I haven't seen him, Rhonda. I've been here awhile."

She broke down entirely then, her tears turning into big, heaving sobs. "I'm…sorry to involve you in this. I just don't know what to do…"

"It's okay, Rhonda. He's a little mixed up right now, but he's not a bad kid."

"I feel…like it's…all my fault." She hung her head down and Sebastian drew her into his arms. She needed a hug right now, and some compassion.

"It's not your fault, Rhonda. He's a headstrong kid. He'll come around."

Sebastian believed that. Having been orphaned at a young age, Lonny was acting out right now, a form of re-bellion at his lot in life. It wasn't easy having a supermodel sister, someone known around the world for her swimsuit layouts. "Tell you what? Let's go for a drive and try to find him together. You know where his friends live?"

She nodded. "Most of them."

"We'll start there."

"Really? You'd do that?" She smiled through her tears.

"Yes. Come on. I bet we find him before the sun goes down." Which was in just two hours, so they really had to move. "Okay?"

Rhonda cupped his face in her hands and kissed him briefly on the lips, her eyes shining with gratitude. "Thank you."

He opened the car door for her. "Get in. We're burnin' daylight."

Rhonda chuckled at his attempt at humor and got into his car. The truth was, he was worried about the kid, too. Boys at that age were reckless, at times. He and Sutton surely had been and they'd gotten into trouble more than once, but nothing like what Lonny was going through. One wrong move could change Lonny's whole life forever.

"The family's buzzing about you dating Sebastian," Sutton said, handing Gracie a cup of Lauren's special hot cocoa, a teasing smile on his handsome face. He had many of the same expressions as his twin, and sometimes it was like a sense of déjà vu being with him.

"Thanks." She warmed her hands up around the mug. They sat at a back table at The Eatery. It was their slow time, the hours between lunch and dinner, when they could all take a breather. "Buzzing how?"

Lauren tugged on her ponytail. "What do you think? They've known you and your family for years. Everyone's thrilled."

"Are they?"

Gracie was a pretty confident woman, but when it came to her place in the Wingate empire, she had her doubts. She certainly hadn't thought she'd be so welcome. Or was it the lottery win that had her in their good graces now?

"You're like family already," Sutton said.

Gracie eyed him, raising her brow.

He got the hint. "Sebastian's been happier lately."

Gracie liked hearing that from Sebastian's twin. The two brothers were incredibly close, and it was as if she was hearing it from Sebastian himself. Although they hadn't parted too happily last evening. Sebastian was losing patience with her.

"So what's on your agenda tonight?" Lauren asked. "Got a hot date with my future brother-in-law or anything?"

"Actually, I do. Soon as I finish up here, I'm going home to change."

"Where's he taking you?" her partner asked.

"I have no idea. He wouldn't say. Other than it's some-place special."

"Special is always good."

Gracie's cell phone rang and she noted the number. "Excuse me. I've got to get this," she told Lauren and Sutton. Then she walked into the office and closed the door.

"Hello, yes, this is Gracie Diaz. Thanks for calling me back."

"No problem, Ms. Diaz. This is Trudy Metcalf from the Royal Birthing Center. I understand you're interested in taking early bird classes. Congratulations, by the way, on your pregnancy."

"Thank you. Yes, I think it's about time I sign up. Although I've been reading everything I can get my hands on about having a baby."

"It's all good. How far along are you?"

"I'm about fourteen weeks now, and I'm in very good health."

"Great, we want to keep it that way. That's what our early bird classes are all about."

Gracie spent a few more minutes on the phone with Trudy, signing up for classes. Once the call was over, it was as if another step in her life's plan was finally coming together. Never mind the morning sickness or the fuller waist or the huge appetite now, signing up for childbirth classes made her pregnancy and the new life she would bring into this world a beautiful reality.

Gracie left The Eatery at five in the afternoon to get ready for her date with Sebastian. She was grateful for

Sutton's and Lauren's support. It meant a lot to her and made her feel a tad bit better about dating Sebastian. She strode into her rental home, proceeded upstairs, stripped off her clothes and stepped into a hot shower. Warmth immediately seeped into her bones, easing her tension with the help of a freshly scented lavender scrub.

After the shower, she took her time drying off, looking at the mirror to examine the subtle changes in her waist. It was a good thing and meant her baby was thriving. "Can't wait to meet you, little one," she murmured.

Gracie rummaged through her closet, looking for just the right dress for her date. Sebastian said he was taking her someplace special, and she wanted to look the part. She pulled out one dress after another, making a small mound on her bed until she hit upon just the right one. It was a creamy taupe with a plunging neckline, blending well with her skin tones, its folds draping a little past the knee. Was it too much? She'd never worn it before. But her decision was made as soon as she tried it on. The fit was perfect, and she wasn't going to be shy around Sebastian.

She fastened a thin gold choker around her neck and added hoop earrings. The look warranted a special do with her hair, so she fussed with it, coming up with a messy uplift that appeared salon-worthy.

With a few minutes to spare, Gracie sat down in the living room and called her mother. She liked to check in with her several times a week. And loved that she could now afford to give her mom and brother a good life in Florida. It meant the world to her. "Hello, Mama. It's me."

"Gracie, my heart, it's good to hear your voice. It's been a few days."

"*Si*, Mama. But just a few. How are you and our little Enrico today?"

"Our little Enrico is getting taller than your mama,"

she said. "He's well. He's out with friends right now. Nice boys. But how about you, Graciella? How is the baby?"

Her mother never could understand her need to have a baby on her own. Alisa Diaz was too traditional to think of conceiving a child any other way. And Gracie finally had confided in her mama the situation with Sebastian. Not the details, goodness no, but at least now she did know know the truth about the baby's father. And her mother was being supportive.

"We're both fine. I am feeling well, Mama. I signed up for childbirth classes."

"That's good. And Sebastian? Will he be going with you?"

"He's… I'm not sure, Mama. But we're going out on a date tonight."

"It is working out, then?"

It was hard for her mother not to push. And she understood that. Alisa simply wanted to see her daughter settled and happy. "*Si*, Mama, but we are going slow."

"How slow? You are already pregnant!"

Gracie chuckled. Her mother had a way of putting things in perspective. "You know what I mean. I want… I want what you and Papa had."

"Ah, I see." Her mother paused and then added, "So your plans have not changed? You won't be coming to Florida to live with us?"

"No, Mama, I won't. Right now, my life is here. My new estate has plenty of room for when you come to visit."

It was past seven when she ended the call. Actually, it was half an hour past, and Gracie looked at her texts to see if Sebastian had been delayed. Nothing yet.

Five minutes later, she was just about to send him a text when his message came through. I'm sorry. Something came up last minute and I have to cancel. I promise to make it up to you.

Gracie stared at the message a long time. It sounded rushed and impersonal and cold.

She texted him back. Are you okay?

She didn't receive an answer until an hour later, when he simply wrote, I'm fine.

Gracie had never been stood up before, and it hit her right in the gut. She was disappointed, for sure, and curious as to what had happened tonight to keep Sebastian from calling her beforehand. From giving her a better explanation. "All dressed up and nowhere to go, Gracie," she murmured. She kicked off her shoes, changed out of her clothes and threw on a pair of comfortable gray sweats. The night she thought was just beginning had come to a grinding and discouraging halt.

In the morning, Gracie stopped by the Texas Cattleman's Club. It was a prestigious club, generations old, that catered to rich and powerful businessmen, and now businesswomen, who lived in the vicinity and had a valued stake in Texas commerce.

Austere, with dark wood walls and furnishings, the club had gone through a bit of transformation lately. It had become more female-friendly, with brighter interiors and updated facilities. Although the old private rooms still existed, the tone of the club had totally changed. But what remained was the rule that one had to be a member or a member's guest to use the facilities. Thank goodness for Beth. She'd invited her countless times to play tennis here, to go to the day spa with her and to use the pool. But now it was her turn to become a full-fledged member, and she was especially interested in the recently updated day care center for the baby.

The receptionist at the desk recognized her. Being Royal's only mega lottery winner had some advantages. "You're Gracie Diaz."

"Yes, that's me."

"It's very nice to meet you. What can I do for you today, Ms. Diaz?"

"Well, for one, I'd like to apply to become a member of the club. I know it takes a vote, but I want to get the process started. If that's okay?"

"Yes, I think that's fine. You do know you need to be recommended, right?"

"Yes, I don't think that should be a problem." Or *would* it? She didn't come from old money. In fact, her money was as new as it could get. But those archaic notions were just that, and she was pretty sure that when Beth and Cam got back from their honeymoon, they would help her. Sebastian could, too, but she didn't want to ask him.

She was still a bit put off about being stood up last night. He'd never called. And she didn't know what to make of that.

The receptionist handed her a form to fill out and she thanked her.

"I was wondering if I could take a peek at the day care center?"

"Why, um, sure." The woman took off her glasses and set them on her desk. "I could probably take a minute to show you."

"That's great, thank you."

Boisterous laughter making its way from the hallway interrupted her thoughts. She turned and found Sebastian walking alongside a gray-haired man. The two were oblivious to anyone else, Sebastian's smile wide. Apparently, whatever crisis he'd had last night, *when he'd stood her up*, was over and done with. He looked like he didn't have a care in the world.

Then suddenly, their eyes met. And she had to give him credit—he didn't flinch or look away when he spotted her.

Instead, he bade the man farewell and headed over to her. "Gracie," he said, "what are you doing here?"

"I'm...checking out the day care center among other things."

The receptionist rose from her desk. "I was just going to show her the room, Mr. Wingate."

Sebastian's eyes lit up. "I can do that. I know where it is. I can take her."

The receptionist exchanged glances with both of them, unsure, and then the phone rang. "Excuse me, I have to get this," she said.

"We'll just be going," he told her and the woman nodded as she took the call.

Sebastian took Gracie's elbow and they walked down a corridor. "I'm so sorry about last night, Gracie. I really missed seeing you."

She stopped in her tracks. "Did you?"

"I did."

"I don't understand why you couldn't call, instead of leaving me hanging."

Sebastian looked away and hesitated. "It's a long story, Gracie." His gaze traveled the length of the hallway, a note of caution in his eyes. "I'll share it with you, but this isn't the place, Gracie. Trust me on this."

He took her hand, entwining their fingers, and the connection warmed her heart. How could one man elicit so many emotions in her? Desire, doubt, anger, joy. They were all there, simmering under the surface. "Come on, let's go check out the day care center. I promise to explain everything to you when I can."

She frowned, but he kept looking at her with those deep green eyes, penetrating her good sense, giving her hope that he had a valid explanation that would clear up her misgivings.

"Okay," she said.

"Great." He flashed her a big smile.

A minute later, they were awash in the bright colors of the day care center, blues and greens, pinks and yellows and oranges.

"Would you look at this?" Sebastian seemed to be in awe. There were five children in the center. Two little girls playing dress-up, yanking out princess costumes from a treasure chest. Three boys were on alphabet mats, messing around with miniature cars. The room was large, and there was a painting station, a reading circle and a polished wood playhouse complete with a second story for the children to frolic on.

"I'm looking," she said, taking it all in, as well.

The woman in charge walked over to them. "Hello, how can I help you?"

"We're just here to observe," Sebastian said. "For the future."

"Well, as long as you're a member, you're welcome to do that anytime. My name is Katherine. Please let me know if you have any questions."

"Of course. Thank you," Gracie said. When the day care worker walked back to the children, she put her hand on her tummy. "It's hard to believe I'll have a little one like this soon."

"*We'll* have," he corrected. "And I'm with you. It's still hard to take in."

"My mama says every baby is a little prize from God," she whispered.

Sebastian gave her hand a squeeze. "I think your mama is right."

She smiled then, and her anger ebbed. Sebastian asked for her trust. It wasn't easy to give, but for the sake of their baby, she had to try.

She had questions for the day care teacher, but they could wait. It was enough to see the place and envision her child here one day, once she became a full-fledged member of TCC. "I should go. I have other appointments."

She began walking toward the exit with Sebastian at her side. Once they reached the parking lot, he took both of her hands in his and gazed down at her. "I have a busy day, too, but I'd like to see you tonight."

She shook her head. "I'm sorry. I'm busy."

"Doing?"

"For a man who likes to keep secrets, you're awfully nosy."

"Gracie."

"Teasing, Sebastian. I'm going to meet with Tom Riley, my Realtor, later on. I'm looking for a little office space of my own."

"Is it like a date?"

Her eyes rolled. "Married, three children."

"Teasing, Gracie."

"Funny, Sebastian." She had to keep on her toes around him. He wasn't slow on the uptake at all.

"So you need office space?"

She nodded. "Yeah, I do, or I will at some point in the future." She had every intention of starting her own event-planning business. It was something she was good at and loved doing. Now that she had the means, nothing was stopping her from looking into it.

Something flickered in Sebastian's eyes at the mention of her future, but he snapped out of it pretty quickly. "How about I come over after? I owe you and want to make up for being a no-show last night."

He caught her in a weak moment and she had a pretty good idea how he was going to make it up to her. The thought sizzled in her mind and made her insides swirl with heat. "Maybe."

He chuckled. "Only *maybe*? I must be losing my touch."

"Believe me, you're not." His touch was just fine. More than just fine. And he proved it by lifting her chin with his knuckles and planting a delicious kiss on her lips.

He gazed at her then, his eyes gleaming with promise. It was really hard to concentrate after a Sebastian kiss. "Good to know," he said. "I'll call you tonight."

Sebastian rode up the elevator to the sixth floor of Wingate Enterprises, which was just outside Royal proper, and entered his executive office. He had a lot on his mind, so he really didn't see Sutton initially, not until he gazed up and found his twin at the bar pouring bourbon into two tumblers.

"Hey, what's up?" he said, removing his jacket.

"Not much, just crisis number twelve."

"Only twelve? Seems like we've weathered more storms than that lately."

Sutton set the tumbler on his desk while he sipped his own drink. "Seems that way, doesn't it? Drink up."

Sebastian gathered his brows. "Force-feeding me alcohol. This must be bad." He sipped bourbon and it warmed his throat going down.

"Not horrible, but not great, either. It seems WinJet is doing fine, and since we've concentrated on the new branding of our hotels, we're solid there. But we're still in need of some good investments to keep our other US holdings afloat."

"Okay," he said, thinking about the ramifications of that. "So we'll find some capital. Somehow."

"How? We're already maxed out. Since the scandal hit the papers, many of our investors are already on edge. They're not going to want to increase their risk any more than they have to."

Sebastian began nodding. "I get that. So what'll we do? Sell?"

"I don't want to do that. We'll lose a fortune, and honestly, some of those smaller companies are worth the trouble. They were Dad's vision and have been with us from the beginning. Jobs are at stake and people's livelihoods."

"I don't want to sell, either." Sebastian took another swig of bourbon. "Maybe we should talk to Mom about this?"

"And go into the belly of the beast?"

Sebastian laughed. "Okay, not my brightest idea. Give me a few days. I'll think of something."

"You got it." Sutton eyed his brother carefully. "So I hear Gracie's going to childbirth classes. You must be excited about that."

Sebastian set his glass down and stared at his brother. "Childbirth classes? This is the first I'm hearing about it."

"Uh-oh. Me and my big mouth. Lauren's going to punch my lights out for this."

"Lauren knows? Am I the last person to find this out?" A knot twisted in his gut. Why didn't Gracie tell him about this? He had every right to know about the classes.

"Sorry, bro. I didn't realize…"

"Not your fault. Gracie still has issues with me. She's being cautious and I get it." He picked up his bourbon and took a swallow. "Actually, I *don't* get it. We're having a baby together. I need to be there. And I don't have a clue why she wants to go this alone."

"Give it time. I mean it wasn't as if you two went about this in the conventional way. You didn't show an interest in her until you learned about the baby. That would put any woman on edge. You have to build up her trust."

"Trust? Okay. I'm rusty at all this. Haven't had a woman in my life since Rhonda."

Sutton eyed him cautiously. "I hear she's back in town."

"Yeah, she is."

Last night, Sebastian and Rhonda had searched high and low for her brother, Lonny. They'd finally found the kid, along with three other delinquent boys, a rowdy crowd if he ever saw one, just outside town.

They'd obviously been up to no good. Lonny took one look at him, and had nearly caved on the spot. Sebastian had calmed the boy down and had a heart-to-heart talk with him. Lonny had confessed to vandalizing an abandoned house, breaking windows, destroying what was left of the furniture. Sebastian had told him he had to report what he'd done to the local police. The kid had been scared, but he'd followed through, with Sebastian and Rhonda right by his side.

Luckily, Sebastian had been able to pull some strings with Judge Haymore, his TCC buddy, the one he'd been speaking to when he spotted Gracie this morning, and the police had let Lonny go with a stern warning, after extracting a promise from him to clean up the mess he'd made. It was good Sebastian had reconnected with Lonny last night, and he hoped like hell he'd gotten through to the boy.

"You guess so? Have you seen her?"

He nodded. "I have. It's not what you think."

"Good, because what I'm thinking..."

"Don't. There's nothing between Rhonda and me but friendship."

"Try to keep it that way." Sutton slapped him on the back. But already his mind had returned to Gracie, and how he could, for lack of a better term, get back in her good graces.

Eight

It ended up being an early evening after all. Tom, her Realtor, had limited spaces to show her, the inventory being low right now. And none of the three places he'd shown her would work. One was too far outside town, another was so small it gave her claustrophobia and the last one was frankly almost on top of Wingate Enterprises. Like right across the street. No can do. But at least she got an idea of what was out there.

Gracie changed into a pair of cozy pajamas, made herself a bowl of soup and put her feet up on the sofa. It was quiet in the house, and at eight thirty, it was too early to go to sleep. For the next thirty minutes, she channel-surfed her flat screen, unable to find anything on TV she wanted to watch. Gracie sighed. She was antsy and restless, which she couldn't figure out since she'd had a full day today. Her cell phone rang, and she rose from the sofa to answer it.

"Hello."

"Hi, it's me." The low drawl of Sebastian's voice made her heart skip a beat.

"Hello, you. I didn't think you'd call. It's late." Actually, it wasn't all that late, but she wasn't going to make this easy for him.

"I wanted to give you time to finish up with your Realtor. How'd it go?"

"Not too well, but I'm sure I'll find something."

"That's too bad. So what are you doing right now?"

"Right now, just relaxing, or at least trying to."

"Ready for bed?"

"Maybe."

"Before you go, can you open the front door?"

Her pulse began to pound. "Open the front door? Why?"

"You'll see."

She walked over to the window and peered out. Sebastian's car was parked in front of her house. Oh, God! What was he doing here? She was a total mess, covered in soft flannel, her hair in a ponytail, her makeup all washed off. Gracie really didn't want him to see her like this, but then, how could she send him away? She sighed, straightened out her pj's, finger-combed her hair and opened the door slowly. And came face-to-face with a big gray stuffed elephant. With pink ears. And then she noticed a bag filled with chocolate raspberry sticks. Not the gourmet kind, and not in a fancy box, but her very favorite from the grocery store. There were flowers, too, a bouquet of at least two dozen roses in various shades of red, from crimson-tipped to bloodred. Behind all that was the man, his face hidden until he peeked out from behind the elephant. "Hi."

Gracie couldn't believe it. "What is all this?"

"An apology for last night. And if you're not up for company, that's okay. I'll just leave this all with you."

"For heaven's sake, Sebastian. Come inside." She ushered him inside the house and they stood looking at each other, his eyes gleaming.

"An elephant?" she asked.

"You have a collection of them, right?"

Oh, wow. How did he find all this out? He knew about her elephant obsession as a kid. He knew her favorite candy. The man had done his homework. "Right."

She took the elephant off his hands and admired it. It was plush and soft and cuddly. "Is this for the baby?"

"It's for you. The baby will have its own parade of animals."

And then there was silence, an awareness between them that sizzled as they stared at each other. Sebastian set the flowers and candy down. "I can go. But I don't want to."

She didn't want him to leave, either. "Stay."

He gave her a heart-stopping smile. "That's all I needed to hear."

Then he pulled her close, his lips claiming hers, hot and hungry and utterly delicious. One kiss became two and then three, and soon Sebastian had her back against the wall, cupping her face in his big, strong hands, making love to her mouth in a frenzy that stole her breath. She was awash with emotion, with crazy desire, and wanted to touch all of him. Wanted to feel his skin under her fingertips. She pulled at his jacket and then his shirt, unable to get to him fast enough between kisses.

He helped her tug off his shirt and toss it away. She stroked his bare chest, loving the feel of his power under her fingertips, loving the heat of his body, feeling his growing desire below his waist. He groaned in pleasure, telling her he loved what she was doing to him.

It was easy for him to find her skin, his hands slipping under her pajama top, pushing up the material, cupping her breasts and thumbing the hardened peaks. "Oh, man," he whispered in her ear. "You're perfect."

It was all too fevered and crazed, as if time was running out, as if they were in some sort of passionate race. Sebastian's kisses made her dizzy, her body pliant in his arms. And so when he slipped his hand along her tummy and then dipped below her navel, separating her pajama pants from her skin, she opened her mouth at the pleasure and moaned his name. "Sebastian."

"I know, sweetheart," he whispered, his fingertips touching her very core. She moaned again and again as he stroked her there, while kissing her lips, touching their tongues. Her release came quickly, hard, loud and fast as she cried out, the immense pleasure splintering her into a thousand pieces.

It was hot and heavy and so very, very good. She was in deep now. Her hard, outer shell cracking, melting, crumbling. She wasn't sure that was enough. But a man who could make her wild like this, who sparked emotions in her that no one ever had, a man who seemed to know her inside and out, was a difficult one to turn away. She was afraid she was falling in love with him.

Sebastian lifted her into his powerful arms and carried her to the bedroom. He knew the way now, and there was comfort in that, that maybe he belonged right where he was. Then he lowered her onto the bed, and she wasn't shy about removing her clothes, then removing what remained of his.

He was beautiful to look at, especially in his aroused state, tall and tanned and broad-shouldered. And his end-of-the-day facial scruff only made him look more devastatingly handsome.

"Gracie," he said, coming over her. "There's never been anyone like you before."

She smiled, her heart warm, filled with love. "I feel the same way."

His eyes beamed bright, right before he joined their bodies. She cooed at the familiar, welcome feel of him and he sighed, as if…he was coming home.

Sebastian lay on Gracie's bed, watching the beauty beside him sleep. She had been resistant, until tonight. Something seemed to have changed in her. He noticed her giving a little bit more, opening up to the possibility of the two of them. Maybe she was starting to trust in him, trust in *them* as a couple?

Hell, it was all confusing. But he wanted what they were experiencing to continue. He wanted their relationship to grow. Yet, at the same time, he wasn't going to overthink this. Too much was at stake. As hard as it was, he was going to try to let things evolve naturally. Gracie couldn't be pushed. He didn't want her to shy away or run scared.

He stroked her head, pushing aside a few stray strands of hair as she slept. It was dawn now, the light streaming into the room, telling him the world was waking up. So was he. He rose from the bed quietly and looked at the time. It was just after 6:00 a.m. and it was time for a shower and a cup of coffee.

Sebastian showered first, dressing again in yesterday's clothes. He'd have to stop by home and pick up a change of clothes. And then a thought struck. How nice would it be to move in with Gracie, have his stuff here, so that they could be together every day?

He scoffed at the notion. She would never go for that. They weren't there yet, but maybe one day they would be. Maybe one day she'd trust him enough to tell him about the classes she'd signed up for. It really bugged him that she'd shut him out of that part of her life so far.

In the kitchen, Sebastian made coffee, and as it brewed, he scavenged around to find something to make for breakfast. He wasn't a great cook, but he could scramble eggs and fry up some bacon. She had turkey bacon, a healthier alternative to the real thing. He got those things started and then poured two glasses of orange juice.

Gracie stumbled into the room, looking groggy, her hair disheveled and her pajama top wrinkled. He had never seen anything more adorable. "Mornin', sweetheart."

She smiled and walked straight into his arms. It was such a pleasant surprise he didn't know what to do with his hands at first, but then he gently wrapped them around her.

"Good morning to you, too." Gracie laid her head on his chest, snuggling into him, and a delicious warmth traveled through his body.

"How did Sleeping Beauty sleep last night?"

She choked back a laugh. "I'm no beauty. I'm a mess."

He hugged her tighter. "Not from where I'm standing. You look cute."

She groaned. "Ugh."

"I'm making breakfast," he announced. As if she couldn't tell by the pungent smell of bacon cooking and coffee brewing. "Are you hungry?"

She turned her face up to gaze into his eyes. "A little. I need a shower first."

"Go, I'll finish up in here. And then I'll serve you."

"You really don't have to do that. But thanks." She broke from their embrace and turned to leave.

"Hey?" he called to her. "You okay?"

She faced him, gathering her brows as if he'd asked a silly question. "I'm...perfect. You said so yourself last night."

"I meant every word."

"Yeah," she said with a tilt of her head. "I think you did."

She left the room with a whimsical smile on her face and Sebastian felt a stirring deep in his belly. It was a good feeling, like the moment he'd spot his presents under the tree on Christmas morning. Suddenly, he could imagine a lifetime of waking up next to Gracie. He welcomed the thought and wondered if they'd ever get there.

"I feel human again," Gracie said a short time later, returning to the kitchen dressed in a tailored pair of slacks and a deep rose sweater. Her hair was still a little wet, the dark locks in a natural part to the side. Her complexion was flawless, her skin smooth. Pregnancy had bloomed on her and he could only smile at her.

"Human and all woman," he replied with a wink. "Come sit down. Breakfast is ready."

"So you're really serving me?" She took a seat.

"Of course. But don't judge me too harshly, sweetheart. I'm not a great cook."

"Because you never had to cook for yourself. You always had someone do it for you."

She said it good-naturedly and he didn't take offense. "I did, up until recently, when my world crashed around me. Hey, I'm not playing the victim here, just so you know. I'm grateful for everything I've ever had in my life."

"Humble, I like that."

"I think you like *me*, too, a little."

She picked up her orange juice and took a sip. "Maybe."

"I just get a maybe? I thought after last night, I'd be a little higher up the scale than that."

She blushed, a full rosy color reaching her cheeks. "Well, the elephant was a nice touch."

Sebastian let out a chuckle. Damn, it was hard getting her to give an inch verbally, but he still thought they were making great progress in the bedroom. What they had there was scalding hot and delicious and that meant something staggering. "Let's eat."

She put her head down to gaze at her food. "And yes, if you must know, I like you, a little." Then she picked up her fork triumphantly and dug into the meal.

Sebastian only shook his head at her.

A week later, Gracie walked into The Eatery during the six o'clock dinner hour and made her way into the kitchen. She'd spent the better part of the afternoon with Tom Riley searching for the right office space for her event business and so far, she wasn't having any luck finding the right space in the right location.

Lauren was at the workstation, overseeing the dishes being brought out for the customers. She glanced over her shoulder and they made eye contact. "Hey, what are you doing here? Thought you had a hot date with Sebastian again. It's been like four nights in a row."

"Five, but who's counting," she said. "And we did have a date, but he canceled at the last minute."

"Oh, sorry to hear that. It happens sometimes." Lauren wiped her hands on a dish towel and walked over to her. "The Wingate twins are notorious for their work ethic. I bet something came up that he couldn't get out of."

"Maybe, but he's canceled twice this week, and I wouldn't mind, but he's very cryptic about why he's canceling. And then apologizes like crazy."

Lauren walked over to her and gave her shoulders a squeeze. "It's not too busy right now and I'm ready for a break. Let's go into the lounge and have a bite to eat. I'd say let's go for drinks, but—" she gazed at Gracie's belly and winked "—that'll have to wait. C'mon, girlfriend, let's sit down and talk. There's a Tex-Mex pizza with our names on it. I'll bring it over."

And just a short time later, Gracie was biting into a pip-ing hot pizza smothered with cheese and veggies, topped with Tabasco sauce and jalapeños. She looked across the table at Lauren. "Hmm, so good."

"It's getting to be a customer favorite." Lauren bit into her pizza and chewed. "This just might be marginally bet-ter than anything Sebastian had in store for you tonight."

Gracie nearly choked on her food and then managed, "Could be."

Lauren smiled, and then she took on a thoughtful ex-pression. "You know, I think Sebastian has a lot on his mind. He and Sutton are worried about their cash flow. They have over a dozen companies that are struggling. It's not public knowledge, Gracie. Maybe that's what he's working on. Sebastian probably doesn't want to bore you with his problems. I mean, you two are on the honeymoon side of dating."

Gracie stared at her friend, her mind spinning. She thought the money the Wingates received from the sale of the house had put them over the top. "Are you saying Wingate Enterprises still needs money?"

Lauren nodded, lowering her voice. "Yes, except for the hotels and WinJet, Wingate Enterprises could use an influx of cash. At least, that's what Sutton tells me. And this is just between you and me."

She nodded. "Of course. Thanks for telling me. I won't say a word to anyone."

Gracie could keep a secret, but she only wished Sebas-tian had confided in her. Why hadn't he? Was it pride? She fought to put off the other places her mind was going.

He needs money for his company.

I have money.

Gracie didn't want to go here. She didn't want to think that Sebastian was using her to get his hands on her money.

"Hey," Lauren said, as if reading her mind. "Sebastian really cares about you. You have to know that by now. He's one of the good guys, Gracie."

Gracie smiled. She was starting to believe that. This past week, they'd had a great time together. The two of them were growing closer, and they were learning new things about each other every day. She wasn't thinking about the way they burned up the sheets, though that was off-the-charts good. It was more, and she saw it in Sebastian's eyes whenever he looked at her.

"I had my doubts about Sutton and that whole mess with the dating mix-up and Sebastian," Lauren confided. "I thought Sutton was tricking me and lying to me…and it was all so confusing. But when it's meant to be, it finally comes together. I sense that with you and Sebastian. Even if you don't see it yet."

"Maybe I'm beginning to."

"Then trust what you're feeling, Gracie. Open up your heart. Let him in."

The thought of opening her heart to Sebastian wasn't novel. Heavens, she'd dreamed of him for years, and now all of her fantasies were coming true. He was the man she'd been attracted to at the masquerade ball. And the father of her child, the man who'd earned her trust. Perhaps it was time to finally accept that. Maybe, against all odds, she was meant to love and be loved by Sebastian. "Thank you, Lauren. I always feel better after I talk to you."

"That's what friends are for."

She was grateful for Lauren's friendship. She reached over to take the other woman's hand. "I'm glad we're friends."

Lauren nodded. "Me, too. I mean, who knows, maybe one day we'll be more than friends. I mean, it'll be cool if all the stars align, and you and I become family. As in sisters-in-law."

And she was amazed Lauren's notion didn't send her into an immediate tizzy.

It felt sort of…right.

The next day, Gracie made an unannounced visit to Sebastian's office. She had a song in her heart as she rode the elevator to the sixth floor of the building and got off. The receptionist greeted her from behind her half-moon-shaped glass desk. "Hello, how can I help you?" the woman asked.

Behind her, the Wingate Enterprises sign, carved out of teak, shone with a glowing polish. Everything in this building spoke of contemporary design and success.

"I'm here to see Sebastian Wingate."

The woman looked at her computer. "Do you have an appointment?"

"No, but if you tell him that Gracie Diaz is here to see him, he might find time."

The woman smiled. "I will do that." She buzzed in, and announced just that.

She could hear Sebastian on the other end. "Please show her in, Lois."

"Right this way." The receptionist had only taken a few steps toward the wide double doors to her left when Sebastian flung them open and spotted her. "Gracie! This is a surprise."

"A good one, I hope." Lois put her head down and Sebastian grinned.

"Thanks, Lois. I'll take it from here. Hold my calls, please."

And then he reached for her hand and tugged. "Come in. Is everything all right?" He shut the doors behind them.

Gracie laughed. "Everything's fine."

"Okay, great." He nodded his head. "It's good to see you."

"It's good to see you, too." His eyes sparkled and she had a good idea hers did, too, as they stared at each for a few long seconds.

Then instinct took over and Sebastian reached for her, just as she reached for him. And the kiss they shared was more than the meeting of their lips—it was a welcome, an invitation, a promise. Sebastian broke off the kiss but hugged her so tight she thought she'd burst from joy. "This made my day," he whispered in her ear. "Seeing you was just what I needed."

"Really? Are you having a bad day?"

"It's better now that you're here." He kissed her again and tenderly brushed a few locks of hair away from her face. The way he touched her, the way he looked at her, brought ribbons of warmth to her heart. Finally, in his arms, she felt safe and maybe a little bit loved.

Maybe Lauren was right, maybe Sebastian didn't want to burden her with his work problems, because he never really brought the subject up. "I didn't want to interrupt you if you were busy, but I took a chance at coming here."

"I'm glad you did."

She broke away from him to look around his office. "So this is where you spend a lot of your time."

"Some days, yes."

She peered out the window, and from the sixth story, she had a breathtaking view of blue skies above and the town of Royal below laid out before her. "Only some days? What do you do the other days?"

"Have meetings with bankers, and lawyers, and politicians."

Gracie made a face.

"I know, it's no fun. But sometimes, I get to see a beautiful woman, and it makes it all worth it."

Gracie spun around and stared into his eyes. "Really?"

"You have to know, seeing you is the best part of my day and…night."

She didn't know. But she was beginning to. And that made her heart open up wider, letting him in, loving him even more than she thought possible.

"I do have a reason for this visit."

"You do? You mean it wasn't just to put a happy face to my day?"

She smiled. "What are you doing on Saturday morning?"

He gave her a puzzled look and shook his head. "I don't know. Seeing you?"

"I need a partner for my early bird classes, and I—"

"Yes." He took the steps to bridge the gap between them quickly. "Yes. I'm your partner, Gracie. I wouldn't miss it."

He put a hand on her tummy, something he'd done many times before in the heat of passion. But this time was different; this caress meant more. She was finally putting her faith in him, letting go of her doubts and tearing down the walls that had kept her from trusting him.

"You have no idea how much this means to me. I want this, Gracie. I want more with you."

"I think I do know," she whispered back. "I want that, too."

Sebastian took her into his arms again and kissed her tenderly. "I can't wait for Saturday now."

"Neither can I."

Gracie sat cross-legged on a yoga mat in the Pregna-Gym at the birth center, Sebastian by her side, as the childbirth instructor introduced herself. "Hi, I'm Maddy, and first of all I want to say congratulations! This is an exciting time in your lives and I'm honored to be a part of it. We'll be together for the next four weeks, getting your mind and body ready to welcome your child into the world. Now, if we can go around the room and find out who you are and what brought you to this class..."

Several couples introduced themselves. When it was Gracie's turn, knowing eyes gazed at her and Sebastian, as if introductions were not necessary. She was the millionaire lottery winner in Royal, and he was one of the most eligible, recently scandalized, bachelors in Maverick County, a Wingate no less. "I'm Gracie, and I want to learn everything there is to know about having a healthy pregnancy and doing what's right for the baby. This is my coach, Sebastian."

Sebastian smiled to the group.

There were six couples in all sitting in the circle, and after the introductions were made, the instructor passed out a workbook and asked them to take a few minutes to look it over. Gracie shared the workbook with Sebastian, and quietly they turned the pages, heads together, seeing a whole new world opening up before them.

"This is surreal," Sebastian whispered. "In a good way."

"I know. Like, in less than six months, the baby will be here."

Sebastian laid his hand over her wrist and gave a squeeze. "Are you scared?"

"A little." Then she faced him. "I've been wanting a baby for so long, but I have to admit it is a bit daunting."

"I'll be with you every step of the way."

She nodded, grateful for his support, noticing wandering gazes landing on them from around the circle. "I think we've been recognized," she said under her breath.

"I think so, too. Are you okay with it?" he asked.

"I guess I have no choice now. But yes, I'm okay."

Sebastian's eyes flickered and his approval was written

all over his face. He kissed her cheek, a sweet little kiss that packed quite a punch. "Me, too."

"Okay, class, now it's time to get our bodies in shape for the athletic event of childbirth. The more work we do now, hopefully the less labor you'll have later. So today, we're going to learn exercises that will tone your bodies and stretch your muscles. But before you do that, grab a pen or pencil, go to the back of your workbook and write down everything you ate yesterday."

The women in the group groaned.

"I know, I'm catching you off guard. And that's the point," Maddy told them. "We're going to get you on the right track with nutrition, too. But that's next week's class. Oh, and be honest, jot down everything you ate, even those chocolate brownies you had yesterday," she said. "I won't judge. I'm here to help."

The class, which was supposed to last an hour and a half, went quickly. Gracie was almost sorry it was over. She'd learned a lot, and actually felt a camaraderie with the others in the class.

"See you next week," one of the guys said to Sebastian. During the break, they'd bonded over football.

"Yeah, see ya."

Sebastian grabbed her yoga mat and took her hand. They walked over to the instructor. "Thank you," Gracie said. "It's a very informative class. I learned a lot."

"*We* learned a lot," Sebastian clarified.

The instructor shifted her gaze from her to Sebastian and smiled. "That's nice to hear. There's a lot to learn in a short time, and I'm afraid it can be overwhelming at times."

"Pregnancy is overwhelming. Period," Gracie admitted.

"You'll do fine. You have a good coach helping you.

My number is in the workbook," Maddy said. "Call if you have any questions about the exercises or anything so far."

"Oh, we will," Sebastian assured her.

"Thanks again," Gracie said.

Once they were outside, Sebastian rubbed his stomach. "I think all these exercises made me hungry."

"Made *you* hungry?" She swatted his arm. "I did all the work!"

"Hey, it's not easy being the coach."

She chuckled, loving that she and Sebastian could finally have some light moments. "Are you complaining?"

"Never," he said, drawing her close. "Being by your side and helping you is my most important job."

Her head tilted to the side. "Really?"

"Yes, never doubt that."

As he leaned in, the deep green flecks in his eyes mesmerized her. And then his hands were cupping her face, his lips claiming hers. She fell into the kiss, right there in front of the birthing center, with cars driving by, for all the world to see.

Suddenly, she felt free, liberated from her doubts and fears.

Sebastian was her life, her future. She couldn't ask for more. And it dawned on her then how much she loved him, how much she needed him in her life.

She circled her arms around his neck. "How would you like to marry me?" Once the words were out, suddenly, she wanted nothing more.

"You want me to…to—"

She nodded. "Marry me."

Sebastian's eyes grew wide, and he backed away. She'd never seen that particular look on his face before, a mixture of disbelief and horror. As if this was the last thing on his mind, the last thing he wanted. And, oh, boy, she hadn't seen this coming. Not at all. Had she misread everything?

"Oh, God. I've shocked you."

"No, yes… I mean…"

Her eyes welled with tears. Sebastian didn't want her. He didn't love her. She'd misread all the signs. Once again, she was that little girl on the outside, looking in. The woman who'd never quite be good enough for a Wingate, regardless of her big lottery win. She was only little Gracie Diaz, daughter of an immigrant ranch worker, someone not in his class, despite everything she'd accomplished in her life. All her innermost fears were coming true, slapping her in the face, breaking her heart.

"Never mind," she said, turning and walking away.

"Gracie, wait."

"Sebastian, please stay where you are. Don't you dare follow me. I can and will take care of myself."

"You're mad and I'm sorry. I…uh…"

"I am not mad," she called over her shoulder, making a dash to her car. She was *humiliated*. How could she have been such a fool to think that Sebastian had fallen in love with her? He'd never said as much—he'd never actually confessed any true feelings for her at all. She'd only presumed. And what a faulty presumption that had been! All the while, he was only interested in the baby. He wanted to insure a place for himself in the baby's life, not hers. "Just leave me alone."

She picked up her pace, leaving him standing there, her dream man now her worst nightmare.

Gracie wiped at her teary eyes, unable to control her emotions tonight. She was confused and conflicted about what had happened earlier. Once she settled at her house, she made a cup of hot cocoa, got comfortable on the sofa and began to rethink things. It was remotely possible she'd overreacted with Sebastian today. He'd been calling and texting, but she wasn't ready to speak to him yet, and she figured, knowing him, that he just might show up on her doorstep tonight.

She didn't want that. It was the *last* thing she wanted. Not while she was so confused.

Maybe she'd sprung her proposal on him too soon. Just because she'd been sure of her feelings, it didn't mean that in that very moment, he was ready to make the same commitment. She'd been pushing him away almost all along, and then, suddenly, she'd done an about-face and decided she wanted to get married. She shook her head, trying to grasp the truth as the pain of his rejection gnawed away at her.

When the doorbell rang, she was both angry and hopeful. Maybe Sebastian had an explanation as to why he'd reacted that way and just maybe some of the blame could be from her highly emotional state. Had her hormones tripped to the moon and was she finally coming down to earth?

She wiped at her eyes again and went to the door.

And was taken totally by surprise, finding Lauren on her doorstep. "Lauren," she said, looking past her, seeing if anyone was with her. Her friend was alone and looking quite distraught.

"You've been crying," Lauren said. "I'm sorry. I ran over here as soon as I heard."

"You heard? Did Sebastian tell you what happened today?"

"Sebastian didn't say a word. I saw it on the news tonight." Lauren wrapped her arms around her, hugging her tight. "I'm sorry. I'm sure there's a good explanation."

Gracie backed away. "You saw what on the news? I only just proposed to Sebastian this morning. How—"

"You *proposed*? That I didn't know. Oh, honey," she said, taking her hand. "Let's sit down."

Lauren tugged her over to the sofa in the living room and both took a seat.

"Are you going to tell me what you're talking about?"

"Maybe it's better if I showed you." Lauren took a tablet out of her purse and clicked a few times. "There's no easy way to explain this…so brace yourself."

Gracie trembled in anticipation. Lauren's expression alone was enough to make her shake with nerves. She bit her lip and gazed at the screen that loaded on the nightly news site. Under the entertainment and lifestyle section, there was Sebastian with his ex-girlfriend, supermodel Rhonda Pearson, in an embrace. The two looked very comfortable in each other's arms. And the next picture was of her and Sebastian, coming out of the birthing center, Sebastian holding her hand and her yoga mat. The headline read: "Wingate Love Triangle? Supermodel or Lottery Winner?"

Gracie's eyes traveled to the text below the photos and she whispered the words as she read them.

"With Wingate Enterprises still struggling, is Sebastian Wingate charming both mega wealthy women into investing in his company? Or is it true love? Which diva owns his heart? His ex-girlfriend, world-famous supermodel Rhonda Pearson, or his apparent baby mama, lottery winner and entrepreneur Gracie Diaz? Either way, Wingate is bound to come out a winner."

Gracie gasped as tears trickled down her face. She was numb, too stunned to feel anything at the moment. Her mind was spinning, and suddenly everything was beginning to make sense. Sebastian standing her up. Sebastian canceling dates at the last minute. Sebastian looking shocked when she proposed to him.

He wasn't at all the man she thought him to be. "I've been such a fool."

Lauren took her hand and squeezed. "It looks bad, Gracie. But I know Sebastian, and he's not capable of doing this to you."

"He's already done it, Lauren. Don't you see? He never wanted me. He wants his baby and his ex-girlfriend. He wants to have it all. And I can't figure out who's worse—him for betraying me and leading me on, or me, for believing I wasn't good enough for him. All my life I felt like I'd never fit into his world. My father worked for the family. He was loyal and dedicated, but he knew his place. I guess I didn't get that gene, because for just a while lately, I was beginning to believe that I was worthy of love, worthy of a Wingate. Now I see how wrong I've been. I'm not only worthy of Sebastian Wingate, I'm far better off without him."

Tears continued to stream down her face.

Lauren squeezed her hand tight. "Gracie, of course you're good enough for Sebastian. There was never any doubt, but I hate that you're writing him off without getting an explanation from him."

"How do you explain the photo, then? Look at them together. He doesn't look like a man who's ready to commit to another woman."

"Gracie, I'm so sorry this happened."

"S-so…am… I." She put her hand over her tummy and thought of the baby she was to have. Sebastian's child. Her heart shattered at the realization that this child wouldn't have the comfort and security of a real family unit. Originally, she'd wanted to have the baby alone, to raise her child as she saw fit. But when Sebastian entered into the picture, she'd started to believe they could become a true family. That dream was way out of her reach now.

She sighed deeply, trying to hold tight to her emotions,

but her tears flowed freely and she couldn't stop them. The ache inside was greater than anything she'd experienced before.

"The a-article s-says that Wingate Enterprises is still h-having money troubles. You and I have talked about this, but I thought maybe things had gotten better...since, since Sebastian never once mentioned it to me."

Lauren shook her head. "Don't think it, Gracie. Sebastian wouldn't use you that way."

Her heart broken, Gracie didn't agree. "Apparently, the news report says differently."

A pounding at her door startled them both. Lauren rose to peer out the window. "It's him," she said. "Sebastian is here."

"I don't want to talk to him."

"Are you sure, honey?"

"I'm sure. I can't, not tonight." Maybe never. "I'm too upset."

"He's a hard one to say no to, but I'll try."

"I don't want to see him or hear his voice now. I'll be in the kitchen."

"Okay, I'll deal with him."

Gracie rose up on wobbly legs and went into the kitchen. She slumped in the chair and waited. A few moments later, she heard muffled sounds from the front door, but thankfully she couldn't make out what they were saying. A long time passed and finally Lauren entered the kitchen. "He's gone. It took some doing. I finally used the baby card, telling him your stomach is already upset and seeing you might jeopardize the baby's health. That got him to leave."

"Good. Thank you."

"He's really hurting, too, Gracie. He says none of it's true."

"What else could he say?"

"He asked me to make sure you're all right. He's genuinely concerned."

For the baby. Not her. The fact remained that he seemed totally horrified when she'd asked him to marry her. That pain just added to the humiliation of seeing him with his ex, of the entire county seeing her in that light. Of basically announcing to the world that Sebastian was the true father of her baby.

How could she forgive any of that?

Lauren began opening cupboards, looking for things. "What are you doing?"

"I'm going to make you some herbal tea. And you need to eat something. I bet you haven't put anything in your stomach for most of the day."

"You'd be right. But I don't think I can eat a morsel right now."

"Tea, then. And I'll make you some soup. If you're hungry later, it'll be waiting for you."

"Thanks, tea sounds good."

Lauren made herself comfortable in the kitchen. It came second nature with her, and there was no doubt whatever she made would turn out delicious. "Thanks for staying with me. I really appreciate it."

"Of course. I'm not leaving until you feel better."

"Oh, then you'll be taking up permanent residency?"

Lauren's shoulders slumped and sympathy filled her eyes.

"I'm sorry. Bad joke. I'll be okay. I just have to…to… I don't know." She sighed. After being with Sebastian these last few weeks, she'd grown so much closer to him. They'd gone beyond the physical. Great sex was one thing, but she thought they'd really made a connection in other ways. They'd had fun together and had a possible future to look forward to. And she'd finally allowed herself the freedom to fall in love with him. That was what hurt the most, the betrayal of her trust. When it had been the hardest thing for her to give.

When the tea was ready and a delicious-smelling vegetable soup was simmering on the stovetop, Lauren took a seat at the table, handing her a teacup. It was a cinnamon-spicy blend perfect for winter and warmed her throat going down. "This is good."

"Hmm. It is."

"Lauren?"

"Yeah?"

Gracie steadied her breathing, trying to calm herself down. "What can you tell me about Sebastian's relationship with Rhonda?"

"Well, I don't know much really. Sutton said that it wasn't what it seemed. But Sebastian's pretty closed-mouth about his relationships."

"Do you think Rhonda broke his heart?"

"That, I honestly don't know," Lauren admitted. "It's something you could find out, when you're ready to speak to Sebastian again."

A lump rose to Gracie's throat. "Will I ever be ready?"

"Well, you're having his child, so I would think at some point you're going to have to be, but you don't have to think about that now. Just sip your tea and try to relax."

"I'll try."

But Gracie knew sleep would be a long time coming tonight. Her heart ached and she didn't figure that was going to get better anytime soon.

Sebastian was up half the night, pacing the floor, wearing out the rug, as his mother would say. He sipped bourbon straight up, too anxious to sleep, too keyed up to think about anything but Gracie and how she was feeling.

Tonight, when he'd gone to Gracie's house, Lauren had laid down the law. Gracie didn't want to hear from him; she didn't want to see him. And how could he blame her? He'd lied to her, omitted the truth and subsequently destroyed the relationship they'd been building. She'd actually proposed to him, and it had taken him by total surprise. He'd reacted badly, and he didn't think he'd ever get the hurt look on Gracie's face out of his head.

But he hadn't hurt her on purpose, damn it, and he was innocent of the claims the news reports had made. There was no love triangle. He *loved* Gracie. And it'd taken him losing her to figure out just how much she meant to him. Suddenly it was all clear, but she wouldn't believe him now if he declared his love.

Rhonda wasn't back in his life, and the innuendo that he was using either woman to bankroll his business had struck him right between the eyes. Nothing was further from the truth. But how could he ever convince Gracie of that?

When his cell phone rang at midnight, he had an iota of hope it was Gracie. But his hope was stifled the second Rhonda's image appeared on his screen. He let it ring a few times, and then finally picked up.

"I'm so sorry," she said immediately.

This wasn't her fault. Other than the fact that she was world-famous and always had some sort of paparazzi following her if they sniffed out a story. But he should've realized that. He should've known that would be the case. Even in Royal. "I had no idea I was being followed. I only wanted to help Lonny, Sebastian. I never meant to hurt you."

"I know that, Rhonda. And I wanted to help him, too. My mistake is that I wasn't honest with Gracie."

"You really care about her, don't you?" she asked softly.

"Yeah, and she's not talking to me right now."

"She's having your baby. I guess I should say congrat-ulations. There's no doubt you'll make a great father, Se-bastian."

"Thanks," he said. "But right now I have to figure out a way to gain Gracie's trust."

"Let me know if I can help in any way."

He didn't think bringing Rhonda into this would help. It could possibly make things worse. No, he had to do this on his own. But first he had to get Gracie to talk to him.

Nine

Gracie lay low for the next few days. She didn't want to see anyone, and she certainly didn't want to do an interview. News vans had parked outside her house for two days, but by the third day, they'd found the next new big scandal and left. Thanks to Sebastian and his lies, she'd been like a prisoner in her own home. The flowers he sent every day had been returned, the notes went unopened. Sebastian continued to text her, continued to clog up her voice mail with messages, until finally, because he'd given her no choice, she decided to confront him.

On Friday morning, she put her long dark hair up in a ponytail, and tossed on a ball cap and sunglasses. Wearing jeans and a big bulky sweater and no makeup, she got into her car, making sure no one was following her, and drove to Sebastian's office on the outskirts of town.

She parked in the large parking lot and sat there, determined to set him straight, make her point and get away from him as quickly as possible. But her heart still ached, and it was difficult to make the move, difficult to get out of the car.

"You're doing the right thing, Gracie," she whispered to herself. She had to put the future she'd always dreamed about out of her mind. Had to make a clean break. Sebastian would be free to date anyone he wanted. She'd make that clear, too. Just thinking of the humiliating photos and articles written about her gave her the incentive she needed to get out of the car and march toward Sebastian's office. As luck or fate would have it, she was nearing the building when she heard her name called from behind.

"Gracie? Is that you?"

She turned to find a blonde-haired, green-eyed Wingate approaching. For a second, she thought it was Sutton, but as he strode closer, she knew it was definitely not him. She'd learned the tiny nuances that other people usually didn't notice to determine it was Sebastian.

He seemed glad to see her, his eyes so very green at the moment, his handsome face filled with hope. A less determined woman might just melt on the spot, but she wouldn't allow that to happen. If she had to confront Sebastian in the parking lot, so be it.

She acknowledged him with a nod.

"Gracie, I've been trying to reach you for days."

"I guess I didn't want to be reached, Sebastian."

"I'm sorry about this whole mess. If you'll let me explain, I'll—"

"I don't want to hear your explanations, Sebastian. I doubt I'd believe them. I only came here to tell you we're through. You can stop sending flowers and notes. They don't mean anything to me." She took a breath, watching the light dim in his eyes, watching his demeanor change instantly.

"You're not even going to hear me out?" he rasped.

"Are you saying you didn't lie to me countless times?"

"I—I… Okay I did, but for a good reason."

"There's no reason that's good enough for me," Gracie said adamantly. "I'm sorry. I don't want to see you anymore. I think it's best this way."

"It's *not* best. You can't break up with me like this. You have to be reasonable and allow me to explain."

His voice held an edge, as if he was barely holding on to his anger. She knew why he was so upset, aside from being caught in the act. It was because of the baby. He wanted an heir, his own flesh and blood, but he didn't want her. Sebastian had never claimed to love her. He'd rebuffed her marriage proposal almost instantly, making her feel unworthy yet again. And worst of all, he may have pursued her solely for her money.

She lifted her chin, more determined now to make things clear. "I won't get in the way of you seeing the baby, Sebastian. I'm not that cruel. You'll have generous visitation rights. The child should know its father. We'll work something out between our attorneys when the time comes."

"We'll work something out between our attorneys," he repeated, his voice a low growl. "That's not the way we should approach this, and you know it, Gracie."

"I know of no other way."

A muscle ticked in his jaw. "I can think of a dozen different ways, and they all start with you letting me explain."

"Ever since we've met, I've listened to your explanations, Sebastian. I've heard about enough this time." She released a quavering breath. "I'm humiliated and hurt and angry enough to cut you completely out of my life. Am I sorry about this? Yes, but it's not my doing. It's yours."

Sebastian closed his eyes briefly. "We can't be through."

His plea broke her heart all over again. "You're free to see anyone you want. You can go about your business and—"

"I don't want to see anyone else! Damn it, Gracie, listen to me. I have no feelings for Rhonda—"

"Stop. Just stop, Sebastian. No more. I have to think about the baby and how this turmoil is affecting my pregnancy. If I do know one thing, it's that you care about this child. At least, I think so."

"Of course I do," he said firmly.

"F-fine, then. If you care about the health of this baby, let me walk away. I need you to. This is hard for me, Sebastian. Maybe you don't realize how much, but I've let you hurt me enough. I can't do it any longer. I don't have the strength."

Sebastian stared at her, his gaze penetrating, and she recognized the exact moment he relented. His face fell, his shoulders slumped and he shifted his stance ever so slightly to let her pass.

She stepped away from him and squeezed her eyes closed, saying a silent goodbye to her dream. Her heart hurt now, more than it ever had. Putting one foot in front of the other, she moved through the parking lot, got into her car, took one last look at Sebastian and then drove off. She was doing what she had to do to protect herself and the baby, yet the pain was almost unbearable.

It was hard to believe that just a week ago, Gracie had proposed marriage to him and he, like a fool, had reacted badly. It wasn't that he didn't love her, he did. He was just coming to the realization that Gracie was his whole world, when she'd proposed and caught him off guard. Now that she'd cut him out of her life, it was a vital wound to his heart, a stabbing pain that ached with every breath he took.

But he loved her beyond belief and he wasn't about to let her go so easily. He'd just have to show her she couldn't get rid of him so fast. That he was in it for the long haul. So he mustered his bravado and entered the birthing center, enduring the stares of the couples who now knew more about him than he'd like. But he was here for Gracie and their baby.

He waited around for Gracie, hoping to prove to her he wasn't going to abandon her, but after a few minutes, the instructor, Maddy, approached him. "Hello again."

"Hi."

"I, um, thought I'd mention," she said quietly, just for his ears, "your partner, Ms. Diaz, dropped out of class."

"She did?"

"Yes, she's going to be taking private classes from now on. I'm sorry."

"No, no. I should've figured. I'm sorry for bringing your place into the public eye like that. It was all one big misunderstanding."

She nodded. "It's okay. Good luck with the baby," she said.

"Thank you."

Sebastian walked out of the place feeling like he'd been sucker punched in the gut. He was angry with Gracie for cutting him out of her life like that, but he was angrier with himself for all the bumbling mistakes he'd made with her. Of course she wouldn't want to show her face in the early bird class, not after all the things that had been printed about her.

She been humiliated, and it had been his fault.

He'd never really given her a reason to trust him. He'd gone about this courtship all wrong, and wow, now he was paying the price.

By six o'clock he was dressed in jeans and a button-down shirt and knocking on his mother's door. It was family dinner time, his mother calling the shots, wanting everyone in the family to sit down with her. She didn't do this often, but when she did, you didn't dare refuse. He was in no mood tonight for a get-together, but his family's name, once again, had been dragged through the mud because of some overambitious news reports that got it all wrong. He owed his family an explanation, for many things.

Ava greeted him at the door with a big hug, and the look in her eyes wasn't what he'd expected. She'd always been a stickler for transparency and expected to be clued in on everything that went on with the family. It surprised him that she wasn't showing her disapproval. She wasn't judging him, but instead was providing unconditional love. "Hello, dear."

"Mom."

"How are you doing tonight? You had a rough week."

"I did, but I'm doing okay."

"Just okay?" Ava asked.

"I may have lost something, *someone*, who I really care about. Mom."

"That's not the man I raised, Sebastian. You're one to never give up, and it's a trait I admire about you. Don't throw in the towel just yet. Gracie will come around."

He doubted that, but his mother's encouragement meant a great deal to him.

"Come, your brothers and sisters are all here."

She led him into the dining room, where the others were already seated, noisily chattering while drinking wine and munching on appetizers. "Hey," he said to everyone, slapping his brothers' backs and kissing the women on the cheek.

Sutton and Lauren were here along with Beth and Cam,

who were back from their honeymoon. Miles and Chloe were in town, as was Aunt Piper, who was sitting beside Brian. Beside them sat their cousins and the women in their lives, Luke and Kelly and Zeke and Reagan. Then, turning toward his baby sister, Sebastian marveled at what an adorable threesome Harley and Grant and little Daniel made. Soon, Daniel would have a cousin, which was a good thing, but would they be close? Would they even get a chance to know each other?

He pulled out a chair and sat down. This dining room in his mother's rental apartment was a far cry from the beautifully decorated oversize one in the mansion they were used to, but it didn't matter. The family was here, and everyone was in good spirits.

After downing a glass of wine, he asked for everyone's attention and apologized to his family. "I'm sorry for bringing our name down again. We've worked so hard to improve our image, but I have to say the news reports and tabloids got it mostly wrong."

"They usually do," Miles said, and others in the room nodded. Being wealthy and famous meant there was a target on your back, and he'd never felt it more than this past year.

"The truth is, Gracie and I *are* going to have a baby. That part was factual. But I only just found out the baby was mine. I guess everyone assumed she'd gotten pregnant through an in vitro procedure, but as Grant knows, the treatments never got that far."

Grant smiled. "My lips are sealed."

As any good doctor would say.

"I'm sorry that you all had to find that out on the news. I wanted to shout it out to the world, but Gracie wanted to wait."

He was met with a round of congratulations and smiles, which bolstered his sagging heart.

His family really had his back, and he needed that right now.

"*The Gossiper* wasn't too kind, either." Sutton had been furious about what that sleazy tabloid had written. "They can all go to—" He stopped himself, realizing Daniel was in the room.

"Thanks, bro. But just so you know, I wasn't going behind Gracie's back with Rhonda. I was trying to help her with her brother, Lonny. My mistake was in not telling Gracie about it."

"Why didn't you?" Lauren asked.

He turned to her. "Lonny was heading down a bad path. He'd gotten in trouble at school and was acting out. And since I'd always bonded with the boy, Rhonda simply asked me to talk to Lonny. He valued my friendship and needed some guidance, and Rhonda asked me to keep this private. If news got out, she feared it would set back any progress I made with the boy.

"Now I might've blown it for good with Gracie. It's killing me that she won't talk to me. I should've been up front with her. I should've trusted her with what I was doing, and now *she* doesn't trust me." Regret tightened the corners of his mouth. "And the worst part? I honestly don't know if there's anything I can do at this point to change her mind. Anyway, this isn't a Sebastian pity party. I just wanted my family to finally know the truth."

They nodded and gave words of encouragement, which meant a lot to him.

And after another round of drinks, Miles spoke up. "Well, I have good news to report, and I'm glad we're all together today to hear it. Thanks to Chloe's heads-up, I finally have proof that dear 'Uncle' Keith did more em-

bezzling than we originally thought. Turns out that while
Dad was recovering from his stroke, Keith took advantage
of the crisis to siphon off huge chunks of money without
us realizing it. And the best news is, the money is all ac-
counted for and we'll have it back in our hands soon. It's
enough to keep our other holdings afloat and enough to
put the family back on track financially."

"That's wonderful news," Ava said. "I still can't believe
I let that crook dupe me for so long. Brian, I'm sorry to
say that in front of you, but we all know you're not like
your uncle Keith."

"He certainly is not," Aunt Piper said in defense of her
much younger boyfriend. Brian might be a Cooper but it
was in name only. He'd proven his loyalty to the family
by helping to expose his traitorous uncle.

"Miles, you've really saved our family," Ava said, with
pride in her eyes. Miles had once been the black sheep of
the family, but he'd come around, and his firm, Steel Security, was a top-notch investigative company.

"Thanks, Mother. But it was all of us. We're all in this
together, the good, the bad, the ugly. And it's been ugly,
but all that's behind us now."

"Yes," Ava said. "We've proven time and again that
we're a family that sticks together."

"It's really great news because," Luke said, taking his
fiancée Kelly's hand, "now Kelly and I can go to Oahu
and get the hotel ready for the big launch without worrying about the family. We plan to spend an entire month
there, and having this peace of mind will help take some
of the pressure off."

"Pressure in paradise?" Harley asked. She and Grant
were leaving in just a matter of days themselves, and so
this family dinner was also a good way to send them off.

"I know, it's tough work, but somebody's got to do it,"

Kelly teased. The family's mood was definitely lightening up. It was good to see.

"Well, since this is a day for announcements, Reagan and I have some good news, too. Seems Sebastian isn't the only one bringing a new little one into the world."

All eyes turned to Luke's brother, Zeke, and Reagan. "While we're in San Diego setting up the new family-oriented resort there, we'll be also using the facilities for our own little ready-made family." He looked to Reagan. "Tell them, honey."

Reagan didn't hesitate. "We're having twins!"

Gasps of joy filled the room. Everyone rose to congratulate Zeke and Reagan, and Sebastian was incredibly happy for them. Seems his family was finally blessed with good news. It only made him wish for a second chance with Gracie. Or was that a third or fourth? He'd certainly messed up his chances.

And after everyone was settled back in their seats, Brian stood up with glass in hand. "I'd like to propose a toast."

The room quieted and all eyes were on Brian Cooper at the opposite end of the table. "But first I have something to say. I can't tell you how sorry I am about what my uncle did to Wingate Enterprises. It was unforgivable and I'm truly glad he's out of all our lives now. But I'm also grateful that despite everything, all of you have welcomed me into your homes and family." He cleared his throat. "And since this is a day for announcements, I'd like to add to the happiness. Ava," he said, garnering her full attention, "you're going to be an aunt again."

His mother's mouth just about dropped to the floor. Her eyes riveted to her sister, Piper.

And Piper acknowledged her with an excited nod of the head.

"Yes, it's true." Piper took Brian's hand and rose, moving to stand beside him. "We didn't want to steal anyone's thunder today. But yes, Brian and I are having a baby. We'll think about a wedding some time down the line, but right now we're excited for this child."

His mother walked over to Aunt Piper. "You robbed the cradle," she said. The entire family watched on with trepidation. Ava and Piper hadn't always been close, so everyone's eyes were on his mother. "Lucky you," she declared finally, wrapping her arms around her sister and hugging her to her chest. "Congratulations," she murmured, turning to kiss Brian's cheek. "May I finish the toast?" she asked him.

He handed her the glass and took a step back. Ava began, "This family…well, we've been through a lot, and I can't say it's always been pleasant. But we survived and are stronger for it. So this toast is for each and every one of you and the new little ones to arrive soon. May we always be close, be loyal, be true. May this family not only survive, but *thrive*. Here's to our family," Ava said, her eyes misting up as she raised her glass.

Glasses clinked, and there were heartwarming smiles all around.

Now, if only Gracie were here by his side, all would be perfect.

Ten

Keeping busy was the only thing keeping Gracie sane at the moment. She'd never felt lonelier in her life. She moved around her house as if in slow motion, thinking back on her time with Sebastian. They'd had something pretty wonderful together that only lasted mere days, but it had been gut-wrenchingly powerful, and now it was gone. He'd stopped calling and texting as she'd asked. It only made her feel hollow inside and so incredibly sad.

Had Sebastian moved on already?

Had he given up on her?

It wasn't that she wanted to speak to him, but if she was being totally honest, a part of her wanted to know he was suffering as much as she was. She wanted to know that he felt the same emptiness. Was that selfish of her?

Why couldn't things just go back to the way they were before?

When her doorbell rang, she quickly opened the door to Beth. "Hi, I'm a little early."

"That's no problem. I'm happy to see you."

"Same here."

They hugged a little longer than usual, Gracie needing the support. She'd called Beth this morning and they'd spoken about her honeymoon with Cam, which had been fabulous. Gracie wanted to explain to Beth about the baby and why she hadn't told her that Sebastian was the father. It was a misstep on her part and she apologized. Luckily, Beth hadn't taken offense. Then they'd lamented about how much they missed seeing each other, and Gracie had invited her over. "Come in. I made lunch for us."

"Something wildly Mexican and tasty?"

"Your favorite. Enchiladas. Come into the kitchen."

It was great having her friend here now, filling the empty void in her heart for a little while. She led Beth into her modest kitchen. "Tea, lemonade, wine? What can I get you to drink?"

"I'd love some tea, Gracie, and if you don't mind me saying so, you look…"

"Terrible, I know."

"No, you could never look terrible. But you're stressed, aren't you?"

She gave her a half smile. "A bit."

"I thought so."

Beth took her hand. "I'm worried about you."

"Don't be, Beth. You know I'll bounce back. I always do."

Beth gave her a skeptical look. "Nice try, Gracie, but this is me and I know you better than that. You're hurting."

She shrugged and offered her friend a seat. "I'll be fine…eventually." She didn't really think so, not with the way she'd been feeling lately, but it sounded good.

Gracie warmed a pot of tea on the stove and then picked

up a pair of pot holders and took the dish of enchiladas out of the oven.

"Oh, those smell delish. Can I help with anything?"

"No, thanks. I'm good." She poured two cups of tea and then placed a salad on the table.

"You're a busy bee to keep your mind off…things. I recognize the traits, Gracie. I'm a lot like that, too."

"Guilty as charged." She dished up the enchiladas, steam rising up off the cheesy topping, and set the plates down on the table. "Here we go."

"Those look wonderful. My mouth is watering."

"Let's dig in. Baby is hungry, too."

Beth's eyes softened immediately as she gazed down at Gracie's belly. "Did you know that you're in good company? We had a family dinner the other night and found out that Aunt Piper is pregnant, too. And so are Zeke and Reagan—those two are having twins, for heaven's sakes. I can't keep up with my family."

Gracie smiled. "I know. That's very good news. Babies bring so much joy. Your family is expanding, isn't it?"

"Yeah, it sure is. Only thing is, Sebastian looks about as frazzled as you do. He's hurting, too, Gracie. He told the family about what happened and apologized for bringing the family's image down again, but none of it is true. He has a good explanation for all of it."

Gracie picked up her fork, and wished Beth would do the same. She was sorry Beth had to find out about the baby through some sleazy tabloid article; she'd wanted to tell her friend herself. But as far as Sebastian was concerned, she didn't want to hear it. She'd never forget the way he'd reacted to her marriage proposal, and if that wasn't her first clue, then him seeing his ex-girlfriend behind her back certainly was. Add in that his company needed cash to completely get out of the red, and she had a rock-solid case of no-can-do.

"I really don't want to talk about Sebastian, if you don't mind."

"I, uh, sure. All I'm going to say is to please think about giving the guy a chance to explain. And now," she said, making a zipping gesture over her mouth, "I promise, no more talk about my brother."

"Thank you," Gracie said. "I'm not a horrible person, you know, but I've been hurt and…"

Beth took her hand. "I get it. We won't talk about it. I'm not judging you. And I'm here if you need me."

"I know you are."

Beth finally dug into her food. She made a satisfied face and sighed quietly as she chewed. "This is heaven."

"I'm glad you like it. It's a foolproof recipe, handed down from my grandmother."

"I love that you're keeping your family traditions alive like that. It's special."

"I do try whenever I can," Gracie said.

"You should be a chef specializing in Mexican cuisine."

"No, I think I'll leave that to Lauren, thank you very much. Actually, I wanted to pick your brain about something else. If you're up to it."

"Sure. What's up?" Beth asked.

"Well, I'm still hoping to become an event planner and open up my own business. I've been looking for a space to lease or buy. But since you're an expert at it, would you mind giving me pointers and tips on getting started? I think I have pregnancy brain."

"That *is* a thing."

"Oh, how well I know it!" she said. "So maybe you can clear up some questions I have and we can go from there."

"Okay, sure. And, Gracie, just for the record, I think

it's admirable that you want to pursue your dream. I know you'll be a success and a great mommy, too."

"That's my goal."

"Okay, so ask away."

It was almost three o'clock before they finished their talk and Beth left. Gracie felt inspired after getting her questions answered. Beth had a wealth of knowledge in the event-planning department. She'd planned so many Wingate parties and charity events in her life, and was generous in sharing the business side of it, as well. With her mind spinning in several directions, Gracie got lost in thought. And so when the doorbell rang again, it took her a few seconds to realize someone was at her door.

"Just a minute," she said. Gracie had given her house-keeper the day off, which had worked out perfectly since she needed to keep busy, and cooking and cleaning had done the trick.

She opened the door and stared into the striking blue-green eyes of supermodel Rhonda Pearson. Her first incli-nation was to slam the door in her face. But she wouldn't do that.

"I know, I'm probably the last person on earth you wanted to see."

They'd never met before, yet the woman assumed she knew who she was. Well, yes, she *was* that famous.

"I'm Rhonda." She put out her hand.

Gracie shook it once—she hated her manners at times. "Gracie."

"May I come in?"

She really wasn't up to this. "It depends."

"Before you think otherwise, Sebastian has no idea I'm here. I guess you could say I'm here at my own risk. He'd actually murder me in my sleep if he found out I came to speak with you."

Gracie had had a fleeting notion to do the same to the two of them when she'd seen them in that cozy scene on the news. It had knocked her for a loop. "And why is that?"

"Can I please come in? I'd love to explain everything."

Gracie sighed. So many people had encouraged her to hear Sebastian out, but maybe this was the next best thing. "Yes, please. Come inside."

She showed Rhonda to her living room and offered her a seat.

"Thank you," the other woman said.

Gracie nodded, took a seat, too, and continued to stare at the gorgeous supermodel. Rhonda's features were picture-perfect, with big turquoise eyes, long, luscious blond hair and a figure that wouldn't ever know a bad fit.

Rhonda seemed confident in her own skin and didn't seem to mind Gracie's staring. It was as if she expected it, which wasn't so much conceited as it was honest. She banked her life on her good looks, flawless skin and body. "So tell me exactly why you are here."

"That's easy to answer. I'm here for Sebastian. One good turn deserves another. Even though he would hate that I came here."

"Yes, you've said that already."

"You see, I'm raising my younger brother, Lonny. And when Sebastian and I were together, Lonny became attached to him. They really got along great. Sebastian was such a good role model to Lonny, and my brother was at his best around Sebastian. Only, when my relationship with Sebastian ended, I thought a clean break would be best for Lonny. But that apparently was totally wrong. Sebastian lost touch with Lonny, mostly because of me. And because his company started having trouble. I didn't realize how much Sebastian meant to Lonny until he started acting out."

Rhonda sighed. "Let's face it, it's not easy having your big sister modeling bathing suits all over magazine covers and being under the scrutiny of the paparazzi. Lonny is at a sensitive age. I mean, do you remember when you were fifteen? It's tough. And there's tons of peer pressure. Anyway, when I came back to town recently to give Lonny a good home life, his rebellion didn't end. It got worse. So I called Sebastian and asked for his help. I knew he could get through to him."

"You're saying Sebastian was meeting you secretly for Lonny's sake?"

"Yes, and it's all my fault he didn't confide in you. I made him promise not to tell a soul, in order to protect my brother. If news got out about him getting into trouble, the paparazzi would've damaged him, permanently, I'm afraid."

"Sebastian lied to me about where he was."

"If he did, I'm sorry. But you see, he bailed Lonny out of a jam. My brother got in with the wrong crowd, and the boys vandalized a building. He could've gone to jail if Sebastian didn't convince him to own up to what he did. Lonny confessed and Sebastian pulled some strings to get a judge to give Lonny a second chance."

"He did?" It was too complicated a scenario to not be true. Gracie could actually see Sebastian helping a young boy out that way. But if she was to believe that, she wished he would've trusted her with the truth.

Rhonda nodded. "Yes, and I'm very grateful to him, but we're only friends now, Gracie. I swear it."

"You broke his heart. I think he'd care more for you than just as a friend."

Sebastian's ex shook her head. "I didn't break his heart. I never wanted out of our relationship. *He* broke up with me, and he let me save face with the public by claiming

I broke up with him. It was silly of me to do that, but Sebastian went along with it for my sake. You see, he's a really good guy."

Gracie pulled air into her lungs. "It's a lot to take in."

"I know, but whatever the press wanted you to believe about me and Sebastian isn't true. And if you'll allow me, let me show you something."

"What?"

Rhonda pulled out her cell phone and scrolled until she found what she'd been looking for. "Here we go. Just hit the arrow for the video." She handed Gracie the phone and she turned the video on. She seemed to be watching a track-and-field event.

"That's Lonny. He's on the track team now in high school. He's always been fast and he loves to run. A short time ago, he might've landed in juvenile detention, but look at him now. He won the race and the coach is very impressed with him. With Sebastian's guidance and a little encouragement from his big sister, Lonny is the happiest I've seen him."

The impact of this wasn't lost on Gracie. She'd known boys who hadn't been that lucky and had gotten into major trouble, only to drop out of school. She had a brother, too, and only wanted the best for Enrico. Just like Rhonda wanted for her younger brother. "This is wonderful to see."

"It is. The only drawback is that you and Sebastian aren't together anymore. And I feel responsible for that."

"It's not your fault. Sebastian is the one who made the mistakes."

"Everyone is worthy of a second chance. Lonny got one, and hopefully Sebastian will, too. Please think about it. Oh, and congratulations on the baby. I know you both will make wonderful parents."

Hope jetted through Gracie's heart. She'd refused

Sebastian's explanations because she'd been extremely hurt. She'd lumped all of his mistakes and her misgivings into one tidy package and labeled it "Unforgivable," and she hadn't thought anything he said would be enough to change her mind.

And now, thanks to a supermodel and a fifteen-year-old kid, she had a better understanding of why Sebastian had done what he'd done. "Th-thank you. And you don't have to worry. Sebastian won't know a thing about this."

"So you'll give him a second chance?"

"I'll think about it."

"Good." Rhonda smiled and glanced at her watch. "I'd better go. I promised Lonny we'd go out for ice cream after his practice today, but he wanted a protein shake instead. I'm so proud of him."

The winsome look on her face filled Gracie's heart. It was as if both of them were getting a fresh start. "You don't want to be late. And thank you, Rhonda. I do appreciate your honesty."

Gracie walked her out and watched her drive off in a sporty silver car, her heavy heart easing a bit learning of Sebastian's motives.

In just two hours, Gracie had a private early bird childbirth class. She closed her eyes and concentrated on that, instead of the eye-opening conversation she'd just had with Sebastian's ex-girlfriend. Gracie sighed, afraid to hope, but even more afraid, not to hope.

The next day, Gracie dressed in a black wool blazer and slacks, with a cozy blue cashmere sweater underneath to keep her warm. The weather had turned nasty, the clouds overhead gloomy. It would've been a good day to stay in, but she'd done enough of that lately. She wasn't about to mope all day. She'd had a very informative childbirth class at her home last night, when the instructor, Maddy, had let it slip that Sebastian had also hired her for a private class. Maddy had kind eyes, and there was a soothing softness in her voice as she spoke. Perhaps she was a bit of a matchmaker. So Gracie didn't call her out on the possible intentional slip but instead questioned Maddy on why she supposed he'd done that. And the woman had simply replied, "He wants to support you when the baby comes."

Every time Gracie thought about that, the frost in her heart thawed a bit. Heck, who was she kidding? She was melting inside, and all signs pointed to Sebastian being a good guy. Still, she couldn't fathom why he'd rejected her marriage proposal.

She headed to The Eatery, opting to do some work this morning. A frigid wind swept her inside and she took off her blazer and weaved her fingers through her tangled hair. She glanced inside the work area, and found Lauren and Sutton, apparently in a private moment.

Quietly, she moved into the back room, giving them privacy.

"Is that you, Gracie?" Lauren called out.

"Don't mind me," she called back. "Go back to what you two were doing."

Lauren walked into the back room and they came face-to-face. "We weren't doing anything other than talking. How are you, Gracie? What are you doing here so early?"

It *was* early for her. She usually didn't start working on the books until nine, and it was only seven thirty. "I, uh, just had to get out of my house. I couldn't sleep, and well, I guess I needed a friend."

Lauren put out her arms, and she walked straight into them. "You've got a friend right here."

"Thank you." Tears came to her eyes. Lauren's friendship meant so much to her.

"Is it about Sebastian?"

She nodded. "I love him, Lauren. And I think I've made a terrible mistake. I'm not sure about anything anymore."

"It's a confusing time."

"It is," Gracie said hoarsely.

"But if you know you love him, why not hear him out?"

"I know, I should." She pulled back to search Lauren's eyes. "Right? Everyone's been telling me to give him another chance…"

"I think you should."

"So do I." The deep voice came from behind and she turned to find Sebastian there. Immediately her heart started pumping hard. "Sorry, I overheard." Then he smiled.

"What on earth?" Gracie looked at Lauren.

She shrugged. "I guess you thought I was with Sutton."

"You know I did!"

"Sebastian came by to talk, the same way you did just now. It seems like kismet that you were on the same page, and we all know this mistaken-identity thing can get really baffling." Lauren gave her an innocent look. "So I guess I'll leave you two alone now."

Dumbfounded, she stared after Lauren, watching her leave the room, and feeling Sebastian's overwhelming presence in the room.

And when she finally turned to meet his eyes, he wouldn't stop smiling.

Her lips curled up, as well. She was glad to see him, too. Even if the twin-switch mistake had happened to her once again. Couldn't one of them style their hair differently or something? They looked identical, and she wasn't really thinking that Sebastian would come to talk to Lauren so early in the morning. So when she'd first walked in, she'd assumed it was Sutton.

"I've missed you, Gracie."

She nodded, unable to speak at the moment. He'd heard everything. And she wasn't angry or embarrassed about it. She was glad. Yes, *glad* that her feelings for him were finally out in the open. She'd been sheltering her emotions for too long. It wasn't healthy, and now she felt liberated. "I've missed you, too."

"There's a lot I want to say to you, but not here. Will you have dinner with me tonight? I want to take you someplace special."

She smiled. "Yes."

Sebastian took a big gulp of air and sighed in relief. The look on his face was filled with gratitude and promise. "I'll pick you up at six."

"I'll be ready."

He grinned. "Until tonight, then."

And he leaned over to kiss her cheek, leaving her to wonder just what he had in store for her tonight.

Gracie could hardly concentrate on what she was doing. Sitting in the back room at the computer, she opened and closed the inventory app for The Eatery half a dozen times, her hands shaking. Excitement and curiosity crowded her mind to the point that there was literally no room inside her head for anything else.

"Why don't you quit for the day," Lauren said, coming to stand beside her at the desk. "You're not going to be able to get anything accomplished today."

Gracie ran her hands down her face. "I think you're right. My heart's not in it right now."

"That's because your heart is where it should be. With Sebastian."

Gracie tilted her head toward Lauren. "Thanks to you."

"Sure, I'll take credit if you want to give it to me. But you have to know that I had no idea Sebastian was coming over to speak to me until early this morning, when he texted me. I think Sutton put him up to it. He said his brother was pretty desperate and needed to talk it out with someone close to Gracie. Me."

"Really?"

"Yes, really. The guy's nuts about you. And when you opened up to me this morning, I couldn't know that he'd overheard. But I'm glad he did. You two have been dancing around each other for weeks now."

"True story." She was ready now to hear Sebastian out. After her conversation with Rhonda, she was ready to give him the benefit of the doubt and try to move forward. Finally admitting that she was in love with him, saying it aloud to Lauren, made it all seem real and attainable. At least, she was willing to give it a try.

"So go home, gussy up and have a good night with Sebastian."

"That sounds like a plan," Gracie said. "Are you sure you don't need me?"

"I'm covered here, and the inventory can wait. Just go."

Lauren was already handing Gracie her blazer. "Keep warm, it's cold out there."

"The baby's keeping me warm." Which was true. Being pregnant had some advantages, like she was never too cold. The added weight and her hormones kept her from turning into a popsicle during the winter season. "You should try it sometime."

"The Eatery's my baby right now. But someday in the future, our children will be playing with each other. I'm sure of it."

"That's a beautiful thought. Thanks again." She hugged

Lauren. Their friendship was rock-solid. Lauren and Beth had given Gracie nothing but support lately. She was lucky to have both women in her life right now.

One hour later, Gracie was home, soaking in a nice hot bath. Her nerves were so rattled she'd lit candles and put on her favorite soft country rock music before stepping into the tub. The only thing missing in the bubbles was champagne and… Sebastian.

Oh, boy. The champagne would have to wait for months, but Sebastian wouldn't.

The hours dragged by, and finally it was time to dress. Gracie chose a slinky scarlet gown, the high-low hemline making a statement of its own. She wore tall heels and her best gold jewelry, along with wide hoop earrings. Glancing in the mirror, she could see her baby bump was evident now, the slightest little rounding of her belly filling her heart with immeasurable pride.

When Sebastian pulled up to her home, she was ready and greeted him at the door.

"Wow," he said immediately. "You look gorgeous."

"Thank you. So do you. Handsome, I mean. Do you want to come in?"

He took her hand. "Trust me, you don't want me to come in. If I did…"

She couldn't argue with his logic. He was right. She'd never get over seeing him look so dashing in a dark suit and tie, his facial hair groomed just enough to make him look sexy and dangerous. She'd missed him, both in and out of bed.

He kissed her cheek again and helped her on with her coat. With a hand to her back, he walked her to his car and opened the door. "Where are we going?" she asked as she slipped into the passenger seat. His gaze roamed over her legs, and a swell of heat shot through her body.

"You'll see."

He was being cryptic all of a sudden, and she didn't know what to think.

"It's someplace special to me. To us."

He started the engine and turned on the music. The song playing was from her favorite band. Softly, she sang along with the tune, her voice no match for theirs, and yet it put a smile on Sebastian's face. Had he remembered her favorite music?

They headed down the road, away from her house, and after ten minutes, he pulled up to the Texas Cattleman's Club. Her brows rose in surprise. What was he up to?

The question in her eyes prompted him to say, "This will all make sense soon."

He helped her out of the car, and hand in hand, they entered the club. After they checked in, the receptionist said, "Everything's ready for you, Mr. Wingate."

"Thank you."

She handed him a key and Sebastian led them down a hallway to a private room. He stopped to open the door and ushered her inside. The room was magical, with dozens of lit candles, a roaring, wood-burning fire in the fireplace and arrangements of beautiful flowers throughout the room. In the middle of all of it, a table was set for two.

She turned to face Sebastian, her face probably revealing her awe. "This is amazing. You did all this today?"

He nodded. "I had to work fast. It was worth it to see the look on your face. But before we talk about the future, I need to talk to you about the past."

Sebastian pulled out a chair for her, and she took a seat. Then, sitting down to face her, he took her hand. It was as if he needed the connection, needed to touch her in order to proceed. "It isn't easy for me to admit this, but I've made a lot of mistakes with you. And I hope to rectify all of them tonight, Gracie. First of all, thank you for hearing me out. I want us to start out with a fresh slate, so I'll admit to not being perfect."

"Nobody is," she said. In her youth, she'd thought of him that way. Her crush had known no bounds. But she was steeped in reality now. "I'm not perfect, either."

"From where I'm sitting at the moment, I'd say you are." He scanned over her face, gazing into her eyes.

She smiled, loving the way his hand was softly squeezing hers, as if he needed her strength to go on.

"I was never after your money. Never. The thought never once crossed my mind. The Wingates are financially sound, and whatever struggles we have will be taken care of professionally. You bought the house, and that helped us, yes, but it was never about money between you and me. In fact, I wasn't thrilled that you thought so little of me."

"I didn't want to, Sebastian, but there were so many other things that confused me, too."

He inhaled. "I know, sweetheart. And that's on me. I wasn't sure about how to convince you about my feelings for you. You seemed to have the notion that I only cared about the baby, that I never wanted you because you weren't good enough for a Wingate. That I never seemed interested in you before this." He released a ragged breath. "But the truth is, I had a thing for you, too, Gracie. I just never acted on it because your father worked for us. And also because you were Beth's best friend. In my mind, you were off-limits. So yes, I never thought of us as a possible couple, but not because I didn't think you were worthy. And certainly not because I felt superior to you.

"More recently, I thought it best not to bombard you with my growing feelings because I didn't want to rush you. You seemed to need time, and I thought I was doing what you wanted. So I held back. Perhaps I shouldn't have.

But I've always cared for you, Gracie. Make no mistake about that."

He squeezed her hand. "You may not even realize it, but you turn heads when you walk into a room. And to know that you're carrying my baby only makes you more beautiful to me."

Tears welled in her eyes. This time, she wouldn't blame it on hormones. This time, it was hearing Sebastian open up his heart that gave her hope and brought on deep emotion.

"About Rhonda," he began.

She held her tongue, keeping her promise to his ex that she wouldn't divulge anything they'd spoken about. Besides, it was better to hear it from him.

"I was only trying to help Rhonda's younger brother…"

Gracie listened to his full explanation and to his apology. She already had forgiven him in her heart. "I understand. It was a good thing you were trying to do."

"I'm still trying. I plan to be in the boy's life to a degree."

"I wouldn't expect anything less, but why didn't you just tell me about it? Didn't you trust me?"

"I—I didn't want to rock the boat. It was hard earning your trust, Gracie, and I wasn't sure I had it at the time. I gave my word to keep Lonny's problems private. It wouldn't have done anyone any good to bring light to his troubles."

She nodded. "I get that, Sebastian. I really do. You were trying to protect Lonny, just like I was trying to protect our baby. I, uh, I probably shouldn't have jumped to conclusions about you. I thought the worst of you, when in my heart, I'd always believed you were a good guy. I guess that's why I was so confused and hurt."

He squeezed her hand once again, keeping their connection solid. "I made a mess of things, but you have to know, I didn't want to fail our baby the way I failed Lonny in the past."

"I understand that." But she had to ask. She had to clear the air, and even though it was hard for her to do, she couldn't let this go without an explanation. "I guess what hurt me the most was when I proposed to you, and you looked like the devil had cornered you in the bowels of hell."

Sebastian began shaking his head. "Oh, man, Gracie. No, that's not how I felt at all. You just startled me, because I'd made so many mistakes with you, I wanted to be the one to do the proposing. I wanted to sweep you off your feet the way you deserve. I wanted to show you how much you meant to me. I had this all planned out in my head, and so—"

"I jumped the gun."

"I was thrilled you wanted to get married, but you deserve a beautiful wedding proposal. Can you understand that?"

Candles flickered, the fireplace shot blue and golden embers up, and Sebastian's love surrounded her. "I can. I do."

"Hold that thought, Gracie. Just hold that thought."

Sebastian rose from his chair and walked to her side. Then he bent his knee and brought out a gorgeous red velvet ring box. Her heart began to pound, and her body trembled as she gazed down at Sebastian, love shining in his eyes. He lifted the box lid to reveal a stunning oval diamond ring surrounded by dozens of tiny diamonds. It was the prettiest ring Gracie had ever seen.

"Gracie, we started out right here in these rooms when I met a wonderful masked woman who knocked me for a loop. I'd never felt that way before, the instant connection we had, the way we responded to each other. It wasn't a fluke that we're together now. We were meant to be, Gracie. I believe that with my whole heart. I love you so much. I love the baby you're carrying, too, and I want this love to continue on until we take our last breaths. Gracie Diaz, my love, will you be my wife? Will you marry me?"

Tears streamed down Gracie's face. She'd wanted this since childhood, and now she believed in Sebastian and his love. She believed they belonged together. She believed in the beautiful family they'd created. "I love you, too, Sebastian. I want nothing more than to be your wife. Yes, I'll marry you. Yes. Yes. *Yes!*"

He took her hand and placed the diamond ring on her finger. Then he pulled her up from the seat and cradled her face in his hands. "I love you, Gracie." And the kiss he bestowed upon her spoke of love and promise and forever. She'd never been happier.

"There's more, sweetheart," he said. He pulled a few papers out of his pocket. "This is the deed to your house. It's in your name now, and all yours. And here's an agreement proving I was never after your money. It says we each keep what we went into our marriage with, so there'll never be any doubt."

"There never will be, Sebastian. Because I'm never letting you go."

He gave her another tantalizing kiss, and then took her by the hand. "Remember that little alcove, when we first—"

"Hooked up?"

"Made love," he corrected and then nuzzled her neck, his mouth working magic on her.

She ached for him. It'd been too long. "Think we can find it again?"

"I'm sure of it, sweetheart." He pointed to the far end

of the room and the hidden space between the fireplace and a large bookshelf. "Right there."

She opened her mouth in awe, surprise and delight, then threw her arms around his neck and kissed him for all he was worth.

He took her hand and led her to the alcove. "This is where it all began…"

"If you wanted to sweep me off my feet, you've succeeded. Sebastian Wingate, you just might be perfect after all."

He touched her belly lovingly and his warmth brought joy to her heart. "That makes three of us, my love."

Epilogue

One year later...

Gracie stood beside the podium, her husband at the helm, his voice deep and proud as he addressed the gathered crowd in the main dining hall of the Texas Cattleman's Club. "Let me start out by saying my wife, Gracie Diaz Wingate, has accomplished so much in her life, and no one deserves this honor more than she does. She's a dynamo, and frankly, this Wingate has trouble keeping pace with her. As you all know, she's incredibly smart. Well, she married me, didn't she?"

The small crowd, including his mother, Ava, and Lauren, Sutton, Beth and Cam, all chuckled at his little joke. The others in their family were off on their own adventures and couldn't be there today.

"She's also a wonderful mother to our beautiful infant son, Mateo." Sebastian choked up and Gracie was one compliment away from tears spilling down her cheeks, as well. She had only to look down at the precious baby in her arms to realize how very fortunate she was. She had a loving husband, a baby she adored and a place in the Royal community now.

"But all personal feelings aside, Gracie Diaz Wingate is a capable businesswoman, restaurateur and horse breeder. She loves each enterprise equally, and has recently opened a new office in the downtown area, where she plans on starting up an events business. I know she's thrilled to be the newest inductee to the Texas Cattleman's Club. So, with that said, I invite my beautiful wife to say a few words before we let the president do the honors."

Gracie handed the baby over to Sebastian, the transfer seamless. They'd been sharing baby duties ever since the little one took his first breath, and loving every second of it. Gracie's mother and brother had been here for the birth and had helped out for weeks while she and Sebastian got the hang of parenting and schedules and sleepless nights.

She stood in front of the podium now, looking into the eyes of her new family and so many other community members and friends. "I stand here before you, humbled and grateful for all the good things in my life. So many of my dreams have come true, two of them standing right beside me." Gracie looked upon Sebastian and Mateo lovingly and then turned back to the small crowd. "But to be here among all of you as part of this club, as part of the Royal community, is an honor I hope to live up to. I hope to make a difference in our town. And I plan to play a very active role at TCC. Thank you all for being here today. It means a great deal to me."

Then the president came up to say a few words. After his speech, Sebastian invited everyone in attendance to enjoy their dinner and music afterward. It had been his idea to celebrate Gracie's induction with a party for family and friends. Gracie loved him now more than ever. He'd proven himself to be the man she'd always hoped he was. The man she'd fantasized and loved for many years.

And now with Wingate Enterprises back on solid ground, Sebastian had only good things to look forward to. She sat beside him at a table, while dinner was being served. Piped-in music flowed throughout the room, and pastries would be served later. She got the feeling Beth had something to do with planning this party in her honor. As a sigh escaped her lips, Sebastian peered at her.

"What is it, sweetheart? Everything okay?"

She nodded and gazed at the two men in her life. "Yes, I'm great." She whispered quietly, "Just a little tired. I can't wait to go home with the two of you."

She lived on the beautiful sprawling land of the Wingate Estate now, in the home she'd decorated with the slightest of touches to make it their own.

"Of course," he whispered back. "It's been a long day."

"I love being with you and Mateo at our home. Maybe he will even sleep tonight."

"If not, it's my turn to rock him. Even though I think he prefers his mommy's arms. Can't say I blame him. I kinda like them, too." Sebastian kissed the side of her neck, his warm breath making every cell in her body come alive. Her husband was such a deliberate temptation, and she loved that about him.

She knew in her heart that the day she and Sebastian fell in love was the day of her true lottery win.

She couldn't get much luckier than that.

* * * * *

COMING SOON!

We really hope you enjoyed reading this book.
If you're looking for more romance, be sure to
head to the shops when new books are
available on

Thursday 7th January

LET'S TALK

Romance

For exclusive extracts, competitions
and special offers, find us online:

MILLS & BOON

THE HEART OF ROMANCE

A ROMANCE FOR EVERY KIND OF READER

MODERN

Prepare to be swept off your feet by sophisticated, sexy and seductive heroes, in some of the world's most glamourous and romantic locations, where power and passion collide.
8 stories per month.

HISTORICAL

Escape with historical heroes from time gone by. Whether your passion is for wicked Regency Rakes, muscled Vikings or rugged Highlanders, awaken the romance of the past.
6 stories per month.

MEDICAL

Set your pulse racing with dedicated, delectable doctors in the high-pressure world of medicine, where emotions run high and passion, comfort and love are the best medicine.
6 stories per month.

True Love

Celebrate true love with tender stories of heartfelt romance, from the rush of falling in love to the joy a new baby can bring, and a focus on the emotional heart of a relationship.
8 stories per month.

Desire

Indulge in secrets and scandal, intense drama and plenty of sizzling hot action with powerful and passionate heroes who have it all: wealth, status, good looks…everything but the right woman.
6 stories per month.

HEROES

Experience all the excitement of a gripping thriller, with an intense romance at its heart. Resourceful, true-to-life women and strong, fearless men face danger and desire - a killer combination!
8 stories per month.

DARE

Sensual love stories featuring smart, sassy heroines you'd want as a best friend, and compelling intense heroes who are worthy of them.
4 stories per month.

To see which titles are coming soon, please visit

millsandboon.co.uk/nextmonth

JOIN US ON SOCIAL MEDIA!

Stay up to date with our latest releases, author
news and gossip, special offers and discounts, and
all the behind-the-scenes action
from Mills & Boon...

 millsandboon

 millsandboonuk

 millsandboon

It might just be true love...

MILLS & BOON
HISTORICAL
Awaken the romance of the past

Escape with historical heroes from time gone by. Whether your passion is for wicked Regency Rakes, muscled Viking warriors or rugged Highlanders, indulge your fantasies and awaken the romance of the past.

MILLS & BOON
True Love
Romance from the Heart

Celebrate true love with tender stories of
heartfelt romance, from the rush of falling
in love to the joy a new baby can bring,
and a focus on the emotional
heart of a relationship.